Praise for Marta

"A warm, loving story

—*RT Book*

"A terrific family story, ... throughout....
Kudos to Marta Perry for such an inspiring novel."

—*RT Book Reviews* on *Mission: Motherhood*

"Marta Perry's warm novel offers some terrific history about the Amish community."

—*RT Book Reviews* on *Hide in Plain Sight*

Praise for Debby Giusti and her novels

"Danger seems to be everywhere, amping up the pace until the surprise reveal. This is not your typical Amish-themed tale."

—*RT Book Reviews* on *Undercover Amish*

"Detailed descriptions and well-developed dialogue create the perfect pace with no lulls in the action."

—*RT Book Reviews* on *Person of Interest*

"The active pace becomes more engaging as the drama intensifies."

—*RT Book Reviews* on *The Agent's Secret Past*

A lifetime spent in rural Pennsylvania and her Pennsylvania Dutch heritage led **Marta Perry** to write about the Plain People who add so much richness to her home state. Marta has seen nearly sixty of her books published, with over six million books in print. She and her husband live in a centuries-old farmhouse in a central Pennsylvania valley. When she's not writing, she's reading, traveling, baking or enjoying her six beautiful grandchildren.

Debby Giusti is an award-winning Christian author who met and married her military husband at Fort Knox, Kentucky. Together they traveled the world, raised three wonderful children and have now settled in Atlanta, Georgia, where Debby spins tales of mystery and suspense that touch the heart and soul. Visit Debby online at debbygiusti.com, blog with her at seekerville.blogspot.com and craftieladiesofromance.blogspot.com, and email her at Debby@DebbyGiusti.com.

MARTA PERRY

Second Chance Amish Bride

&

DEBBY GIUSTI

Undercover Amish

HARLEQUIN® LOVE INSPIRED®

Recycling programs for this product may not exist in your area.

ISBN-13: 978-1-335-46351-7

Second Chance Amish Bride and Undercover Amish

This edition published by arrangement with Love Inspired Books.

www.Harlequin.com

Printed in U.S.A.

CONTENTS

SECOND CHANCE AMISH BRIDE

Marta Perry

This story is dedicated to my husband, Brian,
with much love.

Judge not, and ye shall not be judged:
condemn not, and ye shall not be condemned:
forgive, and ye shall be forgiven.

—*Luke* 6:37

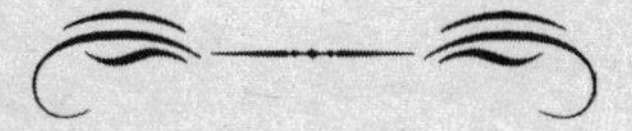

Chapter One

The hospital van bounced over a rut in the farm lane, and Caleb King leaned forward to catch the first glimpse of his home. At last—those four weeks in the rehab hospital after his leg surgery had seemed endless, but finally he was coming back to his central Pennsylvania farm. If only he could jump down from the van, hug his kinder and plunge back into the life of being a dairy farmer.

But he couldn't. His hands tightened on the arms of the wheelchair, and he glared at the cast on his leg. How much longer would he have to count on the kindness of his family and neighbors to keep the farm going?

Caleb glanced toward the Fisher farm across the fields. The spot where the barn had been before the fire was cleared now, and stacks of fresh lumber showed a new barn would soon rise in its place. For an instant he was back in the burning structure with Sam Fisher, struggling to get the last of the stock out before the place was consumed. He heard again Sam's shout, saw the fiery timber falling toward him, tried to dive out of the way…

He should have thought himself blessed it had been only his leg that suffered. And doubly blessed that Sam had hauled him out of there at the risk of his own life.

The van stopped at the back porch. Caleb reached for the door handle and then realized he couldn't get it open. He'd have to wait for the driver to lower the wheelchair to the ground. How long until he'd be able to do the simplest thing for himself? He gritted his teeth. He was tired of being patient. He had to get back to normal.

By the time Caleb reached the ground, Onkel Zeb was waiting with Caleb's two little ones, and his heart leaped at the sight of them. Six-year-old Becky raced toward him, blond braids coming loose from under her kapp, which probably meant Onkel Zeb had fixed her hair.

"Daadi, Daadi, you're home!" She threw herself at him, and he bent forward to catch her and pull her onto his lap, loving the feel of her small arms around him.

"Home to stay," he said, and it was a promise. He hugged her tight. His young ones had lost too much with their mother's desertion and death. They had to know that he was always here for them.

Reminding himself that whatever Alice's sins, he must forgive her, he held out his hand to Timothy, who clung to Onkel Zeb's pant leg. "Komm, Timothy. You know Daadi, ain't so?"

Little Timothy was almost four, and his blue eyes had grown huge at the sight of the lift and the wheelchair. But at the sound of Caleb's voice, he seemed to overcome his shyness. He scrambled into Caleb's lap, managing to kick the heavy cast in the process.

Onkel Zeb winced at the sight. "Careful, Timmy. Daadi's leg..."

Caleb stopped him with a shake of his head. "It's worth it for a big hug from my boy."

Nodding, Onkel Zeb grasped Caleb's shoulder, his faded blue eyes misting over. His lean, weathered face seemed older than it had been before the accident, most likely from worry. "Ach, it's wonderful gut to have you home again."

The driver slammed the van door, smiling at the kinder. "Don't forget, I'll be back to pick you up for your therapy appointment next week." He waved as he rounded the van to go back to the driver's seat.

Caleb grimaced as the van pulled out. "I wish I could forget it. I'd like to be done with hospitals."

"Never mind. You're getting well, ain't so? That's what's important." Zeb started pushing the wheelchair toward the back door, where a new wooden ramp slanted down from the porch. "Sam Fisher and Daniel put the ramp in last week so it'd be all ready when you came home."

"Nice work." Of course it was. His brother Daniel was a skilled carpenter. Caleb tried to look appreciative, but it was hard when he kept seeing reminders of his helplessness everywhere he looked. "Is Sam still helping with the milking?"

"I told him not to come in the morning anymore. With Thomas Schutz working every day, we're getting along all right." Zeb paused. "I was thinking it might be gut to have Thomas stay on full-time even after you're back on your feet. We could use the extra pair of hands."

Caleb shrugged, not willing to make that decision so

quickly. Still, Thomas seemed eager to earn the money for his widowed mother, and he was a bright lad. They could do worse than take the boy on until Timothy was of an age to help.

"At least for now we'll keep him full-time," he said. "And we'll have Edith Berger continue with the house and the young ones."

Onkel Zeb stopped pushing when they reached the door. Caleb glanced up and was surprised at the look of discomfort on Zeb's face.

"About Edith…her daughter has been having some health troubles and needs her mamm. So Edith had to go to her. She isn't coming anymore."

Caleb's hands clenched again as the chair bumped over the doorstep into the house. He could hardly care for the kinder when he couldn't even go up the stairs. "We'll have to find someone…"

His words trailed off as they entered the kitchen. A woman in Plain dress stood at the stove, taking a pie from the oven.

"Here's a blessing arrived this morning that we didn't expect." Onkel Zeb sounded as if he forced a note of cheerfulness into his voice. "Look who has komm to help us out."

The woman turned as he spoke. Her soft brown hair was drawn back into a knot under a snowy kapp. She had on a dark green dress with an apron to match that made her hazel eyes look green. The woman wasn't one of the neighbors or someone from the church. It was Jessie Miller, cousin of the wife who'd left him, and the last person he wanted to find in his kitchen.

For a long moment they stared at each other. Jessie's oval face might have been a bit paler than normal, but if she was uncomfortable, she was trying not to show it. Caleb's jaw hardened until it felt it might break. Jessie had offered her assistance once before, just after Alice left, and he'd turned her down in no uncertain terms. What made her think she could expect a wilkom now?

"Caleb." Jessie nodded gravely. "I'm sehr glad to see you home again."

He could hardly say that he was happy to see her, but a warning look from Onkel Zeb reminded him that the kinder were looking on. "Yah, it's wonderful gut to be here." Becky pressed close to the chair, and he put his arm around her. "What are you…how did you get here?" *And why have you komm?*

"Jessie took the bus and got a ride out from town." Zeb sounded determined to fill up the silence with words, probably because he was afraid of what Caleb might say. "It'll be wonderful nice for the kinder to get to know Cousin Jessie, ain't so?"

Caleb frowned at his uncle, unable to agree. He supposed, if he were being fair, that Alice's family deserved some chance to get to know her children, but not now, not like this.

Before he could speak, Zeb had seized the handles of the chair. "I'll show you the room we fixed up for you so you could be on this floor. Becky, you and Timothy give Cousin Jessie a hand with setting the table for supper. Daadi must be hungry, and Onkel Daniel will be in soon."

Becky let go of Caleb reluctantly and went to the drawer for silverware. Timothy raced to get there first, yanking so hard the drawer would have fallen out if Jessie hadn't grabbed it.

"Ach, you're a strong boy," she said, a bit of laughter

in the words. “Best let Becky hand you the things, ain’t so?” She smiled at Becky, but his daughter just set her lips together and proceeded with the job. Even at her young age, Becky had a mind of her own.

Zeb pushed Caleb’s chair to the back room that had been intended as a sewing room for Alice. The hospital bed looked out of place, but Caleb knew it would be easier to get into and out of than a regular bed.

Once they were inside, Caleb reached back to pull the door closed so no one could overhear. He swung to face his uncle.

“What is she doing here?” he demanded.

Onkel Zeb shrugged, spreading his hands wide. “She just showed up. Seems like word got to Ohio about your getting hurt, and Jessie said she thought she was needed.”

“Well, she’s not.” Caleb clamped down on the words. “We’ll do fine without her, so she can just take tomorrow’s bus right back again.”

“Ach, Caleb, you can’t do that.” His uncle’s lean, weathered face grew serious. “Stop and think. What would folks think if you turned your wife’s kin out of the house? What would the bishop and ministers say?”

“I don’t want her here.” He spun the chair to stare, unseeing, out the window. “I don’t need any reminders of what Alice did.”

“What Alice did, not Jessie,” Zeb reminded him. “It’s not Jessie’s fault. She wants only to help, maybe thinking she can make up a little for what her cousin did.”

“She can’t.” He bit out the words. It was easy telling himself that he had to forgive Alice. It wasn’t easy to do it.

"Even so, you'll have to agree to let her stay for a short visit, at least." His uncle pulled the chair back around to give Caleb the look that said he meant business. "I'll not have you hurting the woman for someone else's wrongdoing."

Onkel Zeb hadn't often given orders to Caleb and his brothers, even though he'd shared the raising of them. But when he did, they listened.

Caleb clenched his jaw, but he nodded. "All right. A short visit—that's all. Then Jessie has to go."

With Caleb out of the room, Jessie discovered that she could breathe again. She hadn't realized how hard this would be.

Caleb had changed over the years, just as she had. She'd first seen him on the day he'd met her cousin, and a lot of years had passed since then. His hair and beard were still the color of a russet apple, and his cheeks were ruddy despite his time in the hospital.

But the blue eyes that had once been wide and enthusiastic seemed frosty now, and lines etched their way across his face. Lines of pain, probably, but maybe also of grief and bitterness. Who could wonder at that, after what Alice had put him through?

Guilt grabbed her at the thought of the cousin who had been like her own little sister. She'd been meant to take care of Alice, but she'd failed.

A clatter of plates brought her back to the present with a jolt, and she hurried to the kinder. "Let me give you a hand with those," she said, reaching for the precarious stack Becky was balancing.

"I can do it myself." Becky jerked the plates away so quickly they almost slid onto the floor. She managed to get them to the round pine table and plopped them down with a clank. "I don't need help." She shot Jessie an unfriendly look.

Had Becky picked up her father's attitude already? Or maybe she saw herself as the mother of the little family now that Alice was gone. Either way, Jessie supposed she'd best take care what she said.

"We can all use a bit of help now and then," she said easily. "I'm not sure where there's a bowl for the chicken pot pie. Can you help me with that?"

Timothy ran to one of the lower cabinets and pulled the door open. "This one," he announced, pointing to a big earthenware bowl. "That's the one for chicken pot pie. Ain't so, Becky?"

He looked for approval to his big sister, and when she nodded, he gave Jessie an engaging grin. "See?"

"I do see. That's just right, Timothy. Do you like chicken pot pie?"

Still smiling, he nodded vigorously. "And cherry pie, too." He glanced toward the pie she'd left cooling on the counter.

Jessie took the bowl, smiling in return at the irresistible little face. Timothy, at least, was friendly. Probably he wasn't old enough to remember much about his mother, so her leaving and her death hadn't affected him as much as Becky.

She began ladling out the fragrant mix of chicken and homemade noodles. The men would doubtless be back and hungry before long. Even as she thought it, Jessie heard the door of Caleb's room open and the murmur of voices.

"Let's get those hands washed for supper," she told Timothy. "I hear Daadi coming." She reached out to turn on the water in the sink, but Becky pushed her way between Jessie and her brother.

"I'll do it." She frowned at Jessie. "He's my little bruder."

Jessie opened her mouth, found herself with nothing to say and closed it again. Her mother's voice trickled into her mind, and she saw again the worried look on her mother's face.

"I wish you wouldn't go. You'll be hurt."

Well, maybe so, but she couldn't let that stop her from doing what was right. She had to atone for the wrongs Alice had done, and if she was hurt in the process, it was probably what she deserved. Given Becky's attitude, she didn't doubt that Alice's daughter was hurting inside, too.

The hustle of getting food on the table was a distraction when Caleb and his uncle returned to the kitchen. Zeb went to the back door and rang the bell on the porch. Almost before its clamor had stilled, Caleb's brother Daniel came in, pausing to slap Caleb on the back.

"So you're home at last. I thought I would have to sneak you out of that hospital."

Caleb's face relaxed into the easygoing smile Jessie remembered from his younger self. "You just want to have more help around here, that's all."

"Can't blame me for that. I've got the carpentry business to run, remember? I can't spend all my time milking cows."

Daniel's gaze landed on Jessie, and he gave her a slightly quizzical look. He'd already greeted her when she'd arrived, so he wasn't surprised to find her there as Caleb had been. Maybe he was wondering how Caleb had taken her arrival. If so, she didn't doubt he'd soon see the answer to that question.

She'd have known Caleb and Daniel were brothers even if she'd never seen the two of them before. Their lean, rangy bodies and strong faces were quite similar, though Daniel's hair was a bit darker and of course he didn't have a beard, since he'd never married.

That was strange enough to be remarked on in the Amish community. At twenty-eight, Daniel was expected to have started a family of his own. She'd heard from the talkative driver who brought her from the bus station that folks around here said the three King brothers had soured on women because of their mother's desertion. If that were true, she couldn't imagine Alice's actions had helped any.

There was another brother, too, the youngest. But Aaron's name was rarely mentioned, so Alice had told her once. He'd jumped the fence to the Englisch world a few years ago and hadn't been back since as far as she knew. Nothing about the King boys was typical of Amish males, it seemed.

Jessie found herself seated between Zeb and Timothy, and she scanned the table to be sure she hadn't forgotten anything. Silly to be so nervous about the first meal she'd cooked in this house. It wasn't like she was an inexperienced teenager.

Caleb bowed his head for the silent prayer, and everyone followed suit. Jessie began to say the Lord's Prayer, as she usually did, but found her heart yearning for other words.

Please, Lord, let me do Your will here. Give me a chance to make a difference for Alice's children.

For a moment after the prayer, no one spoke. The

dishes started to go around the table, and Jessie helped balance the heavy bowl while Timothy scooped up his chicken pot pie. Warmed by his grin, she passed the bowl on to Caleb. He took it with a short nod and turned away.

Zeb cleared his throat. "It looks like you found everything you needed to make supper." He passed the bowl of freshly made applesauce.

"The pantry is well stocked, that's certain sure. Lots of canned goods." She couldn't help the slight question in her tone, since Alice hadn't been here to do the housewife's job of preserving food last summer.

Zeb nodded. "The neighbors have been generous in sharing what they put up. Some of the women even came over and had a canning frolic when the tomatoes and peppers were ready in the garden."

"That was wonderful kind of them." The King family didn't have any female relatives nearby, so naturally the church would pitch in to help. "And someone made this great dried corn. That's a favorite with my little nieces and nephews."

Before anyone could respond, Becky cut in. "You don't have to go back to the hospital anymore, right, Daadi? So we can get along like always."

Zeb's face tightened a little, and he glanced at Caleb as if expecting him to correct Becky for rudeness. But if Caleb caught the look, he ignored it. "I'll have to go for just a few hours each week. It's what they call physical therapy, when they help me do exercises to get my leg working right again."

Becky's lips drew down in a pout that reminded Jessie of her mother. "I thought you were done."

"The therapy will help your daadi get rid of that

heavy cast and out of the chair," Daniel said, flicking her cheek with his finger. "You wouldn't want him to skip that, ain't so?"

Becky shrugged. "I guess not. But only for a little while, right?"

It wasn't surprising that Becky wanted reassurance that her father would be home to stay. She'd certainly had enough upheaval in her young life.

"Don't worry," Caleb said. "We'll soon be back to normal. I promise."

Jessie rose to refill the bowl with pot pie. Caleb glanced her way at the movement, and his intent look was like a harsh word. She knew what he meant by *normal*. He meant without her.

By the time the uncomfortable meal was over, Jessie was glad to have the kitchen to herself while she washed the dishes, though a little surprised that Becky didn't insist on taking over that job, too. The little girl certainly seemed determined to convince everyone that Jessie was unnecessary.

Jessie took her time over the cleaning up, half listening to the murmur of voices from the living room. It sounded as if Caleb was playing a board game with the young ones, and Daniel was helping Timothy keep up with his big sister. The play was punctuated now and then by laughter, and the sound warmed Jessie's heart. Obviously everyone was as glad to have Caleb home as he was to be here.

She was just hanging up the dish towels to dry when Daniel and the children came back in the kitchen and started putting on jackets. "Going someplace?" she asked.

Daniel nodded. "These two like to tell the horses good-night. Timothy says it makes the horses sleep better."

"It does," Timothy declared. "Honest."

"I'm sure you're right," Jessie said. "Do you take them a treat?"

"Carrots," he said, running to the bin in the pantry and coming back with a handful.

"Share with Becky," Daniel prompted, and Timothy handed her a few, obviously trying to keep the lion's share.

Jessie had to smile. "Your mammi used to do that when she was your age," she said.

Timothy looked at her with a question in his eyes, but Caleb spoke from the doorway.

"Best get going. It's almost time for bed."

"Komm, schnell. You heard Daadi." Daniel shooed them out, and the door closed behind them.

"Don't talk about their mother to my children." Caleb's voice grated, and he turned the chair toward her with an abrupt shove from his strong hands that sent it surging across the wide floor boards.

For a moment Jessie could do nothing but stare at him. "I only said that—"

His face darkened. "I know what you said, but I don't want her mentioned. I'm their father, and I will tell them what they need to know about her."

Her thoughts were bursting with objections, but Jessie kept herself from voicing them. "I didn't mean any harm, Caleb. Isn't it better that they hear people speak about Alice naturally?"

The lines in his face deepened, and Jessie felt a

pang of regret for the loss of the laughing, open person he'd once been.

"I won't discuss it. You'll have to do as I see fit during your visit."

He'd managed to avoid speaking Alice's name thus far, and that should have been a warning in itself. Arguing would do no good.

"Whatever you say. I'm just here to help in any way I can."

Some of the tension seemed to drain out of Caleb, but not much. She suspected there was more to come, and suspected, too, that she wasn't going to like it.

"Since you're here, you may as well visit with the kinder for a few days." Instead of looking at her, he focused on the National Parks calendar tacked to the kitchen wall. "I'll arrange for you to take the bus back to Ohio on Friday."

"Friday? You mean this Friday? Two days from now?" She hadn't expected this to be easy, but she also hadn't anticipated being turned away so quickly.

Caleb gave a short nod, still not meeting her eyes. He swung the chair away from her as if to dismiss her.

Without thinking, Jessie reached out to stop him, grabbing his arm. His muscles felt like ropes under her hand, and the heat of his skin seared through the cotton of his sleeve. She let go as if she'd touched a hot pan.

"Please, Caleb. I came to help out while you're laid up. Obviously you need a woman here, and your uncle mentioned that the person who had been helping couldn't any longer. Please let me fill in."

A muscle twitched in Caleb's jaw as if he fought to contain himself. "We'll get along fine. We don't need your help."

He sounded like Becky. And arguing with him would do about as much good as arguing with a six-year-old.

Would it help or hurt if she showed him the letter Alice had written a few days before she died, asking Jessie to do what she could for the kinder? While she struggled for an answer, he swung away again and wheeled himself toward the door.

"Friday," he said over his shoulder. "You'll be on Friday's bus."

Chapter Two

Jessie lingered in the kitchen until Daniel and the kinder returned. Becky and Timothy ran straight to the living room, as if they couldn't bear to be parted from their daadi for more than a few minutes. Daniel, with what she thought might have been a sympathetic glance at her, followed them.

She stood, irresolute, watching the red glow in the western sky over the ridge. It turned slowly to pink, fading as dusk crept into the valley. She wasn't used to being surrounded by hills this way. Her area of Ohio was fairly flat—good farmland. These enclosing ridges seemed to cut her off from everything she knew.

Caleb made good use of the land on the valley floor, and his dairy herd of forty head was apparently considered fairly large here. Where the ground started to slope upward toward the ridge, she'd spotted an orchard, with some of the trees already in blossom. Too bad she wouldn't be here to see the fruit begin to form. Caleb would see to that.

She turned abruptly toward the living room. Best make what use she could of the little time he seemed willing to grant her with the kinder. As she entered, she heard Becky's plaintive voice.

"But isn't Daadi going to help us get ready for bed?" She stood in front of her father's wheelchair, and her look of dismay was echoed by the one on Caleb's face.

"Ach, Becky, you know Daadi won't be able to go upstairs for a bit," Zeb gently chided her. "That's why we fixed up the room downstairs for him."

"I'm sorry." Caleb cupped his daughter's cheek with his hand, his expression so tender it touched Jessie's heart. "You go along now, and come tell me good-night when you're ready."

Timothy was already rubbing his eyes. It had been a big day for a not-quite-four-year-old.

"Komm. I'll help you." When Jessie held out her hand, Timothy took it willingly enough.

But Becky's eyes flashed. "We don't need your help."

The sharp words were so unexpectedly rude coming from an Amish child that for a moment Jessie was stunned. She realized Zeb was frowning at Caleb, while Caleb was studiously avoiding his eyes.

"Becky, I'm ashamed of you to speak so to Cousin Jessie." Zeb had apparently decided that Caleb wasn't going to correct the child. "You go up at once with Cousin Jessie, and don't let me hear you talk in such a way again."

Becky looked rebellious for a moment, but at a nod from her father, she scurried ahead of Jessie and her brother, her cheeks flaming. Jessie, clutching Timmy's hand, hurried after her.

She was quick, but not quite quick enough. Behind her, she heard Zeb's voice.

"Caleb, I should not have had to speak to Becky. It's your job to teach your kinder how to behave."

Caleb's response was an irritable grumble that faded as she reached the top of the stairs.

"That's me and Becky's room," Timothy informed her, pointing. "And that's where Daadi sleeps. Onkel Daniel has that next one."

"Onkel Zeb is sleeping in the little front room," Becky said. "He had to move to make room for you." She shot a defiant look at Jessie.

But Jessie had no intention of responding in kind. Becky must see that rudeness wouldn't drive her away, if that was what the child had in mind. It had been a natural thing in a houseful of men for Zeb to put her into the adjoining daadi haus.

"It was nice of Onkel Zeb to let me use the daadi haus," she said. "He's a kind person, ain't so?"

Becky was forced to nod, and Timothy tugged at Jessie's hand, his sister's rebellion clearly passing over his head. "I'll show you where everything is."

With Timothy's help, Jessie soon figured out how he expected to be gotten ready for bed. She had to smile at his insistence on doing everything exactly the same way as always, according to him. Her brother's kinder were just like that. His wife always said that if they did something once, it immediately became a tradition they mustn't break.

The bathroom was as modern as those in any Englisch house, save for the gas lights. And she'd noticed a battery-powered lantern in the children's bedroom—a sensible solution when a light might be needed quickly. Caleb had done his best to make the farmhouse welcoming for Alice and the kinder, but that hadn't seemed to help Alice's discontent.

Alice had been too young, maybe. Not ready to settle down. She'd thought marriage and the move to Lost Creek, Pennsylvania, would bring excitement. But when life had settled into a normal routine, she hadn't been satisfied.

Jessie had seen her growing unhappiness in her letters. Maybe she'd been impatient with her young cousin, thinking it was time Alice grew up. If she'd been more comforting…

But it was too late for those thoughts. Jessie bent over the sink to help Timothy brush his teeth, but Becky wedged her little body between them to help him instead. *Fair enough*, Jessie told herself. A big sister was expected to look after the younger ones. Maybe if she ignored Becky's animosity, it would fade.

A line from Alice's last letter slid into her mind. *"You were right. I never should have come back here to die. Please, if you love me, try to repair the harm I've done to these precious little ones."*

Jessie's throat tightened. She had begged Alice to stay with her for those final months instead of returning to Caleb. But Alice had been determined, and Jessie hadn't been able to stop questioning her own motives. Whose interests had she had at heart?

Pushing the thought away, she reached over their heads to turn off the water. "All ready? Let's go down and say good-night."

Bare feet slapping on the plank floor, the kinder rushed down the stairs. Following more sedately, she saw them throw themselves at Caleb, and she winced at the kicks his cast took. But he didn't seem to notice.

Caleb cuddled each of them, apparently as reluctant to send them to bed as they were to go. It must have seemed like forever to him since his life had been normal, but she knew him well enough to understand he'd never regret risking injury to help a neighbor. That's who he was, and she admired him even when she was resenting the cool stare he turned on her.

"Go on up to bed now." Caleb helped Timothy slide down from his lap. "Sleep tight."

Smiling, Jessie held out her hands. Once again, Timothy took hers easily, rubbing his eyes with his other hand. But Becky pushed past her to grab Daniel's hand.

"I want Onkel Daniel to tuck me in," she announced.

"Sounds gut," he said, getting up and stretching. "Cousin Jessie and I will see you're all tucked in nice and snug. Ain't so, Cousin Jessie?"

She smiled, grateful that he'd included her. "That we will."

"Let's see how fast we can get upstairs." Daniel snatched up Becky and galloped toward the steps.

"Me, me," Timothy squealed, holding his arms up to Jessie.

Lifting him and hugging him close, she raced up the stairs, and they collapsed on Timothy's bed in a giggling heap. Timothy snuggled against her, seeming eager for a hug, and her heart swelled. If circumstances had been different, he might have been her child.

The unruly thought stuck to her mind like a burr. She remembered so clearly the day she'd met Caleb. He'd come from Pennsylvania for the wedding of a distant cousin, and she'd been asked to show him around. They'd hit it off at once in a way she'd given up expecting to happen to her.

And he'd felt the same. She was sure of it. That afternoon was surrounded by a golden haze in her memory—the beginning of something lovely. A perfect time—right up to the moment when they'd gone in to supper and Caleb had his first look at Alice. She'd turned from the stove, her cheeks rosy from the heat, strands of cornsilk-yellow hair escaping her kapp to curl around her face, her blue eyes sparkling and full of fun.

Jessie wrenched her thoughts away from that long-ago time. No sense at all in thinking about what might have been. They could only live today, trusting in God's grace, and do their best to make up for past mistakes.

Caleb expected Onkel Zeb to chide him again about Becky's behavior once the others had gone upstairs. His defenses went up at the thought. Becky was his child. It was his responsibility how she behaved.

Unfortunately, that wasn't a very comforting thought. He'd let his own reactions to Jessie's presence influence his daughter's behavior. Besides, Onkel Zeb was as close as a father to him…closer, in some ways, than his own daad had been. It had seemed, after Mamm left, that all the heart had gone out of his father. Onkel Zeb had been the one to step up and fill the role of both parents for him and his brothers.

The unfortunate King men, folks said. Mamm had left Daad, and then Alice had left him. Onkel Zeb's young bride had died within a year of their marriage. Daniel was definitely not looking for a wife, and as for Aaron—well, who knew what he was doing out in the Englisch world?

He darted a look at his uncle. Onkel Zeb was studying him…patient, just waiting for him to realize himself what should be done.

"Yah, you're right. I'll try to do better with Becky."

"And with Cousin Jessie," Onkel Zeb pointed out. "She is not to blame for Alice's wrongs."

"And Cousin Jessie." He repeated the words dutifully. "At least she's nothing at all like Alice was. She's plain, not pretty and flirty."

"To the *Leit*, plain is gut, remember?" Zeb's lips twitched. "I'd say Jessie has a face that shows who she is…calm, kind, peaceable. Funny that she's never married. It wonders me what the men out in Ohio were thinking to let her get away."

Truth to tell, Caleb wondered, too. If anyone seemed meant to marry and have a flock of kinder to care for, it had been Jessie. His mind flickered briefly to the day they'd met and winced away again. He had no desire to remember that day.

But Onkel Zeb's thoughts had clearly moved on, and he was talking about how things had gone while Caleb was in the hospital.

"…working out fine, that's certain sure. Sam just can't do enough for us, though I keep telling him we're all right. Guess he feels like he wants to repay you, seeing it was his barn where you got hurt."

"That's foolishness, and I'll tell him so myself. As if any of us wouldn't do the same for a neighbor. Sam's got plenty with his own farm to run. They'd best be getting his new barn up soon, ain't so?"

"Barn raising is set for Saturday." Onkel Zeb grinned. "The buggies have been in and out of Sam and Leah's lane all week with the women helping to clean and get the food ready. Nothing like a barn raising to stir folks up."

Caleb was glad Sam's barn would soon be replaced, but Zeb's words had reminded him of something else. "Maybe Leah would know of someone I can hire to help out with the kinder. What do you think?"

Onkel Zeb shrugged. "Not sure why you want to go looking for someone else when you have family right here eager to do it."

Frustration with his uncle had him clenching his hands on the chair. Before he could frame a response, he heard Daniel and Jessie coming back down the stairs. They seemed to be chuckling together over something, and Caleb felt himself tensing. Irrational or not, he wanted his uncle and brother to share his own feelings about Jessie's arrival.

They came in smiling, which just added to his annoyance. Onkel Zeb glanced at them.

"What funny thing did young Timothy say now?" he asked.

"Ach, it wasn't Timmy at all." Daniel grinned. "Cousin Jessie just didn't agree with my version of the story of the three bears."

Jessie shook her head in mock disapproval. "Even Timothy knew there wasn't a wolf in the story of the three bears. That was the three little pigs."

"Maybe you'd best stick to telling them stories about when you and their daadi were small," Zeb suggested. "And not be confusing the kinder. Or better yet, let Jessie tell the bedtime story."

Caleb could feel his face freeze. Zeb made it sound as if Jessie would be around more than a few nights to tell them stories. She wouldn't.

Jessie seemed to sense the awkwardness of the moment. She turned toward the kitchen. "What about some coffee and another piece of pie?"

"Sounds wonderful gut about now." Onkel Zeb seemed to be answering for all of them.

Caleb almost said he didn't want any. But he caught Jessie's gaze and realized how childish that would sound. So he nodded instead. Jessie's guarded expression relaxed in a smile, and for an instant she looked like the girl he'd spent an afternoon with all those years ago.

It was disconcerting. If he hadn't gone to that wedding, if he hadn't met Jessie and through her met her cousin Alice…what would his life have been then?

Jessie cleared up the plates and cups after their dessert, satisfied that her pie, at least, had met with universal approval. She'd have to take any little encouragement she could get.

Zeb and Daniel had gone to the bedroom to set up a few assistance devices the hospital had sent, leaving her and Caleb alone in the kitchen for the moment. She sent a covert glance toward him.

Caleb had his wheelchair pulled up to the kitchen table, and at the moment he was staring at the cup he still held. She suspected that he didn't even see it. His lean face seemed stripped down to the bone, drawn with fatigue and pain. Today had been a difficult transition for him, but he wouldn't want her to express sympathy.

No man wanted to admit to pain or weakness—she knew that well enough from being raised with six brothers. And clearly Caleb would resent it even more coming from her. The hurt she felt for him, the longing to do something to ease his pain…it would have to stay, unspoken, in her heart.

But the silence was stretching out awkwardly between them. "Becky is…" she began. But the words slipped away when Caleb focused on her.

"What about Becky?" He nearly snapped the words.

That didn't bother her. When folks were hurting, they snapped, like an injured dog would snarl even when you were trying to help it.

"She seems so grown-up for her age. Very helpful, especially with her little bruder."

The words of praise seemed to disarm him. "Yah, she is gut with Timothy. Always has been, especially since…" His lips shut tight then.

Especially since Alice left when he was just an infant. Those were the words he didn't want to say. She could hardly blame him. But if only they could speak plainly about Alice, it might do everyone some good.

"I know how Becky feels. I always felt responsible for Alice after her mamm passed."

Caleb's strong jaw hardened. "I don't want to talk about her. Not now. Not ever. I thought I made that clear."

She wanted to tell him that she understood, but that hiding the pain didn't make it go away. It just let it fester. But she couldn't, because he wouldn't listen. If she had more time…

"I'm sorry. I promise I won't say anything about Alice." *Until the day you're willing to talk.* "But please, think twice about sending me away. The kinder are my own blood, like it or not. I want to care for them, and they need me. You need me."

But she could read the answer in his face already. He spun the wheelchair away, knocking against the table leg in his haste. Impulsively she reached out to catch his arm.

"Please…"

The anger in Caleb's eyes was so fierce she could feel the heat of it. He grabbed her wrist in a hard grip and shoved her hand away from him.

"No." Just one word, but it was enough to send her back a step. "We don't need you. I can take care of my kinder on my own. You'll go on the bus on Friday."

Jessie looked after him, biting her lip. She should have known better than to start her plea by referring to Alice. She'd been trying to show that she understood how Becky felt, but she'd approached him all wrong.

Resolutely she turned to the sink and began washing the plates and cups. If a tear or two dropped in the sudsy water, no one would know.

Caleb might not want to hear it, but she did feel responsible for Alice, just as Becky felt responsible for Timothy. She could only hope and pray Becky never went through what she had.

"You're the older one," her mother had always said. *"You're responsible for little Alice."*

Most of the time she'd managed that fairly well. But when she'd grown older, she'd sometimes become impatient with Alice always tagging along behind her. She'd been about eleven when it happened, so Alice had been only eight. She'd tagged along as always when Jessie and her friends had been walking home from school.

They'd been giggling, sharing secrets, the way girls did when they were just starting to notice boys. And

Alice, always there, always impatient when she wasn't the center of attention, had tried to burst into the conversation. She'd stamped her feet, angry at being rejected, and declared she was going to run away.

Jessie's shame flared, as always, when she thought of her response. *"Go ahead,"* she'd said. *"I won't come after you."*

She hadn't meant it. Everyone knew that. But Alice had run off into the woods that lined the path.

"She'll come back," the other girls had said. And Jessie had agreed. Alice was afraid of the woods. She wouldn't go far. She'd trail along, staying out of sight until they were nearly home, and then jump out at them.

But it hadn't worked out that way. Alice hadn't reappeared. Jessie searched for her, at first annoyed, then angry, then panic-stricken. Alice had vanished.

Jessie still cringed at the memory of telling her parents. They'd formed a search party, neighbors pitching in, combing the woods on either side of the path.

Jessie had followed, weeping, unwilling to stay at the house and yet terrified of what the adults might find. She didn't think she'd been quite so terrified since.

It had been nearly dark when the call went up that Alice had been found. Alice wasn't hurt. They'd found her curled up under a tree, sound asleep.

Alice had clung to Jessie more than ever after that experience. And Jessie hadn't dared let herself grow impatient—not once she'd learned what the cost of that could be. She was responsible for Alice, no matter what.

Jessie tried to wipe away a tear and only succeeded

in getting soapsuds in her eye. Blinking, she wiped it with a dish towel. She heard a step behind her.

"Ach, Jessie, don't let my nephew upset you."

She turned, managing to produce a slight smile for Zeb.

Zeb moved a little closer, his weathered face troubled. "You think it would be better to talk more openly about Alice, ain't so?"

She evaded his keen gaze. "Caleb doesn't agree, and they are his kinder."

Zeb didn't speak for a moment. Then he sighed. "Do you know why I was so glad to see you today?"

"Because you are a kind person," she said. "Even Alice..." She stopped. She'd promised not to mention Alice.

"Even Alice liked me, ain't so?" His smile was tinged with sorrow. "This business of not talking about her—Caleb is making a mistake, I think. You can't forgive if you can't be open."

"Some things are harder to forgive than others."

"All the more important to forgive, ain't so?" He patted her shoulder awkwardly. "Don't give up. Promise me you won't."

She didn't know how she'd manage it, but she was confident in her answer. "I didn't come this far just to turn around and go back home again."

Renewed determination swept through her. It seemed she had one person on her side, at least. And she wasn't going to give up.

Chapter Three

Caleb woke early, disoriented for a moment at not hearing the clatter of carts and trays. He wasn't in the hospital any longer. He was home. Thankfulness swept through him, replaced by frustration the instant he moved and felt the weight of the cast dragging him down.

He was home, and those were the familiar sounds of going out to do the milking. He heard the rumble of Onkel Zeb's and Daniel's voices, and then the thud of the back door closing.

The source of the sound switched, coming through the back window now. Thomas Schutz must have arrived—he was calling a greeting to the others, sounding cheerful despite having walked across the fields in the dark.

Onkel Zeb was right about the lad. They should keep him on, even after Caleb was well enough to take on his own work. That would free Daniel to spend more time with his carpentry business instead of being tied to so many farm chores.

Caleb sat up and leaned to peer out the window. Still

dark, of course, but the flashlight one of them carried sent a circle of light dancing ahead of them. Caleb's hand clenched. He should be out there with them, not lying here in bed, helpless.

Stop thinking that way, he ordered himself. He might not be up to doing the milking or going upstairs to put the kinder to bed, but for sure there were things he could do. The sooner the better.

Using his hands to move the cast, Caleb swung his legs out of bed and sat there for a moment, eyeing the wheelchair with dislike. He didn't have a choice about using it, so he'd have to figure out how to do things with it.

First things first. If he got up and dressed by himself, he'd feel more like a man and less like an invalid. His clothes were not far away, draped on the chair where Onkel Zeb had put them the previous night. That clamp-like gripper on a long handle was obviously intended for just such a situation. Maybe he should have paid more attention to the nurse who'd explained it to him.

Getting dressed was a struggle. He nearly ripped his shirt, and got so tangled in his pants he was blessed not to end up on the floor. But when it was done, and he'd succeeded in transferring himself from the bed to the wheelchair, Caleb felt as triumphant as if he'd milked the entire herd himself.

A few shoves of the wheels took him out to the kitchen. Fortunately Zeb or Daniel had left the light fixture on, since he'd never have been able to reach that. Well, he was here, and a few streaks of light were beginning to make their way over the ridge to the east.

Jessie hadn't appeared from the daadi haus yet. The

small separate house was reached by a covered walkway. It was intended to be a residence for the older generation in the family, leaving the farmhouse itself for the younger family. When he and Alice had married, Onkel Zeb had moved in. Now Jessie was staying there, at least temporarily.

Definitely temporarily. Given how irritable she made him, the sooner she left, the better.

"The kinder need me. You need me." That was more or less what Jessie had flung at him last night. Well, he was about to prove her wrong. He'd get breakfast started on his own. Even if he couldn't go up the stairs, he could still care for his own children.

Oatmeal was always a breakfast favorite. Fortunately, the pot he needed was stored in one of the lower cabinets. Maneuvering around the refrigerator to get the milk was more of a challenge.

Feeling pleased with himself, he poured milk into the pot without spilling a drop. Now for the oatmeal. This would need the gripper, but he'd brought it out of the bedroom with him. Congratulating himself on his foresight, he used it to open the top cupboard door. The oatmeal sat on the second shelf. Maybe he ought to have someone rearrange the kitchen a bit to make the things he'd need more accessible. In the meantime, he could make do with what he had.

Caleb reached with the gripper but found it wavering with the effort of holding it out with the whole length of his arm. A little more… He touched the cylinder of oatmeal, tried to get the prongs open and around it. Not quite… He leaned over the counter, focused on the elusive box, determined to get it down.

He reached, grabbed at it, lost his hold, sent the oatmeal tipping, spilling down in a shower of flakes. The chair rolled with the imbalance of his body. He tried to stop it, and then he was falling, the floor rushing up to meet him. He landed with an almighty thud that felt as if it shook the house.

For an instant he lay there, stunned. Then, angry with himself, he flattened his palms against the floor and tried to push himself up.

"Wait." A flurry of steps, and Jessie was kneeling next to him, her hand on his arm. "Don't try to move until you're sure you aren't hurt."

The anger with himself turned against her, and he jerked away. "It's not your concern."

"Yah, yah, I know." She sounded, if anything, a little amused. "You are fine. You probably intended to drop down on the floor."

Apparently satisfied that he was okay, she reached across him to turn the chair into position and activate the brake. "Next time you decide to reach too far and overbalance, lock the wheels first."

Much as he hated to admit it to himself, she was right. He'd been so eager to show her he could manage that he'd neglected the simplest precaution. While he was still fumbling for words to admit it, Jessie put her arm around him and braced herself.

"Up we go. Feel behind you for the chair to guide yourself." Her strength surprised him, but no more than her calm reaction to what he'd done.

It took only a moment to settle himself in the chair again. He did a quick assessment and decided he hadn't damaged himself.

Jessie, ignoring him, was already cleaning up the

scattered oats. He had to admit, she was quick and capable, even if she was bossy.

"Aren't you going to say you told me so?" he asked.

She glanced up from her kneeling position on the floor, eyes widening as if startled. Then her lips curled slightly. "I have six brothers, remember? I've dealt with stubborn menfolk before. There's no use telling them."

"I suppose one of them broke his leg, so that makes you an expert."

"Two of the boys, actually." She finished cleaning the oatmeal from the floor and dumped a dustpan full into the trash. "Plus a broken arm or two. And then there was the time Benjy fell from the hayloft and broke both legs." Jessie shook her head. "He got into more trouble than the rest of them put together."

He watched as she started over making the oatmeal. Yah, *capable* was the right word for Jessie. Like Onkel Zeb said, it was surprising no man had snapped her up by now. She was everything an Amish wife and mother should be. Everything Alice hadn't been.

Caleb shoved that thought away, even as he heard voices. The others had finished the milking.

Jessie darted a quick glance at him. "No reason that anyone else needs to know what happened, ain't so?"

He had to force his jaw to unclamp so he could produce a smile. "Denke."

Jessie's face relaxed in an answering grin.

Onkel Zeb came in at that moment—just in time to see them exchanging a smile. He cast a knowing look at Caleb.

Caleb started to swing the chair away, only to be stymied because the lock was on. Still, he didn't have to meet his uncle's gaze. He knew only too well what Zeb was thinking.

All right, so maybe Jessie wasn't as bad as he'd made out. Maybe she was deft and willing and good with children. But he still didn't want to have her around all the time, reminding him of Alice.

Jessie's heart had been in her mouth when she'd heard the crash in the kitchen, knowing Caleb must have fallen. She'd been halfway along the covered walkway, and she'd dashed as fast as she could for the house door. When she'd entered the kitchen…

Well, it had taken all the control she had to put on a calm exterior. Even so, her heart hadn't stopped thumping until he was back in the chair and she could see he was all right.

She set a bowl of oatmeal down in front of him with a little more force than necessary. He was fortunate. Didn't he realize that? He could have ended up back in the hospital again.

A stubborn man like Caleb probably wouldn't admit it, even to himself. Any more than he'd admit that he could use her help. Apparently it would take more than a broken leg to make him willing to have her near him.

She slipped into her chair as Caleb bent his head for the prayer. Then she started the platter of fried scrapple around the table. Timothy took a couple of pieces eagerly, but she noticed that Becky didn't serve herself any until she saw her father frown at her. Obviously Jessie wasn't going to win Becky over easily.

Jessie's heart twisted at the sight of that downturned little mouth. Becky looked as if she'd been meant by nature to be as sunny a child as Timothy, but life had gotten in the way. If only Jessie could help…but there was no sense thinking that, unless she could change Caleb's mind.

The men were talking about whether or not it was too early to plant corn, all the while consuming vast quantities of food. Jessie had forgotten how much a teenage boy like Thomas could eat. He seemed a little shy, and he was all long legs and arms and gangly build. Tomorrow morning she'd fix more meat, assuming Caleb didn't intend to chase her out even before breakfast.

"Sam says he'll komm on Monday and help get the corn planted," Zeb said. "Told him he didn't need to, but there was no arguing with him."

Jessie noticed Caleb's hand wrapped around his fork. Wrapped? No, *clenched* would be a better word. His knuckles were white, and she guessed that the fork would have quite a bend in the handle when he was done.

Caleb wouldn't believe it, but that was exactly how she felt when he refused to let her help.

Timothy tugged at her sleeve. "Can I have more oatmeal?"

"For sure." She rose quickly, glad there was something she could do, even if it was only dishing up cereal.

"I love oatmeal." Timothy watched her, probably to be sure she was giving her enough. "Especially with brown sugar. Lots of brown sugar," he added hopefully.

"A spoonful of brown sugar," Caleb said firmly, coming out of his annoyance. Jessie met his eyes, smiling, and nodded, adding a heaping spoonful of brown sugar that she hoped would satisfy both of them.

"Shall I stir it in?" she asked, setting the bowl in front of Timothy.

He shook his head vigorously. "I like it to get melty on top." He sent a mischievous glance toward his uncle. "Onkel Daniel does, too."

Daniel laughed. "You caught me. But I'll need lots of energy at the shop today. New customers coming in to talk to me about a job." He looked up at the clock. "Guess I should get on my way."

With Daniel's departure, everyone seemed ready to finish up. Soon they were all scooting away. Left alone with the dishes, Jessie looked after them. She'd think Becky was old enough to be helping with the dishes. Probably her desire to take over didn't extend to the dishes. She'd certain sure been doing that at Becky's age. But she wasn't going to be here long enough to make any changes.

When she'd finished cleaning up the kitchen, Jessie followed the sound of voices to the living room. Becky stood backed up to the wheelchair, a hair brush in her hand. "It's easy, Daadi. Just make two braids, that's all."

Jessie stood watching, oddly affected by the sight of the vulnerable nape of the child's neck. Caleb had managed to part Becky's long, silky hair, and now he clutched one side, looking at it a little helplessly.

Gesturing him to silence, Jessie stepped up beside him and took the clump of hair. For an instant she thought he'd object, but then he grudgingly nodded. Jessie deftly separately the hair into three strands and began to braid.

Caleb watched the movement of her fingers so intently that she imagined them warming from his gaze.

If he were going to be doing this he'd have to learn… but of course he wouldn't. He'd find some other woman to take her place once he'd gotten Jessie out of the way. Maybe he already had someone lined up.

But it couldn't possibly be anyone who'd love these children more than she did. She'd come here loving them already because they were all that was left of Alice. Now she'd begun to love them for themselves… Timothy with his sparkling eyes and sunny smile, Becky with her heart closed off so tightly that she couldn't let go and be a child.

Feeling Becky's silky hair sliding through her fingers took her right back to doing the same for Alice, laughing together as she tried to get her wiggly young cousin to hold still. From the time Alice's mother died, she'd been a part of Jessie's family—the little sister Jessie had always longed for. To help raise Alice's kinder, to have a second chance to do it right this time…that was all she wanted. But with Caleb in opposition, apparently it was too much to ask.

The braiding was done too quickly. She showed Caleb how to do the fastening and then stepped back out of the way while he took his daughter by the shoulders and turned her around. "There you are. All finished."

"Denke, Daadi." Becky threw her arms around his neck in a throttling hug. "I'm wonderful happy you're home."

"Me, too, daughter." He patted her.

The thump of footsteps on the stairs announced Timothy. He jumped down the last two steps and ran into the living room. "I brushed my teeth and made my bed," he announced. "Can I show Cousin Jessie the chickens now?"

"She'll like that," Caleb said solemnly. Then he gave her a slight smile. He turned to Becky. "You go along, too."

For an instant Becky looked rebellious, but then her desire to please her daadi won, and she nodded. Timothy was already tugging at Jessie's hand. Together they went through the kitchen and out the back door.

"The chickens are this way." Timothy pulled her toward the coop. "Reddy is my very own hen. I want to see if she has an egg for me."

"In a minute." She tried to slow him down. "Look. Is that someone coming to see us?"

Jessie pointed across the pasture toward the neighboring farm. A woman and a little boy walked toward them, the boy carrying a basket by the handle. He couldn't have been much more than four or five, and he held it carefully as if mindful of his responsibility.

"It's Jacob and his mammi." Timothy dropped her hand to plunge toward the new arrivals. "Look, Becky." His sister nodded and joined him at a trot.

Jessie stood where she was and waited, unsure. This was obviously the wife of the man who'd been helping so much. It was in their barn that Caleb had been injured, and Jessie had formed the opinion that Leah and Sam were close friends of his. That being the case, she wasn't sure what kind of reception she was likely to get.

Leah and Jacob drew nearer. Caleb's kinder had reached them, and Timothy was chattering away a mile a minute to Jacob, who just kept nodding. Taking a deep breath, Jessie went to meet them.

"You'll be Jessie. Alice's cousin." The woman's

smile was cautious. She was thirty-ish, probably about Jessie's age, with a wealth of dark brown hair pulled back under her kapp and a pair of warm brown eyes. "Wilkom."

"Denke." It was nice to be welcomed, even if Leah sounded as though she were reserving judgment. Jessie smiled at the boy. "And this must be Jacob."

The boy nodded, holding out the basket to her. "Shoofly pie," he announced. "For you."

"I wasn't sure what you needed," Leah explained. "But I thought a couple of shoofly pies were always of use."

"They surely are," she replied. "Denke."

A lively controversy had already broken out between Timothy, who wanted Jacob to look for eggs with him, and Becky, who thought he'd rather play ball.

"You should do what your visitor wants," she informed her brother loftily.

"Chickens first," Jacob said. "Then ball."

Jessie couldn't help smiling as the three of them ran off toward the chicken coop. "Jacob is a man of few words, I see."

Leah's face took on a lively, amused look that Jessie suspected was more normal to her than her cautious greeting. "Especially when he's around Timothy. Does that boy ever stop talking to you?"

"Only when he's asleep." She looked after them. "I wish Becky..."

"I know." Leah's voice warmed. "If only Becky would loosen up and talk about things, she'd be better off."

"You see it, too, then. It's not just me."

Leah shook her head, and that quickly, the barriers between them collapsed under the weight of their common concern for the child. “No, it’s not just you. She may be worse with you, though, because…” She stopped, flushing.

“Because of my relationship with her mother. I know. I don’t blame her.”

“Still, she must learn to forgive her mother, or she’ll be carrying the burden around with her for the rest of her life.”

Leah’s insight touched Jessie to the core. “That’s what I think, too.” Unfortunately, Caleb didn’t see it that way.

Leah seemed to measure her with a serious gaze. Finally Leah gave a brisk nod. “Maybe you’ll be able to reach her while you’re here.”

“I won’t be here long enough, I’m afraid. Caleb… well, I am leaving tomorrow.”

“You mean Caleb is insisting you leave tomorrow, ain’t so?” Leah frowned. “I’ve known Caleb King all my life, so I guess I understand. Everyone knows the King men have always been unfortunate with women. It’s turned him sour, I fear.”

Jessie stared at her. “I heard something like that from the driver who brought me out from town, but I wasn’t sure whether to believe it.”

“They’ve had a string of unhappy situations with women, that’s certain sure,” Leah said. “Zeb losing his young wife, and then Caleb’s mammi running off and leaving the three young ones. And after what happened with Alice…well, it’s not surprising folks think so. Or that it’s made Caleb bitter.”

She hadn’t realized just how deep that belief ran from the way Leah spoke of it. Poor Caleb. She knew full well that his attitude wasn't surprising. She just wished she could make a difference.

Leah was watching her, and Jessie had to say something.

"You are wonderful kind to care so much about your neighbors. I just wish we could get to know each other better."

"Yah, I wish it, too." Leah clasped her hand, smiling. "Maybe you could dig in your heels and refuse to leave. Then what would Caleb do? He couldn't carry you out."

They were still laughing at the image when the kinder came running up to them. "Can we help with the barn raising on Saturday, Leah?" Becky looked more enthusiastic than Jessie had ever seen her. "Please?"

"You'll have to ask your daadi. If he says so, we'd certain sure like to have your help. There's lots you can do." Leah held out her hand to her son. "Now we must be getting home to fix lunch. We'll komm again when we can stay longer." She gave Jessie a warm glance. "I hope you'll be here."

"It was wonderful gut to meet you, anyway. And we appreciate the shoofly pies."

Timothy grabbed the basket handle as they walked away. "Can we have some shoofly pie, Cousin Jessie?"

"I'll help carry it," Becky said. "Let's ask Daadi about the barn raising."

They headed for the house, the basket swinging between them, and Jessie followed, smiling a little. For a moment there, in her enthusiasm for the barn raising, Becky had looked like any happy little girl. Somehow the glance gave Jessie hope. That child existed in Becky, if only she could bring her out.

Caleb sat at the kitchen table with a cup of coffee, looking a little startled at the excitement of the children. They swung the basket onto the edge of the table and rushed at their father.

"Daadi, we saw Leah and Jacob." Timothy rushed the words, wanting to be first.

"Leah says we can go to the barn raising on Saturday if you say it's all right." Becky wasn't far behind. "We'll help."

Caleb seemed to have mixed feelings about the barn raising. Was it the fact that he'd been injured when the old barn burned? Or maybe just the thought that ordinarily, he'd be up on the beams with the rest of the community, making sure the barn was finished for his neighbor?

"Barn raising is for grown-ups. I don't know how you'd help," he said.

"Jacob says he's going to carry water. I could do that." Timothy straightened as if to emphasize how tall he was.

"We could carry the food Cousin Jessie fixes. Leah said they could find something for us to do." Becky didn't look at Jessie when she said the words, but apparently she didn't mind using her if it meant she'd be allowed to help.

Apparently Caleb hadn't told them she was leaving tomorrow.

She touched their shoulders. "Why don't you give Daadi a minute to think? You go and wash your hands, and I'll cut the shoofly pie."

When they'd stampeded toward the bathroom, she turned back to Caleb. "I guess the young ones don't know I have to leave tomorrow. I'll explain to them."

"You don't have to do that."

She frowned slightly. "You mean you'd rather explain it yourself?"

"No." His voice was gruff. "I mean I've been thinking about you leaving. Maybe I was a bit hasty. If you want to, you can stay. But just until I get back on my feet again. That's all."

It wasn't the most gracious of offers, but she was too relieved to boggle at that. She felt as if an intolerable pressure had been lifted from her heart.

"Denke." Jessie struggled not to let her emotions show in her voice. "I would like that, Caleb."

Her time was still limited, but at least she had been given a chance. A quick prayer of thanks formed in her mind.

Please, dear Father. Show me what to do for these precious children.

Chapter Four

Following the noise late Friday morning, Caleb rolled himself into the kitchen. It had turned into a beehive of activity since breakfast, with racks of cookies cooling while Jessie pushed another pan into the oven. Both Timothy and Becky were intent upon baking projects, Timothy with a dish towel tied around him like an apron. Young Thomas leaned against the counter, seeming right at home with a handful of snickerdoodles.

"What's going on?"

His voice brought all the activity to a halt for an instant. Thomas straightened up, flushing and trying to look as if he didn't have his mouth full of cookies.

Jessie straightened, as well, closing the oven door. She was flushed and smiling, and with her eyes sparkling, she didn't look as plain as he'd thought. "We're baking for the barn raising tomorrow. All those workers need plenty of fuel."

"Look, Daadi." Timothy waved a fistful of dough in the air. "I'm making the little balls, see? When Cousin Jessie bakes them, they'll be snickerdoodles."

Caleb wheeled himself closer to the table. "I see. What's Becky doing?"

"I'm rolling them in cinnamon and sugar." Becky's attention was grabbed by the dough Timothy had in his hand. "That's not how to do it, Timothy. They're supposed to be round. Let me."

Timothy flared up instantly. "This is how I do it. You do your own."

Becky reached out to take the dough from him, but before it could turn into a fight, Jessie was there.

"Becky, can you help me? I need these cookies moved to the cooling tray to make room for the next batch. You're old enough to be careful not to touch the hot pan, I know."

Distracted instantly by the thought of doing something Timothy wasn't allowed to do, Becky abandoned the battle over the shape of Timothy's cookies, and peace reigned.

Thomas seemed to sidle toward the door, and Caleb waved him back. "Stay and help if you want." He pushed his chair through the doorway and out onto the back porch.

The sun's rays warmed his face, and he inhaled the familiar aroma of the farm, overlain by the baking scent coming from the kitchen. He should have been grateful just to be home instead of fretting about all that he couldn't do, but it was hard to be helpless.

Still, if he could manage a little more each day, he'd see progress. He just had to make up his mind to it. The sooner he was back on his feet, the sooner life would return to normal. Without Jessie's disruptive presence.

Hands on the wheels, he rolled himself carefully down the ramp, pleased when he reached the bottom without incident. He turned toward the barn and spotted Onkel Zeb and his brother coming toward him.

"You're out and rolling!" Daniel exclaimed. "Gut work." He grabbed Caleb's shoulder, his face creasing in pleasure.

Maybe Daniel's pleasure was mixed with relief. If the past weeks had been hard on Caleb, they'd been hard on everyone else, too.

"I had to get out," Caleb said. "If you wander into the kitchen, you might get sucked into helping with all the baking that's going on for tomorrow."

"That doesn't scare me off." Daniel headed for the steps. "I'll talk Jessie into a bag of cookies to take to the shop with me." He waved in the direction of his carpentry shop, located in its own building about twenty yards beyond the barn.

"Don't say I didn't warn you." He turned his attention to his uncle. "Thomas is in there, but he looks like he's doing more eating than helping."

Onkel Zeb shook his head. "I don't know where that boy puts it all. He's as skinny as a rake, and he eats all the time." He put his hand on the chair handle. "Headed for the barn?"

"Seems like a gut jaunt. The doctor said to keep busy."

"He probably also said to be careful not to overdo." Zeb moved as if to push the chair toward the barn.

Caleb tried to turn the wheels on his own, but it was a lot harder than he'd expected on the gravel lane. He gritted his teeth and put more muscle into it. He'd have to try harder. Zeb grasped the handles and pushed, too.

For a moment they didn't speak, but then Onkel Zeb

cleared his throat. "Seems like you decided Cousin Jessie can stay."

"For a while," Caleb said quickly. He didn't want any misunderstanding on that score. "Just until I get back on my feet."

"What made you change your mind?"

He couldn't see his uncle's face since he was pushing the chair, but he should have known Zeb would want an explanation. And he didn't have one, not really.

"I got to thinking about what you said. About her being kin to the young ones." He hesitated, remembering how he'd felt when Jessie had interceded to braid Becky's hair and then stepped back to let him take the credit. "I have to admit, she seems to care about them."

"She must, giving up her business to komm all the way from Ohio to help, ain't so?"

Caleb blinked. "Business? What business? I thought she just lived with her brother and his wife."

"She does. She helps out a lot there, too. But she has a business of her own, making baked goods to take to the Amish markets in a couple of towns. Way I hear it, it's turned into quite a success."

Caleb stopped pushing and swung to face his uncle. "How do you know all this?"

"All you have to do is talk to get to know a person." There was a chiding tone to Zeb's voice that made itself heard. He meant that Caleb should have done the same.

Caleb ducked away from the implied criticism. "I guess that's why she looks like she does about all that baking she's doing," he muttered.

"How does she look?"

Caleb shrugged. "I don't know. Happy, I guess."

Pretty. Not beautiful, the way Alice had been when they'd met, but appealing in her own way.

"If she's used to baking for market, I guess she'd take a little thing like a barn raising in her stride." Onkel Zeb frowned a little. "As for the barn raising, are you wanting to go over for it?"

Caleb's jaw tightened, and he slapped the chair. "Not likely I can be much help, is it?" Besides, he wasn't sure he wanted to visit the site of his injury so soon. He'd relived the accident enough times already.

But Onkel Zeb's frown had deepened. "Sam's been doing a lot for us while you've been laid up. Seems like it's only neighborly to go over for a spell. Visit with folks, anyway. I was thinking you could use the pony cart. It's low enough that it wouldn't be hard to get in, and the chair could go in the back."

When Caleb didn't answer right away, his uncle shrugged. "Think on it, anyway."

It wasn't easy to hold back when Zeb gave him the look that said he'd be disappointed in Caleb if he didn't go. So he supposed he'd be hauling himself into the pony cart tomorrow.

But as for his uncle's other expectation—well, why should he be interested in finding out more about Jessie's life? She'd be gone soon enough, anyway, and he wouldn't have to think about her at all. That would suit him fine, wouldn't it?

Jessie brought the pony cart up to the bottom of the ramp on Saturday. She'd been wryly amused at the expression on Caleb's face when he'd realized he'd have to let her help him get to Sam and Leah's, since Zeb and Daniel, along with Thomas, had gone as soon as they'd eaten breakfast.

She stopped the black-and-white pony so that the cart was directly in front of Caleb waiting in his wheelchair. Timothy and Becky were on either side of him, Timothy bouncing up and down in excitement.

"Here we are." Jessie hopped out of the cart and scooted around the wheelchair. "I think it will work best if the chair is right next to the cart seat." She moved it into position as she spoke and then set the brake.

Caleb didn't say anything, but he looked as if he held quite a few words back. He reached out for the cart. She intercepted him.

"Better let Becky get up there first, and she can steady the cast and help lift it in. Right, Becky?"

"For sure." She was already scrambling in, eager to help her daadi.

"Me, too." Timothy pouted.

"We need you to hold the chair steady so it doesn't wobble when Daadi pushes off it. You think you can?" Jessie asked.

"Sure. I'm strong." He seized the arm of the wheelchair and planted both feet, gritting his teeth.

"I can swing myself over." Caleb sounded for all the world like his son. He grasped the rail on the cart seat. It was lower than a buggy, but still higher than the wheelchair.

"A little extra help never hurts." Before he could object, Jessie slid her arm around him. "Ready? Go."

She hadn't given him time to argue, but she felt him stiffen, probably not liking her so close.

And they were close, very much so. Caleb grasped

her shoulder with his free hand, his body pressing against hers for what seemed a long moment. Fighting not to react, Jessie concentrated on lifting him. Becky grabbed the cast, and in a moment Caleb was seated in the pony cart, breathing heavily.

She was breathless, too, but not from the exertion. She hadn't expected—well, whatever it was she'd felt when she'd held him against her.

Nothing, she told herself fiercely, and knew it wasn't true. It seemed the feelings that had been aroused that long-ago afternoon were still there, ready to flare up. Maybe that was why her mother feared coming here would hurt her.

While the kinder argued about who was going to sit next to Daadi, Jessie folded the wheelchair and lifted it into the back of the cart. Then she placed the tins of cookies in with it.

"Just hush," Caleb said. "One of you should walk over with Cousin Jessie since there's not room for all in the cart. Who will it be?"

Neither of them wanted to, she thought with a stab of pain. Of course they'd both rather go with Caleb. "It's all right," she began, but before she'd finished, Timothy had hopped down.

"I'll walk with you, Cousin Jessie." He took her hand. Her heart gave a thump at the feel of his small hand put so trustingly in hers. Mamm had been right—being here hurt, and leaving would hurt even more.

But that didn't matter. Nothing mattered except helping Alice's children face life happily again.

Timothy beguiled the short walk by talking about what kind of barn he'd build when he was big enough. Jessie encouraged him even while she was keeping an eye on the pony cart and hoping Caleb wasn't overestimating his strength. But the cart arrived safely, and she could see several of the men helping him down and establishing him in the wheelchair. He was probably delighted that he didn't have to rely on her this time.

They had barely reached the fringe of the crowd of helpers when a smiling teenage girl appeared. "I'm helping to look after the kinder. Timothy, why don't you come along so your cousin can help the women with the food?"

Timothy switched over happily enough, spotting his friend Jacob with the other children. Jessie wasn't surprised that the girl knew who she was. Everyone in Lost Creek probably knew it by now. How they felt about it was another matter. Everyone here had known Alice. They had known what she did to her family. Would their attitude toward her carry over to Jessie?

Another teenager had gathered up Becky, and Caleb was surrounded by a group of men, so Jessie headed for the pony cart to get the cookie tins. Leah would probably want them brought to the kitchen, and the sooner she managed to face these people, the better.

The kitchen buzzed with activity. Women unpacked food and tried to put just one more casserole in an already crowded oven. Jessie hesitated inside the screen door, searching for Leah, and spotted her wedging a dish onto the refrigerator shelf.

Jessie made her way to Leah, aware of furtive glances from the other women. "Leah?"

Leah turned, her face warming with a smile even though she looked as distracted as any homemaker would who had a few too many people in her kitchen.

"Jessie, I'm wonderful glad you came. Did Caleb make it, as well?"

Jessie nodded. "He used the pony cart. Easier to get into with his cast."

"Gut, gut. He'll be wanting to be outside after all that time in the hospital." Leah glanced around as a pan clattered in the sink.

"You're busy," Jessie said quickly. "Where do you want these tins? They're snickerdoodles and whoopie pies."

Leah looked for an available flat surface and didn't find one. "Let's put them in the pantry for now." She led the way. "My shelves are getting empty now that the winter is over."

The pantry still looked very well stocked with Leah's canning, but Jessie found an empty shelf and slid the tins onto it. "Is there something I can do to help?"

Leah rolled her eyes. "Everyone asks that, but just now, I need to get organized. Once it's nearly time to serve the men, I'll need everyone's hands. Until then…"

"You'd prefer our space to our presence," Jessie said, smiling. "I understand. I'll be back."

When she returned to the kitchen, she saw that most of the other women, having deposited their offerings, were scattering outside. Leah would have organized some reliable workers, probably kinfolk, to be her aides, and they'd work best without interference. Jessie was too used to the routine of this sort of work frolic to have any doubts.

Outside, Jessie paused on the back porch to get her bearings. Long tables, probably the same ones that would be turned into benches for worship on Sunday, were already set up, and the teenage girls had the young ones corralled a safe distance from the barn going up. She caught a glimpse of Becky and Timothy chasing around with other kinder in some sort of game.

The barn was already taking shape, as the men had been hard at work since dawn. They swarmed over it like so many purposeful bees, each worker knowing the task assigned to him. Sam and Leah must be sehr happy to see their whole community contributing to their new barn. She could well remember the day the new barn had gone up on her brother's farm—he hadn't been able to stop smiling all day.

Jessie searched for Caleb almost without planning it. His wheelchair was placed next to a long wooden table that held supplies the workers would need. Even from here, she could see the tension in his figure—the way his hands gripped the arms of the chair as if he'd propel himself out of it. Watching the work go on without him must have made him feel more helpless than ever. Maybe it would have been best…

"Don't worry too much about Caleb." The unexpected voice came from behind her, and Jessie swung around to see an older woman watching her with sympathy in her face. "There, my husband is talking to him. Josiah will keep him from fretting."

Jessie suspected her cheeks were red. "I didn't… I mean…"

"Ach, I know." The woman patted her arm. "I'm Ida. Ida Fisher, Sam's mother." She gestured toward the addition to the farmhouse. "We moved into the daadi haus a few years back to give Leah and Sam's family more space. And you are Alice's cousin, komm all the way from Ohio to help out."

Jessie nodded cautiously. This woman, at least, didn't seem to harbor ill will toward her because of Alice. "I arrived on Wednesday."

"I know," she said again, chuckling this time. "The Amish grapevine works wonderful fast here in Lost Creek. Are you finding your way around all right?"

"It's fine. Onkel Zeb is a big help. And Timothy isn't shy about telling me how things should be done."

"He's a talker, that one. Such a sweet child. He and our little Jacob are growing up gut friends, just like his daadi and Caleb always were. So you don't need to worry that Caleb will get into mischief trying to help. Josiah is looking out for him, and Sam will, too. The two of them have taken care of each other more times than I can count—even when the barn was burning."

"That was when Caleb was hurt, ain't so?" She'd heard only a brief reference to the accident since she'd been here.

"The Lord was watching over both of them that day, that's certain sure." Ida's blue eyes misted with tears. "They were getting the animals out when they saw a burning timber coming toward them, Sam says. Caleb jumped, but it came down right on his leg."

Jessie touched Ida's arm in quick sympathy. "I'd guess Sam got him out, ain't so?"

Ida nodded, blotting the tears away with her fingers. "Yah, he did. I'm being foolish, crying when they're both safe. But that's how those two boys always were, getting into trouble together and pulling each other out."

"Caleb's fortunate to have such gut friends and neighbors to help him, especially since Alice..." Jessie stopped, not really wanting to talk about Alice with someone she hardly knew.

"Poor Alice." Ida shook her head. "The way I see it, she's paid for whatever mistakes she made. It's way past time for forgiveness."

Jessie's throat was tight. "I wish everyone felt that way."

Ida studied her face as if searching for answers. Whatever she saw seemed to satisfy her, because she gave a short nod.

"Maybe your visit will help. Make Caleb and the rest of the community face what they're feeling. The gut Lord forgives us in the same measure that we forgive others. That should give all of us pause, ain't so?"

Jessie nodded, and Ida gave her hand a little pat. "I see Josiah has gone off to check on something. May be a gut time for you to see if Caleb needs anything."

Was that a hint? If so, maybe she'd best follow it. Sam's mother seemed the kind of wise woman her own mother was, who always saw beneath the surface of other folks.

At least Ida was ready to be friendly, as was Leah. Perhaps Jessie's acceptance here wouldn't be so difficult after all.

She stopped a step or two short of Caleb's chair. He hadn't noticed her, probably because his gaze was intent on the workers busy erecting the framing for the barn's loft. Well, she couldn't just stand here.

"They're working quickly." A foolish comment, but at least it drew Caleb's attention.

He glanced at her and then gave a short nod. Impossible to tell what he was thinking when he wore that stern expression.

"It's going to be a bit larger than the last one, according to Sam," he said just when she thought he wasn't going to speak. "He's been impatient to get it up."

Jessie's tension eased. At least he was talking to her. Maybe she could distract him from thinking that he ought to be up there, balancing on a beam, hammer in hand.

"Close to a month they've been waiting, so Onkel Zeb says. No wonder he's eager to see it done."

"Yah, he says it was one thing after another—first delays at the sawmill, then bad weather, then Elias Stoltzfus down with the flu."

"Elias Stoltzfus?" Stoltzfus was a common enough name among the Pennsylvania Amish, but she hadn't heard of him since she'd been here.

"He's planned every barn in Lost Creek in the last forty years. No one would think it right to start building without him. Especially Elias." There was the faintest twinkle in Caleb's eye.

"I see. Moses Miller is the barn planner out in our community. If he doesn't walk it out first, no one will start to build." In fact, folks were starting to wonder what would happen when Moses, already eighty-four, couldn't go on.

Caleb glanced at her in a way that was almost friendly. "Guess there are as many things the same out in Ohio as there are different."

"I guess so. I keep expecting to see bicycles, but I gather that's not part of your tradition."

Caleb shrugged. "I've heard tell bicycles are allowed out in the Ohio communities because folks tend to live farther apart."

That hadn't occurred to Jessie before, but maybe

it was the reason. There certainly seemed to be a big concentration of Amish farms along this road, whereas in Ohio, they'd more likely be interrupted by Englisch homes.

"Probably that's why." She saw that he was staring at the men working the very top of the barn. "I suppose you're one of those who likes to work up top."

He actually chuckled at that. "I guess. The first time I was a bit scared, but when I got up there, it felt pretty good. And Sam… Sam was never afraid of heights. He was climbing to the top of the big oak tree when he wasn't much more than Timothy's age."

"Better not let Timothy hear you saying that, or we'll be coaxing him down, ain't so?"

"You've noticed he's a bit sure of himself."

"You could say that." Relief bubbled up in Jessie that they were actually talking together as though they were kin, maybe even friends.

"He's always been that way. Crawling out of his crib at ten months, he was." Caleb's smiling gaze met hers—met and held for a long, breathless moment.

They both looked away, and Jessie prayed that color wasn't flooding her cheeks. "Well, I… I came over to ask if there is anything you need."

"No. Nothing." Caleb grabbed a box of nails from the table next to him and began counting them as if the success of the barn raising depended on knowing how many nails were used.

"I'll go along and help with the lunch, then."

Jessie went hurriedly toward the house, imagining she felt people looking at her. Watching her every move with critical eyes.

Nonsense. Folks had better things to do than to

think about her. Some teenagers put plates and napkins on the tables, and women were starting to head into the kitchen. She'd be needed to help carry things out.

They'd feed the workers first, of course. That was always how it was done. That way the builders could have a bit of a break to let their food digest before getting back at it. If it was like most barn raisings, they wouldn't want to leave today until the barn was under roof, if not completely ready to use.

After the men had eaten, the women and children would take their turn at the tables, enjoying the plentiful food. Always enough and more—that was the Amish table. And then there'd be all the cleaning up to do.

She searched for Timothy and spotted him still running, maybe a little slower than before. The boy had plenty of energy, but he was likely to tire out before too long. That might be a good excuse to get Caleb to go home, as well. He'd been out of the hospital only a few days, and he'd probably been told to take it easy, although he wouldn't want to admit it.

Taking a deep breath, she prepared to plunge into the maelstrom of activity in the kitchen. All of the other women seemed to have the same idea, but the service was surprisingly orderly. Each person picked up a dish handed over by Leah or one of her helpers and then filed out with it, passing those still waiting in line.

With the assembly line working at full speed, it wouldn't take long to have everything out to be served. Jessie's thoughts fled back to Caleb. He might need someone to help the wheelchair across the grass. But of course one of the men would assist him. He didn't need her.

Jessie grabbed the dish of whipped potatoes that was handed to her and hurried back out the door, following the lead of the woman ahead of her in placing her dish. Then she started back, not sure whether there would be a second round of deliveries.

The entry line seemed to have slowed to a crawl, so Jessie stopped on the porch. A glance back told her that the men were already taking their places on the long benches, and she spotted Caleb with his wheelchair situated at the end of one table. So that was all right.

She tore her attention away from him in time to hear the conversation of the women ahead of her, who were just inside the screen door.

"...terrible, having the nerve to come here and move in on Caleb after what her cousin did. I'm surprised Caleb let her stay."

Jessie was frozen in place, cold hands clasping one another.

"Caleb had better watch out, that's all," the other woman said. Jessie caught just a glimpse of her when she moved—an older woman, sharp-featured, wearing black. "A helpless widower with two young children... She's out to trap him, that's what. Did you see her watching him? Not content with her cousin breaking his heart...now she's after him herself."

Jessie took a step back, then another. She had never been so mortified in her life. How could anyone possibly think that about her?

Well, she'd wondered how she'd be accepted here, hadn't she? Now she knew.

Chapter Five

Caleb didn't want to admit how much the barn raising had taxed his strength, but by Sunday morning he had no choice but to face it. He wasn't the person he'd been before the accident, and there were days he feared he never would be.

He tried to shake off the feeling as he struggled into the wheelchair. That process was getting easier, he reminded himself. The doctors had been right to insist he spend two weeks in the rehab hospital. Without that time, he wouldn't have been ready to come home.

Now for today's challenge—going to worship. This was church Sunday, and folks would expect to see him there. Their community, like most in Pennsylvania, held worship every other Sunday. He wheeled himself out to the kitchen.

Jessie was already at the stove while Onkel Zeb, Daniel and the kinder sat at the table eating. Jessie's smile looked a little strained as she spooned up oatmeal for him and poured a mug of coffee.

Now that he thought about it, she'd seemed unusually quiet after they'd returned home from the barn raising yesterday. He gave a mental shrug. He didn't understand what made Jessie tick, and that was just fine. He'd been pushed by circumstance into accepting her help, but that didn't mean he wanted to be friends.

Daniel gave him a sidelong look as he took his place at the table. "You sure you should be going to worship today? Nobody would blame you if you stayed home."

He glared at his brother. "I'm fine." He bit out the words. Daniel shrugged, not impressed by his ill humor. Or maybe thinking it showed he wasn't fine at all.

"I want to be at church," he added, modifying his tone so nobody could accuse him of being cranky. "I've missed it. Anyway, that's where we belong on a church Sunday, ain't so?"

"That's certain sure." Jessie put a bowl of scrambled eggs on the table and then took her seat. "I suppose a lot of the folks who were at the barn raising were from your church district?" Her tone made it a question.

"Most of them," Onkel Zeb said. "Some were from the next district over. Here, each bishop has two districts. Is it that way out in Ohio?"

Jessie nodded, her mind seeming to be on something else. Whatever it was, it had taken the sparkle from her eyes.

Caleb frowned. But he worried how he would manage just getting to worship. He didn't need to be wondering about Jessie.

Daniel and Onkel Zeb had obviously given some thought to the problem of transporting him to worship. They'd rigged an improvised ramp to lift him to the level at which he could move over to the buggy seat. He and Daniel would go in the smaller buggy, while Onkel Zeb took Jessie and the kinder in the family buggy.

He barely suppressed a sigh once he was settled on the buggy seat. Daniel picked up the lines and released the brake before he spoke. "I don't want to get my head bitten off, but don't push yourself too hard."

Caleb pushed down the frustration that wanted to release. "Sorry," he muttered. "I hate seeing everyone else carrying my load."

"Guess I'd feel that way, too," Daniel admitted. "But you'd do the same for every one of us, ain't so?"

Caleb grunted. "It's easier to be on the giving end."

His brother grinned. "Maybe the gut Lord decided to teach you some humility."

Was that true? If so, the Lord had surely found the hardest way of doing it—forcing him to depend on Jessie, of all people. The idea was enough for him to chew on the rest of the short ride to the Stoltz farm, and he still hadn't finished with it when they arrived.

Daniel took the buggy right up to where folks were gathering outside the barn—men and boys arranging themselves in one line while women and girls did the same in another. Soon they'd be filing into the Stoltz barn for worship, going from oldest to youngest, as always.

Several men hurried forward to help, and Caleb was lifted down and installed in the wheelchair almost before he had time to brace himself. Becky and Timothy came running over, trailed by Onkel Zeb and Jessie.

Funny. He took another look. Jessie's strained expression seemed to have intensified. Was it possible she was nervous about meeting all these people who were as close to him as family?

"I'll sit by you, Daadi." Timothy grabbed the arm of the wheelchair, bouncing up and down.

"No." Becky's pout had returned. "I want to sit next to Daadi."

"You'll sit on the women's side, like you always do," Onkel Zeb said firmly.

"No, please, Daadi. I want to sit with you."

Jessie didn't speak. She just looked at him, and Caleb knew she was waiting for his verdict. But there couldn't be any question, could there?

"Becky, you always sit on the women's side. Go with Cousin Jessie now."

Jessie held out her hand, smiling at his daughter. "Komm. I need you to show me where to go in the line."

Becky folded her arms mutinously, and Caleb's patience snapped. "Rebecca Jane, stoppe! Go to your cousin this instant!"

He'd spoken so sharply that several people nearby turned to look at him. Becky's lips trembled. Annoyed with her and disgusted with himself, he spun the chair away.

What kind of father was he turning into? What was wrong with him?

"Komm." Jessie's voice was soft, but it reached him, and he felt sure she'd taken Becky's hand. "Folks are cross when they're in pain, ain't so? We just have to understand and love them, anyway."

If it was possible for him to feel any more ashamed than he did already, Jessie's words would have done it.

Jessie breathed a silent prayer that Becky would understand. Then Becky took her hand and led her toward the lineup of women and girls. As they passed the single young women, Becky hesitated, glancing up at Jessie.

Jessie answered the question in the child's face. "At home I sit with the women who are about my age, even though they're all married but me." Becky obviously hadn't known where to put her, which wasn't surprising. Everyone from her rumspringa group was long since married, and it had seemed foolish to sit with younger and younger unmarried girls. She had no plans to be married, so the day she'd joined them had been a silent announcement, if any were needed, that she considered herself a spinster.

Not a pretty term, but it was true. She'd given up the idea of marriage a long time ago.

Now the question was how to avoid the women she'd heard talking about her yesterday at the barn raising. She cringed inside at the memory of those hurtful words. *Forget them*, she ordered herself, but since she'd been saying the same thing all night, the command didn't seem to be working.

She'd had only a quick glimpse of one face, so how would she know them for sure? And for all she knew, everyone here was thinking the same thing, even if they weren't so outspoken about it.

Fortunately, before Jessie could sink any deeper, she saw Leah gesturing to her. Relief lifted her heart. She had one friend here, at least. That was something to thank the gut Lord for.

Leah greeted her with a smile. "Komm, sit with us."

"Denke." Leah couldn't know how thankful she really was. "Becky is showing me around this morning."

"Gut." Leah touched Becky's cheek lightly. "I'm

glad you're taking care of your cousin. And everyone will be sehr happy to see your daadi back in worship this morning."

Becky nodded without speaking, still looking on the edge of tears. Jessie could almost believe the child pressed a little closer to her. Maybe it was possible to break through the barriers Becky had put up between them, but she certain sure didn't want it to be at the cost of Becky's close relationship with her daadi. This was proving much trickier than she had imagined when she'd left home so full of hope.

The line started to move then, so there was no time for more. But Becky's hand stayed in hers all the way into the barn and while they filed into the rows of benches on the women's side of worship.

The two rows of mammis and small children were so placed that they had the rumspringa-age girls in front of them and then the row of young girls who were deemed old enough to sit together in worship. Their older sisters and mothers would keep a close eye on them. Jessie smiled a little, remembering the day her brother's oldest had begun to giggle in worship and been escorted, face flaming, back to sit with her mamm.

Sitting on the hard backless benches for three hours could be a challenge. Jessie let her gaze slide covertly to the men's side, where she saw with relief that Caleb was in his wheelchair, pulled up to the end of a bench next to his brother and little Timothy. At least he hadn't stubbornly insisted on moving to the bench, where his cast would have had little or no support.

"I hope Caleb is not overdoing it." Leah had mastered the gift of whispering just loudly enough to be heard by her neighbor.

Jessie nodded. “Me, too. But he’s…” She let that trail off, not wanting to seem critical.

“Stubborn.” Leah supplied the word, the corner of her mouth twitching. “I know.”

The song leader began the long, slow notes of the first song, with the rest of the worshippers joining in. Jessie had no need to consult the book of hymns to join in the familiar words. Next to her, Becky sat very straight, adding her small voice to the song of praise.

Jessie was relieved that the service was familiar from her own church district. There were always differences in custom from one district to another, but from what she had seen so far, Caleb’s was very similar to hers in Ohio except for some minor differences in what technology they accepted.

Had that made Alice feel at home when she came here? Or would she have felt stifled by it, with her longing for change and adventure unmet?

Jessie discovered her fingers were twisting together in her lap, and she forced them to be still. Everyone had been happy when Caleb started courting Alice. Apparently Jessie had been the only one to question whether Alice was actually ready for marriage. If she had spoken out then, might it have made a difference?

But she hadn’t. She’d been hamstrung by the undeniable fact that she had thought she would be the one Caleb wanted. Anyone might think she was speaking out of her own disappointment.

Jessie didn’t think other people’s opinions would have stopped her, if only she hadn’t feared in her own heart that it might be true that she felt jealous.

Probably the result would still have been the same. *Accept*, the faith counseled. *Accept what God sends as His will.* She'd tried. She was still trying.

Halfway through the long sermon, given today by the bishop, Becky began to sag. Leah eased her arm around the child, wishing with all her heart that Becky would relax against her and accept the love she had to share.

The bishop was talking now of the love the shepherd had shown, leaving the ninety-nine behind to seek and save the one who was lost. Love for his people seemed to shine in Bishop Thomas's face as he spoke, and Jessie warmed to him. She felt for a moment as if he talked directly to her. She wasn't exactly lost, but she was alone in a strange place. Maybe Bishop Thomas was someone she could turn to if necessary.

Becky jerked upright when Leah's two-year-old, Miriam, kicked her legs fretfully as she sat on her mamm's lap. As if it were catching, Becky began kicking her feet.

Jessie pulled her attention away from the bishop's preaching on the lost sheep and exchanged looks with Leah. Both of them were obviously familiar with the efforts involved in keeping small children quiet during a long worship service. And Jessie couldn't help wondering how many people were watching her with critical eyes, ready to seize on the slightest mistake on her part.

Drawing out a white handkerchief, Jessie began shaping it into, if you used considerable imagination, a bunny. She slipped it over her fingers and made it hop over to Becky. Her attention captured, Becky made the bunny hop along her own lap.

Little Miriam made a grab for it and was thwarted by her mother. Smiling, Leah hushed her small daughter and passed another handkerchief over to Jessie so that she could produce a second bunny. In two minutes the kinder were happily…and silently…playing. Peace reigned until the end of worship.

As they rose from the final prayer, Leah turned to her, smiling. "That was a lifesaver, Jessie. You must show me how to do it."

"For sure. But they fall apart pretty fast, I'm afraid."

Becky was tugging at her, so she moved out of the way of the men and boys who were rapidly changing the benches into the tables that would be used for lunch. Later they'd be loaded onto the church buggy, ready to be taken to the next host residence for worship.

Leah was saying something about her fretful daughter when Jessie's attention was drawn away by a voice that was only too familiar. An older woman, filing out of a seat a few rows behind her, spoke to the woman next to her. The words didn't matter, but the voice… the voice was that of the woman who'd said those hurtful words yesterday at the barn raising. When Jessie looked closer, she recognized the sharp-featured face.

Jessie waited a moment before turning to Leah. "Who is the woman just going out two rows behind us?"

"The one in the black dress with the gray hair? That's Ethel Braun. Bishop Thomas Braun's wife."

Jessie's heart sank to her shoes. The bishop had preached about love and forgiveness, and she'd been drawn to him, eased by his words. All the while his wife spread hateful rumors about Jessie. It didn't look as if she could expect any understanding from the bishop.

* * *

Why does it matter what anyone else thinks? Jessie, sitting in the living room rocker with a stack of mending that evening, tried to dismiss the reactions of Caleb's community from her mind. She had made a friend in Leah, and some of the other young married women had cautiously approached her, so the prospect of being accepted wasn't entirely bleak. Besides, her job here was to make things better for Caleb and the kinder, not to worry about her own popularity or lack of it.

How Alice had expected her to do that was another question. The last letter from Alice had laid a burden on her, but not even Alice had suggested how Jessie might make things right with the family she'd left behind. Alice probably hadn't known—she'd just had a glimmer of hope that her older cousin would solve her problems, as Jessie so often had.

Jessie picked up one of Becky's dresses from the mending basket. The hem had pulled out—a simple enough fix, but it made her wonder who had been taking care of the mending and sewing for the family. Neighbors or relatives, she supposed, but if so, they'd allowed it to pile up fairly high. She'd have several evenings' work just to catch up.

Caleb cleared his throat, and she glanced at him. He'd seemed engrossed in the newspaper, so she'd respected his silence. But now he was frowning, glancing first at her and then down at his hands.

"About Becky..." He came to a stop, frown deepening.

"What about her?" Jessie kept her voice even, wondering if this would be another warning about what she should or shouldn't say to his daughter.

"I heard what you told her this morning. After I was so short with her."

"I'm sorry if I spoke out of turn." She swallowed a number of things she would have liked to say.

"It's not that." He looked directly at her, and she was startled by the pain in his face. "You were right in what you said. Becky shouldn't question doing what she's told, but there was no reason for me to tell her so harshly."

What could she say? He was right, of course, and yet she understood. "Being sick or in pain does make a person a bit short-tempered."

"It's important that Becky listen." He seemed to be arguing with himself. "But I… I wonder if I should say anything to her about it. If I should…"

"Apologize?" she finished for him. Jessie made several stitches in the hem to give herself time to think. "It's a hard decision. But I remember a time when my daad and one of my brothers were at odds most of the time." Her lips curved upward, remembering. "Joshua was fourteen, and thought he knew all the answers about everything. He got sassy with Daad at a time when Daad was worried about the milk tank leaking. He was afraid we were going to lose a whole day's production and maybe risk the contract with the dairy. Anybody smart wouldn't have butted in at a time like that."

"Joshua wasn't smart, I take it." Caleb's interest had been caught.

"Not as smart as he thought he was, anyway. Josh was the last straw, and Daadi blew up at him." She paused. "He was sorry afterward, that was certain sure.

He'd always been fair, and it was like he'd let himself down, as well as Josh."

"Yah, it does feel that way." Caleb ran his hand through his hair in a frustrated gesture. "What did he do about it?"

"At first I didn't think either of them was willing to be the first to speak. But then Daad said he was sorry, that he shouldn't have taken his worries out on Josh. Josh just stood there for a minute. Then a couple of tears spilled over, and the next thing he was crying and saying it was his fault." She grinned. "Which it was, but he finally grew out of being so obnoxious."

Caleb's smile flickered. "Yah, I have little brothers, too. Denke, Jessie."

For once it seemed they were really communicating, without all the barriers between them. Something that had been tied up in knots inside Jessie began to ease.

There was a clatter at the back door as Onkel Zeb, Daniel and the kinder came in from doing the evening chores. Not that the little ones would be much help, as small as they were, but that was how children learned—by standing beside an adult, first watching, then helping, then finally doing it all by themselves.

Jessie folded the mending. "I'll go up and get things ready for bed."

They'd fallen into a routine already in the few days she'd been there. By disappearing upstairs to prepare for the kinder's bedtime, she gave Caleb a few minutes alone with them. He'd need it tonight if he intended to tell Becky he was sorry for his anger.

Jessie understood his hesitation. It wasn't easy to admit you'd been wrong, especially when the other person had been wrong, as well. Caleb wouldn't want

Becky to get the idea that it was all right for her to disobey, but he wanted to be honest with her, too.

Taking her time, Jessie got everything ready. Then she started downstairs quietly, ready to retreat if it seemed Caleb was still having a private talk with Becky. But when she reached the spot from which she could look into the living room, all seemed fine. Timothy was on the floor, showing his daadi something about his farm animal set, while Becky cuddled on Caleb's lap.

Relieved at the sight, she went on to the living room, smiling. "This looks like a happy group."

"I was showing Daadi the brown-and-white cow I have. I named her Brownie. Do you think that's a gut name for a cow?" Timothy's blue eyes were very serious.

"Very gut. It describes her, doesn't it?"

He gave a decided nod, and she suppressed a grin at his determination.

"If I had a cow, I'd name her Buttercup," Becky said, leaning against her daadi's shoulder. "Do you think I could have a calf to raise all by myself, Daadi?"

"In a year or so," Caleb said. He smoothed back the strands of blond hair that had slipped out of her braids, and the tender look on his face told Jessie everything was all right between them now.

Even as she thought it, Caleb's gaze moved to her face with a smiling acknowledgment that her words had helped. Her heart swelled. They seemed to have reached a truce, and that was surely enough to be going on with. Perhaps they could even be friends one day.

Caleb glanced at the clock. "Time you young ones were in bed. Put the farm set away now, Timothy."

For an instant Timothy pretended not to hear. Jessie knelt next to him. “Should Brownie go into the barn for the night?” She “walked” the cow toward the barn.

“I’ll do it,” Timothy said, his smile instantly restored. He set about putting the pieces away, and in a moment Becky slid down from her daadi’s lap.

“I’ll help.”

Jessie stood, smiling. That sort of cooperation was sweet to see between sister and brother. In a normal Amish family, there might be another baby or two by now, and they’d be sharing time and attention, but for Becky and Timothy, there was no other sibling. Or cousin, either, for that matter, and Daniel showed no sign of getting serious about anyone. Maybe he, like everyone else, believed the King brothers to be unfortunate in love.

She waited while Becky and Timothy kissed their daadi. When she bent over to detach Timothy, who had a tendency to use Caleb’s cast to climb on, Caleb caught her wrist. She raised startled eyes to his, wondering if he could feel her pulse pounding.

“Denke,” he said again, softly.

He let go, looked away, and time moved on at its usual pace. But for a moment, it seemed to have stopped indefinitely.

The kinder were already scrambling up the stairs, and Jessie hurried after them with more speed than dignity. She couldn’t let Caleb imagine she had any feelings for him. She just couldn’t.

Timothy was already at the bathroom sink, brushing his teeth, but Becky lingered in the bedroom.

“Cousin Jesse, could I have my hair in one braid for the night? So it won’t get tangled?”

"For sure." She tried to keep her elation from filling her voice. Becky was actually letting her do something. This was a red-letter day indeed.

They sat side by side on the bed while Jessie unpinned the silky soft hair and ran the brush through it, careful of any tangles. As she started winding the strands into the loose braid that would be comfortable for sleeping, Jessie found herself slipping backward in time.

Wasn't it just yesterday that she'd done the same thing for Alice? She'd been so glad to have a small girl cousin, since Mamm and Daadi hadn't provided her with any sisters. Alice had been a pleasant change from the boys, who never wanted to sit still for a minute and certain sure wouldn't let her brush their hair.

"There we go."

The bottom of the braid was well below Becky's shoulder blades, and Jessie rested her hand against the child's back as she found the band to secure the braid. How small and fragile Becky seemed in this quiet moment, with the vulnerability of her nape exposed. Jessie was swept with an intense wave of protectiveness.

After Jessie fastened the band, Becky shook her head so that the single braid swung from side to side. "Feels gut."

"Your mammi used to say that, too. You look very like her." The words were out before Jessie remembered that she wasn't supposed to mention Alice to the kinder.

But she didn't have time to worry about that, because Becky's reaction was too violent to let her think of anything else.

"I'm not! I'm not like her!" Becky burst into a storm

of weeping and threw herself onto the bed, her whole body shaking.

For an instant Jessie froze, aghast at the reaction to her simple words. Fortunately it seemed no one else had heard. At least, no one came hurrying to see what was wrong.

She bent over Becky, almost afraid to speak for fear of saying the wrong thing again. "I'm sorry, Becky. I didn't mean to upset you. Please forgive me." She kept her voice soft and gentle, praying silently for guidance.

Oh, Lord, help me know what to do for this troubled child.

Becky's sobs eased. "I don't look like her. Not one little bit." Her voice had returned nearly to normal, interrupted only by a little hiccup.

"If you say so." Jessie hesitated, wondering how much she dared to say. "Is it bad to look like her?" She carefully didn't speak Alice's name.

Sniffing a little, Becky sat up, nodding. For an instant, Jessie thought that was all she'd get by way of explanation. Then Becky blinked away the tears. She stared down at the floor.

"Daadi might not like me if I look like her," she whispered.

Jessie felt as if Becky had grabbed her heart and squeezed it. She couldn't seem to get her breath. How could the poor child have come up with this idea?

But she knew how, didn't she? Caleb, and his determination never to speak of Alice.

She focused on Becky, praying she might feel the love in Jessie's heart. "Your daadi loves you and Timothy more than anything in the whole world, no matter what you look like. I promise you."

Becky pierced her with an intent stare. "Are you sure?"

"I'm sure," she said. "If you were purple with blue-and-white stripes, your daadi would still love you just the same."

That brought the smile she'd hoped for to Becky's face. But it didn't solve the problem.

Caleb should be made to know and understand the harm his attitude was doing to Becky. If Jessie tried to tell him, though, he would turn on her with all the anger bottled up in his heart. The brief truce between them would be over.

He wouldn't listen to her words. But somehow he had to be made to see the truth.

Please, Lord. I don't think I can do this. Please, help me.

Chapter Six

Getting ready for the visiting therapist to arrive on Monday morning, Caleb found he was still a bit uneasy about Jessie. The plan was to have the therapist come every week, while he went to the clinic periodically. Not that it was any concern of his, but she was, in a sense, his guest, and she'd seemed distracted, almost worried, since they'd come home from worship on Sunday.

Even now, while she cleaned up the kitchen after breakfast, Jessie acted as if she was preoccupied with something other than the job in front of her. Maybe she was bored. The thought slid into his mind. After all, Alice had become bored with this life quickly enough.

That was probably unfair. Jessie had spent many years as an adult helping with her brother's children and doing all the things any Amish woman would take for granted. She wouldn't have expected anything else here.

But at the moment he'd rather think she was bored, illogical as it was, than assume he was in some way responsible for her feelings. He hadn't invited her here.

That justification didn't seem sensible, even to him.

The sound of a car pulling up next to the house put an end to his fruitless imaginings. "That'll be the therapist," he said.

Jessie swung around as if she hadn't realized he was in the room. "Ach, yah, that's who it will be." She dried her hands on a dish towel. "I'll get the door."

The kinder came stampeding down the hall at the sound of the vehicle. "We'll go," Becky said. "We'll get it, Cousin Jessie."

Jessie smiled and nodded, but she followed them. Just as well, since even Becky didn't have much Englisch yet. In September, when she started first grade, she'd begin learning the Englisch an Amish person needed to get along in the world. But around the house and with other Amish folks, Pennsylvania Dutch was spoken.

Becky pulled the door open almost before the man had finished knocking, but then, as Caleb had expected, she was struck dumb with shyness, stepping back and blushing. Thankfully Jessie had reached them by then.

"Please, komm in. Caleb is expecting you."

"I'm Joe Riley." He was young, with reddish hair and freckles, and he grinned at the kinder in a friendly way. "Who are you?"

"This is Becky, and this is Timothy." Jessie touched them lightly as she said their names, and then she switched from Englisch to Pennsylvania Dutch. "Give the gentleman room. He's here to help Daadi with his exercises."

Still speechless, the children backed into the kitchen from the entryway.

The therapist raised his eyebrows at Jessie. "And you are?"

"Cousin Jessie," she said. "Caleb is here." She ushered him into the kitchen, and Joe came over to shake hands with Caleb.

"We met before you were released from rehab, didn't we? I bet you're enjoying being back in your own house after all that time in the hospital. And having some good home cooking, too, right?"

Caleb nodded, wondering why all the therapists he'd run across were so unwaveringly cheerful. "Yah, that's so. It's good of you to come to the house."

"That's my job." Joe set a duffel bag on the table. "We can't just let you sit in that chair when you get home. Have to help you build up your strength so this leg won't be as weak when the cast comes off."

"Yah, I know." Caleb took himself to task for sounding unwelcoming. The man was here to help him, and the more Caleb worked at it, the faster he'd get back to doing the things he wanted.

"Just remember that the leg will be wasted some after all this time in a cast. Even after it comes off, you'll still have to work on getting the strength back in it."

Maybe the therapist thought he needed the cautionary words. He probably did, since he'd seen the cast as the enemy.

"Where would be the best place to work?" Caleb asked.

Joe looked around. "This would be a good spot. Nice smooth floor and not much to trip on. If it's okay to move the table and chairs, that is." He glanced at Jessie as if rearranging the kitchen was up to her.

"Yah, it's fine," Caleb said. This was his house, not Jessie's.

"I'll take the chairs into the dining room." Jessie suited action to words and the kinder, catching on even though Joe had spoken in Englisch, hurried to help.

It was quickly done, and then Joe grabbed one end of the table while Jessie took the other. They put it against the far wall.

"Great! Now we can get to work." Joe was relentlessly happy, and Caleb expected he'd be relentless about pushing him, as well.

"The children and I will get out of your way." Jessie shooed the children gently toward the other room. "Just call if you need anything."

They began with some of the simple routines he'd done in the rehab hospital. After a few minutes Joe called a halt.

"Okay, obviously I don't need to start with building upper body strength. I guess a farmer already has plenty of that, not like somebody who sits at a desk all day."

Caleb hadn't expected to find this process amusing, but he was returning Joe's grin. "Yah, when you're tossing hay bales around, you build up a few muscles."

"Let's get on to the hard stuff, then." Joe bent to check the cast and the pulse in Caleb's ankle. "See, what happens is that this leg is losing muscle all the time it's in the cast. Right?" He glanced at Caleb's face to make sure he was following. "So we want to keep the muscles working as much as possible. That's going to help you move around more easily with the cast on, and also keep you from losing too much. Okay?"

He always seemed to want agreement with his statements, so Caleb nodded. Maybe that was the therapist's way of ensuring that his patient was on board.

"I want to get back to my regular work," Caleb said, "so whatever you say to do, I'll do it. I'm needed here, and I can't run a dairy farm from a wheelchair."

"You might be surprised at what people can do from a wheelchair," Joe said, his face serious. "I worked with a farmer up north of here who couldn't get around without a chair, and he did all right. He even rigged up a lift he could work himself to get from the chair to his tractor."

Maybe Joe meant that to be encouraging, but Caleb didn't care to picture that kind of a life for himself. He would get his strength back, and everything would be as it had been.

"All right," Caleb said. "Let's get to work."

Caleb almost regretted his words over the next half hour. Joe worked him every bit as hard as he'd expected, and Caleb felt convinced that the cast was getting heavier with every repetition.

By the time Joe stepped back with a satisfied nod, he was breathing about as hard as Caleb was. He stood for a moment and seemed to be considering something.

"I'm going to give you a bunch of exercises to do on the days I don't come." He pulled a couple of printed sheets from his bag. "But they're not things you can easily do on your own. What we really need is someone to help."

Before Caleb could respond, Joe had spun and walked into the living room. "Hey, Jessie? Could you come and give us a hand?"

"For sure."

Caleb's jaw tightened at Jessie's quick assent. If Joe

expected him to accept Jessie's help with the exercises, he was mistaken.

Jessie and Joe came back to the kitchen, the kinder trailing along behind, their eyes round with curiosity. "Caleb will have to do this routine on the days I don't come, and it's not something the client can do alone. Can I count on you to help?"

Jessie's face didn't give anything away, but Caleb thought she didn't like the idea. Still, she'd never say so. He knew she'd consider it her duty.

Jessie answered as he'd expected. "I'm wonderful glad to help any way I can. What do you want me to do?"

Caleb had to stop this before it went any further. "Jessie has enough to do with the kinder and the house. I can work on my own."

"Sorry." Joe's smile flashed, but he sounded firm. "You really can't. Not and do what needs to be done. This definitely requires another person."

"Then my uncle can help," Caleb said impatiently.

"Is that the older man I saw working outside when I came in? Looks like he already has plenty to keep him busy."

"He does," Jessie said. "I'm the logical person to help Caleb." She turned to the children and spoke quickly without giving him time to argue. "You'll help me with Daadi's exercises, ain't so?"

"We'll help. We'll do a gut job, Daadi. We really will." Becky was solemn in her assurances, and Timothy ran over to scramble up into his lap.

"Looks like you're outvoted," Joe said. He gestured with the papers to Jessie. "Here are diagrams that show exactly how the exercises are supposed to be done. I'll demonstrate them to you, just to be sure."

Jessie nodded, her head bending over the papers. Her soft brown hair was parted in the center and swept smoothly back under her kapp, and the column of her neck was slim and strong. There was determination in the firm line of her jaw. If Jessie thought she was going to give Caleb orders…

But was that really what bothered him about this idea? Or was it the fact that he wasn't sure how he felt about working so closely with her?

"I want to help plant the garden!" Timothy ran alongside Jessie that afternoon, while Becky trailed behind.

"For sure you're going to help," Jessie assured him. "And Becky, too."

Becky's face gave her feelings away so readily. She wanted to participate, and yet she was resentful of each new chore Jessie took over. "Onkel Zeb planted the garden last year," she pointed out.

"He'd like to do it this year, but he's been wonderful busy since your daadi got hurt, so I said we'd help." Jessie glanced at Becky. "He got it all ready for us, and he said you were a big help last year."

Becky's face brightened. "I was. And I'm bigger this year, so I can do even more."

"We'll make a gut job of it, then, with such gardeners." They'd reached the plot not far from the kitchen that had been plowed and harrowed. "Onkel Zeb says we should wait a week or two for the tomatoes and peppers, but we can already plant a lot of the vegetables."

Using the corner of a hoe, she marked out a furrow

for each of the kinder and gave each one a seed packet. "Drop just a seed or two at a time," she cautioned, remembering her small nephew planting by the handful.

But these two seemed happy enough to follow directions. Jessie moved along with them. "Not too deep," she cautioned when Timothy poked a hole with his finger. "Remember, when the seed sprouts, it has to work its way clear up through the soil so it can reach toward the sun."

"How long will it take?" Timothy eyed the seeds he'd just planted. "I want to see it sprout."

"Some seeds take a week. Some take two or even longer." Thinking of her nephew's activities, she added, "You can't dig it up to see if it's sprouting, you know. If you do that, it will never grow."

Timothy's mouth turned down. "But I want to see it."

"You will," she assured him. "When it's ready, it will pop up through the ground. A couple of little leaves will start to open. Then you can watch it grow bigger every day."

"Then we'll water it," Becky added. "That will help it grow."

"Yah, that's so." Jessie smoothed the soil over a few more seeds. "Jesus said that our faith is like a tiny seed planted inside us. He helps it grow just like the sun helps the plant grow, until it's strong and healthy and able to do good things."

She wasn't sure Timothy was getting it, but Becky seemed to mull over her words. "Good things like helping other people," she said finally. "Onkel Zeb says a good deed is like a lighted candle in a dark room. It helps folks see."

"Onkel Zeb is a wise man," Jessie said, relieved. She had wondered who was teaching them the gentle examples of faith from everyday life that an Amish mother imparted without even thinking about it. It sounded as if Zeb had sensed that need in Becky and Timothy and was trying to fill the gap.

They'd reached the end of the third row of planting when Timothy leaped up. "Daadi's coming out!" He charged toward the porch, closely followed by Becky, their feet making small prints on the row of newly planted seeds.

Jessie got up slowly. She and Caleb hadn't spoken to each other since the physical therapist left, and she hesitated to bring up the subject. Clearly Caleb hadn't wanted her to be the one to assist him, and she hadn't really wanted to, either.

But she felt quite sure that their reasons were very different. Caleb didn't want to be beholden to her because he resented her presence—or maybe more accurately, he resented the fact that she was a reminder of Alice.

Her reasons were much more complicated. Over the years, she'd convinced herself that she couldn't be blamed for having feelings that had started before Caleb had even so much as seen Alice. And anyway, those feelings had long since faded to the vanishing point.

Unfortunately, she wasn't quite as sure of that fact as she had been. And being close to him, helping him with his exercises, touching him…that could be very dangerous to her emotions. To her heart, which still seemed vulnerable where Caleb was concerned.

The kinder were helping Caleb down the ramp in

the wheelchair. Or at least, he was letting them believe they were helping him, which amounted to the same thing in making them feel useful. Her mother always said that a useful child was a happy child, and Jessie agreed. It seemed to her that the worst thing a parent could do was to do everything for a child.

She watched as they approached the garden, Becky very intent and serious as she pushed the chair and Timothy holding on to the arm to ease it along. This opportunity to be with Alice's kinder and help them might be as close as she ever got to parenthood, and she was determined to do it well.

She still had her many nieces and nephews, she reminded herself. But each of them had two parents, and none of them had Becky and Timothy's desperate need.

The chair came to a halt at the edge of the plowed earth. "Look, Daadi." Timothy darted along the row. "I planted all these seeds. They'll grow into carrots."

"We put the seed packet on a stick at the end of each row so you can tell what's planted there." Becky tapped the one closest to her. "They're like little flags, ain't so?"

Caleb nodded and then glanced at Jessie. "Zeb usually takes care of the garden. You didn't have to do it."

He sounded like his daughter, resisting any change in the order of things.

"Zeb has plenty on his hands right now," Jessie said lightly. "He was happy to let us take over the planting. Besides, I love planting the garden. At home, my nieces and I always take care of the vegetable patch and the flowers."

Caleb's hands tightened on the arms of the chair.

"Yah, you're right. Onkel Zeb is taking on too much for a man his age."

"Better not let him hear you say that about him," Jessie said lightly, hoping to distract him.

But Caleb just glared at the cast. "I'd like to take a saw to this thing."

A quick glance assured Jessie that the children were at the far end of the garden, out of earshot. "Then you'd never get back to the way you were, ain't so?" Could he feel her sympathy? "It's wonderful hard to be patient."

"It is." His hands eased as if he'd needed someone to recognize how difficult this was for him. "Where's Zeb now? Do you know?"

"In the barn. He said something about fixing a few weak stall boards." She made her tone casual. "Maybe he could use someone to help hold the boards."

Caleb's smile flickered briefly. "Trying to make me feel useful, Jessie? I've seen you do that with the kinder, distracting them from being quarrelsome."

She couldn't help laughing. "I was just remembering something my mamm always says…that a useful child is a happy child."

Surprisingly enough, he took that well. "Maybe grown-ups aren't so different." He raised his voice. "Becky! Timothy! Komm help me out to the barn."

The kinder ran down the lane between the rows. "I'll push," Becky declared, getting there first.

"No, I will." Timothy's face puckered.

"You are both needed to push," Caleb said. "The chair doesn't go so well on the rough ground."

"We can do it," Becky said. She made space for her brother, and they both began to shove.

Jessie hurried to keep pace with them, suspecting

another hand might be needed to get up the incline to the barn door. Caleb rolled the wheels with his hands. He must be tired after this morning's hard workout, but he didn't show it.

Caleb darted a quick look at her, and then his gaze dropped. "You never told me about your business out in Ohio."

It took a moment for Jessie to process the unexpected words. Finally she shrugged. "There didn't seem to be a reason to."

"Or an opportunity?"

She shook her head slightly, but it was probably true. They hadn't had many casual conversations, and she tended to pick her words carefully with him.

"Zeb told me about it. He said you gave it up to come and help us."

"I couldn't be there and here, could I? It seemed more important to be here."

"Why?" His eyes met hers, challenging. "Why was this important to you?"

Jessie hesitated. She glanced at the kinder, but they didn't seem to be paying any attention to the adults' conversation. "I grew up being responsible for...for my little cousin."

She wouldn't say the name, afraid of provoking an explosion, and as it was, she was dangerously close. Still, Caleb was the one who'd forced the question.

"I guess I still feel responsible. If I can do something to right a wrong, then I want to do it. I need to do it."

Jessie couldn't bring herself to look at his face, afraid of what she'd read there. He reached out suddenly to grab her wrist, covering her hand on the chair, and her breath caught.

"You aren't…" he began.

But she wasn't to know what he might have said. Becky gave the chair a big shove. "We can take it the rest of the way. We don't need any help."

Jessie let go and watched the children struggle to get the chair into the barn. She wanted to assist, but not at the cost of upsetting Becky.

What had brought on that sudden reaction on the child's part? The fact that Caleb had been momentarily occupied with Jessie? She wasn't sure. But each time she took a step forward with Becky, it seemed to be followed by a plunge backward.

As for where she stood with Caleb…she didn't even want to think about that problem.

Caleb grasped the wheels, helping propel the chair onto the barn floor. It began to roll faster once it hit the worn wooden floor boards.

"Stop pushing now or you'll send me right into Beauty's stall."

For some reason, the kinder seemed to find that hilarious, and they scampered into the barn, giggling. Jessie followed a few paces behind. It took a moment for his eyes to adjust to the dimness after the bright sunshine outside.

He'd wanted to say something to Jessie, but clearly now was not the time, not with Zeb and the kinder around. Later, maybe. Or was it best to leave the whole subject alone? She couldn't atone for what Alice had done, if that was what she'd meant. Nobody could.

"Ach, you've made it all the way to the barn." Beaming, Onkel Zeb rose from squatting by a stall door. "Looks like you had some helpers."

"Yah, I did." He rolled the chair toward the stall. "Now it's my turn to help. I can reach the stall bars from the chair, anyway."

Zeb gave Jessie a questioning look as if wanting reassurance that he could manage. Caleb tried not to let it annoy him. Onkel Zeb was only acting out of love.

Whatever Zeb saw on Jessie's face must have satisfied him, because he nodded. "I could use an extra pair of hands, that's certain sure."

Becky darted forward to join them. "I'll help, too."

"You already have a job," Caleb said firmly. "That garden isn't going to plant itself. We're counting on you."

He saw the faintest suggestion of a pout forming on his daughter's face.

"Onkel Zeb and I will komm see it when you're done, ain't so, Onkel Zeb?"

"For sure," Zeb said. "Don't forget to water the seeds when you get them in."

"We won't." Timothy grabbed Jessie's hand. "Let's hurry. I want to water." They started toward the door.

"I do, too." Becky, distracted, hurried after them.

Zeb waited until they'd disappeared before he chuckled. "What one does, the other wants to do, as well. You boys were just the same when you were that age."

"I guess we were." For a moment his thoughts strayed to Aaron, his youngest brother. What was he doing out there in the Englisch world? Was he well? Did he ever regret jumping the fence?

But there was little point in worrying over something he couldn't control or asking questions with no answers. He had enough of that right here at home.

Somewhat to his surprise, Caleb found he had little

trouble figuring out how to work from the chair. He and Zeb labored together as they always did, with the exception that Zeb fetched things he couldn't reach. His spirits began to lift. Maybe he wasn't so helpless after all.

Zeb hammered a nail into place. "Folks were sure glad to see you at worship yesterday. Seemed like it had been an awful long time."

"For me, too." He frowned slightly. "Jessie was quiet after we got back from church, ain't so?"

His uncle considered, lean face solemn. "Maybe folks weren't as happy to wilkom her as they were to see you."

"She doesn't know anybody, I guess, other than Leah and Sam and their family."

Zeb looked at him as if waiting for more. When it didn't come, he set a screw for the door with a tad more forced than necessary. "Whenever someone brings a visiting relative to worship, folks gather round to meet them. Make them feel at home."

"So?" Maybe he knew where Zeb was going with this, but he didn't want to admit it.

"So, did you see anybody gathering around Jessie yesterday? I sure didn't. A few of the women smiled in passing, but that was about it."

"You think it's because they know she's Alice's cousin." He toyed with the nails in his hand, turning them over and over.

"Not just because she's Alice's cousin. Because most folks know how you feel about Alice and all of her kin."

Caleb tossed the nails into the toolbox. "I never said a word to anyone."

"You didn't have to. You think folks are dummies?

They know you well, Caleb. Your actions speak louder than your words. Half the county probably knows you feel like Jessie pushed her way in here."

Caleb wanted to defend himself. Unfortunately, the small voice of his conscience was telling him there was something in what his uncle said.

If Jessie meant what she said to him earlier about making up for what Alice had done… But he didn't know for sure. Maybe she was trying to justify her own actions.

Or was he just trying to justify his?

Chapter Seven

Jessie sat in the rocking chair that evening, working her way toward the bottom of the mending basket. The room had a pleasant feeling of peace with the day's work done. Onkel Zeb was replacing the wheels on a broken toy while Becky and Timothy built a barn with blocks.

She shot a quick glance at Caleb. Once again he was holding a newspaper, but he didn't seem to be reading it. Did her very presence make him uneasy in his own home?

Jessie pushed that idea away. She had to be patient, and so did Caleb. Today she had referred to Alice very obliquely, and he hadn't bitten her head off. Maybe that was progress.

"We need some more pieces for the roof," Becky said. "Where are the rest of the green ones?"

"I'll find them." Timothy's method of searching involved diving into the block box headfirst, giving them a view of the seat of his pants.

Jessie couldn't help smiling. Caleb, meeting her gaze, was smiling, as well, and for a moment they shared their amusement. Then Timothy resurfaced, red in the face, clutching the long green blocks they were using for the roof. "I got them."

He was taking the blocks to his sister when he noticed the small shirt Jessie had pulled out of the basket. He hurried over to her. "Hey, that's my shirt. It was lost."

"Not lost. Just hiding in the mending basket." She held it up against him and chuckled. "I think you won't be wearing this one again."

Timothy held his arm out to see how short the sleeve was. "I grew, didn't I?"

"That's certain sure. You're getting bigger all the time." Jessie folded the shirt on her lap. "What shall we do with it? Can I use it to make patches in a quilt?"

"Whose quilt? Will it go on my bed?"

"If you want." She might not possess the artist's eye for a quilt that her sister-in-law did, but she usually had something in progress, and she took a lot of satisfaction from the quilts she made.

"Can I help?" Becky still sat on the rug by the barn, but she was watching them.

"Yah, you can. Do you like to sew?"

"I never tried." She looked at her hands as if assessing the possibility of their wielding a needle.

"Well, then, it's time you did. We'll collect some quilt patches and plan a project for you."

Jessie was ridiculously elated. It was the first time Becky had shown any enthusiasm for doing something with her, and at six, it was time she was introduced to sewing. Normally a mother, grandmother or aunt would have done it already, but Becky was missing all of those.

And whatever memories she had of her mother must have been sad ones. She was five when Alice died—old enough to see, if not understand, those last weeks of life. If only Jessie had been able to convince Alice to stay with her instead of coming home…

But Alice was determined. She had left Caleb and the kinder when Timothy was just a baby, and she hadn't contacted anyone. The only explanation she'd left behind had been a short note saying she was sorry. Jessie had wondered about postpartum depression, but Alice had been dissatisfied with her life for a time before that pregnancy.

Jessie's family had searched, of course, but it was easy for an Amish person to hide in the Englisch world. It was only when Alice was seriously ill with the cancer that took her life that she'd resurfaced, announcing that she intended to go back to Caleb for whatever time she had left.

Jessie had tried to dissuade her. She'd written, urging Alice to reconsider, to live with her and let Jessie care for her. But Alice had thought she could reconcile with the family she'd left.

Jessie, convinced it could only cause harm, had taken an endless series of buses to get to the address in Chicago that Alice had given her, only to be too late. Alice had gone back to Caleb.

Jessie eyed him covertly. How had he taken Alice's return? He'd accepted her back into his house because she was his wife. But Jessie couldn't believe he'd been glad to see her. And under the circumstances…

It was past, and it was futile to go over it again, but Jessie longed to replace the unhappy memories Becky must have with some happier ones of Alice. She was the only person who could tell the children stories of "when Mammi was a little girl," but Caleb wouldn't allow it.

Daniel came down the stairs just then, obviously dressed to go out. Zeb raised an eyebrow.

"Are you finally using the courting buggy for its right purpose, Daniel?"

Daniel gave a good-natured grin. "If that happens, I'll be sure to tell you. Tonight I'm meeting with that Englisch couple who's talking about having me do new kitchen cabinets for them." He shrugged. "Not sure it's the best thing for me right now, though."

"That would be a big job for you, ain't so?" Caleb looked concerned, and Jessie thought she knew why. He was afraid Daniel might turn the job down because he was needed to help Caleb. "Why wouldn't you take it?"

Daniel hesitated. "It'd take a lot of time. And an extra pair of hands, most likely. I'm used to working on my own."

"If you're thinking we need you here, don't." Caleb bit out the words. "I can hire another man if need be."

Daniel shrugged again. "We'll see what happens. I'd best find out what they want first." He scurried out as if eager to escape an argument.

Jessie bit her lip to keep from offering an opinion that wouldn't be welcomed. She realized the children were staring after their uncle, so she laid the mending aside.

"It's about time for bed. Shall we put away the blocks?"

For a moment she thought she'd have a protest on her hands, but after a quick look at her daadi's face, Becky began cleaning up. Jessie helped Timothy slide the barn they'd built into a corner out of the way. As long as he didn't have to tear his barn apart, he seemed willing enough.

In a few minutes she was shepherding the kinder upstairs. At a guess, Zeb and Caleb would take advantage of being alone to discuss this possible job of Daniel's and how it would affect them.

When Becky and Timothy were ready for bed, they unfortunately didn't seem ready for sleep. That always seemed to be a problem as the days grew longer. The daylight slipping into the room around the window shades convinced little ones they should stay up longer, even when they could hardly hold their eyes open.

"Tell us a story, Cousin Jessie." Timothy paused in the act of jumping on his bed. "Tell us a story before we go to sleep."

Becky didn't seem to be listening. Or at least, she was pretending not to be interested, busy settling her Amish faceless doll under the covers.

"A story. Now, let me think." Jessie looked into Timothy's blue eyes, so like Alice's, and the idea popped into her head. She couldn't tell them about Alice—or could she? If she didn't use Alice's name, Caleb would never know. And she wouldn't really be breaking her agreement, would she?

After a short struggle with her conscience, she gave in to the temptation.

"Once upon a time there were two little Amish girls," she began. "Their names were… Anna and Barbie."

"Were they twins?" Becky's attention seemed to be caught.

"No, no, they weren't. Anna was the big sister, and Barbie was the little sister. But even though they weren't twins, they liked to do things together, and Barbie would always say, 'Me, too, me, too' whenever Anna was doing something."

"Like me," Timothy said, grinning.

"Like you," she agreed, reaching out to tickle him. "So one day, they decided to go up the hill and pick blackberries."

"It must have been summer," Becky said wisely.

"Yah, it was. August, when the wild blackberries are ripe. So they each took a pail, and they went up the path to where the blackberries grew." She noted that Timothy had stopped wiggling and settled onto his pillow.

"The berries were so big and fat and juicy that they couldn't stop. They'd picked half a pail full each in no time at all. Anna picked the ones up high, and Barbie picked the ones on the bottom. They were just talking about what to make with the berries when what do you think Barbie saw under the blackberry brambles?"

"A bird," Timothy murmured sleepily.

"No, a turtle," Becky said.

"You're both wrong. It was a great big black snake. When Barbie saw it, she let out a huge shriek, threw her bucket into the air and ran as fast as she could go down the path. And the snake, who had been taking a nice nap in the shade of the bushes, went spinning around in a big circle and raced up the hill in the opposite direction as fast as it could go."

Becky giggled. "The snake was scared, too."

"I wouldn't be scared..." Timothy's words were interrupted by a huge yawn.

Jessie tucked the covers around him. "So Anna picked up all the berries she could find and took them back down the hill. Anna and Barbie helped their mammi make a big blackberry cobbler for supper, and they each had two pieces."

His eyes were closed. Jessie bent and kissed his cheek lightly. Then she went to Becky's bed. To her pleasure, Becky let her tuck the covers in and didn't even turn her face away from Jessie's kiss.

"Good night. Sleep tight," Jessie murmured. She went softly across the room and out into the hall.

When she turned from closing the door, her pulse gave a little jump. Zeb stood a few feet away.

"Ach, you startled me," she said softly. "I didn't know you'd komm upstairs."

"Just wanted my pipe." He gestured with it and then glanced at the door to the children's room. "I was in time to hear the story you were telling the kinder."

Something about his steady regard made her nervous. "Picking blackberries. It was maybe not as exciting as Onkel Daniel's version of fairy tales."

"It's best not to be too exciting when they're going to sleep, ain't so?" He paused for a moment. "Thing is, I'd heard that story before."

Jessie's breath caught. "When…when was that?"

"A long time ago now. Alice happened to see a black snake in the garden. Scared her, I guess. She mentioned the day she went picking berries with her big cousin and saw the snake."

Jessie pressed her hands together. She'd never thought of that. "Does Caleb know?" If he did, and the kinder mentioned the story…

Zeb shook his head. "He wasn't here that day. She didn't want him to know she'd been so foolish, she said."

"I see." She tried to still her whirling thoughts. "Are

you going to tell Caleb I told the kinder a story about their mammi?"

Zeb lifted an eyebrow. "I didn't hear you mention Alice, ain't so?"

Jessie felt herself relax. "I don't wish to upset Caleb, but it seems..."

"Yah, I know." Zeb's voice sounded weary. "No good can come of bottling everything up. I've tried and tried to convince Caleb of that, but he isn't ready to listen."

"No." They stood together for a moment, and she knew that they understood each other. "I haven't repeated that story to anyone in a long time. But it...it made my little Alice seem real to me again. Maybe one day, the kinder will remember it and know it was about their mother."

"Maybe one day you'll be able to tell them yourself," Zeb said.

"Maybe," she echoed, but she doubted it.

"I like scrambled eggs better than anything." Timothy was his enthusiastic self at breakfast a few days later. "Don't you, Onkel Daniel?"

Daniel considered, head tilted and eyes twinkling. "Better than chocolate cake? Or whoopie pies?"

"Well, but... I mean for breakfast. Cousin Jessie wouldn't give us whoopie pies for breakfast."

Caleb glanced at his son. Funny how quickly Timothy had accepted Cousin Jessie as the authority on what he had for breakfast. After a week, he acted as if Jessie had been here forever.

At the moment, Jessie was entering into the fun, talking about how a whoopie pie could be a breakfast food and making Timothy giggle. She seemed to have overcome whatever had depressed her spirits on Sunday.

Maybe Zeb had been wrong in what he'd thought was going on. Maybe people were sensible enough to know that Jessie wasn't responsible for what Alice had done. The thought made him uncomfortable. Why was it sensible for others to think that when he himself acted as if blaming Jessie was okay?

He risked a glance at her face again. He didn't blame her, exactly. He just didn't like being constantly reminded of Alice. That was natural enough. Not Jessie's fault, but not his fault, either.

"More coffee?" Jessie had just filled Onkel Zeb's cup, and she stood next to Caleb, the coffeepot in her hand.

He nodded and watched the hot liquid stream into the heavy white cup he used. A simple gesture, refilling the coffee cups, but one that Alice had ignored often enough. It was a silly thing to have bothered him. After all, he could pour his own coffee.

"Maybe a little slice of that shoofly pie with my coffee," Daniel said. "A man's got to keep his strength up, after all." He grinned, looking as if he expected a tart response to that.

"You'll need it, if you're going to take on that kitchen job," Onkel Zeb said. "Did you make up your mind yet?"

Daniel shook his head as Jessie put a slab of shoofly pie in front of him. "Still have to work out all the figures before we get to an agreement. And I may not have the time and manpower to do it."

"I told you I'd hire another person to help on the

farm until I'm rid of this cast." Caleb knew he sounded testy, but he couldn't help it.

Daniel eyed him. "Not so easy as you might think. Thomas is a fine helper, but I'm not sure where we'd find another like him."

"We can manage," Zeb said. "If someone has two good legs, I can teach him what to do."

"Is it possible…" Jessie began, and then fell silent when they all looked at her.

"Go on, Jessie," Zeb urged. "You have an idea?"

"Well, I just wondered if maybe there were things Caleb could do to help Daniel with the project—things he could do from the wheelchair that would free up Daniel's time."

Caleb swallowed his instant response. He shouldn't reject the idea just because it came from Jessie.

Daniel brightened, but then shook his head when Caleb didn't respond. "It would be too much for him."

"No. It wouldn't." No matter where the idea came from, it was a logical one. "If you lowered one of the work benches so I could reach it from the chair, there's plenty I could do. Better than sitting here feeling useless."

"That could make all the difference." Daniel gulped down the rest of his coffee and pushed his chair back. "I'll get started on those figures. Maybe you can come out to the shop after your exercises and we'll see if we can make it work." He beamed at Jessie. "Gut thought, Jessie."

Becky's fork clattered onto the table. "I'm done." She slid off her chair and started from the room.

"Take your plate to the sink first, please," Jessie said before Becky could make her escape.

"I want to go outside." Becky's face set in the pout that Caleb was seeing too often.

"Do as Cousin Jessie says, Becky." The least he could do was back Jessie up when she was right. Becky shouldn't be allowed to develop rebellious habits.

Becky just stared at him for a moment. Then, without a word, she came back, picked up her plate and utensils, and carried them to the sink.

"Denke, Becky," Jessie said. Ignoring Becky's lack of response, she began to clear the table with quick, deft movements. "When I've finished, will you be ready to start your exercises?"

Caleb suspected she thought he'd argue, but he wouldn't. He'd do whatever was necessary to get back to his normal self, including accepting help from Jessie.

By the time Jessie had pushed him through his first few exercises, Caleb was beginning to wonder if he really was willing to do anything to regain his strength. Jessie was much more of a taskmaster than he'd expected.

He stopped, panting a little at the exertion of attempting to lift his leg multiple times. "That's enough of that one."

"Just three more. Komm, you can do three more."

Caleb's temper flared in spite of himself. "I ought to know how many I can do."

"And what do you think the physical therapist would say to that?" she chided. "Now, if you were Becky's age, I could offer you a whoopie pie for doing it all ten times."

His momentary annoyance fizzled. "Are you saying I'm acting like a six-year-old?"

"What do you think?" Her eyes twinkled. "I'll help. Just three more."

Steeling himself, he managed to push himself through three more leg lifts.

"Wonderful gut," Jessie said. "You see? You can do whatever you put your mind to."

She sounded as if she had a routine for encouraging rebellious patients. "This can't be the first time you've done this—helped someone komm back from an injury, I mean."

"You remember all those brothers of mine, don't you? If one wasn't damaging himself, another one was. Mamm was too soft on them to make them exercise. And when Daad busted his leg…ach, if you think you're pigheaded, you should have seen my daad."

Jessie hadn't often relaxed like this when she talked to him. It was nice to see the affection in her eyes when she spoke of family.

She'd had a full, rich life in Ohio with her kin and her business, and she'd left it behind out of her need to help his family. She'd come here knowing what her reception would most likely be. He thought of what Zeb had said about the attitude of the church family and felt a prickle of guilt.

"It's gut you had a chance to get acquainted with Leah so fast. She's been a wonderful gut neighbor to us."

"I can see that. It's been nice to get to know her a little and to feel she's ready to be friends. Especially since I don't know any other women here."

Caleb hesitated, but Zeb's words still rankled. "Did you talk to some of the other women after worship?"

"A few." Jessie's gaze slid away from his, and she

busied herself getting out the elastic bands for his next set of exercises.

"Some of them must have made you feel wilkom." He was pushing, because he needed to know if his uncle had been right or not.

Jessie was silent for a long moment. At last she shrugged. "I'm sure they usually do so. But folks here know I'm Alice's cousin. They're bound to be resentful. I can't be surprised that they are not eager to accept me."

Caleb's fingers tightened on the arms of the chair. "You mean it's because of me. Because I am unforgiving." He stopped, aghast at what he'd said. To be lacking in forgiveness for the wrongs done to him by another person was to live in defiance of God's law.

"I don't... I didn't mean that," he said quickly, stumbling over the words. "I've forgiven Alice." *Over and over.* So why did he have to keep doing it?

"Have you?" Jessie's face twisted in what he thought was grief and hurt. "Sometimes I think forgiveness has to keep happening again and again, each time we think of the person who has wronged us. Until one day, we finally know we are free, and can think of them without pain."

He felt he was seeing Jessie for the first time. She might act sure of herself and competent, but inside there was pain and guilt.

"Yah." He found he was reaching out instinctively, clasping her hand in his. He could feel the flutter of her pulse against his skin and hear the catch in her breath. "Have you been able to forgive her and be free?"

Jessie's eyes met his, and the barriers between them

slipped away for the moment, at least. She sighed. "I'm getting better at it, I think. Maybe, one day…"

"One day," he echoed. He would like to live without this tight ball of anger and resentment inside him. He just didn't know how to get rid of it.

Her lips trembled a bit. "If I can help Becky and Timothy, perhaps I will go the rest of the way."

The lump in his throat made it hard to get the words out, but they had to be said.

"I'm sorry. Sorry I've made it more difficult for you, sorry for treating you as if you were to blame." His fingers moved against her skin. "Forgive me."

Whatever she might have answered was lost in a cry from the doorway. He turned, still clasping Jessie's hand, to find his daughter standing there, staring at them.

"Daadi! What are you doing?"

The anger in her small face shocked him. Maybe Jessie was right. Maybe Becky did need help.

"I am thanking Cousin Jessie for assisting me with my exercises," he said evenly. Jessie slipped her hand from his and stepped away, bending to pick up the exercise bands. "And you are being rude, Rebecca. You had best go to your room and think on it."

Becky stared at him with angry eyes. Then, with a sharp, cutting look at Jessie, she turned and ran toward the stairs.

Chapter Eight

Jessie couldn't get the expression on Becky's face out of her mind. She had been angry, yah, but upset, too. And then there were her own emotions to contend with. Maybe Caleb hadn't felt anything. Maybe it had all been her—her longing, her imagination, creating a momentary link that hadn't been real.

Caleb had certainly been quick to get back to his exercises after the interruption. Everything they had said to each other was strictly business. The minute they'd finished, he had headed out to the workshop, waving away her offer of help.

Thankfully Daniel must have been watching for him. From the kitchen window she saw Daniel hurry from his shop along the gravel lane to intercept his brother and push the wheelchair on its way. The shop was even farther from the house than the barn. Caleb was stubborn, that was all. She just hoped he wasn't so stubborn he'd hurt himself.

Jessie turned away, occupying herself with the fabric fragments she'd been gathering for the quilt project she wanted to start with Becky. A small nine-patch quilt, suitable for a doll's cradle—that was a good beginner project. In fact, it was the one her mamm had started her on all those years ago.

Mamm would have done the same with Alice. Jessie felt sure of it, even though she didn't remember the specifics. Mamm had been determined to do all she could after Alice's mother passed.

Jessie had enough scraps to start the doll quilt. Whether she'd have any cooperation from Becky was another question.

Picking up her sewing bag, she went into the hall and called up the stairs. "Becky and Timothy? Komm down for a minute, please."

Timothy bounded down the steps as he always did, his feet thudding on each tread. Becky came more slowly, running her hand along the rail. Jessie had thought she might have been crying but could see no sign of tears on her face.

"I have my sewing bag here, and I thought maybe you'd like to start on a sewing project. There are a lot of scraps in the scrap bag, so we could make a little quilt or maybe a pot holder together."

Timothy would no doubt want to do whatever his sister did, but the project she had in mind for Becky would be beyond his abilities. Still, she could find something to keep him busy.

"I want to make something." Timothy ran over to her and tugged on the bag. "Komm on, Becky."

"No." When they both looked at her, Becky managed to ignore Jessie. "I'm going to collect the eggs. Komm with me, and I'll show you how to do it."

Timothy looked a little hesitant, and Jessie suspected

she knew why. He was a bit scared of the chickens, especially the bad-tempered Rhode Island Red.

"You're not scared, are you?" Becky knew just how to prompt him to do what she wanted.

"I'm not scared of any chicken. I'll get the basket." He ran toward the back door, and Becky followed him.

Jessie set her sewing bag on the floor next to the rocker. She'd known this wouldn't be easy, especially with Becky. Maybe she should have waited a bit longer to allow time for her to get over her little snit at seeing her daadi holding Jessie's hand.

At the moment, she'd best get outside so she could keep an eye on the egg gathering from a distance. She could logically be checking on the garden, couldn't she?

Jessie was bending over a few green leaflets that were already above ground while she watched the children approach the chicken coop. Becky, carrying the egg basket, unhooked the door and stepped right in. Timothy held back for a minute as the hens rushed toward Becky in hope of food. Then Becky said something to him, and he stepped into the enclosure.

If this helped Timothy get over his fear, it would be a good thing. He followed his sister under the shelter of the roof where the laying boxes waited. If the hens had been cooperative, this shouldn't take long.

Jessie let her gaze stray toward the workshop. How was Caleb getting along? If only he could do something, even if it wasn't his usual work, he'd be happier. Time hung heavy when a busy person suddenly had no responsibilities.

A squawk from the henhouse captured her attention. She craned her neck, trying to make out what was happening. Timothy's voice alerted her—he was yelling for his sister, and the red hen was chasing him.

Jessie got up quickly. Before she could go more than a few steps, Becky had reached her brother. She shoved him out the door and slammed it behind her. Timothy let out an anguished howl, and Jessie ran. That wasn't fear. It was pain.

When Jessie reached them, both children were outside the chicken coop. Becky was crying nearly as hard as Timothy was.

Jessie caught them, turning them toward her. Her heart pounded so loudly she could hardly hear. "What's happened? Who is hurt?"

They both tried to answer at once, and she could make no sense of it at all.

"Hush, now. I can't understand you when you're crying. Who is hurt?"

Becky managed to check her sobs. "Timmy. I didn't mean it. I slammed the door on his finger."

"Ach, now, we know you didn't mean it." She drew Timothy close against her. "Komm, Timothy. You must let me see your finger so I can tell how badly it's hurt."

"Don't touch it," he cried. Reluctantly he held his hand out, and she took it gently in hers.

"I think maybe you'll live, ain't so?" The small finger was red and puffing up a little, and an open scrape didn't make it look any better. But judging by the way he was moving his finger, it probably wasn't broken. He started to cry again, and she picked him up, holding him close against her.

"It will be all right. I promise. Komm, Becky. Let's go in the house and fix your bruder's finger, okay?"

Tears still dripped down Becky's cheeks, but she

nodded. At least they'd both stopped wailing. Jessie took a cautious look toward the workshop, but obviously the men hadn't heard the commotion. Just as well. She'd like to get everyone calmed down and cleaned up before trying to explain this to Caleb.

Becky hurried ahead of her to hold the door open, and they went into the kitchen. Still cradling Timothy against her shoulder, Jessie pulled a handful of ice from the gas refrigerator.

"Becky, will you get a clean dish towel from the drawer for me?"

Nodding, Becky hurried to obey. Having something useful to do seemed to calm her tears a little. She rushed back with the towel.

Jessie sat down at the table with Timothy on her lap, detaching him from her shoulder. "We're going to put ice on your finger. That will help it stop hurting. Will you let Becky hold your hand steady?"

Sniffling, Timothy nodded, extending his hand toward his sister. Suppressing a few sniffles of her own, Becky took his hand gingerly. She held it while Jessie wrapped the towel around the ice and put it gently against the injured finger. Timothy winced at first, but then he seemed to relax when he realized it wouldn't make matters worse.

"Gut job, Becky. Timothy is a brave boy, ain't so?"

"Is it broken? Like Daadi's leg?" Becky's voice wavered.

Timothy actually brightened at that idea, convincing Jessie that he wasn't badly hurt. "Will I get a cast?"

"No, I don't think it's broken. But it has a nasty scrape. We'll need to put a bandage on it, won't we, Becky?"

Becky nodded and ran to the kitchen drawer where first aid supplies were kept. She brought the whole box back with her.

"Gut. We'll keep the ice on just a little longer, I think." She affixed the bandage in place and held the ice against it, then tried a smile for the two of them, who still looked woebegone. "We're going to have to teach that red hen who is boss, ain't so?"

Becky's face seemed to crumple again. "It wasn't the hen. It was me. It's all my fault!" She bolted from the room before Jessie could stop her.

Jessie bit her lip. She'd tried not to interfere, but this time she had to. Becky couldn't go on like this, flaring up about things and then running off. Somehow she had to get through to the child.

But first, Timothy must be taken care of. His bottom lip was trembling again, no doubt in reaction to his sister's tears. She was reminded of her mother, saying that there were times when every mammi needed an extra pair of hands. Maybe she wasn't Becky and Timothy's mammi, but right now she was all they had.

"Becky feels bad because you got hurt, ain't so?" She smoothed Timothy's hair back from his rounded forehead. "She loves you."

Timothy snuggled against her. "Do you think Daadi cried when he got hurt?"

She suppressed a smile. "I'm sure he felt like crying, even if he didn't. Lots of times grown-ups do."

That seemed to satisfy him. After another minute of snuggling, he started to wiggle. "Maybe a cookie would make my finger feel better."

Jessie dropped a kiss on his hair. "I don't know

about your finger, but I'll bet your tummy would like it. How about a snickerdoodle and a glass of milk?"

He nodded, and she set him on his own chair and got out the promised snack. He was using his hurt finger normally by the time he'd had a bite, so it was safe to assume he'd be okay. Now for Becky.

"I'll see if Becky wants a snack. You wait here for us, okay?"

"Okay," he said thickly around a mouthful of cookie.

With a silent prayer for guidance, Jessie climbed the stairs toward the children's bedroom.

Becky lay on her bed, both arms wrapped around her pillow. Her face was buried, but her shoulders still shook with muffled sobs. She looked so small and vulnerable that Jessie's heart ached.

She sat on the edge of the bed. When Becky didn't move, Jessie leaned over to put her hand on the child's back.

"Timothy is eating snickerdoodles. I think that means his finger feels much better. That's gut, ain't so?"

Becky didn't respond. Well, Jessie hadn't expected it to be as simple as that. Whatever troubled Becky, it was bigger than the question of her brother's finger.

"You feel bad because Timothy got hurt, I know. But it was an accident. Accidents happen to everyone. All we can do is try to be more careful."

That got a response from Becky. She shoved herself up on her elbows and pounded the pillow. "It's my fault! He's my little bruder. I have to take care of him."

"I know. I have little brothers, too." *And once I had a little cousin.* "But we can't always stop them from getting hurt, no matter what we do."

"It's my fault. It's always my fault...just like when Mammi went away."

Jessie's heart seemed to stop. She had to repeat the words over in her own mind before she could take them in. Becky was blaming herself for Alice leaving. Why hadn't any of them seen that?

"Becky, listen..." She swallowed her words. Careful...she had to be very careful in what she said now. "Why would you think it was your fault that your mammi left?"

"Because it was. If I'd been better, or prettier, or..."

"Ach, Becky, don't!" She put her arm around the thin shoulders, ignoring the way Becky stiffened at her touch. "That's not true. It isn't. I know."

"How do you know? You weren't here." Becky's jaw set, reminding her of Caleb.

"No, I wasn't." *I wish I had been.* "But your mammi wrote to me all the time. Every week she wrote. And you know what she said about you?"

That caught Becky's attention. She actually turned to look at Jessie. "What?"

Jessie risked stroking her hair. "She said she had the prettiest little daughter ever. She told me all about what you did...when you took your first step, when you got your first tooth, everything. She was so very pleased with you, and she loved you so much."

"Then why did she go away?" The rebellious note was gone from her voice. Poor child. She wanted so much to know it wasn't because of her.

But how did Jessie answer her in a way that a six-year-old could understand? "I don't think even your mamm really understood why," she said carefully. "She was very young when she got married, and maybe she hadn't grown up enough yet. And sometimes she got really sad. Not because of what anyone did but just because of something inside her. It was like being sick. We don't blame people or get angry with them for being sick, do we?"

Jessie's own thoughts seemed to clarify as she tried to explain to the child. Who could say why Alice had been the person she was? Maybe having her mamm die when she was so young had started something inside her that none of them had understood.

"No, but..."

"No buts," Jessie said gently. "One thing we know for sure. It wasn't your fault that your mamm left. I promise."

Some of the tension eased out of Becky's face. She sat up, leaning against Jessie's arm for a precious moment before pulling away.

Becky wasn't entirely convinced. No one ever gave up a deeply held belief because of a few simple words.

Jessie knew that. She knew because looking into Becky's face was like looking into a mirror and seeing her own pain.

Just like Becky, she'd been telling herself that what Alice did was her fault. But Alice, no matter what problems she had, had been a grown woman, not a little girl.

There might be nothing Jessie could do about her own feelings, but there was something she had to do about Becky's. She must talk to Caleb about this, whether he wanted to hear it or not. Healing Becky's hurt would take effort on all their parts, not just on hers.

Caleb pushed the wheelchair through the back door and into the kitchen. No help needed, he told himself.

There might be things he couldn't do, but he wasn't helpless, and that was a wonderful gut feeling.

He found Jessie alone in the kitchen, cutting up a chicken at the counter. "Chicken tonight, yah?"

He'd keep the talk between them light and casual. No more conversation that led to revealing emotions, and definitely no more touching. He still seemed to feel her pulse beating against his palm, and that wouldn't do.

Jessie's smile seemed a little strained. She was probably as uncomfortable about what had passed between them as he was. Not that it had meant anything.

"Chicken and homemade noodles, just like my grossmammi always made."

"I remember." Jessie's family had spread the wilkom mat on his first visit to Ohio, and her mother and grandmother had stuffed him until he was ready to burst. "Are yours as gut as hers?"

"I wouldn't go that far," she said lightly. She glanced at the clock. "You were out at the shop for two hours or more. You must be ready for a rest."

He shook his head, helping himself to a snickerdoodle from the cookie jar. "It felt great to be working again. Not that I'm anywhere near the craftsman Daniel is. He always had a feel for wood, even when he was a kid. I'm an apprentice compared to him."

"Even an apprentice can be helpful," she said, moving the heavy Dutch oven onto the stove. "This job… it's important to Daniel, ain't so?"

"Very. If he satisfies an Englisch client, he'll probably get a lot more orders. He shouldn't miss a chance like that. Even if all I can do is attach hinges and finish the wood, it frees Daniel up to do the hard part."

Jessie leaned against the sink, drying her hands. "You could reach everything all right?"

"Daniel fitted up a makeshift workbench that's just the right height for me." He slapped his palms on the arms of the chair. "Even if I'm stuck in this thing, I can still work. I..."

Caleb stopped. Here he was blabbing away about it as if he was some kind of hero for helping his brother, after all Daniel was doing for him. That was bad enough, but worse, he'd completely ignored the fact that it had been Jessie's suggestion in the first place.

Jessie was looking at him with some concern, probably because he'd stopped what he was saying in midstream. He shook his head.

"Ach, I'm forgetting the most important thing. You're the one who thought of it to begin with. Denke, Jessie."

She gave a quick shrug. "You would have, I'm sure."

Maybe, but she had first. He glanced around the kitchen, belatedly aware of how quiet it was. "Where is everyone?"

"Your uncle had to run over to the feed mill, so he took Becky and Timothy with him. They should be back soon." Now it was her turn to hesitate. "While they're out, I'd like to have a word with you about Becky."

"If it's about her being sassy this morning..." He was caught in a cleft stick. He could hardly say it was none of her business when she was taking care of his kinder.

"No, not that." A faint flush rose in her cheeks. "It's something that happened later. She told Timothy she'd show him how to gather the eggs from the chickens, so they went out to the coop."

If that was all, it hardly seemed worth her bringing it up. "I'm surprised he went. He's a little bit scared of the chickens."

"I know. But he wanted to appear brave to his sister, so he went." She hesitated. "I know Becky does that by herself, but I kept an eye on them since Timothy was going."

Caleb gave an impatient nod. Jessie was picking her words carefully over nothing, it seemed.

"I heard a ruckus and went running. I'm not sure exactly what happened, but I think that bad-tempered red took off after him. He was trying to get out, and in all the fuss, Becky accidentally shut the door on his finger."

"He's all right?" He must have been, if he'd gone off to the feed mill with Onkel Zeb.

"He's fine." Her face relaxed in a smile. "I think they were both more scared than anything. I took care of the scraped finger, and Timothy was happy again in no time."

"Well, then..."

"But Becky wasn't." Jessie looked at him, her hazel eyes dark and serious. "I found her upstairs crying her heart out. She was blaming herself, you see, for Timothy getting hurt."

He frowned. "I'm more used to boys than girls. I don't recall my brothers being upset about something like that, but Becky is more sensitive. That's all."

"You're thinking I'm making a mountain out of a molehill."

Jessie's comment was so near the truth that he had to smile. "Aren't you?"

"It was what else she said that troubles me." Jessie took a breath. "She said she was to blame for Timothy getting hurt. Just as she was to blame for her mammi going away."

The words hit Caleb like a blow to the stomach. For an instant it seemed the wind had been knocked out of him. He finally got his breath so he could speak. "She couldn't think that."

"She does." Jessie's lips trembled. "I'm sorry. I know you don't want to hear it. And you don't want me to mention Alice. But it's no use trying to handle her leaving and her dying that way. Don't you see?" She leaned toward him, almost pleading. "Becky has that guilt in her heart, foolish as it is. You can't make it go away by pretending it isn't there."

He spun the chair away from her, because he was afraid of what his own face might betray. "Didn't you tell Becky she was wrong?"

"Of course I did." Now it was Jessie who sounded impatient. "I tried to get through to her. I told her how often her mammi talked about her in letters, and how happy she was to have a sweet little daughter." Jessie's voice tightened on that. "Alice did love them, you know. Despite what she did."

Caleb wanted to push everything away, because it hurt too much to talk about it. But Jessie… Jessie had come too far into their lives for that, like it or not.

"I'll talk to her," he said, trying to sound sure of himself. "I'll convince her it wasn't her fault."

"I know you'll try to make it better. But it's not easy to let go of the burden of guilt, no matter how irrational it may be. Becky..."

"All right!" He couldn't take any more. "I'll do what I can. Just leave it alone for now."

Chapter Nine

Had Caleb tried to talk to Becky about her mother or not? Jessie sat with her sewing basket at her feet that evening, wondering. Somehow she thought not. Caleb's stoic expression might not reveal his emotions, but Becky would be showing the effects if he'd said anything.

Becky was quiet, for sure, but it was the same quiet that she'd maintained since her bout of crying earlier in the day. Maybe Caleb had had no opportunity to get Becky alone for a serious talk. Or maybe he was avoiding the job, unwilling to open that box of trouble.

Jessie could understand. It was always tempting to pretend that nothing was wrong, sometimes even convincing yourself. After all, she'd convinced herself that she'd done everything she could to keep Alice from coming back here to die. But had she? Had she been able to disentangle her own feelings from what was best for everyone?

And then there was the realization that she and Becky were doing the same thing—blaming themselves for what Alice had done. Becky was clearly wrong. She could have done nothing. Jessie would like to say the same of herself, but she couldn't quite convince herself.

Life could be like the tangle of thread she'd discovered in her sewing basket—impossible even to find an end to pull.

She could fix the thread with a pair of scissors. The same wasn't true of relationships among people.

Smoothing out a couple of the fabric squares she'd cut, she started to pin them together for a small quilt. Timothy, deserting his toy barn, came over to see.

"What are you making, Cousin Jessie?" He fingered one of the pieces and narrowly missed pricking himself on a pin. "What will it be?"

"It'll be a quilt when it's finished." She smiled at him. "But it won't have any pins in it then to stick you."

"Gut." He gave a little shiver as if imagining himself wrapped in a quilt with pins. "Can I do it?"

She glanced at Caleb, wondering if he'd object to his son learning to use a needle. But he seemed intent on something he was jotting on a tablet.

"Sure thing. Let me get you some pieces of your own to sew." She found a couple of scraps and held them together. "The needle goes down through the material and then back up through. Try putting it in right here."

His little face intent, tongue sticking slightly out of the corner of his mouth, he managed to push the needle through and promptly dropped it so that it hung by the thread. "I did it."

"Yah, you did. Now keep pulling on the needle until the thread is tight. Next we'll come back up through the material." Experience with her small nieces and nephews had taught her that it was too much to expect him to make a complete stitch in one movement.

She took a covert look at Becky and discovered that she was watching them. Good. She was interested. Now to reel her in. "There's some material here if you'd like to try, Becky."

Becky hesitated and then came over. She stood in front of Jessie with her hands linked as if to show that she wasn't really all that intrigued.

"Why don't you pick out two pieces of different colors you think would look nice next to each other."

She handed Becky the basket and began threading a needle for her, stopping only to help Timothy in his efforts to stab the material without stabbing himself.

In a moment Becky had pulled a stool over and settled in next to Jessie. As she'd imagined, Becky's little fingers were quite nimble, and she soon got on to the idea of making small, even stitches. Her line of stitches wasn't quite straight, but it was very good for a first try.

"Look at that. You've done this before, haven't you?"

Becky smiled. "Leah showed me a little bit, and I practiced. It's fun."

"My fingers are tired," Timothy announced. "I need to put my horse in the barn." He dropped his material in Jessie's lap and reached for the horse, then paused. "Tell us another story about the big sister and little sister. Is there one with a pony in it?"

Jessie really didn't want to tell her thinly disguised story in front of Caleb, but it seemed her chickens had come home to roost. She glanced at Zeb, who gave a tiny shrug. At least Caleb wasn't paying much attention.

"Once upon a time, Anna was teaching Barbie how to drive the pony cart. Their pony was named Snowflake. Know why?"

Timothy blinked, shaking his head, but Becky grinned. "It was white, ain't so?"

"That's right. It was a pretty little white pony, but when they drove the cart through a puddle, she got all muddy. So they decided to give her a bath."

She spun out the story, seeing that Timothy's eyes were growing heavy while he listened. He leaned against her knee, patting the toy horse.

"So when the pony was sparkling clean, Anna and Barbie led her up toward the house to show Mammi. But they didn't watch where they were going, and before you knew it, Snowflake saw a nice freshly plowed garden and thought it would be a great place to roll."

Timothy started to giggle, anticipating what the pony would do, and Becky grinned.

"So Anna and Barbie grabbed the rope and pulled as hard as they could, but they couldn't stop that determined pony. She rolled and rolled right in the dirt. And then she stood up and shook herself, and the wet dirt flew all over Anna and Barbie until they were even dirtier than Snowflake. Mammi came out, and they thought she'd be mad, but instead she laughed until the tears rolled down her cheeks."

The kinder laughed almost as much as Mammi had that day, especially Timothy, who found the image of the mud-splattered little girls hilarious.

Once again, just telling the story seemed to bring Alice alive again for her. It hurt, yes, but at the same time it was comforting. Those we lost did live on in our memories, it seemed.

"Time to get ready for bed," she said firmly when Timothy suggested another story. She shooed them toward the stairs and was about to follow when Caleb said her name.

Jessie paused, looking back at him.

"That story..." Caleb hesitated. "Would I be right in thinking it a true story?"

So he knew. Had Alice told him at some point, or was it just obvious from her own emotions?

"Yah, it was true."

He nodded, his eyes going dark with pain. "I thought so."

She waited for him to forbid it, but the words she anticipated didn't come.

"All right," he said at last. "All right." His voice was heavy, and her heart ached for him. But she knew better than to comfort him. He couldn't accept that, not from her.

Caleb stared down at the cast on his leg for a few minutes, hearing the sound of Jessie's retreating footsteps. He'd been so sure he was right to forbid any talk about Alice. That part of their lives was over, and the best thing they could do was forget.

But he'd been wrong, if doing so had allowed his daughter to blame herself. He still wasn't sure how to fix it, but perhaps letting Jessie tell her stories was a step in the right direction.

"Something is wrong," Onkel Zeb observed. "Will you tell me?"

Caleb moved his shoulders restlessly, trying to get rid of the weight of the guilt. "I'm not hiding it," he muttered, knowing that was exactly what he was doing. From himself, most of all. "Becky got upset this morning, and she told Jessie something she's kept secret from the rest of us." He forced himself to display a calm he didn't feel. "Becky says it's her fault that her mother went away."

For a long moment there was silence. Onkel Zeb shook his head slowly, his face sorrowful. "Poor child. Poor little child."

"I should have known." The truth burst out on a wave of pain. "I should have been the one to find out, not Jessie."

"Maybe it was easier for Becky to say it to Jessie instead of you."

"I'm her daad. She barely knows Jessie." Resentment edged his tone.

"How could Becky tell you?" He asked the question and just let it lie there between them. Onkel Zeb had always done that when the brothers tried to evade responsibility that belonged to them. His uncle looked at him steadily until Caleb's gaze fell.

Caleb's throat grew tight. "I never spoke of her mother. She must have thought she couldn't. So she kept it to herself. Brooded on it, most likely. And I never realized."

That was the bitterest thing of all—he hadn't realized something was wrong. Becky had lost all the laughter and sunshine she'd once possessed, and he hadn't even guessed at the cause.

"It won't be easy to change her mind," Zeb observed.

"That's what Jessie said. It will take more than just telling her it's not her fault to make her really believe it."

"Cousin Jessie has a gut heart," his uncle observed. "And a sharp eye where the kinder are concerned."

"I don't deny that. I just wish..."

He didn't know what he wished. That she'd never come here? But if he hadn't broken his leg, if she hadn't come and insisted on staying in spite of his order, how long would it have taken him to find out what was happening with his daughter?

"Your parents' failings hurt all three of you boys." His uncle's voice was heavy. "Look at the results. You married a girl who was nowhere near ready to be a wife and mother. Daniel smiles and guards his heart from love. And Aaron runs away entirely."

"You can't blame all that on Mamm and Daad. They didn't mean to hurt us."

"Not meaning to has caused a lot of trouble." Onkel Zeb sounded more severe than Caleb could ever remember. "And now you. You didn't mean to hurt Becky by your silence. But it happened. If you are not careful, your kinder will be as afraid of loving as you are."

Caleb wanted to argue. The words boiled inside him, but he couldn't let them out. If there was even a chance that Onkel Zeb was right, he must do something. Must change. And the pitiful thing was that he didn't know how.

"Onkel Daniel says he saw a few ripe strawberries in the strawberry patch." Jessie kept a firm hold on Timothy's hand as they approached the patch that lay between the barn and Daniel's workshop. He was only too likely to run right over the plants in his eagerness.

"I want to pick lots," he exclaimed.

"It's too early for there to be lots," Becky said wisely.

"That's right." Jessie smiled at her, relieved that Becky seemed a little more herself this morning.

"Not like when Anna and Barbie picked the blackberries," Becky said, eyes already focused on the green plants. "Maybe we can have enough to eat, though."

"Or make a rhubarb strawberry cobbler. Onkel Zeb said Daadi loves that," Jessie said. Jessie stopped at the edge of the strawberry patch and knelt to capture Timothy's wandering attention. "We walk only on the path between the plants, ain't so? And we move the leaves very, very gently to look."

"And only pick the really red ones," Becky added. "I'll watch him, Cousin Jessie."

Jessie nodded. Becky still wanted to look out for her little brother, and that was how it should be. But she didn't seem quite so determined to push Jessie out of the picture.

Could Jessie say the same for Caleb? Maybe, at least a little. He could have been angry the previous night when he'd realized her stories were about Alice. He hadn't been. Grieved, yes, but he would put his own pain aside if it meant helping his children.

"I found some," Timothy shouted, and Jessie stepped carefully over the row to look.

"Yah, those are fine to pick. Yum, they'll be delicious."

"I got some, too," Becky began, and then gave a startled yelp. "Look what's here! Komm, schnell."

Jessie picked Timothy up and swung him over the

row of plants he was about to step on. They found Becky squatting next to a turtle.

"Not a snake, like the story. A turtle," Becky said. She touched the shell with the tip of her finger. "Is it dead?"

"No, he's just hiding in his shell. He's afraid of boys and girls, I think. He's called a box turtle."

"Why?" Timothy wanted to know.

Jessie grinned. "I have no idea. But my daadi said that's what this kind of turtle was, and I believed him."

"Did you find one when you were my age?" Becky asked.

"Just about. My brother and I were picking strawberries when we found him. We put our initials on his shell, so whenever we saw him we knew he was our friend."

"Can we do that?" Becky jumped up. "I'll get a crayon."

"We need something more lasting than crayon. Why don't you run over to the shop and ask Onkel Daniel for a permanent marker?"

"Okay." Becky leaped over the rows of berry plants and streaked off toward the shop.

"Does the turtle eat the berries?" Timothy clutched his berry container close to his chest.

"I don't know, but I'm sure there will be enough for all of us. You could watch him and see."

Timothy squatted, staring intently at the turtle, who seemed equally intent on staying safe in his shell and peering out at Timothy.

Amused, Jessie concentrated on picking the ripe berries along the edges of the rows. If the children's attention lasted, they might get a pint or more, and the berries along the edges should be picked before they attracted the attention of hungry birds.

"Daadi's coming," Timothy said, looking up from his absorption.

Jessie's heart gave a little thump when she spotted Becky pushing the wheelchair toward them while Caleb propelled the wheels with his hands. She almost jumped up to help but caught herself. Better to let Becky do it and give them a chance to talk.

But it looked as if their thoughts were only on the turtle. Becky waved a marker in one hand. "Daadi wants to see, too."

"We'll bring the turtle to him." Jessie picked the creature up carefully and carried it to a spot on the edge of the patch where Caleb could examine it easily.

"Here we are. I suspect he'll stay in his shell until we leave. Becky, will you put a *B* for Becky or an *R* for Rebecca?"

Becky knelt, uncapping the marker. "A *B*, 'cause mostly I'm Becky. Where shall I put it, Daadi?"

Caleb gave the question serious consideration, but his eyes twinkled a little. "Why don't you do one side and let Timothy do the other?"

Becky nodded and advanced the marker toward the shell. She hesitated, the pen wavering a bit. "Cousin Jessie, will you hold it still?"

It seemed highly unlikely the turtle would venture out of its shell, but she nodded, steadying it until Becky had put a small *B* on one side.

"Now me, now me!" Timothy squished his way between them. "Hold him still, Cousin Jessie."

"Gently now," Jessie cautioned.

"You don't need to press hard," Caleb added, lips quirking as he and Jessie exchanged a glance.

Jessie's heart warmed for no good reason. But just for a moment he'd reminded her of the optimistic young man she'd spent an afternoon with a long time ago.

And lost my heart to, a small voice whispered. She did her best to ignore it.

"Sehr gut," she said when Timothy had managed a wobbly *T* on the ridged shell.

"Just like you did, ain't so?" he said, and turned to his father. "Cousin Jessie and her brother did that when they were our age."

"Did you ever put your initial on a turtle, Daadi?" Becky asked.

"No, I don't think so." Caleb hesitated, and Jessie saw his brown eyes darken a little. Odd how quickly she had learned to read his moods. He was thinking of something that saddened him.

Caleb reached out to pull Becky into the circle of his arm. "But once I put a *C* for Caleb and an *A* for Alice on that big old apple tree by the paddock. That was when I was courting your mammi." He smoothed a strand of Becky's hair back. "I'll bet you can find it if you look. Komm back and tell me, yah?"

Becky's eyes had widened at the mention of her mother. She nodded tentatively as if not sure that was the best thing to do. Then she ran off toward the apple tree, with Timothy in hot pursuit.

It took Jessie a moment or two to be sure she had mastery of her voice. "That was gut for her to hear, I think."

"I hope so." His voice was sober. "Onkel Zeb said..."

He let that trail off, and his face closed down. Apparently she wasn't meant to know what Zeb had said. But whatever it was, she suspected it was good advice. She was almost afraid to speak for fear of ruining the step forward he'd taken.

Caleb was looking after his children, who were circling the apple tree. "I hope you…we are right about this."

Her heart clutched at the way he'd coupled them together in the responsibility. "Yah."

Finally Caleb looked at her, something a little rueful in his gaze. "Any thoughts on what to do next?"

Was he seriously asking for her advice? She couldn't quite accept that he was relying on her, but she did have an answer if he wanted one.

"Becky said once that she didn't want to look like her mammi, because you wouldn't like that." She stopped, afraid she'd gone too far.

Caleb brushed a hand at his forehead as if brushing away cobwebs. "She does look like Alice. I never realized…" He shook his head slightly. "Becky shouldn't feel that way about how she looks. But being pretty isn't everything."

Jessie forced a smile. "I'm afraid it's the first thing a young man notices."

But he didn't put it off lightly. "A gut heart is worth more than a pretty face."

Did he mean that as a compliment? She found herself ridiculously elated, even while thinking that no woman especially wanted to be praised for her plain looks. Now, if a man found beauty in the person who had the good heart—well, perhaps that was reaching for the moon.

Jessie reminded herself that she had long since become satisfied with the life she had. It wouldn't do to let being here make her long for something that was out of reach and always had been.

Chapter Ten

It was an off Sunday, so Caleb wouldn't have to sit through another worship service wondering if folks were feeling sorry for him. Like most Amish church districts, worship here was held every other Sunday. In the intervening week, a family might travel to worship with a neighboring district or spend a peaceful day at family gatherings.

Peaceful. Somehow that didn't exactly describe today's visiting. The whole family was invited to Zeb's cousin Judith's house for her usual immense family meal, giving opportunities for everyone to speculate on Jessie's presence among them.

At the moment, he, Onkel Zeb and Daniel were lingering over coffee in the kitchen, watching Jessie packing the pies she'd made into a basket.

Daniel put his mug in the sink and went to peer over her shoulder. "You're not going to take all four pies to Cousin Judith's, are you? We'll be fortunate to get a slice. If you left them for us..."

"And go empty-handed?" She set the fourth pie on the rack in the basket. "We can't do that. And I don't think you'll go hungry if it's like any family meal I've ever gone to."

Daniel grimaced, and Caleb knew just what he was thinking. "The food will be wonderful gut, but I'd just as soon stay home if I had my way."

Before Jessie could react, Onkel Zeb chuckled. She looked at him inquiringly.

He grinned. "Ask Daniel why he doesn't want to see my cousin."

Jessie couldn't know it was a family joke, but she did as he directed. "Why, Daniel?"

"Onkel Zeb can laugh. It's not him she's after," Daniel grumbled. "Every single time I see Cousin Judith, she wants to know why I'm not married yet."

"And then she starts talking about all the young women she thinks would be perfect for him," Caleb added, grinning at his brother's discomfort. "If he's not quick on his feet, he'll find himself courting someone without even knowing it."

"You should talk," Daniel retorted. "She's starting to think about you now. She's probably lining up available widows. She says the kinder need—"

"Time to hitch up the carriage," Onkel Zeb said loudly, covering the end of that sentence.

For an instant Caleb was startled, but then he saw Becky and Timothy coming and understood. Just as well if the kinder didn't hear any speculation about him remarrying, which he wasn't going to do, anyway.

Jessie jumped into the momentary silence. "Becky, will you wrap up a couple of the oatmeal cookies for you and Timothy during the ride to Cousin Judith's?"

Becky's slight frown vanished, and she trotted over

to Jessie. "Two for Timothy and two for me, yah?" She reached for the cookie jar on the counter.

Caleb nodded. "That's gut. Timmy, you go along and help Onkel Daniel hitch up. It's time we were on the road."

The awkward moment passed. Daniel sent an apologetic glance toward Caleb and went out, Timothy at his heels.

He couldn't very well blame Daniel. Or Cousin Judith, for that matter. Speculation about the marital prospects of bachelors was common in the Amish community, and the blabbermauls had been gossiping about the King brothers for years.

Jessie was supervising while Becky tucked a snowy napkin over the pies in the basket. She seemed to have an instinctive awareness of Becky's need to help, and she went out of her way to invite that assistance. Jessie was thoughtful when it came to the children. He had to give her that. She seemed to have noticed things in a little over a week that he hadn't picked up on in a year.

He didn't like that idea, but he couldn't seem to dismiss it, either.

Soon they were all assembling outside to climb into the family carriage for the ride to the farm where Cousin Judith lived with her youngest son and his family. There were sure to be plenty of cousins and second cousins there, all curious about Jessie. Did Jessie realize that?

Her expression was as serene and composed as always, but he thought he detected a hint of worry in her eyes. While he wondered whether he should say something, Onkel Zeb supervised loading everyone into the carriage. Before Caleb quite understood what was happening, he found he was driving, with Jessie sitting beside him.

"You can tell Jessie about the valley along the way," Zeb said blandly. "She hasn't had a chance to see much of anything since she came."

What Jessie thought about that, Caleb couldn't say. She was glancing across the field, and the brim of her bonnet hid her face from him.

Daniel seemed to be teasing Becky in the back of the carriage—Caleb heard her giggle. He glanced back. "Don't get the kinder all riled up before we reach Cousin Judith's," he warned. "Not unless you want to be responsible for calming them down again."

"Hey, I'm just their onkel," Daniel protested. "I'm supposed to be fun."

"How about a game of I Spy?" Jessie suggested. "You can look for signs of spring. I spy a willow tree that has its leaves out. What do you see?"

Of course both of them started naming things, trying to top each other. Since Jessie couldn't very well keep turning around, Onkel Zeb and Daniel took over the game, and they were soon completely engrossed.

"That was a gut idea," Caleb said under the cover of their noise. "Denke, Jessie. Daniel always did like to stir things up."

"When he's a father, he'll learn," she said, smiling a little.

"If," Caleb muttered, thinking of what Zeb said about the influence their parents' troubles had on them.

She shrugged, obviously not wanting to venture an opinion on the subject.

They passed two other Amish buggies headed in the other direction, no doubt on the same mission they were. Each buggy had a husband and wife in the front, of course, and he was suddenly very conscious of Jessie sitting beside him. What was she thinking? Any casual observer might assume they were husband and wife.

Onkel Zeb had no doubt thought of that. He was getting as bound on mischief as Daniel was, in his own way. What did he think was going to happen?

Caleb had been silent too long, and he saw that Jessie was looking at him with apprehension. He cleared his throat, trying to find the right way to reassure her.

"I thought maybe..." He ran out of words, not sure what he wanted to say.

"Yah?" Her eyebrows lifted.

The game was still going full blast in the back of the carriage, and he and Jessie might as well have been alone. "If you're feeling a bit nervous about being pitchforked into a lot of family...well, I don't blame you, I guess."

"It is a little scary," she confessed. "I suppose I met some of them at...at the wedding." She rushed over that part. "But I probably won't remember names."

His jaw tightened at the mention of his wedding to Alice, but he forced himself to go on. "Nobody will expect you to, except probably Cousin Judith. You won't be able to dodge her."

"Wants to have a shot at me, does she?" Jessie seemed to make an attempt at lightness, but he didn't think she felt it.

"It's certain sure she'll want to know all about you and not be shy about asking." He should have realized it would be an ordeal for her, meeting all these people who had strong feelings about what Alice had done. "They'll be polite, I think." He hoped. "If you get caught in an uncomfortable conversation, you can always say you have to check on the kinder."

"I'll be fine." In a turnabout, she was the one reassuring him. "Denke, Caleb." She smiled, her eyes warming as she looked at him. "It's gut of you to think of it."

Her smile touched him. She was going into a difficult situation, but she wouldn't let it get her down. It seemed Jessie had a tough core of strength to go along with the tenderness she showed his kinder.

Looking back on it that evening, Jessie had to admit that the afternoon had gone better than she'd anticipated. Zeb's cousin Judith had been terrible inquisitive, that was certain, firing question after question at Jessie until she'd begun to sympathize with Daniel's reluctance to face her.

Then suddenly the inquisition stopped. Apparently she'd passed some sort of test and had gained Judith's grudging acceptance. And where Cousin Judith led, it seemed the rest of the family followed.

Jessie had come home with a copy of Cousin Judith's precious recipe for pon haus, she'd exchanged quilting ideas for youngsters with a second cousin who had daughters about Becky's age, and she felt she'd begun to make some friends.

Now the house was quiet. The kinder were long since asleep, and Daniel had gone off on some mission of his own that he'd seemed disinclined to talk about. A girl? She'd wondered but hadn't asked.

Onkel Zeb, suppressing his yawns, had headed for bed early, and Caleb had disappeared into his own room at that point. Had he been reluctant to be left alone with her? She wondered, but her relationship with Caleb was tentative at best, so she tried to take things as they came.

Besides, she enjoyed these last few moments of tidying the kitchen for the next day, feeling the house sleep around her. It was almost as if she belonged here, as if this were her own house, her kinder asleep upstairs, her…

"Jessie, surely you can stop working now. It's late."

Startled, Jessie swung around from the sink to find Caleb in the doorway. The memory of the direction her thoughts had been headed made her cheeks warm.

"Ach, I'm enjoying it. My mamm always says that tidying the kitchen the last thing at night sets it up for a fine morning's start."

"Looks wonderful tidy to me already. You should see it when it's just us and Onkel Zeb here." He wheeled himself around the table, closer to her. "If it's Daniel's turn to do the dishes, they pile up until there aren't any left to eat from."

"He can't be as bad as all that. Although I confess, my brothers are a menace when left alone in the kitchen." She dried her hands on the towel. Was he hinting that it was time she retired to the daadi haus?

But he didn't seem in any hurry. "I remembered that I hadn't told you I have an appointment with the doctor tomorrow morning. The van is going to pick me up at nine."

"I should think he'll be happy with your progress. You're getting stronger every day." That wasn't an exaggeration. In the past week he'd done things he hadn't even attempted when she'd first come.

"Yah, it's been better. It's that boss I have forcing me to exercise, ain't so?"

When Caleb's eyes crinkled in amusement, his whole face changed, warming until she hardly remembered the steely expression he'd worn that first day. Her heart lifted in response, making her think she'd best give herself another lecture about her attitude toward Caleb.

"I'm only doing my job," she said, unable to keep from smiling back. "You're the one who is working hard at it. You have the will to get back to normal, and that's the most important part."

Getting back to normal. To Caleb, that meant seeing the last of her. Ironic that the harder she worked to help him, the sooner she'd leave.

"Being at Cousin Judith's today…it wasn't bad after all, ain't so?" he asked.

Her smile widened. "I began to sympathize with Daniel when she started questioning me. I felt like she turned my head inside out to see what was in there."

"Yah, Cousin Judith has that effect on people. She claims she's old enough to say what she wants, but as far back as I can remember, she always has. What was she asking you?"

Jessie hesitated, but he seemed to want to know. "Actually, she was asking about Alice. About why we were so close."

She waited for Caleb's expression to shutter as it usually did at the mention of Alice. But although he frowned, he didn't turn away from the subject.

"I guess she didn't know about Alice's mamm dying when she was so young. I don't think we ever talked about it."

It was a measure of success that he acknowledged that much, she thought. "Yah, well, I don't suppose it mattered. She understood when she realized that Alice was much more like a little sister to me."

She darted a cautious glance at Caleb, and found that he was studying her gravely with a hint of question in his eyes.

"There's more to it than that," he said slowly, with an air of feeling his way. "It seems like you hold yourself responsible for...well, for what she did wrong."

Jessie brushed a hand across her forehead, trying to banish the memories. "Maybe so. I guess I never got over thinking that I had to take care of her."

He didn't speak for a moment, and the old farmhouse was very still around them...so still she could hear the ticking of the clock on the shelf.

"Why?" Caleb spoke abruptly. "Tell me why, Jessie." He reached out to circle her wrist with his fingers as if he'd compel her to tell him the truth.

She found she was shaking her head. "It...it's nothing."

Caleb leaned over to grasp one of the kitchen chairs and pull it close to the wheelchair. "Sit down and tell me. I want to know why it's important to you. You don't have to atone for what someone else did wrong."

Jessie sank down on the chair, as much because her knees were wobbly as because of the pressure of Caleb's hand. "I was the big sister. That's how my mamm put it after Alice's mother passed. She would try to be a mamm to Alice, and I must be her big sister."

Caleb nodded. "You mentioned that, and I could just hear your mamm saying it." He waited as if he understood there was more she had to tell.

"I tried. I really wanted to be a gut big sister. But I failed." The taste of failure was still there. "I just... I suppose I got tired of always having to include her. One day, after school, we were walking home." The memory never really left her, but it wasn't easy to say out loud. "Alice got mad because I was talking with the other girls. I wasn't paying attention to her."

"Ach, Jessie, every big brother or big sister feels that way sometimes. Plenty of times I told Daniel and Aaron to get lost."

She couldn't smile as he'd obviously intended. "That's what she did. Really. She ran off into the woods and I... I didn't go after her. The other girls said she'd jump out at us when we got home, but she didn't. Alice was lost."

"What happened?"

"I went back. I looked in the woods, called to her, all the time getting more and more frantic. I couldn't find her. Finally I had to go home and tell Mamm and Daad what I'd done."

His fingers moved soothingly on the palm of her hand. "Somebody found her, yah? And she was all right?"

"Daadi called out all the neighbors. We searched and searched." She still remembered how terrifying it had been. "I followed along behind Daad, feeling so guilty. Someone finally found her asleep under a tree."

"So no harm was done." Caleb was obviously struggling to understand. "Maybe you were thoughtless, but that shouldn't make you carry a burden the rest of your life."

She shook her head. He didn't understand. Maybe he couldn't.

"I was responsible, but it was worse than that. When Alice flounced off into the woods, I was actually glad. I finally had time alone with my friends. Then, when I couldn't find her, I knew how wrong that had been."

"Ach, Jessie, if anybody could be too responsible, it must be you." His voice was gentle, maybe a little amused, but kind.

The trouble was that she couldn't tell him the rest of it, because it involved him too closely. How could she admit that she'd resented it when he picked Alice? How could she say that she might have kept Alice from coming back here to die if only she'd tried harder? Maybe she could have spared Caleb and the kinder if she'd been wiser and more determined.

"You want to make amends for the harm Alice might have done to Becky and Timothy." Caleb's fingers tightened on hers, and she forced herself to look at him. "I do understand that, Jessie. You came because you thought you could make a difference."

"Yah, I did." She was finding it difficult to breathe, sitting so close to him in the quiet house, feeling his hand encircling hers as if it was the most natural thing in the world. "You don't agree?" She made it a question, longing to have this much, at least, clear between them.

"At first all I wanted was to get rid of you, but…" His voice trailed off, and she felt his gaze on her face as if he were touching it. "You showed me some things about my kinder that I should have seen for myself, Jessie. I'm grateful." He leaned toward her, his eyes intent. "This hasn't been easy for you. I'm sorry if I made it harder."

She'd never expected an apology from him…never

thought he'd admit that her presence had helped. She ought to have spoken, but her lips trembled.

Caleb was scanning her face. He was so close that she could see a miniscule scar on his temple, hear the intake of his breath.

"Jessie." He said her name softly. He leaned even closer...so close that in a moment their lips would touch.

And then footsteps sounded on the outside steps, and the back door rattled. Caleb snatched his hand away, spinning the chair around so that by the time Daniel came inside, they were several feet apart.

Jessie managed to compose herself, to speak rationally to Daniel. But all the while her heart ached. Now she'd never know if Caleb would have kissed her. And she'd never know if he was glad or sorry that Daniel had stopped him.

The next day, Caleb still couldn't quite believe his actions. How had he come so close to Jessie? Another moment and he'd have kissed her.

He could only be thankful Daniel had come in when he did. If Caleb had acted on the impulse of the moment, he'd have made all their lives unbelievably difficult.

Frowning out the window of the van taking him home from his doctor's appointment, Caleb automatically noticed the greening of the pastures. The spring rains had been plentiful this year, thank the gut Lord.

Another reason for thanks was that he'd had an appointment this morning. It had given him a reason to get out of the house early, cutting short any chance of a conversation with Jessie. At the breakfast table, awkwardness had been avoided by the kinder babbling away about the spring program at the Amish school this week. They took it for granted that the whole family would be going. Becky, especially, couldn't wait. She'd been picturing herself in school come fall.

And she'd included Jessie in her imaginings, as if naturally Jessie would be there to pack her lunch and walk her to school on the first day. Jessie had answered her without committing herself, carefully avoiding a glance at him.

Which brought him right back to the problem he'd caused. He'd thought he was being generous, encouraging her to talk about her reasons for coming. He'd felt it was the least he could do, given all the ways she'd helped them.

Maybe he'd even been thinking he should tell her she was welcome in his house for as long as she wanted to stay. But then he'd turned that possibility upside down by giving in to the wave of attraction.

It might be better, safer, if Jessie left. She'd made him realize that he still had longings for a woman to spend his life with, that there might be hope of a normal relationship with someone. But not with Jessie, carrying the baggage of her involvement in Alice's life. That would be a disaster.

His gaze landed on the crutches that lay on the floor of the van. The doctor had been so pleased with his progress that he'd actually given him permission to start using them a short while each day.

It was thanks to Jessie that he'd made such progress. Once he was on crutches, he'd be on his feet, in a way. On his feet—that was what he'd told Jessie. She could stay until he was on his feet again.

He didn't have time to follow that thought to its difficult conclusion, because they were pulling up to the house.

"Here we are," the driver announced cheerfully, coming around to maneuver the lift that would lower the wheelchair to the ground. "Looks like someone is here to help."

It was Onkel Zeb who'd come out to the van. How long would it take him to start asking questions? Caleb knew perfectly well that Zeb had been aware of the strain between him and Jessie at breakfast. His uncle didn't miss much.

"Back already?" Zeb nodded his thanks to the driver and grabbed the handles of the wheelchair. "What did the doctor say?"

"That I'm doing fine." Caleb took the crutches the driver handed him. "See?"

"Ach, he's not going to let you start using crutches already, is he? He said it would be six weeks, and it's not near that."

"I won't use them all the time," Caleb admitted. He was tempted to skirt what the doctor had actually told him, but he didn't have any desire to do something stupid and ruin all the progress he'd made. "He said I could try them a couple of times a day for a few minutes at a time. Just to see how it will feel to be back on my feet again."

Zeb surveyed him severely. "How many minutes? And where are you allowed to try it? Are you supposed to have help?"

Caleb couldn't suppress a smile. "You sound like a mother hen, ain't so?"

"Mother hen or not, you just answer me." His uncle

took up a position in front of the chair, plainly intending that Caleb wouldn't go anywhere until he'd answered.

Caleb sighed. There was no getting away from Onkel Zeb when he was in this mood. "Yah, someone must be with me. No more than fifteen minutes at a time. And only in the house. Satisfied?"

Onkel Zeb gave a crisp nod. "Jessie and I will see there's no cheating, that's certain sure, so don't even think it." He started pushing the chair up the ramp to the back door.

Jessie. Caleb frowned at the crutches he was carrying. If he wanted it, he now had an excuse to send Jessie away. After what happened between them, that might be the smartest thing he could do, no matter how wrong it felt.

Chapter Eleven

"That's enough for now." Jessie put as much steel into her voice as she could, her hand steadying Caleb as he tried to balance on the crutches.

She forced herself not to quail at the angry look he sent her.

"I can judge better than you when I've had enough."

"The doctor is the one who knows better than either of us. According to Onkel Zeb, he told you no more than fifteen minutes at a time." She moved the wheelchair into position behind Caleb.

"Onkel Zeb talks too much," he muttered, but he reached back with one hand for the chair. The crutch slid from under his arm, and she grasped him to ease him into the chair.

"If you overdo, you'll just risk a setback. You don't want that, ain't so?"

For an instant he looked as if he'd snarl at her, but the expression slid away into one more rueful. "Yah, you're right. I get impatient."

"That's only natural." She set the crutches in the corner of the hall, which they'd decided was the best spot for practicing. "But look at how far you've komm just since you got home from the rehab hospital. No one would believe you could do so well in a few short weeks."

He needed the encouragement, she suspected, as well as the cautioning. He was eager to get back on his feet. She feared a big part of that was his determination to get rid of her.

Sure he was settled, she headed back to the kitchen. From the moment he'd gotten his body upright with the help of the crutches, she'd been expecting him to say they could do without her now.

She couldn't fool herself just because he'd seemed so kind the previous night, encouraging her to share her feelings about Alice. That momentary connection between them had been smashed by the wave of longing that seemed to come from nowhere.

Caleb was regretting it today—she'd seen it clearly in the way he'd withdrawn from her at breakfast. Probably he'd consented to let her help with the crutches only because Daniel and Zeb were both out this afternoon, and he had just enough sense to know he couldn't do it alone.

The back door slammed, and Becky and Timothy rushed into the kitchen, Becky carrying a few eggs in a basket.

"Leah is coming," Becky announced.

"And Jacob, too," Timothy added.

"Gut." She gestured to the containers of rhubarb they'd picked that morning. "It's time we were making a batch of jam."

"I'll help," Becky said immediately. "Timmy will play with Jacob, but I'll help."

Jessie hesitated, trying to find the right way to say she'd rather not have a six-year-old around boiling syrup. But Caleb made it unnecessary to disappoint her.

"I need your help this afternoon, Becky. I have to finish sanding those cabinets before Onkel Daniel gets home. I'm counting on you."

Becky sent one regretful glance toward the rhubarb, but the lure of working with her daadi won out. "I like to sand. I'll do it just the way you showed me." She hurried to get behind the wheelchair. "I can help push you up the ramp to the workshop."

"I can, too," Timothy said, obviously determined not to be left out. They headed out the back door, arguing about who should push the chair.

Jessie heard them exchanging greetings with Leah. In a few moments the children's voices faded and Leah came in, smiling.

She set a plastic pail of berries onto the counter. "I have enough strawberries that we can do a few jars of strawberry rhubarb, I figured. Looks as if Caleb is going to keep the kinder out from underfoot while we're making jam. It's just as well, ain't so?"

"There's nothing worse than a burn from boiling sugar syrup," Jessie said. "I've never forgotten the time my mamm and I let Alice help, and she got it on her fingers. I had to chase her across the kitchen to grab her and stick her hand in cold water."

Leah lost no time in starting to wash and cut berries, since Jessie had everything they'd need laid out and the rhubarb already prepared. "I decided I'd help when my mamm was pouring out peanut brittle. That really hurts. Poor Alice. No wonder she lost her head."

She paused, looking at Jessie. "Alice was like a little sister to you. I know that makes it hard to hear how some folks here talk about her."

Jessie nodded, trying not to think of the hurtful words. "I understand how folks feel. After all, they had Caleb and the kinder to care for when she ran off. But it's still difficult." She measured sugar carefully. "I'm grateful that you understand. Alice was…" She stopped, not wanting to say too much.

"Go on," Leah said. "You can talk about her to me, even if Caleb probably isn't ready to hear it."

But Caleb had let her talk last night, hadn't he? Was it possible his bitterness was ebbing?

"Alice was always so bright and cheery. It was like having a ray of sunshine in the house, my daad said. Such a smile she had, and how she'd laugh at the silliest things. You couldn't help but be charmed by her."

"Caleb was, that's certain sure." The pile of berries grew higher in Leah's bowl. "He told me once he'd fallen in love as soon as he set eyes on Alice."

"That's so." Jessie tried to ignore the little pang in her heart at the memory. "He'd traveled out to Ohio for a wedding, and Mamm and Daad offered to house some of the overnight guests. So he came to our place."

"And saw Alice and fell hard," Leah said. She shook her head. "I can't say I think that's a gut way of doing it. Sam and I knew each other all our lives. There wasn't much we didn't know about each other when we married."

"Actually, when he got to the farm, Alice wasn't home. Mamm had me show Caleb around and keep him company." But that wasn't the part Leah wanted to hear. "When we got back to the house, Caleb walked into the kitchen and saw Alice. He stared like he'd never seen a girl before in his life."

She tried to keep her voice light, but the memory was so strong. She'd walked in happy, enjoying Caleb's presence, eager to introduce him to the rest of the family. And then she'd seen him staring dumbstruck at Alice, and all the joy had faded from the day.

She realized Leah was watching her and gave herself a little shake. "The syrup is almost ready. How are the berries coming?"

"About done," Leah said. "Jessie..."

There was a questioning note in her voice, and it was a question Jessie didn't want to answer. She'd never confided her feelings about Caleb to a soul, and she wouldn't now.

"Yah?" She smiled brightly, and Leah seemed to understand.

"I'll scald the jars," she said instead of the question that obviously hovered on her tongue.

They busied themselves with their jobs, and it wasn't until several minutes had passed that Leah spoke again.

"Funny." She glanced around the kitchen. "It must be quite a few years since anyone made jam in here. The last few years, Caleb insisted I take the rhubarb and the berries, so I made jam and brought half over here."

"I noticed someone had stocked the pantry shelves," Jessie said. "I should have known it was you." She poured hot jam carefully into a jar. "I suppose Caleb's mamm did a lot of canning."

"I guess." Leah began wiping jars and capping them. "I don't remember her all that well, and everything changed once she left." She shook her head. "I've wondered sometimes how the boys would have turned out if she hadn't gone away."

"They were affected, that's certain sure." She thought of Becky and Timothy. She'd just begun to make some headway with them. If only Caleb didn't insist on her going away too soon…

"And then Becky and Timothy went through the same thing," Leah said, her voice heavy. "Almost seems like it runs in families, though I guess that's silly. Still, they've been much better since you've been here."

"I hope I can make a difference for them."

Leah eyed her, speculation in her face. "Maybe you'll be here for good. It's time Caleb gave those kinder a mother and himself a wife."

Heat flooded Jessie's face. "Don't matchmake, please, Leah. It's impossible."

"Why?" Leah didn't seem ready to give up her idea. "Nobody could love those kinder more than you do, and it's plain you care about Caleb. So just tell me why not."

"I can't. It would be wrong." She felt as if she couldn't breathe. "I let Alice down. I wasn't there when Alice needed me. It would be wrong to take her place."

"Nonsense," Leah said robustly. "Alice was a grown woman who made her own choices. That's no reason you and Caleb and the kinder should suffer."

All Jessie could do was shake her head. After those moments when they'd felt the strength of the attraction between them, Caleb probably felt just as guilty as she did. No matter what she might wish, Alice would always stand between them.

By the time he spotted Daniel's buggy pulling up to the barn, Caleb had sent the kinder out to play while he finished the cabinets. The soothing, repetitive nature of the work gave him plenty of time to think. Unfortunately, his thoughts just kept going around in circles.

One part of him kept saying that now that he was better, he had a good excuse for sending Jessie back to Ohio. And a good reason, too, given the way he'd responded to her last night. But his conscience insisted that it would be wrong to send her away just because he hadn't been able to control his desires. Her reason for coming was admirable, even if he thought she was overreacting with her guilt.

Daniel came in, arms full. He stacked supplies on one of the work tables and looked over Caleb's shoulder. "You've got a lot finished. Denke, Caleb. I don't see how I'd be able to do this job without your help."

Caleb shrugged off his thanks. "You should think of bringing in an apprentice once I'm back to work. Especially if this job leads to more. Once this client's neighbors see your work, you may have more than you can handle."

Daniel seemed unimpressed. "Sometimes I think they just want to say their cabinets are Amish-made."

"As long as they hire you, what difference does it make?" Caleb studied his brother's face, wondering at the slight frown he wore. "You and I might know that being Amish doesn't automatically make you a fine craftsman, but that's what you are."

"I guess so." Daniel's face relaxed in a smile. "I'm too picky. I want them to hire me because I'm good, not because I'm Amish."

"So you're both. They win both ways." He was relieved to see the smile. People who didn't know his brother well might have been fooled by his carefree exterior, but Caleb knew how conscientious he was. Daniel would always do his best, no matter what it cost him.

Daniel focused on organizing the supplies he'd brought in, and Caleb went back to putting the final touches on the cabinets. Even though he didn't come by the work naturally like Daniel, it was still a pleasure to feel the wood grow smooth and silky under his hand. They worked together in comfortable silence.

Then Daniel looked at him with a question in his face. "You didn't tell me about the crutches. Did you try them out earlier, or were you waiting for me to get home?"

"Already done," Caleb said. "Jessie helped me." He considered. "I'd say it went pretty well for the first time. Made me feel normal again to be standing and moving."

"Sehr gut." Daniel hesitated. "You're not going back to using that for an excuse to get rid of Jessie so soon, are you?"

Caleb evaded his eyes. "I don't know. I'll maybe soon be well enough we could just have someone in for a few hours a day to watch the kinder, ain't so?"

"No." Daniel leaned against the workbench, frowning. "Not if you mean to subject us to Onkel Zeb's cooking again."

"Do you ever think of anything but your stomach?" Caleb tried to keep his voice light. He didn't want to talk about Jessie leaving. He was already having enough trouble with the idea.

"It's important," Daniel protested. "Besides, Jessie's wonderful gut with the kinder. I'm not saying it's like having a mamm of their own, but I don't know who'd be any better. Do you?"

Caleb gritted his teeth at the direct question. It hit too close to the bone. "Why don't you think about getting married to some nice girl? Becky and Timothy would love to have an aunt."

Daniel turned away. "Just haven't run across the right one, that's all."

"Is it?" Caleb felt a sudden longing to see someone in the family make a success of love. "Are you sure it's not because of…well, because of Mamm? And because of the mess I made of marriage? You shouldn't give up on the idea because of that."

"I could tell you the same thing, ain't so?" His brother's quick gaze challenged him. "Seems to me you're the one who's given up on being happy."

The words seemed to hang in the quiet room between them. Caleb clamped his lips together. He wasn't going to respond. Not now. Maybe not ever.

Chapter Twelve

Nothing was any pleasanter than having the family sitting together in the living room as the sun slipped behind the ridge. Jessie paused in her mending to let her gaze rest on Caleb, relaxed in the easy chair he'd insisted on moving to from the wheelchair. He had a newspaper in his hands, but he looked over it at Timothy and Becky, playing more or less quietly together on the floor.

Jessie could understand his insistence on getting out of the wheelchair. Every small step he took toward recovery was important to him, even if it was as simple as sitting in his usual seat.

Funny how quickly this rocker had become hers. Onkel Zeb had gone automatically to the end of the sofa, pushing her mending basket over next to her as she reached for it.

Daniel had disappeared in the direction of his workshop after the chores were done, saying he wanted to get his materials ready for the next day. He'd shaken his head, smiling a little, when both his uncle and his brother offered to help.

"I want to plan the work out in my head," he'd said. "You'll just be a distraction."

That was probably the best way he could have picked to dissuade Caleb from going out with him. Caleb had thrown himself into work in the shop, no doubt from his need to repay Daniel for all the farm work he was doing. That determination was a measure of Caleb's personality, she suspected. He hated being dependent more than anyone she'd ever known.

Perhaps the accident was God's way of confronting Caleb with that, but she knew he wouldn't want to hear it.

Following his gaze to the two children, she found herself smiling. Timothy had reached the point of taking her presence as a fact of life, and it never seemed to occur to him that she wouldn't always be there.

As for Becky…well, Jessie couldn't entirely suppress a sigh. Becky had been much more cooperative lately, and any resentment she might have felt over Jessie's presence seemed to have disappeared that day that she'd sobbed her heart out and Jessie had comforted her.

But Becky still wasn't the happy, carefree little girl she was meant to be. She accepted Jessie, but the closeness Jessie longed for hadn't been forthcoming.

How could she reach the child and make a difference to her if Becky didn't let her guard down? They needed a situation that would encourage Becky to talk, and Jessie hadn't yet found it. She thought longingly of the hours she and her mamm had spent chatting about anything and everything while they washed the dishes each evening. But if she tried to engage Becky that way, Timothy would be right there, determined not to be left out.

She glanced down at the sewing in her lap and remembered her thought about introducing Becky to quilting. The quilt squares she'd cut were still in her basket, but she and the kinder had been busy with other things and it had slipped her mind. Maybe now was the time to introduce it.

As she tucked the mending away and began taking out the quilting squares, Becky crossed the room to her daad. "Daadi, you didn't forget going to the school tomorrow, did you?"

"No, for sure I didn't." Caleb put the paper down. "You'll be going to school every day come September. We'll go so we can all get a gut look at it."

Timothy, overhearing, pouted. "I want to go to school, too."

"You'll see the program tomorrow," Jessie reminded him. "Then you can imagine what it's like when Becky is there."

"I wish I was older," he declared, but the pout receded.

Onkel Zeb chuckled. "You won't feel that way in a few more years, young Timothy."

Timothy looked a little puzzled at that, but he noticed the patches Jessie was laying out on her lap, and that distracted him.

"What are those, Cousin Jessie?" He poked at a patch with one finger.

"These are the quilt squares. Remember? I showed you some before, and you tried sewing. When these are all stitched together, they'll make a small quilt, just big enough for a doll or a teddy bear. I'm trying to see which patches will look best next to each other."

"Can't you just make them all the same?" he asked.

"Silly," Becky said, showing off her experience. "Quilts always have different colors on each patch."

"I guess they wouldn't have to, but they're prettier this way," Jessie said, peacemaking. "It's called a nine-patch, because I'll put one in the middle and eight around it." She laid out a sample on her skirt. "Then you sew them together for the quilt."

Becky reached out tentatively and rearranged one of the squares. Encouraged, Jessie smiled at the child. "Do you want to pick out some squares, Becky? I have lots of them. You'll stitch them together just like you sewed that practice piece the other night."

Becky hesitated, and Jessie held her breath, hoping she hadn't sounded too eager. Then Becky nodded.

Jessie scooped the rest of the fabric squares from the basket and fanned them out. "Which ones would you put together?"

Timothy started to reach in front of Becky for a square, but Onkel Zeb called his name.

"Timothy, komm over here. Let's see if I remember how to make a lamb from a piece of wood."

Timmy scrambled over to his great-onkel, hanging on him as he got a penknife out. Jessie looked her thanks at him. Zeb, at least, understood what she was trying to do.

Becky quickly got into the idea of laying out the squares into a pattern, and Jessie smiled at the intent look on Becky's face. When she concentrated so hard, she very much resembled her daadi. Jessie glanced at Caleb and found him watching her. His face softened into a smile, and for a long moment they just looked at each other.

Then she felt the heat rising in her cheeks and focused on the fabric again. What did that stare mean, if anything?

"How about these two together?" She put a brown square against a black one.

Becky wrinkled up her nose. "Too dark," she said decidedly. "Maybe this." She picked up a rose-colored piece and laid it out next to the black.

"Very nice." Jessie felt a slight inward twinge. That rose piece was from a dress Alice had in her early teens. She'd looked like a flower in it.

Finally the squares were arranged to Becky's satisfaction. "Now we sew them together, ain't so?"

Jessie nodded. "I'll thread a couple of needles," she said, taking out the spool. "Why don't you match up the edges of two squares so they're just right?"

Becky pulled a stool over next to Jessie and picked up two of the squares. Her forehead wrinkled into a frown of concentration as she focused on matching them exactly. Like her daadi, she wanted to do everything perfectly.

"Now we start to stitch them together." Jessie showed Becky how to move the needle, picking up a small stitch. "It will be hard at first to sew a straight line, but it will get easier with practice."

Becky managed to get two stitches more or less in place before she pricked her finger and stopped to suck on it. She eyed Jessie. "You learned to sew when you were my age, ain't so?"

"Yah, that's right. My mamm taught me. I used to stick myself sometimes, too." She smiled at the memory. "My mamm said that my fingers would get better long before the nine-patch was finished. And she was right."

Becky stuck her needle in the fabric again. "Did you make one like this?"

"Yah, but different colors. It was in my doll cradle for a long time. Alice made one for her bear, I remember."

She was smiling until she saw the rigid look come over Becky's face. How foolish of her—she'd said the one thing that might turn Becky against the idea of quilting. But the girl couldn't go through life refusing to do anything her mother had done, could she?

Becky put the sewing down carefully and got up from the stool. "I don't want to sew anymore now." She went to Onkel Zeb, seeming instantly absorbed in what he was doing.

Frustrated, Jessie frowned at Caleb. Hadn't he said he'd work on showing Becky it was okay to be like her mammi? As far as she could tell, he'd never bothered to do it.

Caleb returned her look with one that was half ashamed and half stubborn. She ought to have been angry, but instead she felt only sorrow. Helplessness. What would break this cycle of blame and guilt that kept Caleb and his children trapped in this difficult place?

Caleb grasped the arms of the wheelchair as Onkel Zeb moved him into place at the rear of the schoolroom, Jessie following with the children. Several of Caleb's friends and neighbors got up, greeting him, making room on the benches for everyone.

He'd wanted to come to the school program on crutches, but Zeb had talked him out of it, reasoning that it would be hard to maneuver in the crowded room without tripping someone. He'd been right, that was certain sure. It looked as if the whole church was here. Everyone wanted to see the scholars put on their program—one of the few times Amish children performed for others, since that idea smacked of being prideful.

The one-room school hadn't changed, it seemed, since he'd been a scholar here. The alphabet still marched across the wall over the top of the chalkboard. Someone had put a Wilkom Friends sign on the board, decorated with flowers in colored chalk.

Becky had wiggled her way next to him on the end of the bench, and now she pulled at his arm. "Where will I sit when I'm a scholar?"

Putting his arm around her, he pointed to the small desks at the front of the room. "You'll be right up there. Teacher Mary wants the first-graders up front so she can help them."

His daughter stood to scan the front row of desks, now occupied by the schoolchildren who were waiting and eager to begin. "I want that one, on the end," she whispered in his ear.

"Maybe you'll be there, maybe not. It's Teacher Mary who decides."

Becky looked slightly mutinous for a moment, but then she nodded and relapsed into silence, her small face grave.

What had happened to the bright, sunny child she used to be? His conscience struck him a blow, and he glanced at Jessie. She seemed to know.

They hadn't spoken about last night. In fact, Jessie seemed determined to ignore the incident.

Not so Onkel Zeb. He'd had plenty to say once he got Caleb alone. And Caleb knew he was right. It was his responsibility to help his daughter come to terms with what her mother had done. He'd told Jessie he would. But when it came right down to it, he hadn't been able to find the words.

Fortunately, the program started before he tied himself in too many knots trying to rationalize his failure. No one could think of anything else while the young scholars were saying their pieces and singing their songs.

He had to smile, remembering the school programs of his youth. There was the year he'd completely forgotten his lines and stood there, turning red, until the teacher had prompted him. To say nothing of the time Aaron had knocked over a whole display of posters by backing into it.

Timmy, seated on Jessie's lap so he could see better, was wiggling, but Becky sat rapt, totally engaged in every line. Her lips moved silently along with the songs.

Caleb smiled, watching her, and found himself automatically looking at Jessie, wanting to share the moment with her. She was looking at Becky, as well, but then she glanced at him. Her serene face curved in a smile, and it was hard to look away. How could it be that he was communicating wordlessly with her?

His gaze dropped. He didn't want to feel that comfortable with her. It was yet another reminder that he had to move forward, and he didn't know how.

When the program ended, everyone began moving

outside for the picnic and games that always closed out the school year. The chatter of the crowd was immediate, and he was kept busy answering questions about his health.

Willing hands lifted the chair down the single step out of the white frame schoolhouse, and Zeb pushed Caleb toward the picnic tables where the scholars' mothers were busy putting out food. He spotted Jessie taking the kinder to the table and knew he didn't have to worry about them. Jessie would take care of them.

Zeb parked him next to a group of men. "You stay here and catch up on all the news. I'll bring you a plate."

"No need to pile it into a mountain," Caleb called after his uncle. Zeb seemed to think he would recover faster if he was stuffed with food. Just like an Amish mother, he was.

Caleb found it rejuvenating to join in the talk of the weather, the crops, who was planting what, who'd increased his dairy herd and who was having trouble with the cooperative dairy. The ordinary topics of life in a farming community were of vital interest to no one but the folks who lived there. To them, such things were crucial, and just chatting with the others made him feel a part of it again.

The group dispersed as they finished eating, some to join the ball game that was starting, others to watch and cheer.

"Looks like the kinder are done eating," Zeb observed, nodding at Becky and Timothy, who were running toward the swings.

Caleb's gaze lingered on Becky. For once she was laughing, distracted from her troubles. She ought to have been that way all the time. He glanced at Zeb and found his uncle watching him.

"Yah, all right." Caleb frowned at him. "I know what you're thinking. And you're right. I have to try harder with Becky. It's just...difficult."

Zeb took a breath before he spoke, a sure sign he was weighing his words. "You're finding it hard."

"I'm finding it impossible," Caleb said flatly. "Jessie thinks I ought to be able to talk normally about Alice to the kinder, and I can't. It keeps coming out stiff."

"You think maybe that's because you haven't really forgiven her yet?"

Caleb smacked his palms on the arms of the chair. "I've tried. The gut Lord knows I've tried. I think I've done it, and then the anger and resentment pop back up again."

"Ach, Caleb, what do you expect? That's what forgiveness is like. If you found it easy, it surely wouldn't be real. You forgive, and then the next day when the feeling comes up again, you forgive again. One day you'll know that this time it will stick."

"That's what Jessie says. I hope you're both right," he muttered with no great confidence.

His uncle gave him a stern look. "You know what to do. Take it to the Lord. He will help you. And when you understand what the next step is, take it. Whether you want to or not."

Caleb nodded, feeling the reluctance drag at him. Yah, he knew what the next steps were. To apologize to Jessie. And then to speak naturally about Alice to his daughter.

Muttering that he was getting some coffee, he maneuvered the chair toward the table where he'd last seen Jessie.

The wheels moved quietly over the grass, newly mown for the event, and probably the bishop's wife and her daughter-in-law didn't hear his approach.

"I saw how they looked at each other," Ethel Braun was saying. "They should be ashamed of themselves."

"Maybe you misunderstood…" the daughter-in-law began timidly.

"I did not! I'd never have thought it of Caleb. That woman is out to trap him into marriage just like her cousin did, and we all know how badly that turned out."

He could back up silently. Pretend he hadn't heard anything. Nobody wanted to start an argument with the bishop's wife. Bishop Thomas himself was kind and reasonable. What he'd done to deserve a woman with such a sharp tongue, nobody knew.

But he couldn't let it go. He knew how much killing a rumor of that sort took. If he didn't scotch it today, half the county would be wondering tomorrow. Jessie didn't deserve that.

"Excuse me." *Be polite*, he told himself. *No matter what you're thinking.*

The two of them swung around. The younger woman went scarlet when she saw him. But the bishop's wife just looked more sharp-featured than ever.

"Caleb." For a moment he thought she was going to ignore the whole thing, but then she gave a short nod. "I suppose you heard what I said. I suppose I hurt your feelings, but…"

"I'm not easily hurt by gossip," he said bluntly, forgetting his resolve. "But Cousin Jessie has done nothing, and it's not right to spread rumors about her."

Faint, unbecoming color stained her thin cheeks. “Are you accusing me of being a blabbermaul?”

If the shoe fits, he thought but didn’t say.

“When you talk that way about an innocent woman, what am I to think? Jessie has been nothing but kind in helping my kinder and taking care of the house during this difficult time.” He was building up a head of steam. He should have stopped, but he couldn’t. “She knew she would be facing rejection by coming here, but she came, anyway.”

She came, knowing what she’d have to contend with, and he hadn’t been much help. It was time he made a fresh start.

He spun the chair around and froze. Jessie stood there, and it was obvious she’d heard the whole thing.

Chapter Thirteen

Jessie started down the stairs to the living room that evening after she'd gotten everything ready for putting the kinder to bed. She stopped abruptly when Caleb's voice reached her.

"...didn't you want to make a quilt with Cousin Jessie? I thought it would be nice to do."

Jessie froze, pressing her hands against the wall as she strained to hear what reply Becky might make.

"I don't know," Becky mumbled. "I just didn't want to."

Caleb cleared his throat as if talking had become difficult. "You know, your mamm was really good at sewing things. I think you would be, too."

If only Jessie could see their faces. Then she might know what they were thinking and how Becky was reacting. But she was afraid to move for fear of interrupting them.

Caleb was actually doing what she'd hoped. She could hardly believe he was able to speak that way to Becky. True, he didn't sound very comfortable, but at least he was trying.

"I don't know," Becky said again, and Jessie could imagine the confusion she must feel. Her mother hadn't been spoken of in this house for what would seem a long time to a child.

"Maybe you could ask Cousin Jessie to show you a little more about quilting before you decide you don't like it," Onkel Zeb suggested.

"Yah, that's a gut idea." Caleb sounded relieved at the helpful interruption.

"I'd like a doll quilt," Daniel said. "Make me one."

Becky giggled, and Jessie decided it was safe to go the rest of the way down. "And what would you do with a doll quilt?" she asked, keeping her voice light. "It would only cover one of your hands."

"Or one foot," Becky said, her face alight.

"Wrong, both of you." Daniel swung Becky up toward the ceiling, gave her a hug and set her down again. "I'd wrap it around my coffee thermos to keep it hot when I go to work." He shot a glance at Onkel Zeb. "Ready to help me load those cabinets on the buggy?"

"Sure thing. You'll want to put some padding between them. And a tarp on top to protect them overnight."

"Sounds gut. I want to make an early start tomorrow." Daniel ruffled Timothy's hair. "About bedtime for you, ain't so? I'll see you in the morning."

Timothy dropped a wooden horse in the toy box and flung his arms around Daniel in a hug. "See you in the morning," he echoed.

There was a little spell of silence when the two men had gone. Jessie smiled at the children. "I think it's time to tell Daadi good-night now. Don't you?"

Timothy shoved the toy box against the wall and

went to hug his daadi. But Becky hesitated, looking at Jessie. "Can we sew a little bit more tomorrow?"

It took an effort to hide her pleasure. "For sure. I'd like that."

Apparently satisfied, Becky nodded before she trotted over to tell Caleb good-night. Above the child's head, Jessie's gaze met Caleb's. *Thank you.* She mouthed the words, and Caleb nodded. Unable to stop smiling, she walked up the stairs with Becky while Timothy scurried up ahead of them.

The usual routine of putting the children to bed seemed doubly precious to Jessie that night. The kinder had grown so dear to her. Just the fact that Caleb was supporting her made her feel more a part of the family, so much so that she couldn't bear the thought of leaving.

Maybe that was what Mamm had been thinking when she'd worried about Jessie coming here. That she'd give her heart away and not be able to take it back.

Jessie sat down on Timothy's bed, and he and Becky hopped up on either side of her. She snuggled them close. "What kind of story will it be tonight?"

"A story about a rabbit," Timothy said quickly. He'd been engrossed in the story of Peter Rabbit lately.

"Peter Rabbit?" she suggested. "Benjamin Bunny?"

"We already heard those," Becky said. "Tell us a story about an Amish girl who had a rabbit."

Becky seemed to like making her use her imagination when it came to bedtime stories. "All right, but you'll have to help me."

Thinking quickly, Jessie began a story that relied a little on the fact that her cousin had once raised rabbits.

She encouraged the children to fill in details of color and place, loving the way their imaginations caught hold.

When the story had wound its way to the end, with the bunny safely back in his hutch after his adventures, she tucked them in, bending over Timmy for one of his throttling hugs. When she went to Becky she paused, as always, for any sign that an embrace would be welcome. She found Becky looking up at her solemnly.

"Cousin Jessie, am I like my mammi?" It was said in a very small voice.

Jessie's heart ached. What was the right answer to that question?

"You're like your mammi in some ways, and like your daadi in others," she said. "Parts of each, all mixed up to make a special Becky."

Apparently it was the correct response. Becky smiled and lifted her head for a good-night kiss, putting her arms around Jessie's neck in a long hug.

Jessie went back down the stairs slowly, knowing that when she reached the living room, she and Caleb would be alone. They had to talk about what the bishop's wife had said, didn't they? The fear that he'd think she was trying to trap him nagged at her. She had to face it, but what she really wanted was to go straight to the walkway that led to the daadi haus and hibernate there until morning.

But that would be cowardly. So she walked into the living room, knowing that Caleb would be waiting for her and not looking forward to it any more than she was.

She began to talk when she entered the room, afraid

she'd panic if she waited any longer. "Caleb, about what happened at the school..."

"I'm sorry," he said abruptly. His jaw was like iron.

"Sorry for what? You didn't do anything."

"I don't think I honestly realized the harm I was doing by how I thought about...about Alice. I thought it was my own business. But it must have been obvious to everyone else in the community."

She took the chair next to him. "You had every right to be angry with Alice, Caleb. I know that better than anyone."

"Yah. But I hardly considered how folks would act toward you because of it."

"They haven't all been like the bishop's wife," she hurried to assure him. "Leah has been kindness itself, and many others have been friendly."

That didn't seem to make him feel any better. "I should have thought. Just like I should have seen what was happening with my Becky." He shook his head and seemed to fight for control. "Why, Jessie? Why did Alice act as she did? Why couldn't she be happy with the life we had?"

Her throat was tight with pain, and she struggled to speak. "I don't know. But I thought from the beginning that she was too young. She hadn't...hadn't settled yet, inside herself. It was like she was always looking for a place to belong."

Caleb turned a tortured face to her. "That's what I wanted to give her."

"I know. You did your best. We did, too. From the time her mamm died, she was like one of our own, but..."

"But you failed. I failed, too."

She put her hand on his arm, helpless to comfort

him. "We did our best. Somehow what we offered was never enough to fill the empty place inside her."

"No." Caleb sucked in a deep breath, and some of the tension seemed to seep out. "When she came back, I thought at first she was sorry. That she wanted to make up for what she'd done. But I guess she just wanted a place to die."

On that subject, at least, she could reassure him. But it meant revealing things she'd never intended to say.

She pressed her fingers against her temples. "It's not…not quite that way. Really. I offered to have her. We could have moved into the daadi haus at my brother's. I would have taken care of her." She paused, trying to find the truth of her emotions at that painful time. "I should have tried harder. Maybe she knew how angry I was with her, even though I tried to forgive."

"Forgiving isn't easy." He shook his head. "It wasn't your fault."

They would each have to carry their own burden in that regard, it seemed.

"There's more," she said. "When Alice was here at the end, she wrote to me. She hadn't been writing regularly for a long time, but she did then. She…she said she came back because she hoped to put things right in the little time she had left. So, you see…"

His fingers tightened painfully around her wrist. "She wrote? You have a letter she wrote when she was dying?"

She nodded, helpless to do otherwise.

"Why haven't you shown me?" He clamped his mouth closed for a moment. "Never mind. I wouldn't give you a chance, would I?"

"No. And I didn't want to hurt you."

"Hurt me?" He said it as if it sounded ridiculous. "I want to see it. I must see it."

She looked at him for a long moment, not sure if this was wise. But what else could she do, now that he knew?

She nodded, rising. "I'll get it." She looked down at his hand, still taut around her wrist.

He grimaced, letting go. "Sorry," he muttered.

"It's nothing." She turned, heading for the kitchen and the door that led to the daadi haus, a sense of dread weighing on her heart. Would knowing what Alice wrote hurt him? Or heal him?

Caleb found he was gripping the arms of the wheelchair so tightly that his fingers were white. He relaxed them deliberately, one by one, trying not to think of anything else.

His thoughts didn't cooperate, racing ahead to what Alice might have written. Jessie had so clearly not wanted to show him. But Jessie, he'd begun to see, had a tender heart under her practical exterior. She couldn't bear to hurt anyone.

Did she imagine anything could be worse than the hurt he'd already endured? It was better to know everything.

He heard the door, and then Jessie's footsteps sounded lightly in the kitchen. He waited, praying that Onkel Zeb and Daniel wouldn't return too soon. For this he needed privacy.

He watched her come through the doorway and turn toward him. The letter was in her hand, and he couldn't tear his gaze away.

It was only a couple of seconds, but it seemed forever until she held the envelope out and sank into the chair next to him.

Now that he had it, he couldn't seem to muster the courage to look at it. He turned it over and over in his hands. "How is it I knew nothing about her writing to you?"

"I don't know."

"I wouldn't have stopped her from writing to you." The words were laced with bitterness. Was that what Alice had thought of him toward the end? That he'd have been mean enough to suppress her letters?

"I know you wouldn't. I'm sure she knew that, as well. Maybe she didn't want to talk about it."

"To me," he added to her words. "Zeb wrote the address. I know his writing."

"Does it matter?" Jessie's tone was gentle. "She'd have known how busy you were, and I'm sure things were strained enough already. It would have been natural to ask Onkel Zeb to do it."

"I guess." He knew what he was doing. He was delaying the moment when he'd actually have to read Alice's words. Being a coward.

The thought propelled him forward, and he opened the envelope.

The notepaper was worn and creased as if Jessie had read it time and again. He unfolded it and began to read.

> You were right, Jessie, like always. I shouldn't have come here. I thought I could do some good.
>
> No, I promised I wouldn't lie to myself anymore. I wanted forgiveness for myself. Selfish,

I guess, but I did think it might help Caleb and the children.

I was wrong. Caleb can't forgive me. Oh, he says the words, but I can see the bitterness in his heart. I should know. I put it there. He can't forgive, and I'm only hurting the children by letting them see me this way. It's not so bad for Timmy. He's just a baby, and he'll forget.

But Becky…dear Jessie, please do what you can to help my little daughter. Don't let her grow up bitter and lonely.

I'm always asking things of you, ain't so? But never anything as important as this. Please, Jessie. I pray that you can do what I can't.

Don't grieve too much for me. It was only when I faced death that I knew what a mess I'd made of living. But I have confessed and asked the good Lord for forgiveness. I rest on His promise to forgive.

Try to remember the silly little cousin who always wanted to be like you, and let the rest slip away to dust.

Caleb's eyes stung with salty tears, and he closed them tightly, struggling to gain control as he let the letter drop in his lap. Poor Alice. Poor, foolish Alice. She had grabbed for what she thought she wanted, only to find it turn to ashes.

"All she asked of me was forgiveness." He struggled to get the words out. "But I couldn't give it." He slammed his fist on the arm of the chair as if that would help.

"Don't, Caleb." Jessie took his tight fist in her hand. "You did your best. That's all anyone can do."

He turned blindly toward her, fighting not to give way. "If only..."

"I know."

Jessie put her hand tentatively on his back, the way she would comfort one of the children. He leaned against her arm as if it were the most natural thing in the world. He could feel the caring flow from her to him, soothing his battered heart.

"There are so many things I could have done better." Speech came more easily now. "Words I could have spoken. Acceptance I could have shown."

"The same is true for me. I keep thinking there was something more I could have done to keep her from coming back here when she was dying. It would have spared you and the kinder so much."

"Don't think that." He enclosed her hand in both of his. "None of it was your fault. The responsibility was mine. I took the vows, not you. I am to blame."

"Ach, Caleb, it's a gut thing the Lord knows we're only human. We all make mistakes. Alice, too. She knew that. Didn't you see what she said? She confessed and accepted God's forgiveness. We must do the same."

"Onkel Zeb told..." He paused, not sure he wanted to go on. But who should he say it to but Jessie, who was so deeply involved? "He told me I was passing my doubts and lack of trust on to the next generation. Folks already say the King boys don't fare well in love. If I didn't change, one day they'd be saying that about Becky and Timothy, too."

Maybe he hoped she'd deny that, but she didn't. "Onkel Zeb is a wise man," she said softly. "But you have already begun to make that right, ain't so?"

"Only because you've been here to guide me." He

managed a rueful smile. "With me fighting you every step of the way."

"Not as bad as that," she said. "Becky is more open already, thanks to you."

He shook his head. "Not me. You. If we have changed, it's because of you, Jessie."

He looked into her eyes and seemed to become lost in their depths. He leaned toward her, longing filling him. Not for comfort this time, but for her. For Jessie herself.

He touched her cheek, feeling the smooth skin beneath his fingers. She flushed, her lips trembling just a little. And then he leaned across the barrier of the wheelchair arm and kissed her.

It was a long, slow kiss, gentle at first but deepening as he felt her response. He inhaled the sweet, feminine scent of her, heard her breathing quicken and felt her lips warm. Her hand touched his nape tentatively, then more surely as she leaned into his kiss. The world seemed to narrow until it encompassed only the two of them.

Slowly, reluctantly, she drew back. "I don't… I'm not sure. Is this right, for me to care about you this way?"

He put his finger across her lips. "You have been so intent on making the rest of us free to move ahead. Now you have to do the same for yourself. It can't be wrong to hope for a better future, can it?"

He saw the doubt ebb from her face, to be replaced by the gentle smile he loved.

"No. Hope is never wrong."

Chapter Fourteen

It was still dark in the kitchen when Jessie began getting breakfast ready, but the sky was lightening in the east, and it would soon be day. Dairy farmers got up early. That was part of the business, and this morning Caleb had insisted on going out to the barn with the other men. There might not be much he could do, but he was determined to take another step toward normal life.

A smile touched Jessie's lips. Once, normal had meant getting rid of her. Now…now it meant something much different.

She cautioned herself not to expect too much, but it was impossible. Caleb wouldn't kiss her that way unless he intended marriage. They weren't teenagers, smooching with one after another on the way to finding a life partner. At their age, a person didn't get involved without it being serious.

She must convince Caleb that they couldn't rush into anything. They'd have to give the children time. But…

Daniel came in, bringing a blast of chill early morning air with him, and gave her a sharp look. "What are you smiling about?"

"I'm not," she said, schooling her face to her usual calm.

"Sure you were. What's up?" He helped himself to a mug of coffee and leaned against the counter to drink it.

She shrugged, thinking she'd have to be more careful if she didn't want everyone talking about her and Caleb. "Just thinking about plans for the day, I guess. I've filled a thermos with coffee for you, and your lunch is packed. Do you have time for breakfast, or should I wrap something up?"

Daniel glanced at the clock and straightened. "I'd better get going. Just give me a couple pieces of the shoofly pie. That'll be enough."

Nodding, Jessie wrapped up half the pie, knowing how Daniel liked to eat, even though it never showed on his lean frame. He grabbed lunch pail, thermos and the bag into which she'd put the shoofly pie.

"Denke, Jessie. I'll have it on the way to the job."

He went out, the door banging behind him. She heard him exchange a few words with the others, so they must be on their way in. She began dishing up oatmeal from the pot on the stove as the kinder thudded their way down the stairs.

Breakfast was a time for chatter about what the day would hold. Jessie tried resolutely to keep from catching Caleb's gaze, but every time she glanced at him, he was watching her with a warmth in his face that was a sure signal to anyone studying him. She'd warn him to be more careful.

She was on pins and needles throughout the meal,

sure he was going to give them away. Somehow they got through without it happening, although she did think Onkel Zeb was looking at them a little oddly.

At last the kitchen emptied out except for her and Caleb. He shoved his chair toward her.

"We're finally alone. I thought they'd never finish breakfast." He caught her hand.

She sent a quick look around to be sure they were really alone. "Ach, Caleb, you have to be more careful. I'm sure Onkel Zeb thought something was going on, the way you kept looking at me."

"But I want to look at you, my Jessie." He drew her down for a quick kiss. "It's a good morning when we're together. Ain't so?"

"Yah." She cupped his cheek with her hand for a moment. "But I mean it about being careful not to let anyone suspect our feelings."

"Why not? Why not just let them know that we're going to marry?"

"Are we?" she asked, smiling in spite of her efforts to stay sober.

"Of course we are. If you go around kissing men the way you kissed me without marriage in mind, all I can say is that I'm surprised at you."

"Silly. I don't go around kissing anyone. Except you," she added. She yanked her mind away from the joy of joking with him. "But it's best if we don't let anyone in on it, at least not yet." She could see the objection forming in his thoughts and hurried on. "For the children's sake, Caleb. We should move gradually. They'll need time to adjust."

"We doubtless won't convince anyone to marry us

until fall," he pointed out, reminding her of the traditional season for weddings. "Isn't that time to adjust?"

"Yah, but I want to be positive sure that Becky has accepted me before expecting her to think of me as your future wife."

"And her mother," Caleb added. "They'll be happy. Why wouldn't they be? But I guess you're right. We don't want any setbacks now, that's for sure."

"Denke, Caleb. I knew you'd understand."

He smiled. "So long as you understand that I'll need to snatch a kiss now and then. Just to keep me going."

"I think we can manage that," she said gravely, while her eyes danced.

He lifted her hand to his lips and dropped a light kiss on it. "So much to look forward to. Soon I'll trade this big cast in for a smaller one, I'll be able to do more, and we'll be busy making plans for our marriage. I feel as if I've come out from under a dark cloud."

"I know. I feel it, too."

"Then come here and give me a kiss before everyone comes back again." He drew her down, cradling her face in his hands. "One to last through the morning," he said, kissing her lightly. "And another…"

Something…some sound…had her turning to look around.

"What's wrong?" Caleb sobered at once.

"I…nothing, I guess. I thought I heard something."

"Just the house making noises as it settles," he said, and he pulled her back to him for a long, satisfying kiss.

Caleb, trying to sweep the workshop floor, decided that sweeping was best done by someone who had two feet to stand on. It was difficult to manipulate the broom and impossible to manage the dustpan from a wheelchair.

He glared at the heavy cast on his leg. He'd be wonderful glad to be rid of it. Maybe, when he went to have it checked tomorrow, they'd decide he could make do with the small one that would let him be more mobile.

Leaning back in the chair, he gave himself up to thoughts of the future. The initial euphoria he'd felt last night when he'd realized he loved Jessie had already subsided to a quiet contentment. That was as it should be, wasn't it?

When he'd met Alice, he'd tumbled into love without a single sensible thought in his head. They'd hurried into marriage because they couldn't bear to be parted, and probably because he'd feared losing this wondrous thing that had happened to him.

How long had it taken to see that they hadn't known each other at all? By the time they did, it was too late.

Everything was different with Jessie. Not less, only different. He'd moved slowly from distrust to wariness, then to cautious acceptance and finally to love. It had been so gradual that he almost didn't realize it was happening until he'd known, for certain sure, that what he felt was love.

He'd rebelled at first at not sharing their happiness with everyone right away, but probably Jessie was right. They needed to do what was best for the kinder. They'd be happy, wouldn't they? They already loved Jessie.

But it was worth taking their time so it was the right moment to tell them. When they did…

The door rattled, and Onkel Zeb came in on a wave of warm air filled with the scent of spring. "Getting stuffy in here, ain't so? Let's see if I can get one of these windows open." He began wrestling with the front window.

"Let me help." Caleb moved the wheelchair into position, and together they managed to push the balky window up. "That's better. Smells like spring, ain't so?"

Zeb nodded. "Soon it'll be summer. The corn we planted is showing green already."

"Gut." Caleb smacked the arms of the chair. "The sooner I get out of this, the better."

"I'm thinking we should tell Thomas we'll keep him on until fall, at least. He'd be glad to know his steady work will go on." Zeb glanced around the shop. "Daniel had best get moving on finding an apprentice. He'll need someone soon."

"Any ideas?" Caleb pushed away from the window, reflecting that Onkel Zeb was never happier than when he was taking care of them.

"I hear tell that Zeke Esch's second boy, Eli, is wonderful gut with his hands. Zeke says he likes working with wood. Seems to me he'd be a good possibility. Zeke would like to see the boy settled in a trade."

Caleb smiled. Things would probably work out just the way Onkel Zeb had in mind. They usually did. The future was falling into a new pattern, it seemed. Not bad, just different.

He realized that his uncle was studying his face. "Anything you want to tell me?" Zeb asked.

"What makes you say that?" Caleb parried, playing for time. It was all very well for Jessie to say they should keep their plans to themselves, but she hadn't reckoned with Onkel Zeb's sharp eyes.

"Ach, I can see as far as the next person. You're different today. And Jessie is, as well."

He'd never been very good at keeping secrets from his uncle. At least he could tell him part of the truth.

"Last night Jessie let me see the letter she got from Alice just before she died. You knew about it, didn't you?"

"Yah, I did." Zeb's face grew sorrowful. "I went to see if she needed anything, and she was just finishing it. I helped her address it and mail it. I didn't know Jessie still had the letter."

"So you don't know what it contained?"

"No. I thought Alice probably wanted to say goodbye to Jessie. They'd always been close."

"She did." Caleb's throat felt rough. "She also said that she'd come back hoping for my forgiveness. And that she hadn't gotten it." He cleared his throat so he could speak. "It made me feel pretty small that she knew I hadn't really forgiven her."

"It's not easy. You know that. It doesn't happen all at once."

"I see that now. The letter opened my eyes to the fact that I've been holding on to my resentment. Reading it…sharing it with Jessie…it seemed as if that set me free. I could forgive…forgive Alice and forgive myself."

Zeb clapped his shoulder, his face working. "Always best to get things out in the open, ain't so?" His voice was husky. "Things heal better that way."

"Yah, they do. I'm out from under a heavy weight. Jessie…" But he'd best be careful what he said about Jessie if he didn't want to give them away.

He saw, through the open window, Jessie hurrying toward the shop. "Here she comes now."

Jessie came in, sweeping the room with a quick glance. "Becky's not here?"

"No. I haven't seen her since breakfast." Caleb's thoughts readjusted. "What's wrong?"

"Ach, nothing," Jessie said quickly, but he saw the little worry line between her brows. "I thought she had gone to gather eggs, but she hasn't come back. Timothy is busy looking for strawberries, and he doesn't know where she is."

"She'll be around here somewhere," Caleb said, vaguely disturbed but not wanting to upset her.

"Most likely she's fallen asleep somewhere," Zeb said. "I mind the time we were looking all over the place for Daniel, and he was up in the hayloft. He'd been hiding from you, and he fell sound asleep."

"That must be it," Jessie said. "I'll have a look around."

"We'll hunt for her, too." Caleb shoved his wheelchair toward the door, his fear mounting.

Jessie hurried ahead as he went out, stopping briefly to talk to Timothy. Reassuring him, most likely.

Common sense told Caleb there was nothing to worry about. Becky had to be here somewhere. Onkel Zeb was probably right, and she'd fallen asleep.

Reaching the house, he went up the ramp as fast as he could. Jessie would have looked in the house already, but it wouldn't hurt to check again.

He went through the downstairs rooms, calling Becky's name. Nothing. He yanked open the cellar door. There was no logical reason why she'd have gone down there, but he sat at the top and shouted her name.

Useless. He was useless, trapped in this chair. He couldn't even go upstairs or down to the cellar in search of his daughter. He shoved the chair to the bottom of the steps leading to the second floor and grasped the newel post. If he could keep hold of the posts, maybe he could pull himself up.

Common sense intervened. Jessie would have looked upstairs first thing. Still, he shouted Becky's name up the steps. No response came.

Back outside again, he could see his son just coming around the corner of the barn from the strawberry patch. Caleb began pushing himself in that direction.

In another moment, Jessie and Onkel Zeb came out of the barn and stood, conferring with each other. Why were they just standing there? Why weren't they hurrying?

Frustration driving him, he tried to move faster, but the chair didn't cooperate on the rough ground. He shoved impatiently and the chair slewed to the side, caught in a rut in the grass. Angry, he yanked at it, overbalancing as he tried to free the wheel. Another angry pull and the whole chair tipped over, spilling him onto the ground.

He had a glimpse of Zeb and Jessie running to help him as he shoved himself up onto his hands. The cast had taken a jolt, but he didn't think anything was injured. He didn't have time for that now in any event.

Jessie reached him, grasping his arm, but he shoved her away. "Never mind me. Just find my child."

She took a quick step back and then busied herself with righting the chair and holding it steady while Zeb helped him into it, scolding all the time.

"Don't be so foolish. It won't make things better if

you get hurt." Zeb settled him in the chair. "Let Timothy help you to the phone shanty in case we need to call for help."

"What are you going to do?" He ignored Jessie, trying to hide the irrational resentment that was building inside him.

"I'm heading up toward the woods. Jessie will go over to Leah and Sam's place."

"If they haven't seen her, I'll ask them to help look," Jessie said as Zeb struck off toward the woods. She put her hand on the chair. "Please, Caleb, go back."

He pushed her hand away. All the darkness he thought he'd banished came storming back, flooding his mind.

"I trusted you with my children. I should have known better."

Jessie whitened. Then she spun and set off for Leah's at a run.

Somehow Jessie managed to keep putting one foot in front of the other as she crossed the field toward Leah's farmhouse. Caleb blamed her. The love he'd shown so briefly was swallowed up in anger at her failure to keep his children safe.

He couldn't blame her more than she blamed herself, though. Her heart twisted in her chest. She had lost Alice. Now she had lost Becky. What kind of person was she, to let down the people she loved?

A failure. She should have taken better care of them. The only thing to do now was pray she could find Becky safe.

Then...then she'd have to go. She'd come here with

hopes of doing good, but she'd ended up doing harm. So leaving was her only option.

Please, God, please, God. She prayed in time with her hurrying footsteps. *Please let me find her. Please keep her safe.*

Blinking tears away, she saw Leah coming toward her. Breaking into a run, Jessie reached her.

Before she could speak, Leah had clasped both her hands. "It's all right," she said quickly. "You are looking for Becky, yah?"

Jessie nodded, breathless.

"She's safe. Really." She patted Jessie's hands. "Calm down before you talk to her."

"Yah." She took a breath, thankfulness surging through her. *Thank You, Lord. Thank You.* "Where is she? How did you find her?"

"She's in our barn loft. She's okay. I saw her climbing up. She looked as if she were crying, so I thought it best to say nothing and let you speak to her. Whatever it is, I didn't want to make it worse."

"Denke, Leah. We've been searching everywhere for her. She...she ran off." It was an admission of failure. "Thank the gut Lord she's safe. You're sure she hasn't left?"

"I've been keeping an eye on the barn door. She hasn't come out. I was just going to send one of the kinder for you when I saw you coming. I'll send him to let Caleb know she's safe."

"Denke," Jessie said again. The word didn't seem enough. "I'll go to her."

"I'll walk with you," Leah said. Gesturing to her oldest boy, she gave him quick instructions as they went.

Jessie felt Leah's gaze on her face as they walked together toward the new barn. She'd have to explain it to Leah later. Now, she must concentrate on the child.

They stopped at the door to the barn, which stood ajar. Leah squeezed her hand in silent encouragement and then turned away. Taking a breath, praying for calm, Jessie walked into the barn.

It was very quiet. The barn was empty of animals at this time of day. Then she heard a small scraping sound from above, and a few fragments of hay drifted down from between the boards of the loft. Becky was almost directly above her.

"Becky," she called. "Where are you?"

Nothing. She imagined Becky freezing, scarcely breathing, like a small animal caught in the beam of a flashlight.

Jessie crossed to the ladder that led to the loft. "Becky, will you come down?"

Again there was no answer. She began to climb, knowing Becky could hear her coming.

When she reached the top she paused. Becky was curled on top of a hay bale against the front wall of the barn, her figure rigid, her face turned away from Jessie.

Relief swept over Jessie at the sight of the child. She was here. She was safe. The rest could be dealt with, surely.

Walking softly, she crossed to Becky and sat down on the bale next to her. Her prayers reached to God for wisdom, for guidance. When the silence stretched on too long, she spoke softly.

"I'm wonderful glad you're all right, Becky. Daadi was very worried about you."

For a moment there was no response. Then Becky

began to cry. "I saw," she said, between sobs. "I saw Daadi kissing you this morning."

"Yah, I thought that must be it." So there had been something to that sound she'd thought she heard this morning. They should have been more careful. This was just what she'd feared—that letting the kinder know about their relationship too soon could ruin everything.

"It made you angry?" she asked.

Becky shook her head, hiccoughing a little. "Not… not angry, exactly. I was…mixed up. Mammi died. Daadi got hurt. Then you came, and I didn't want to like you, but I did. Everything keeps changing." She ended on a wail.

Jessie's heart ached for her. Poor Becky. She was just six. *Everything keeps changing.* How could she understand all the things that had been happening in her short life? It wasn't fair to expect her to.

Jessie could fill in what Becky didn't say. She'd just begun to trust Jessie, and then she'd seen Jessie with her father. No wonder she didn't know what to think. Who could she trust to be there for her?

"I know, Becky. I know." She put her arm around Becky's shoulders, feeling her tremble. But Becky didn't pull away, so Jessie drew the child against her. Sometimes everyone just needed to be held.

They sat in silence for a few moments. Jessie struggled for an answer. For the right words to say. *Gut Lord, guide me*, her heart cried.

She stroked Becky's hair. "It's hard to take so many changes in your life. Not just for you, but for everyone. When your mamm died, I lost someone who was a much-loved little sister to me."

Becky clutched her hand. "She did bad things. Everyone said so."

It sounded as if "everyone" had been careless of what they'd said in front of a small child. "She made mistakes," Jessie said gently. "We can't stop loving someone for making mistakes." She dropped a light kiss on Becky's forehead. "I could never stop loving you no matter what."

Jessie bit her lip. What she'd said was true, but what would Becky think when Jessie left?

She tilted Jessie's face up so that she could see her expression. "Listen to me, Becky. No matter where I go or what I do, I will always love you. And Daadi will always love you…always, always, always. You can be sure of that."

Becky nodded slowly as she struggled to process Jessie's words. She was trying to believe, but her doubts and fears couldn't be cleared up so easily. They were bound to continue, and Jessie's heart seemed to break at knowing she wouldn't be here to help her.

"I think we should go home to Daadi now. What do you think?"

Becky scrambled to her feet. "Daadi. I want to see Daadi."

Together they crossed the loft and climbed down the ladder. They set off. Becky trotted ahead a few steps. Then she stopped, came back and took Jessie's hand. Together they walked toward home.

Caleb saw Becky and Jessie coming toward him across the field. Relief and joy surged through him, closely followed by anger. If Jessie had found her in Sam's barn, why had it taken so long? She should have known he'd be frantic to have his child in his arms again.

He couldn't possibly stay where he was and wait patiently for Becky. He began wheeling himself over the bumpy grass, fighting to keep the chair upright. Zeb came running to grab the wheelchair.

"What are you doing? They're coming. Becky is safe. Do you want to fall again? You won't help matters by getting yourself hurt just when you can see that Becky is fine."

Caleb ground his teeth together, but he had to admit that his uncle was right. It also wouldn't help matters to get into an unseemly tussle with Onkel Zeb over control of the chair.

It seemed to take forever, but it was surely just minutes. When they reached the mowed grass of the yard, Becky let go of Jessie's hand and raced toward him. She flung herself at him, hiding her face in his shirt.

Caleb held her close, murmuring to her. "It's all right. You're here now. It's all right."

He should talk to her about how wrong it had been to run off that way, but not now. Now he just had to hold her and rejoice that no harm had come to her.

Jessie reached them. "Caleb..." Her voice was tentative.

"Not now." He was sharp, but he couldn't help that. He couldn't talk to Jessie without losing what little control he had, so he'd best calm down first.

Regaining his control on that subject took longer than he'd have imagined. Jessie must have realized that, because she went about her usual routine without attempting to speak. The rest of the day passed, and still he hadn't made time to talk to Jessie.

It wasn't until he was lying in bed, staring at the ceiling, that he realized what was really troubling him. Before Jessie came, he'd been…if not happy, at least content with his life. He'd resigned himself to staying single, knowing he could never trust his heart to a woman after Alice. Having Jessie here had shown him how foolish he'd been. He couldn't bar all women from his life because of what Alice had done.

More than that…he couldn't completely blame Alice for what had gone wrong between them. If she'd been too young, too heedless, for marriage, he hadn't been that much better. He hadn't seen the problems for what they were when they began to arise, and he hadn't coped.

But that didn't mean he should fall in love with Jessie. He came back to the source of his anger. He'd trusted her with his children, and look what had happened. The fear he'd felt when he'd realized Becky was missing came surging back.

The sky had begun to lighten along the eastern ridge when he pushed through to what he really felt. He was afraid. Afraid that this love he felt for Jessie wasn't strong enough, afraid that he was jumping into a relationship again, afraid to trust.

You trusted her, one part of him argued. *You trusted her with the kinder, and she let you down.*

She couldn't keep her eyes on them every second of the day, he reminded himself. No one could…and no one should. No kinder could grow up properly if parents protected them that much.

The endless argument was giving him a headache. He had to stop this, had to decide what he was going to say to Jessie. A pang struck him. Jessie must have suffered, too, when she'd seen Becky was gone. She must have told herself that it was just like the day Alice had run off.

He pushed himself upright, sitting on the edge of the bed. Ready or not, the day was beginning. He'd dress, head to the barn, try to be useful. Before he knew it, the van would here to take him to have his cast checked.

Maybe when he returned, he'd have come to some conclusion about what to say to Jessie.

By the time Caleb left for his appointment, Jessie knew what she had to do. She'd waited throughout the early morning for Caleb to speak…to say something, anything, that would tell her what he was feeling.

But he'd said nothing. He'd avoided her eyes and talked to everyone else. She'd failed. And she knew she didn't have any choice.

Leaving the kinder in Onkel Zeb's care, Jessie walked across the field to Leah's house. She found Leah in the kitchen, rolling out pie crust.

"Jessie! What brings you here so early?" Then she got a glimpse of Jessie's face and dropped the rolling pin. She came quickly to her side, wiping flour from her hands with a tea towel. "What is it? Something has happened. Surely Becky hasn't run off again, has she?"

"No, nothing like that." Jessie hadn't intended to explain anything. She'd thought she'd ask her favor and be on her way. But the sympathy on Leah's face undid her. She blinked back tears. "Caleb blamed me for what happened with Becky. He won't even talk about it."

"You have to make him understand."

She shook her head. "I can't. He won't listen to anything I have to say." She tried to smile, but it was a miserable effort. “Funny, isn’t it? Becky ran off because she saw Caleb kiss me.”

“You and Caleb…well, all I can say is that it’s about time.” Leah hugged her. “All the more reason you have to make him listen.”

“I tried to talk to him, but in a way he’s right. I was responsible for Becky. She was upset enough to run away, and I never saw it.”

“Ach, you can’t blame yourself for everything. A child Becky’s age can be gut at hiding her feelings. And poor Becky’s had lots of practice, ain’t so?”

Jessie had to admit that was true. Hadn’t Becky been convinced that her daadi wouldn’t like her if she looked like her mammi?

“There’s plenty I could say to Caleb, but it’s no use if he can’t listen. The only thing is for me to go back home.”

“Jessie, no.” Leah’s arm was around her, comforting her the way Jessie had comforted Becky. “Don’t run away.”

“I have to.” She closed her eyes against the pain. “Please don’t argue with me, Leah. Just…help me.”

She could almost feel Leah’s internal struggle, but finally Leah asked, “What can I do?”

“Will you drive me to the bus? I’ll need to leave Zeb with the kinder, and Daniel is at work.”

Leah clamped her lips closed. She nodded.

“Gut. Come in about an hour. I’ll be packed and ready by then.” Jessie made for the door, but not in time to prevent Leah from getting in the last word.

“I’ll do it. But I still think you’re wrong.”

Right or wrong, she didn’t have a choice, she told herself as she headed back across the field to the place she now thought of as home. Caleb blamed her. He hadn't trusted her. How could she imagine that they'd be able to build a life together without trust?

Caleb wheeled himself off the lift when the van brought him home again, looking ruefully at the heavy cast still on his leg. His hopes that it might be replaced today were dashed. The technician who worked with him would say only that the doctor would be in touch once he'd received the report. Still, she'd said it with a smile, and Caleb had decided to interpret that as a positive sign.

He waved goodbye to the van driver and turned toward the house. Where was everybody? Usually someone came out when he returned to see if he needed help.

No sooner had he thought it than the door opened and Becky and Timothy hurtled themselves onto his lap. With a jolt, he saw that they were crying.

"Here, what is it? What's wrong with the two of you? Are you hurt?" He glanced at Onkel Zeb, who'd followed them out, but Zeb was uncharacteristically silent.

"Becky." Caleb pulled her back so that he could see her face. "You must tell me what's happened to cause all these tears."

Becky nodded, gulping. "It's Jessie. Jessie went away. She's gone!" Her words escalated into a wail.

"Jessie left? Where did she go?" He couldn't make sense of this. "What do you mean, she's gone?"

"Leah is taking her to town to catch the bus," Onkel Zeb said. "Jessie said she had to go home." His expression accused Caleb.

Becky cried, "She said she had to go, but..."

Timothy cut off his older sister. "She can't! Who will tell us stories and tuck us in? We need her more than anyone."

"We love her," Becky said. "And she loves us. It's all my fault for running away."

"Hush, now. Nothing's your fault." He tried to grab on to something that might make sense. "Why did you run off, Becky? That's not like you."

Becky sniffled. "'Cause I saw you kissing Jessie. I… I didn't know what to think. I just wanted to be by myself and figure it out."

For a moment he was speechless. "Becky, I didn't know."

"Jessie said you loved me and Timothy more than anything. She said she'd never stop loving us. But now she's going away."

"Daadi will stop her," Timothy declared. "Daadi will bring her home."

"Please, Daadi?" Hope kindled in Becky's eyes.

If Jessie left, he could stop asking himself difficult questions. He could stop dealing with painful truths.

Jessie was loving and honest all the way through. If he blamed her for anything, it was just an excuse not to blame himself.

Hugging his children, he looked at Onkel Zeb. "Will you bring the carriage? We'd best go if we're going to catch them before Jessie gets on the bus."

Zeb broke into a huge grin. Then he trotted toward the barn, shouting at Thomas to help him harness the mare.

They must have harnessed up in record time. In moments they'd brought the family carriage over. With the help of Zeb and Thomas, Caleb hoisted himself up into the seat.

"What are you waiting for?" he said. "Get in."

Still grinning, Zeb helped the young ones into the carriage and climbed in himself. Caleb clucked to the mare, and they were off.

He took the turn onto the road and snapped the lines, urging the mare faster. They'd have to step on it if they were to be in time.

"Faster, Daadi, faster," Becky urged, sliding off the seat to stand behind him. "Hurry."

"I'll go faster, but you sit properly on your seat and hold on. I don't want to lose you."

He'd come close to losing both of them…all wrapped up as he'd been in his own pain. If it hadn't been for Jessie, he might well have done so.

Onkel Zeb had been right all along. Jessie was probably the only person in the world who could break through to him, because she was hurting just as much as he was. Alice had broken her heart, too. And Jessie had reacted by reaching out to help him despite his rejection.

Once she'd accepted that this was no ordinary, sedate drive, the mare outdid herself, pacing along as if she were pulling a racing sulky instead of a family carriage. Caleb's pulse was pounding in time with the hooves, it seemed. If they didn't make it before Jessie left…

He could write. He could even go out to Ohio after her. But the need to catch her pushed him on. The time for righting wrongs was now, the very minute he realized how wrong he'd been.

They rounded a bend in the road, and the children shouted in excitement.

"There! Leah's buggy. Hurry, Daadi, hurry," Becky said. She was leaning forward as if she could make the buggy go faster.

He closed the gap between the buggies. Surely Leah would hear another buggy behind her, but she didn't slow down. He slapped the reins, the mare put on a burst of speed, and they passed the other buggy. Caleb signaled and pulled slowly to the side of the road, keeping one eye on the mirror to be certain Leah was doing the same. She was, and in a moment both buggies were parked, one behind the other.

Caleb turned, trying to get a look at Jessie's face, but he couldn't. Gritting his teeth, he accepted what he had to do. If only he'd thought to toss the crutches in the buggy before they left.

Swinging his good leg over the step, he lifted the cast, using both hands to move it over, as well.

"Caleb, wait..."

He ignored Onkel Zeb's warning and swung himself outward, grasping the railing with both hands and swinging his legs down. He'd get his feet on the ground, then work his way along the side...

His grip slid, he was losing control, he was falling...

Arms closed around him, supporting him, and he knew without looking that it was Jessie. She held him with both arms clasping him close, so that he could feel her ragged breath.

"What are you trying to do?" she scolded, her voice shaking. "Break the other leg?"

"No." He got one arm around her while he held on to the carriage strut with the other. "Trying to keep you from doing something so foolish as leaving us. Don't you know that we…that I…can't possibly get along without you?"

What else could he say? His thoughts spun frantically. What would show her how much he loved her? What would convince her to stay with them?

She was looking at him, a question in the clear depths of her eyes. "You didn't say anything," she said. "You wouldn't talk to me. How could I know what you were thinking?"

He smoothed his hand down the slender curve of her back. "Ach, Jessie, you should know by now how foolish I am. I had to fight my way through a sleepless night of arguing before I saw the truth for what it is. I love you. Alice's flaws were only human. I forgive her. And I ask God's forgiveness for my mistakes."

Her face softened, warmed. "I'm wonderful glad to hear it."

He found he could breathe again. He wasn't too late. "I'm not done making mistakes myself, you know. I need you, because you keep me straight about who I am. And I love you. For keeps." His heart seemed to be pounding so loudly he couldn't hear anything else. "Please, Jessie. I know you love my kinder. Can you love me, as well?"

She began to smile, and it was like the sun coming out in her face. How had he ever thought her plain? She was the most beautiful sight he'd ever seen. If only she'd speak and say the words that would put him out of his misery. He became aware that the children were hanging out of the carriage over their heads, listening to every word.

Well, why not? This was their future, too.

Jessie's smile encompassed all of them. "I love Becky and Timothy. And I love you, too. All of us belong together."

Caleb's heart was too full for speech. The doubting and anger and bitterness had been a thicket he'd hacked his way through for years, but now the struggling was over. He'd gotten there—to a place of peace and forgiveness.

He could only hold Jessie close and listen to his heart sing with joy. God had taken their broken pieces—his and Jessie's—and fit them together into something wonderful...something that would last a lifetime and beyond.

Epilogue

Spring had come to the valley again. The bulbs Jessie had put in last fall seemed eager to affirm the new life spring brought, sending green leaves unfurling tentatively in the sunshine.

"Mammi, Becky's coming. I see her. Can I run and meet her? Please?" Timothy tugged at her apron, his favorite way of ensuring her attention.

Jessie gave him a quick hug, loving the way it sounded when he and Becky called her Mammi. She looked down the path Becky followed when she walked back and forth to school and spotted her skipping along with Leah's kinder.

"Yah, you can. Mind you stay right with her and don't tease."

Without lingering to respond, Timothy darted across the yard toward the path. Caleb, fixing the pasture fence with Onkel Zeb and Thomas, waved to him and then started toward her.

Jessie walked to meet him, loving the ease with which his lean figure moved now. It had been a long haul, getting his leg back to its normal strength, but he'd made it. Now no one could tell it had ever been injured.

Recovering his strength had meant recovering his confidence, too. Like most men, Caleb could never be content until he could do all the things he expected of himself. He and Onkel Zeb had increased the dairy herd this spring, and with Thomas working full-time, they were able to manage the work among them.

A good thing, too, because Daniel's business had really taken off in the past year. The successful completion of the kitchen project he'd done for the Englischers had brought him as much business as he could handle, and he had taken on two apprentices to work alongside him.

Now, if only Daniel could find a good woman…

Caleb reached her and put his arm around her for a quick hug. "What are you thinking about, looking so serious?"

"How happy we are," she said, returning his hug. "And how I wish Daniel would find someone to love."

"Don't go making matches," Caleb warned. "He'll fall in love one day, and that will be it for him. You'll see. After all, it happened for us, ain't so?"

She nodded, wondering if he'd ever realized that she'd loved him since that first day when he'd come to her parents' farm. "Yah, and just when everyone was giving up on you."

He smiled. "It wasn't everyone's business. Just yours and mine."

"And Becky's and Timothy's," Jessie reminded him.

"Them, too," he agreed. He pressed his hand lightly against her rounding belly. "And this little one's."

Jessie put her hand over his, love overflowing her

heart. "I never thought to be as happy as I am right now."

He held her closer. "Me, also. God has given us the gifts we didn't even know to ask for."

Contentment flooded through her. Caleb was right. Even when they hadn't known what was best for them, God had known. He had seen them through the pain and brought them to this joy, and she was forever grateful.

* * * * *

UNDERCOVER AMISH

Debby Giusti

To My Husband—My Hero

Blessed be the Lord, because he hath heard the voice of my supplications. The Lord is my strength and my shield; my heart trusted in him, and I am helped: therefore my heart greatly rejoiceth; and with my song will I praise him.

—*Psalms* 28:6–7

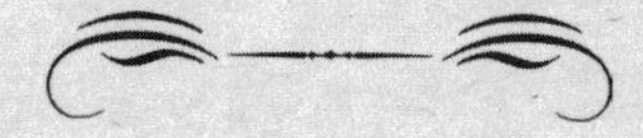

Chapter One

"Hey, lady, that woman on TV looks just like you."

Hannah Miller ignored the wizened old man with the scruffy beard and bloodshot eyes, who undoubtedly was talking to her since she was the only woman in the gas station. Instead of responding, she handed her credit card to the attendant behind the counter. "Twenty dollars on pump four."

Averting her gaze from not only the older man but also the cluster of guys ogling the model on the cover of the latest edition of a men's sports magazine, she squared her shoulders, raised her chin and hoped she looked more confident than she felt. A truck stop off the interstate was the last place Hannah wanted to be in the dead of night, but she needed gas. She also needed to find her sister Miriam and to learn the details of her mother's death as well as the whereabouts of her youngest sister, Sarah, who had disappeared along with Miriam.

Refusing to be deterred, the old guy with the beard pointed to the flat-screen TV hanging on the wall. "Check it out, lady."

As much as she didn't want to respond to his comment, she couldn't stop from glancing at the television. Her heart lurched and a tiny gasp escaped her lips. Her middle sister's face stared back at her from the thirty-two-inch screen.

A reporter, holding a microphone, stepped toward Miriam as the news video continued to play. "Ms. Miller, do you have any comment about the man who murdered your mother?"

"No comment." Miriam pushed past the reporter and climbed aboard a Gray Line bus.

"The suspected killer is dead," the man with the mike continued, "along with a deputy sheriff who was involved in Leah Miller's death. Now her daughter Miriam is leaving Willkommen. A spokesperson for the mayor's office said the tragedy is an isolated incident. The crime rate in the town and surrounding Amish community is low, and tourists shouldn't be discouraged from visiting the area."

The video ended and the late-night news anchor returned to the screen. "That footage, shot six weeks ago, is the last taken of Miriam Miller, although there is speculation she returned to Willkommen and is hiding out in the North Georgia mountains. The police now suspect the carjacking that claimed Leah Miller's life could be tied to the disappearance eight months earlier of Rosie Glick, an Amish girl believed at the time to have run off with her *Englisch* boyfriend."

Hannah's heart pounded and a roar filled her ears. Seeing the news feed made the information she'd learned about her family only hours earlier even more real. She desperately needed space to recover her composure, but the insistent bearded man sidled closer.

"'Spect your last name must be Miller." He raised his voice. "Except for your blue eyes, you look so much alike that you've got to be kin to that woman on the news whose mother was killed. Gunned down in a carjacking was the story I heard."

Hannah pursed her lips and hoped her icy glare would convince the attendant who still held her credit card not to divulge her name. Evidently the kid behind the counter was smart enough to pick up on her cues. He returned her card without comment.

She glanced at the group of men near the magazine rack who had stopped perusing the cover model to stare at her. Feeling totally exposed, she returned the credit card to her wallet, all the while her neck tingled and heat seared her cheeks.

One of the men, dressed in a blue flannel shirt and navy hoodie, shrugged out of the group and hurried outside. If only the other men would leave, as well. Not that they were doing anything wrong, but the last thing Hannah wanted was to call attention to herself.

She tucked her wallet into her purse, grabbed the sales receipt and hurried into the ladies' room, needing a private place to come to terms with what had happened. Her head throbbed and she fought to control the tears that burned her eyes. Her mother was dead, Miriam was gone and her younger sister Sarah had disappeared. When Hannah had left home three years ago, Sarah had just turned eighteen.

Deriding herself for her insensitivity to her family's need, Hannah hung her head in shame. Why hadn't she tried to contact them in all that time? In spite of the angry words exchanged the night she'd left and her fear that law enforcement had been called in, Hannah should have been the better person and made an attempt to reconnect. For so long she'd blamed her mother and Miriam. Now they were gone from her life and her heart ached too much to blame anyone but herself.

Hannah had been selfish and thinking of her own needs, not the good of the family. Although the three girls raised by a flighty, self-absorbed mother hardly deserved the name "family." The disjointed reality of their dysfunctional life had, at times, seemed anything but close-knit or loving.

Plus, the old man was wrong. Any resemblance she had to Miriam was slight. After what she had learned the night she'd left home, it was no wonder she had always felt like an outsider. The accusation and the memory of the secret her mother had revealed remained an open wound.

The last thing she'd expected to find today on her cell phone was Miriam's garbled voice mail. Her sister's heartbreaking message—at least what Hannah could decipher—had been almost too much to bear.

According to the television footage, Miriam hadn't been seen in Willkommen since she'd boarded the bus six weeks ago. The possibility of finding either sister seemed remote, yet Hannah wouldn't give up her search until she found Miriam *and* Sarah.

Needing to get back on the road, Hannah splashed cold water on her face, wiped it dry with a paper towel and hurried to her car, grateful that the older, bearded guy, now chatting with the men by the magazine rack, failed to notice her departure.

Nearing her car, Hannah sensed she wasn't alone and turned to see the man in blue flannel. He glanced at her through narrowed eyes before he opened the door to his black Tahoe and settled into the driver's seat. Something about the guy chilled her blood. Was it his bushy brows and pensive stare or his long hair pulled into a ponytail? His jeans and work boots were crusted with Georgia clay, making him look like he belonged on a backhoe instead of in the well-detailed SUV.

Unnerved by the man's penetrating gaze, she unscrewed the gas cap, inserted the nozzle and began pumping, all the while watching the guy pull his black SUV onto the roadway, heading toward the highway. For whatever reason, she felt a sense of relief.

Once her tank was full, she slipped behind the wheel of her small, four-door sedan and turned left toward Willkommen. Surely the town couldn't be too far away.

The road was windy and narrow and angled up the mountain. A sign for Pine Lodge Mountain Resort caught her attention. Closed For Renovation read the small banner that hung over the larger placard.

A light drizzle began to fall. Hannah flipped on the windshield wipers and squinted into the night. If only visibility was better. The temperature dropped as the elevation increased. She upped the heater, but even with the warm air blowing straight at her, she still felt cold and totally alone.

Usually she welcomed solitude. Tonight, she found the night too dark and eerie. Had it been along this road where her mother had been killed?

Her gut tightened and another tide of hot tears burned her eyes. She blinked them back, swallowed the lump that filled her throat and focused even more intently on the narrow mountain road.

A warning light flashed on her dash. She leaned

closer and tapped the glass, unsure of what was wrong. Her heart pounded as she watched the temperature gauge rise. She clicked the heater off but the needle continued to climb.

She groaned, pulled to the side of the road and killed the engine. Staring into the darkness, she gulped down a lump of fear. She was too far from the gas station to walk back, and she hadn't passed another car for more than twenty minutes. If only someone would happen along.

"Lord—" she bowed her head "—I'm just starting on my walk of faith, but I trust You're with me. Send help."

She glanced up to see headlights in the rearview mirror.

"Thank You, Lord." She exited her car, grateful when the vehicle pulled to a stop behind her sedan. A man stepped to the pavement. Hannah squinted in the glare from his headlights and put her hand to her forehead to shield her eyes. Something about the guy stirred her memory. He neared and her pulse ricocheted as she recognized the blue flannel shirt.

His car had been headed for the highway when he'd pulled out of the gas station. Why had he turned around?

"Looks like you've got a problem." His voice was deep with a hint of Southern twang.

"You're right about a problem," she replied, keeping her tone even and hoping he didn't hear the tremble in her voice. "My engine seems to have overheated."

"Mind if I take a look under the hood?"

"Sure. Thanks." Only Hannah wasn't sure about anything, especially the strange man with the ponytail.

"You wanna pop the hood?" he asked.

She tugged on the release and then stood aside as he peered into the engine.

"Looks like you've got a hole in your radiator."

"But how—?"

"No telling, lady. Willkommen's not far. I'll give you a lift."

An overwhelming sense of dread washed over her. "If you could send someone from a service station, I'd prefer to stay with my vehicle."

"There might not be another car along for hours," he cautioned.

Wary of his advice, she held up her hand. "If you could send help, I'd be most grateful."

"I can't leave you out here." His smile seemed more like a sneer. "Come on, lady. I won't hurt you."

"I never said you would." She stepped back from the car and from the man whose lips suddenly curved into a seductive grin.

Her pulse raced. Fear threaded through her veins.

He moved closer and held out his hand. "Sure you wouldn't like a ride to town?"

"No, thanks."

"Come on, honey."

She wasn't his honey, nor did she like the tone of his voice.

Flicking her gaze over her shoulder, she eyed the thick forest that edged the roadway. Would it provide cover? Enough cover?

He stepped closer and reached for her hand.

She drew back. "What do you want?" she demanded.

"Information. That old guy at the gas station was

right. You've got to be related to the woman on the news."

Hannah shook her head. "I don't know what you're talking about."

He retrieved his cell from his pocket and pulled up a photo. "This is the woman. You look just like her."

Hannah peered at the picture of her sister and fought to control her emotions, seeing Miriam's bruised forehead and her matted hair.

The lewd man stepped closer. "She left Willkommen weeks ago. Some folks say she returned. If so, I need to find her."

"I… I can't help you."

His face darkened. "Look, lady, I'm working with the police. They need to question her."

She didn't believe him, but instead of arguing she squared her shoulders and raised her chin. "Why don't you just climb in your car and return to town?"

The finality of her tone must have convinced him she wouldn't change her mind. He started to step back but then lunged for her. "Where is she? Where's Miriam?"

Hannah screamed. He grabbed her arm. She slipped out of his hold and ran into the woods. The tall pines blocked the moonlight and darkness surrounded her like a pall.

She tripped, righted herself and ran on.

His footfalls came after her, drawing closer.

She increased her speed, not knowing where she was headed or what she would find.

Lord, save me.

A clearing lay ahead. The moon broke through the dark cloud cover, bathing the rolling landscape in light that would mark her as an easy target if she continued on. She angled away from the clearing and forged deeper into the forest. Stumbling over a branch, she threw out her hand to block her fall. Her fingers brushed against a ladder.

She felt the rungs and stared up into the night, seeing the faint outline of a platform at least twelve feet off the ground.

Movement in the brush warned of the man's approach.

Hannah scurried up the ladder and climbed onto the platform. Lying down, she placed her ear to the floorboards and worked to keep her breathing shallow. Even her labored pull of air could alert him to her whereabouts.

The guy ran straight ahead into the clearing. Before the moon passed behind the clouds, Hannah could make out his features. Why was the guy interested in Miriam?

Dear God, don't let him find me.

Her heart pounded so hard she thought it would surely shake the platform.

The man backtracked. He stopped at the foot of the ladder. The platform swayed as he stepped onto the first rung, then the second and the third.

She was trapped at twelve feet above ground and about to be found out by a man intent on doing her harm.

Be still, she chastised her heart, ricocheting in her chest.

She could hear his raspy breath as he stopped his climb and remained poised halfway up the ladder.

"Where...are...you?" he demanded, his voice low

and menacing. "I know you ran this way, but I don't see you anywhere."

A lump filled her throat. In half a second he would scramble to the top, grab her and—

She gritted her teeth to keep from screaming.

Leaves rustled behind the stand as if someone or something was scurrying through the fallen debris, heading back toward the parked cars.

"I've got you now," he whispered, sounding jubilant. In a flash, he climbed down the ladder and ran to catch up to whatever squirrel or possum or raccoon that had saved Hannah, at least for the moment.

Over the roar in her ears, she could hear him disappear into the night. Opening her mouth, she gulped air and trembled from the fear that had wrapped her tightly in its hold.

Thank You, God.

She lay still for a long time, listening to the forest and allowing her anxiety to calm. Breathing in the serenity of the moment, she closed her eyes and, at some point, drifted into a light slumber.

With a jerk, she awoke. Rubbing her neck, she started to sit up. Just that quickly, the sound of footsteps returned. Her gut churned and she bit her lip to keep from moaning in distress.

After all this time, why was he coming back?

Again, she flattened her body against the platform, willed her heart to remain calm and blinked back hot tears that stung her eyes.

This time he would find her. He neared, then stepped onto the ladder, one foot, then another and another as he climbed higher.

Faintly in the distance, she could hear the rev of a

car engine as a vehicle headed down the mountain, but all she could think about was the man on the ladder.

He stopped for half a second, then raised a rifle and laid it on the wooden deck.

Her chance. Her only chance. She grabbed the weapon and pointed it straight at the wide-brimmed hat and full face that appeared over the edge of the platform.

A sliver of moonlight peered from between the clouds as Lucas Grant climbed over the top of the ladder onto the deer stand. Just that fast, his heart stopped, seeing the woman staring at him wide-eyed. Her long hair and oval face made him think of Olivia.

Then he saw the rifle—his .30-30 Winchester—aimed at his gut.

"Put the gun down, lady, before one of us gets hurt."

"Who are you?" she demanded, her gaze wary and tight with fear. Although she squared her shoulders and raised her jaw, the hint of uncertainty was evident in her voice.

"Lucas Grant. This is my property. My deer stand." He let the information settle for half a second then added, "Seems you're trespassing. So, if you know what's good for you, ma'am, you best hand over my .30-30."

He pursed his lips and pulled in a breath as she hesitated longer than he would have liked.

"I won't hurt you, ma'am, and I don't aim to do you harm."

She tilted her pretty head, wrinkled her brow and looked at him through what appeared, even in the dim moonlight, to be troubled eyes.

"You're Amish?" she asked, the surprise evident in her voice.

He glanced down at the black trousers and blue shirt, knowing it was the suspenders that made her come to that conclusion, along with the wide-brimmed felt hat and the black outer coat that hung open.

"I work at an Amish bed-and-breakfast," he said, unwilling to provide more information.

Her brow wrinkled even more. "So you're not Amish."

He shrugged. "Call me Amish in training."

"What?"

He held out his hand. "Ma'am, let's get rid of the weapon and then we can make our introductions."

Instead of reassuring the woman, his comment seemed to have the opposite effect. She gripped the barrel more tightly and inched her finger even closer to the trigger.

Not where he wanted it to be.

She leaned forward, her brow raised. "Did you have anything to do with the man at the filling station?"

He took off his hat and raked his hand through his hair, trying to follow her train of thought. "What filling station?"

"Just off the highway. I stopped for gas and directions. A man followed me."

Some of the pieces were falling into place. "That's why you climbed the deer stand."

Her shoulders slumped and her eyes glistened with what he imagined were tears.

"Ma'am, I'd never hurt a lady. You don't have to worry. I won't hurt you and, if you give me a description of the man who came after you, I'll notify the local authorities."

"The Willkommen police department?"

He shook his head. "It's a county-run sheriff's department, although Sheriff Kurtz is in rehab, recovering from a gunshot wound. One of his deputies is holding down the fort, so to speak."

"Crime must run rampant on this mountain." The sarcasm in her reply was all too evident.

"You're not from this area?" he asked, hoping to steer the conversation onto a more neutral topic.

She shook her head but didn't offer a verbal response.

"Where's your car, ma'am?"

"Broken down on the side of the road not far from here. A warning light signaled the engine had overheated. I pulled off the road."

"That's when the man came after you?"

She nodded. "A few minutes later. I had seen him at the gas station."

"He followed you?"

"I'm not sure. He was headed toward the highway when he first left the station. He must have turned around."

"And he chased after you?" Lucas asked.

"That's right," she said with a nod. "I ran into the woods. He came after me and started up the deer stand. Thankfully, an animal rustled the underbrush and distracted him. He ran toward the sound, probably thinking it was me. Eventually, I heard a car engine and presume he drove off in his SUV when he couldn't find me."

Needing to gain her trust, Lucas pointed in the direction of the road. "You stay here and I'll check the roadway to make sure he's gone."

As much as he didn't want to leave the skittish woman, Lucas wanted to ensure the man had driven away as she'd suspected. He quickly made his way through the thick underbrush until he had a clear view of the roadway. A Nissan sedan sat at the side of the road. No other vehicle was in sight.

He returned to the deer stand. "It's Lucas," he announced as he started up the ladder, relieved to find her waiting for him at the top.

"I saw one car and only one car. A Nissan," he informed her.

"That's mine."

"Then the guy's gone. How 'bout we climb down the ladder? I can check the engine and see what's wrong with your vehicle."

She didn't respond.

"Unless you want to stay on this deer stand all night," he added.

The temperature had dropped even lower. Lucas could feel it in his leg. The wound had healed but the memory lingered. If the dampness bothered him, it had to be chilling her, as well.

Her jacket was light and her head and hands were bare. A slight mist had started to fall and she appeared to be shivering under her bravado.

"Not sure how you feel about a cold rain on a chilly night, but I'd prefer to seek shelter and stay dry."

Her shoulders relaxed. Evidently he was making progress. "I don't want to pry, ma'am, but you haven't told me your name."

"It's Hannah." Her finger inched away from the trigger. "Hannah Miller."

"Pleased to meet you." He hesitated before extending his hand. "Now, if you'll pass me the rifle, we can get out of the rain."

She sat for a long moment. Then, with a faint sigh, she handed him the .30-30. He checked to make sure the chamber was clear.

"I'll go down first. You follow." Swinging his good leg onto the ladder, Lucas started to climb down. Unsure how he'd handle the situation if she failed to move, he smiled to himself when she scooted to the edge of the platform.

"Easy does it, Hannah. One foot at a time. Take it slow. I've got your back."

The woman had been agile enough to climb up the deer stand. Surely she could climb down, as well. Still, he didn't want any missteps. Everything, including ladders, turned slippery when wet, and the last thing he wanted was any more harm to befall the pretty woman who had changed his plans for this evening.

In a flash of clarity, he realized her unexpected entry into his life could upset the peaceful existence he'd been living for the past eleven months. He'd turned in his badge, left law enforcement behind and found solace in the Amish community. Even more important, he'd gotten right with the Lord and found a simpler way to look at the world.

Savannah, Georgia, his years in law enforcement, and what had happened on that dock front were merely a memory. A painful memory that he chose to ignore. Except in the middle of the night when he awoke in a cold sweat, knowing his partner, Olivia, had died because of his delay in responding to her call for help.

He shook his head to send the thoughts fleeing then dropped to the ground and watched the woman with the long legs and free-flowing hair trudge down the ladder.

Her foot snagged on the second-to-last rung. Without thinking, he caught her in his arms. She was slender and soft, and smelled like a fresh floral bouquet. He hadn't been this close to a pretty woman who tugged at his heart in eleven months and, for a long moment, he was transfixed by her nearness.

She bristled. He dropped his hold and took a step back, unsettled by the mix of emotions that played through his mind. A twinge to his gut told him getting close to Hannah Miller might be dangerous to his health.

"Are you okay?" He wasn't sure of the response she would provide, but he knew all too well that he was anything but okay. The woman had an effect on him that was difficult to define. Confused and befuddled might be accurate descriptions of the way he felt.

Gripping his rifle in one hand, he pointed to the trail that wove through the forest with the other. "The path will take us to the roadway near to where you left your car."

She swallowed hard and tugged on the bottom of her jacket before nodding. "I didn't realize there was a path."

"It's hard to see at night unless you know where you're going."

"Maybe you should take the lead," she suggested.

"Sure."

"You're positive the guy's gone?" she asked as if

needing to be reassured that Lucas wasn't leading her into danger.

"I told you, your car was the only one I saw. You mentioned hearing a vehicle heading down the mountain."

Without waiting for a reply, Lucas started walking and was relieved when he heard her following. As nervous as she seemed, he wouldn't be surprised if she tried to run away. But then, where would she go? Her car was broken down, a man had followed after her, and she was halfway up a mountain road few people knew about and even fewer traveled.

He pushed back a branch from one of the saplings and turned to glance over his shoulder. "Are you okay?" he asked again.

"I'm fine."

The mist changed to a steady drizzle. Her hair was matted with rain that ran over her shoulders and down the front of her jacket.

"Fine" was a stretch. She looked cold and about as comfortable as a drenched kitten.

His heart went out to her, but then he realized his mistake. He knew nothing about Hannah Miller, yet a man had chased her through the woods. Maybe that was why Lucas had built the deer stand six months earlier. Had the Lord placed it on his heart to do so, knowing a woman on the run would need a place to hide?

He was still a neophyte when it came to having a relationship with the Almighty. The Good Lord was working on making him a stronger believer and more willing to accept the precepts of the faith he had picked up from the Amish with whom he worked.

Thankfully, they had embraced him with open arms,

but he was the one holding back because of the burden he carried in his heart. He'd asked God to send someone into his life who could remove the plank that weighed him down.

So far, God hadn't answered that prayer.

"Oh," Hannah gasped.

He turned to grab her arm before she tumbled over a fallen log. She nodded her thanks and leaned closer as she regained her footing.

His pulse hammered in his ears. What was it about this woman that caused him to take note? She was pretty. But lots of women were.

Maybe his protective nature had kicked into overdrive. Once a cop, always a cop, even after eleven months off the job. Still, he'd worked lots of investigations in Savannah and had never felt so engaged with a victim or a witness to a crime. Something about Hannah was different, and whether he liked it or not, he felt sure his life was about to change. For better or worse? Only God knew and, at the moment, He was silent.

Chapter Two

Lord, keep me safe, Hannah prayed as she stared at the second man tonight who had peered into her car's engine.

"Shine the light this way," Lucas asked.

She angled her cell to where he pointed, grateful for the flashlight on her phone.

"Looks like there's a hole in the radiator," Lucas said, confirming what the horrible man in the flannel shirt had already told her.

The bad news was easier to accept from the helpful guy wearing suspenders.

She glanced at the road that disappeared around the mountain. A nervous tingle wrapped around her spine. The lewd guy who'd wanted information about Miriam could come back, especially if he expected to find Hannah huddled in her car, seeking shelter from the rain.

Lucas seemed oblivious to the danger. Although there was no telling what he was thinking with half his face hidden under that wide-brimmed felt hat he wore.

Swallowing hard, she gathered her courage to say

what played heavy on her mind. "Do you think he'll come back?"

Lucas glanced out from under the hood of the car and flicked his gaze to the mountain road. "We'll see his headlights in plenty of time."

His comment lacked the reassurance she needed and wanted. Would they really have enough warning to hide if the man returned? Or could a car traveling at a rapid rate of speed surprise them both?

The Good Samaritan's nonchalance troubled her. Surely he wasn't in cahoots with the guy in blue flannel. She shook her head ever so slightly and sighed, refusing to go down that road. Better to think of Lucas in a favorable light. So far, he'd done nothing to cause her concern.

Besides, the Amish were peaceful folks. Weren't they?

Yet he'd said he was almost Amish. What did that mean?

"If we had some water, we could fill the radiator and drive until it ran dry." Lucas extracted himself from under the hood. "That might give us enough time to get to the B and B."

"Where you work?"

He nodded. "But as I mentioned, we need water." He held out his hand, palm up. "And more than a sprinkling of raindrops."

"I've got a case of water bottles in the trunk of my car," she shared. "I went to the store after work—"

"And forgot to unload your groceries?" he added with a knowing smile.

Even in the darkness, she could see the dimples in his cheeks and the sparkle in his eyes.

"I planned to help with the youth at church," Hannah explained. "The kids are always thirsty."

"What changed your plans?"

She avoided his gaze. "It's a long story." One she didn't need to share. "Let's fill the radiator and see how far we get."

After unlocking her trunk, Hannah grabbed as many bottles as she could carry. Lucas did the same. He jimmied a tiny portion of cloth into the hole in the radiator, and then, together, they poured water into the reservoir.

"Looks like it's holding." He held out his hand when she pulled the keys from her pocket. "I'll drive. The roads can be tricky at night."

She liked his take-charge attitude and the smoothness with which he closed the hood, scooped the empty plastic bottles into her trunk and held the passenger door open for her. She settled into the seat and watched as he rounded the front of the car and slipped in behind the wheel.

The road twisted and turned, and she was grateful Lucas was driving. She glanced at her watch. Half past midnight.

Coming to an intersection, he turned right. A road sign pointed left to Willkommen. "Isn't that where I want to go?"

"The town is still a distance from here. The B and B is closer." He glanced at the clock on the console. "It's late, and you've got a radiator that's losing fluid. If we get to the Amish Inn, I'll be more than grateful. You can stay there overnight. The rooms are clean and comfortable and off the beaten path. You won't have to worry about the guy who followed you."

"How can you be sure?"

"I wear a lot of hats," he said with another smile that played with her heart. "One of them is security."

"But you weren't working tonight?"

"That's right. My shift starts at six a.m."

She hated to pry but another question came to mind. "If you don't mind me asking, how'd you get to the deer stand without a car?"

"I live in a house on the inn's property. There's a shortcut on the other side of the mountain. It's a good hike, but doable. When the parcel of land went for sale, I purchased it some months ago and built the tree stand as a place to go to be alone."

"Sorry I interrupted your serenity."

"Not a problem." He flashed another upbeat glance her way. "Glad I could help."

A comforting warmth settled over her. Then, realizing her error, she sat straighter in the seat. She wouldn't succumb to Lucas's charm. She'd been involved with one man too many. No reason to let herself make another mistake.

Lucas might be good-looking, but handsome men could break a girl's heart. She knew that too well. She had the scars to prove it. Not physical but emotional.

She'd built a wall around her heart. Unfortunately, she'd allowed someone entry and learned a very painful lesson that had forced her into seclusion over the last six weeks. Using a prepaid burner phone with a new number and changing her email address so he couldn't reach her had been good decisions. Moving to Macon and starting over had been a bit more difficult. Along with making a new life for herself, she'd fortified that wall around her heart even more. No one could find a way in.

Not even an almost-Amish guy with a killer smile.

Lucas tensed. His eyes locked on the rearview mirror and a muscle twitched in his neck.

"What's wrong?" Hannah asked.

"Headlights, coming this way. Looks like it could be an SUV."

"A black Tahoe?" she asked, rubbing her hands over her arms.

"I can't be sure of the make and model nor the color, but I don't want to take any chances." He glanced at the temperature gauge. "We can try to outrace the vehicle or hole up someplace and wait until it passes."

"What about the leak in the radiator?"

"You've got more water. We can refill if need be." Although putting extra stress on the car wasn't a good option.

Grateful when a narrow dirt roadway came into view, Lucas turned onto the path, guided the car behind an expanse of pine trees and cut the engine. "Hopefully we won't be seen."

"I'd like a little more reassurance." She tugged at a strand of her wet hair and stared through the trees at the all-too-close roadway. "What if it's the guy who came after me and he spots us?"

"Then we'll go to plan B."

Her eyes widened. "Is there a plan B?"

"Not yet, but we'll handle that problem when it arises."

As much as he wanted to make light of a very serious situation, Lucas knew cars on the mountain road were few and far between. Not that he would share that bit of information with Hannah. She was anxious enough.

"By the way, thank you for coming to my aid," she said, her voice barely a whisper.

He glanced at her for a long moment and then turned his gaze back to the road. "My mama taught me to be a gentleman, and gentlemen don't leave ladies at the top of their deer stands."

Out of the corner of his eye, he saw her shoulders visibly relax. She let out an almost-inaudible sigh of relief. As her tension seemed to ease, a tightness constricted Lucas's chest and sent a pulse of heat up his neck. He didn't have medical training but he doubted the reaction had any physical basis, and that worried him. Who was Hannah Miller and what was she doing to his peace of mind?

As the SUV passed, she touched his arm. "It looks like the Tahoe from the gas station. I told you, he had headed for the highway, yet when I broke down, his was the first car to happen by."

"The guy must have known you'd be stranded on the side of the road," Lucas said. "Did you lock your car when you went into the station?"

She thought back. "I had gotten out expecting to pay at the pump, then realized I needed to pay the attendant. I left the car unlocked."

"Which means he could have jabbed the hole in your radiator."

"Except I'd been driving for hours. The engine was still hot. Wouldn't steam and water spray out?"

"He could have worn insulated gloves to protect

his hands. If he closed your hood before you returned to your car, you wouldn't have noticed the problem."

She nodded and stared into the night. "I went to the ladies' room, which gave him ample time."

"Did anyone tail you on the highway?"

"Not that I noticed."

Had the guy taken advantage of a woman driving along an isolated road late at night or was Hannah a known target?

"A pretty woman on a desolate back road..." Lucas didn't need to finish the thought.

Hannah leaned closer. "Did you hear about a mountain hijacking that ended with an older woman dead and two younger women captured?"

The question took Lucas by surprise. "How does that involve you?"

Maybe Hannah was a marked woman after all.

"The murdered woman was Leah Miller."

"You're related?"

Hannah nodded. "She was my mother. My younger sister Sarah was taken. Another sister, Miriam, was supposed to have found refuge with an Amish family named Zook. Do you know them?"

"That's a common name around these parts. Do you have first names?"

"Unfortunately, that's all the information I could decipher from the garbled voice mail Miriam left on my cell. The guy in the flannel shirt who came after me mentioned her name. He wanted to know where she's holed up."

"We need to talk to the deputy sheriff and learn more about the hijacking. Maybe he'll know the Zooks and how to find your sister."

Maybe he would know about Hannah Miller, as well. She'd gone from being a stranded motorist with a guy on her tail to a person of interest in a murder and kidnapping case. Lucas had distanced himself from law enforcement, yet crime and corruption seemed to have found him in the middle of the North Georgia mountains, which was both ironic and unsettling.

Reason told him to give Hannah a wide berth, but he couldn't walk away from a woman in need. Especially a woman whose circumstances tugged at his heart.

"Stay in the car," he said, opening the driver's door. "I'll add more water and then we'll be on our way. There's a fork in the road not far ahead. Just like the previous intersection, the fork to the left goes to Willkommen. We'll veer right toward the Amish Inn. Chances are good the car that just passed us is headed to town."

Lucas refilled the radiator, crawled back into the car, started the engine and pulled out onto the road. The rain eased, but the overhanging trees and thick underbrush that lined the road hung heavy with moisture. The headlights cut a path into the dark night.

As he guided the car to the right at the fork, the moon peered through the clouds. Stretched out around them were rolling hills that led to higher peaks in the distance. They drove in silence for some distance until fenced pastures marked their approach to the B and B. A three-story, rambling inn, painted white with black shutters, wraparound porches and two stone fireplaces came into view. The scene, no matter how many times he saw it, filled Lucas's heart with a sense of home.

"I'm sure everything will look more welcoming in the light of day," Hannah said.

Evidently the bucolic scene that warmed his heart caused her unease. She worried her fingers as if she didn't know whether to be relieved or concerned about what she saw.

"The inn sits at the end of the entrance drive," he explained, hoping to reassure her. "The building closer to the road is the Amish Store and produce mart. Fannie Stoltz owns the place. She's Amish and lives in one of the two houses at the far side of the property. The two Amish homes don't have electricity or technology. The rest of the property runs on solar power backed up with propane generators. The majority of the guests are *Englischers* who want to enjoy the peace of the Amish way but still have their comforts, such as indoor plumbing, electric lights, heat in the winter and air-conditioning in the summer."

"So it's not Amish?"

He smiled. "It's about as Amish as most folks want to get. Fannie is a widow. The inn was a way she could provide for herself."

"She has children?"

He shook his head. "But she's got a big heart."

"You're sure she won't mind me arriving this late at night."

"We won't wake her. I've got a master key and will set you up in a room. Tomorrow we'll explain your late arrival."

Lucas pulled her car close to a rear maintenance shed. "I'll have the mechanic check out your car in the morning. Calvin can fix anything. Even a radiator."

Rounding the car, he opened her door and then pulled her tote from the trunk. Together they hurried along the path that led to the inn and climbed the steps to the expansive front porch.

Lucas keyed open the door and stepped back to let her enter first. A small table lamp glowed halfway down the entrance hall. He placed Hannah's tote on the floor by the table and checked the log book.

"Room three is available," he whispered to keep from waking the other guests.

"Are you sure this is okay?"

"Of course. We all work together at the inn."

He grabbed the key off the peg where it hung and opened the door to the downstairs wing, then motioned her to the left. "It's the last door on the right, a corner room with great views."

He unlocked the door and held it open for her. She stepped into the room and flipped on the overhead light. Her gaze took in the double bed with fluffy pillows and hand-stitched quilt. A dresser and overstuffed chair filled one side of the room across from a door that led to the private bath.

A small latched rug warmed the floor, but the room was still chilly. Lucas adjusted the thermostat on the wall. "You'll get heat soon enough. Extra blankets are in the bottom drawer. Breakfast runs from six thirty until nine a.m. To get to the dining room, turn left and head to the end of the hall."

He stepped past her and checked the latches on the windows in the bedroom and bath.

"Lock the door after I leave. In the morning, I'll let Fannie know you're here." Lucas glanced around the room. "Do you need anything else?"

"Towels?"

"In the bathroom."

"Then I've got everything I need. Thank you, Lucas. I… I'll see you tomorrow."

He nodded. "I'll be on the job by six. Get some sleep. Morning will come soon enough."

With determined steps, he headed for the door then glanced back. "Don't worry. You'll be safe here."

Stepping into the hallway, Lucas felt a sense of relief. He had checked the windows and cautioned Hannah to lock her door. The guy from the gas station wouldn't find her tonight.

Once clear of the house, Lucas stopped to listen to the sounds of the night. Small creatures scurried through the underbrush and the croak of bullfrogs sounded from the nearby pond, but little else could be heard. No cars, no planes overhead, no chatter from guests who were hopefully enjoying their slumber.

He should have been relieved, but tonight something wasn't sitting well within him. He scanned the pastures and the mountains in the distance. Tired as he was, he couldn't pull himself from this observation spot as if everything was warning him to stand guard.

What had he overlooked?

"Gott," he said as his Amish neighbors did. "Show me through Your eyes what I am to see."

The night settled heavy around him, yet still he remained.

The light in room three, where Hannah stayed, went out. His eyes again scanned the fields, the outbuildings, the paddock and stable. A dog barked in the distance.

Foolish of him to remain for so long when the night was quiet. Ready to return to his house, he saw the glow of ambient light from afar. Headlights?

His spine tightened. Was it the man from the filling

station? Had he taken the turn to Willkommen and then doubled back when he'd failed to find Hannah once again broken down on the side of the road?

The lights drew nearer. Lucas moved to the retail store and stood behind the building, hidden from anyone passing by yet with an unobstructed view of the road.

The vehicle's motor filled the night. Lucas watched a dark SUV pull toward the entrance to the property and slow to a stop.

He stepped from the shadows and hurried toward the car, bending to catch sight of the driver through the tinted windshield.

Although Lucas couldn't make out his features, he saw the driver startle, no doubt surprised to see someone approaching, before the late-model Tahoe accelerated. Georgia clay conveniently covered the rear license plate, obscuring the number. The left taillight was out.

The SUV passing the inn could have been anyone, except Lucas hadn't been a cop for six years in Savannah not to know the simplest conclusion was usually the best. Everything in his gut told him the man at the wheel was the guy from the gas station and, for whatever reason, he was intent on finding Hannah Miller. Was he interested in finding her sister Miriam? Or was he focused on Hannah? Whatever the case, one thing seemed certain. If the man found either woman, he planned to do them harm.

Chapter Three

Hannah woke to the clip-clop of horses' hooves. She slipped from the bed and pulled back the curtain, then smiled, seeing a farm wagon stop at the side of the Amish Store. She checked her watch. Six thirty.

In the distance she saw Lucas hurrying along a path. He approached the Amish farmer. Together they unloaded boxes and hauled them into the store, then shook hands on the porch before the man climbed onto his wagon and headed back to the main road.

The sun was barely up, yet everywhere she looked groundskeepers and farm hands, many wearing typical Amish garb, were already hard at work. Dropping the curtain back in place, she hurriedly dressed and followed the scent of coffee to the dining area.

Entering the room almost took her breath away at the sight of the ceiling-to-floor windows that looked over the rolling hills, gardens and mountains beyond. Starched, white tablecloths and napkins dressed the round tables set with blue china that matched the curtains and made the room seem bright and cheerful.

A woman, probably midfifties, wearing a simple,

calf-length dress and white apron approached Hannah. Her hair was pulled into a bun topped with a starched cap. Her round face and twinkling brown eyes were warm with welcome.

"You must be Hannah. Lucas told me about you." The woman took Hannah's hand. "I am Fannie Stoltz. I run the inn, and I am happy you can stay with us. Your room was to your liking?"

"Oh, yes, it was perfect. I slept better than I have in years."

The Amish woman's smile increased, and then she tilted her head. "Perhaps the reason your sleep is not usually sound can be worked out while you are here. The simple life sometimes lets us see more clearly that which is important. The world frets about too many things that should not have power over our well-being. Here—" She spread her hands and glanced through the windows at the rolling hills. "Here our focus can turn to that which is most important."

Finding her sisters was Hannah's number one priority, but she didn't want to disturb the innkeeper with troubling thoughts of two missing women. Instead she chose a timelier topic. "You probably need my credit card."

The woman waved her hand. "We will deal with that when you are ready to check out. Now you must eat." She pointed to a table by the window. "You may sit wherever you like, but this is a nice spot. Lucas is mending a broken fence. Perhaps he will join you in a bit."

A young woman wearing the same garb as the innkeeper filled Hannah's cup with a robust coffee made even richer with the thick cream Hannah added to the hot brew.

"The cream is from our own dairy," the young girl said with pride. "You would like the regular breakfast or do you have dietary needs?"

Probably eighteen at the most, the server had alabaster skin and rosy cheeks that spoke of wholesome living. Even without makeup, the girl was beautiful.

Breakfast was hearty and delicious. Lucas never showed up and Hannah tried to squelch the disappointment she felt. Surely he would be on the grounds. She would find him there.

"Breakfast was wonderful," she told the server before leaving the dining room.

Hannah returned to her room and grabbed her jacket. Hopefully her car would soon be fixed so she could drive to Willkommen. She needed information to locate Miriam, and she didn't have time to while away the morning, enjoying the pretty scenery.

Opening the hallway door that led to the alcove, she nearly ran into a Hispanic man wearing jeans and a navy polo.

"Morning, miss. You are going somewhere?" he asked.

"Just for a walk."

He tapped the board where the keys hung. "You leave your key here when you are gone. The cleaning staff must make your bed and bring fresh towels."

"I wasn't thinking." She dropped her key onto the wall peg attached to her room number.

"You are the new guest?" he asked.

Hannah nodded. "That's right. I arrived last night."

"Someone gave me a note." He held out a folded sheet of white paper. "It is for you, yes?"

Seeing her name written on the outside, she nodded. "Who's it from?"

The man shrugged. "I know only to give it to the new lady."

Unfolding the paper, she smiled seeing Lucas's signature at the bottom of the page. *Meet me at the gazebo after breakfast. I want to show you around the property.*

Tucking the paper into her pocket, she thanked the man and hurried out the door. The musky scent of moist earth hung in the air and filled her with anticipation for the new day. She pulled her jacket around her shoulders and scurried to where Lucas had parked her car last night outside the mechanic's shed.

An African American man, midfifties with a lean face and slender build, greeted her. "I'm Calvin Crawford. You must be Hannah. Lucas said your radiator had sprung a leak."

"Sprung a leak" wasn't Lucas's assessment last night. Evidently he wanted to downplay what had happened. Not that she wasn't grateful. She didn't want to call attention to herself or to the incident on the mountain road.

"I'll have your car ready to drive within the hour, miss, if that works for you."

"Lucas assured me you could fix anything, Calvin."

The man laughed. "Anything involving motors or engines. Only wish I could do more to heal the human heart."

Seemed the mechanic was a bit of a philosopher.

She glanced at the various paths that ran through the property. "Which way leads to the gazebo?"

"Take the walkway on the left. It leads over the hill. You'll see the gazebo. It's not far."

With a quick thank-you, she hurried along the path he had indicated. Topping a slight rise, she smiled, seeing in the distance the lovely gazebo, painted white, with a curved roof and rimmed with colorful winter pansies. The setting would be an ideal spot to sit with a good book or to chat with a friend.

Although she didn't see Lucas, she continued along the path that led to a shaded area of trees and bushes. The thick undergrowth and tall poplars blocked her view of the surrounding pastures, the gazebo and the inn. The temperature dropped and even the overcast sunlight failed to reach into the dense, albeit well-landscaped, thicket. A gurgling stream ambled along the bottom of the steep incline. She walked to where a wooden walking bridge crossed to the other side. As peaceful as the hidden spot appeared, Hannah's thoughts fluttered back to the woods last night.

Her heart thumped and her pulse kicked up a notch. She wiped the palms of her hands along the arms of her jacket, all too aware of her body's reaction to the memories that played through her mind.

A twig snapped. She turned toward the sound. The world stood still as her mind tried to make sense of what she saw. A man. The same man from last night, wearing a hoodie covered with a blue flannel shirt.

She blinked, hoping to send the vision scurrying.

In that instant he started running straight toward her.

A scream filled the silence. Her scream as she raced

over the bridge and up the hill. Rapid footsteps and his labored pull of air followed her.

Full from breakfast, she struggled to stay in the lead. The path wove through the wooded area and then into the open. She pushed on, seeing the pasture in the distance. Lucas stood, with his back to her, on the hillside.

"Help!" She flailed her arms and tried to get his attention as she kept running. Her lungs burned and she could barely draw enough air.

The guy was behind her. Too close.

His hand grabbed her shoulder. She jerked, trying to pull free, and stumbled forward. The path rose to meet her.

Air whizzed from her lungs as she crashed onto the asphalt.

"Where is she?" the man screamed. "Where's Miriam?"

He grabbed her arms and dragged her toward the underbrush. She tried to lash out at him, but the world spun out of control.

Lucas. He would save her.

Then she realized he didn't even know she was in danger.

Standing on the rise of the distant pasture, Lucas saw it play out in a flash. Hannah running along the path that led to the gazebo. A man following close behind.

Dropping his tools at the fence where he had been working, Lucas charged down the grassy knoll.

"Hannah," he screamed.

The wind took her name and scattered it over the hillside. He pulled his radio from his belt and called for help. "Mayday! Gazebo path. Beyond the bridge. A guest attacked."

He moaned, seeing the man dragging Hannah into the underbrush. Lucas increased his speed, wishing his legs would carry him faster. He cut across the clearing, screaming all the while.

Her attacker glanced up. For half a second, he stared at Lucas, who opened his arms and raced forward. The attacker released his hold on Hannah and disappeared into the woods.

Lucas hurried to where she lay and dropped to his knees beside her. Her forehead and cheek were scraped raw from the fall. Her breathing was shallow.

He wove his fingers into her hair, searching for blood. "Hannah, talk to me. It's Lucas. Tell me you're all right."

Why didn't she respond?

She moaned and relief flooded over him.

"What…what happened?" She blinked her eyes open.

"Do you remember anything?"

"The man from last night." She grabbed Lucas's arm. "Where is he?"

"Gone. You're okay. He won't hurt you."

"But you said to meet you at the gazebo."

"What?"

"Your note."

Which he hadn't written.

"I was trying to find you, Lucas, but…"

She closed her eyes.

Fear tugged anew at his heart.

Her eyes reopened. "If he comes after me again—"

Footsteps sounded. She raised her head.

Lucas turned as many of the Amish men and women who worked on the property ran toward them, responding to his call for help.

Turning back to Hannah, he took her hand. "There won't be a next time. I promise you, Hannah."

Lucas thought of Olivia and realized the fallacy of his words. What happened once could happen again. Just as before, a woman was in danger, and if the attacker returned, Lucas might not be able to save her in time.

Chapter Four

Hannah appreciated Lucas's help, but she refused to be coddled and tried to stand as the workers flocked around her.

"Are you all right?" one of the men asked.

She nodded, but the ground shifted and her knees went weak. Lucas caught her.

"Easy does it," he cautioned. His strong arms provided support as a wave of vertigo washed over her.

"Thank you," she whispered, grateful for his help.

"You stood up too fast," he said.

"Fannie's coming." A workman pointed to the golf cart cresting the rise of the hill. Calvin was driving, and the innkeeper sat next to him on the front seat. They raced along the path and braked to a stop near the small crowd that had gathered.

Fannie hurried toward Hannah and wrapped her in her arms. "You are hurt. What happened?"

Lucas quickly filled the innkeeper in as together they guided Hannah toward the golf cart. Lucas helped her onto the back seat and scooted in next to her.

Fannie returned to the front. “Please, drive us to the inn, Calvin.”

“I’m okay.” Hannah tried to reassure them as the golf cart sped along the paved path. Her back and shoulders ached, and a wave of vertigo hit whenever she moved her head.

Lucas stared at her as if he could see through her attempt at bravery. She steeled her spine and blinked her eyes to block out the diffused rays of light that made her head pound all the more.

“You need a doctor,” he announced. “As soon as Calvin fixes your radiator, we’ll take your car to the clinic in town.”

“It’s almost ready to drive,” Calvin assured him.

“The clinic is just off the square on West Main Street,” Fannie said, her eyes filled with concern. “Doc Johnson accepts walk-ins, and the inn will cover any medical expenses.”

“That won’t be necessary,” Hannah insisted. “I’m just tired and need to rest. I’ll feel better as soon as I get some sleep.”

“A concussion can cause fatigue,” Lucas cautioned. “We’ll let the doc check you over before any naps.”

He turned to Fannie. “While we’re in town, we’ll stop at the sheriff’s office and file a report about the incident.”

“I am grateful for your help,” Fannie said. “Will you also find out how Sheriff Kurtz is doing with his recuperation? He has been in rehabilitation for some weeks. I sent him a note that he should have received by now.”

“Would he have information about the carjacking?” Hannah asked.

Fannie’s brow furrowed. “I have not heard of this.”

"A woman was shot and two women were taken captive more than six weeks ago," Lucas quickly explained, although he didn't mention Hannah's relationship to those involved.

Fannie patted her chest and tsked. "How can so much bad happen around us? This area used to be peaceful, which is how I describe the inn in the brochures. Now I am fearful for my guests' safety."

"I feel so bad," Hannah said. "I'm sorry to upset your tranquility here at the inn."

"I am more worried about you," Fannie assured her. "We must make certain this man does not hurt you again."

Hannah had left Knoxville and her sisters and mother in the hope of making her own way in life and finding a place to call home, which she was beginning to realize might never be in her future. She bit her lip and blinked back tears at the realization of what her future would most likely be.

Lucas must have sensed her upset. He circled her shoulders with his arm and pulled her closer, cradling her to him. "It's okay. The man's gone. I won't let him hurt you."

Hannah nodded her thanks and tried to smile. Lucas seemed sensitive to her needs and, at the moment, she needed the reassurance of his embrace.

Calvin pulled the golf cart to a rear door that led into Fannie's office.

"Let me help you," Lucas offered as he hopped out of the golf cart. Taking Hannah's arm, he supported her as she stepped onto the path.

As much as she appreciated his concern, Hannah

didn't want to go to town. Willkommen meant traveling the road where she'd first been assaulted by the guy in flannel. She wanted to stay put at the inn. She would lock the door to her room and curl up under the hand-stitched quilt and sleep until she forgot about everything that had happened. But how far back would she have to go?

Memories assailed her of growing up and being the odd child who didn't fit in. Her mother had told Hannah the truth about who her father was on the night she had left home. The same night her mother had accused her of being a thief. Hannah shook her head to block out the memories. She never wanted to remember the pain she'd felt. Better to be a woman on the run, trying to escape her past, than to open the door that needed to remain closed. Now and forever.

"I don't want to go to town, Lucas. I never should have come to Willkommen. It was a mistake."

"Hannah, you need to see a doctor. I'll stay with you. You won't be alone."

She stared deep into his brown eyes. Lucas didn't know who she was or anything about her family. What would he think if he knew the truth about her father?

She shrugged out of his hold, needing to stand on her own two feet. She didn't need anyone's help. If her mother had turned away from her, how could she trust anyone else?

Lucas didn't understand Hannah's need to be so independent. She seemed to change in a heartbeat, at first allowing him to help her and then backing away as if he was the one out to do her harm. She reminded him of someone who had been hurt, badly, and feared getting hurt again.

Lucas could relate.

Only his worst enemy was himself.

Hannah took a step forward. He reached for her elbow to steady her faltering gait. "The door leads into Fannie's office. There's a couch inside where you can rest and relax."

Her pallor had him worried, along with the lack of luster in her eyes. More than the wind had been knocked out of her sails.

"There's a small step." He pointed to the rise and held her arm as she navigated through the doorway and into the welcoming warmth of the office.

With Lucas's help, Hannah lowered herself onto the couch. "Thank you," she said, her voice little more than a whisper.

Fannie followed them in and drew water into a glass in the small sink at the rear of the room. "Take sips," she suggested as she passed the glass to Hannah.

"I'm really fine," she assured them both before she raised the glass to her lips.

Lucas returned to the golf cart to speak privately to the mechanic. "How long before the car will be ready?"

"Give me fifteen minutes," Calvin said. "I'll bring the car around."

"Thanks, Calvin. Let's keep this trip to town between us."

"You think someone at the inn might be involved?"

Lucas shook his head. "I'm not speculating on anything, but the fewer people who know Hannah's whereabouts, the better."

"Don't worry. You can trust me."

Lucas smiled. Calvin was a good man and an outstanding mechanic.

Returning to the office, Lucas was concerned by the worry he saw in Hannah's gaze and the lack of color in her face.

"We'll leave in about fifteen minutes," he announced, looking first at Fannie and then at Hannah. She must have realized her own fragile condition because she didn't object.

"My purse is in my room. I'll need identification and my medical insurance card."

"Stay where you are," Fannie insisted. "I'll get it."

She stepped out of the room and soon returned with the handbag. "Hector Espinoza is waiting in the hallway, Lucas. He wants to talk to you."

Lucas hesitated, confused by the request.

"Hector said he delivered a note to Hannah," Fannie explained. "He heard what happened and was worried he might be in trouble."

Hurrying into the hallway, Lucas spied Hector, hat in hand, a doleful look on his full face, and motioned him into a corner alcove that was out of sight from anyone walking along the main hallway.

"Who gave you the note?" Lucas quickly asked.

"The Amish girl who works in the store."

"Belinda Lapp?"

"*Sí.* She helps her mother."

"You saw her in the store?"

The man shook his head. "On the trail. She said you wanted the note delivered to the new guest. She described the woman. Belinda had shelves to stock, so she could not go to the inn herself. She said you told her that I would deliver the note."

"Was anyone with Belinda?"

"No, senor." Again Hector shook his head. "She was alone."

"Did you read the note?"

A look of surprise washed over Hector's full face. "I would never do that."

"But you found the lady?"

"She was in the main entryway. She is younger than the other guests. I did not have a problem identifying her."

"What happened after you gave her the note?"

"I returned to the barn."

"And Belinda?"

"I did not see her again."

"Thanks, Hector. You did the right thing in telling me. I know you were trying to help. Next time Belinda asks for a favor, talk to me first."

"*Sí*, I will do that. And the lady?" His dark eyes were narrow with worry. "The lady is going to be all right?"

"I think so. Now go on back to work, but don't let anyone talk you into anything again."

Hector left the inn through a rear door.

Lucas glanced out a nearby window to the store visible in the distance.

Why would an Amish girl be part of an attempt to do Hannah harm? Knowing she was in good hands with Fannie, he followed Hector outside and double-timed it toward the store.

A bell rang over the door and the smell of homemade soaps and fresh-baked bread accosted Lucas at the entrance.

Joseph, the Amish teen who worked with Belinda, looked up from where he was dusting shelves.

"Where's Belinda Lapp?" Lucas asked as he neared the counter.

"She has gone home for the day."

Lucas didn't understand. "The day has just started."

"*Yah*, but she did not feel well."

"And her mother?"

"She is not here, either."

"Both of them are sick?" Lucas asked.

The boy shrugged. "Both of them are not here. I do not know anything except what Belinda has told me."

Returning to the inn, Lucas pushed open the door and stepped into Fannie's office.

She was sitting next to Hannah on the couch, fanning the younger woman with a newspaper.

"What happened?"

"She got light-headed and almost passed out. She needs medical care, Lucas. Calvin parked her car at the rear of my office."

"We'll leave now."

He encouraged Hannah to stand and helped her outside.

Fannie opened the passenger door and wrapped a throw around Hannah's legs. "Lucas will get the heater running soon to warm you."

Before climbing behind the wheel, he hesitated for a moment. "Lydia Lapp didn't come to work today," he told Fannie. "Her daughter, Belinda, is the one who gave Hector the note to deliver to Hannah."

"I trust Lydia, but Belinda seems more interested in young men rather than in getting her work done."

"Have you seen her with anyone recently?"

"I saw her talking to a man this morning," Fannie admitted. "I told her that the store was open and she needed to get to work."

"Can you describe the guy?"

Fannie shook her head. "I was more focused on Belinda and her need to return to work."

"I'll talk to her when I get a chance. Hopefully she's not involved with the attacker, but stranger things have happened."

Fannie glanced into the car and patted Hannah's hand. "I will pray the doctor finds you well."

Hannah gave her a weak smile, which didn't bolster Lucas's spirits. He needed to get her to the doctor, but he also needed to talk to Belinda Lapp. Innocent though she seemed with her white apron and prayer *kapp*, the girl might know something. Lucas needed to find out what.

Chapter Five

Hannah disliked doctors as much as she disliked cops. Yet Lucas insisted on taking her to the medical clinic in Willkommen. The receptionist greeted them warmly before handing Hannah a pile of forms to fill out.

"I'm feeling better, Lucas," Hannah assured him. "You can leave me here and run errands or pick up supplies for the inn. I'll be fine."

He shook his head. "I'm not leaving. I want to know what the doctor has to say. Besides, I don't want you running out on me."

In spite of her aching head, she almost smiled. "Would I do that?"

He laughed quietly. "You look as skittish as a colt ready to bolt. You need to tell the doctor everything that happened."

"I'll tell him that I took a fall."

"That you were thrown to the ground forcefully, hit your head and have been woozy ever since."

"If I tell him all that, he'll keep me for observation."

"Which would probably be best. I'll be in the waiting room. Send the nurse to get me if you need anything."

The doctor was duly concerned about Hannah's condition when he finally entered the examination room more than an hour later.

"You've got a significant hematoma on your head, Ms. Miller." He glanced at her over the top of his bifocals and pursed his lips. "We need to make certain there are no complications before we decide how to proceed."

"I really don't think all the fuss is necessary."

"I'll order lab work and a CAT scan," the doctor suggested, "and go from there. Fortunately, a mobile imaging service is on site today."

Hannah knew arguing was useless.

The scan was painless and she was surprised to see Lucas waiting for her when she came back to the exam room. "I thought you would have gone to the sheriff's office by now."

"We'll go together as soon as you're released."

Four hours later they left the clinic with instructions for Hannah to rest. Lucas placed his hand on her back and escorted her to the car.

"You need to take it easy."

"I'm a guest at the inn. It's a relaxing place. I don't need a doctor to tell me to relax."

Except she didn't mention the man who had tried to do her harm. She wouldn't focus on that or on him.

"The sheriff's office isn't far," Lucas assured her.

"I'd rather not talk to law enforcement today."

"I know, but we need to notify the authorities about what happened."

She sighed. "What can they do?"

"Hopefully they can be on the lookout for the guy with a burned-out taillight."

The sheriff's office was small but tidy. A deputy greeted them. He introduced himself as Lamar Gainz and motioned for them to sit in chairs across from his desk.

Lucas took the lead and quickly explained about the attacker who had accosted Hannah last night and again today on the trail.

"Do you know the man's name?" the deputy asked.

"I saw him for the first time at a filling station." She explained about the hole in her radiator and how the man had stopped to offer his so-called help.

"He threatened you?" Gainz asked.

"His comments were offensive. I feared for my safety and ran into the woods. He followed."

"Did he hurt you?"

"Not then. Not until today."

At the deputy's prompting, she provided a description.

"And he was the same man who came after you today?" the deputy asked.

She nodded. "That's correct. It has something to do with my sister Miriam Miller. The man mentioned needing to know where she was. I'm hoping you have information about a carjacking she was involved in. My mother was killed and my young sister Sarah was kidnapped."

The deputy's eyes widened. "You're related to Miriam Miller?"

Hannah scooted forward in the chair. "I saw on a news report that Miriam left Willkommen. Do you have any information as to her current whereabouts?"

"You probably saw the clip about her boarding the bus. The local news station has run it frequently over the last few weeks."

Hannah nodded. "That's the one."

"Your sister left Willkommen but then returned to the area some days later. While here, she stayed with the Zook family, Abram and his sister Emma."

The deputy glanced at Lucas. "I doubt anyone at the inn would know Zook. He kept to himself. His farm is located a distance outside of town. From what I heard, Ms. Miller decided to join the Amish faith. I believe she and Mr. Zook planned to marry."

Hannah's eyes widened. "Are they at the farm now? I need to see my sister."

"'Fraid that can't happen. The carjacking was front-page news in our local paper and was picked up by radio and television stations in Atlanta. Lots of newsmen came to town looking for information. Abram was worried about Miriam's safety, so they left the area. Ned Quigley has been the acting sheriff while Sam Kurtz has been out on medical leave. Ned and Sheriff Kurtz are the only people who know how to get in touch with Abram."

"Then I need to talk to the acting sheriff," Hannah insisted.

"Yes, ma'am, but he's tied up at the Georgia Bureau of Investigations headquarters in Atlanta at the moment. Don't expect him back for a few more days."

"Give me his number and I'll call him."

The deputy nodded. "You could, but I doubt he'll divulge any information about their whereabouts."

"But Miriam is my sister," she reminded the deputy.

"Yes, ma'am, but that's the way they wanted it kept so no one could come after her."

"I don't understand."

"There's speculation a human-trafficking ring has been working in the area. When your sister's car was stopped on the mountain road, two men captured Miriam and her sister Sarah."

Hannah's heart thumped harder hearing her younger sister's name. "Do you know where I can find Sarah?"

He shook his head. "There's an ongoing investigation, but so far nothing has turned up. Your mother tried to protect Miriam when one of the men grabbed her. Guess Mom went after the guy. That's when she was killed."

"Would anyone else have information? Perhaps the sheriff who was injured?"

"Sheriff Kurtz? He's leaving rehab tomorrow, although I'm not sure where he's going after that. He needs to find a place to recuperate."

"Surely he has an apartment or home."

"Indeed he does, but that doesn't mean he can take care of himself. He'll need time to regain his strength."

"I want to talk to him," she demanded.

The deputy nodded. "I'll gladly give you information as to where he's staying once he lets me know his plans."

She raised her hands in frustration. "Can you tell me anything else about my sisters?"

"Only that Miriam was in good health and she seemed happy."

"Happy that our mother was dead and our younger sister kidnapped?" Hannah asked, unable to understand his comment.

"Happy with Abram, ma'am. Those two make a nice couple."

She wasn't convinced. "Are you sure my sister is safe with Zook? If what you said is true, Miriam might not be acting rationally. I never thought she would become Amish."

The deputy glanced at Lucas and then back at Hannah, making her realize her last comment may have been out of line.

"It's not that the Amish aren't good people," she said, hoping to walk back her comment. "But I can't see her settling down with an Amish widower, which is what she said he was on her voice mail."

"Abram's a good man," the deputy chimed in. "His wife died three years ago. He's had a hard time getting over her death."

"Can you assure me that Mr. Zook didn't abscond with my sister? For all I know, he could be working with the traffickers."

"Ma'am, Abram would never harm a woman."

"Yet he's keeping my sister's whereabouts secret."

"Which means the traffickers won't find her." Lucas squeezed Hannah's hand. "We'll find out more information when we talk to the sheriff."

Although she appreciated Lucas's optimism, she still had questions. "Did Miriam say anything about our mother?" she asked the deputy.

"Only that she was sometimes hard to handle due to her ALZ."

Hannah leaned closer. "You mean Alzheimer's?"

"Yes, ma'am. Your mother hoped to reconnect with her sister. That's why the girls brought her to Willkommen." The deputy shrugged. "Sad part was that the hijacking happened before they ever arrived in town."

"I didn't know my mother had a sister."

"Annie Miller's her name, as I recall, although Miriam could never locate her."

"What about my mother's burial?"

The deputy frowned. "Sorry to say that, due to the murder investigation, her body hasn't been released yet."

Hannah's heart sank. "It's been more than six weeks."

He nodded. "With the sheriff in the hospital, things are taking a little longer."

A lot longer, she wanted to say. "Would you see when her body can be released? I'll make the arrangements."

"Yes, ma'am."

But not today. She wasn't up to picking out a casket or planning an internment.

"Where did the carjacking take place?" Lucas asked, changing the subject, for which she was grateful.

"A few miles past the Zook farm and the Beiler dairy. The road angles up the mountain to the county line. The Petersville police have jurisdiction on the other side of the county line. That's where your sister abandoned her car when she escaped from the cabin where she was being held."

"How far away was the cabin?" Hannah asked.

"A couple miles." He turned to Lucas. "An old guy named Ezra Jacobs lived near the road that leads up to Pine Lodge Mountain Resort. The two sisters were held not far from his place."

"What about Sarah?" Lucas asked. "Has anything been done to find her?"

"Here's the problem," the deputy admitted. "One of our men was injured in a vehicular accident the day Miriam's abandoned car was found by the river. He's been hospitalized in Atlanta since then."

"The accident was in connection with the carjacking?" Lucas asked.

"Not that we can determine, although nothing can be ruled out at this point. With Sheriff Kurtz needing medical care and Ned Quigley at GBI, it leaves us short-staffed. We haven't received any leads for a few weeks. Miriam described the guy who took her younger sister as tall and slender with red hair. He shouldn't be too hard to spot, but so far, no one has seen him."

Hannah hung her head, thinking of the last time she'd seen Sarah, the night she'd left home. Her younger sister hadn't wanted Hannah to leave.

Swallowing hard, she glanced up at the deputy. "Please let me know if any information surfaces about either of my sisters. I'll be staying at the inn for at least a few days."

She turned to Lucas. "I'd like to visit the Zook farm and see it for myself, if we have time."

"Follow the main road out of town, heading west," the deputy told Lucas. "You'll see the farm just after the fork in the road. Two Amish lads, the Keim twins, are helping to maintain the property and livestock while Zook is gone. Tell the boys who you are."

He glanced at Hannah. "They don't have information about Abram or Miriam's whereabouts."

"What about Isaac Beiler?" she asked.

"His dairy isn't far from the Zook place. I haven't seen him or his wife and son for a few days. His wife's name is Emma. She's Abram's sister. I'm sure she'd like to meet you."

Hopefully Emma would provide more information and know how to contact Miriam.

"This case has all of us concerned," the deputy continued. "Plus, there was a young Amish girl who went missing some months earlier."

"Rosie Glick?" Hannah asked.

The deputy raised his brow. "You've heard of her?"

"Her name was mentioned on the late-night news report. She was thought to have run off with a boyfriend."

Gainz nodded. "That's right. Most folks think that's what happened, but when you've got a case like this with two women captured and another killed, you have to wonder if there's something we didn't see in the Glick investigation."

Lucas leaned closer. "Can you provide any more information about Rosie?"

"Only that she was seeing a young man in the area. A non-Amish guy."

"An *Englischer*?" Lucas asked.

"Exactly. His name was Will MacIntosh."

"You mind providing an address so we could talk to him?"

"Don't see how that would hurt if you can track him down. He left town the same time—that's why we thought they were together. His family used to live around here. The father wasn't the nicest of men."

"How old was Rosie when she disappeared?" Hannah asked.

"Seventeen. She would have had a birthday since

then. The boy was three years older. The sheriff put out a BOLO on both kids but nothing turned up."

Gainz wrote directions on a piece of notepaper and handed it to Lucas. "You can talk to the girl's parents, although they might not be very welcoming. You know how the Amish stick to themselves."

He glanced at Lucas's clothing. "Sorry. I didn't mean to insult you."

"The Amish stick to themselves because they live apart from the world, Deputy. Not in the world."

"Sometimes their lives interact with worldly issues and that's when law enforcement gets involved, but that's something you might not understand."

Lucas scowled. Evidently he didn't appreciate the deputy's inference that someone dressed Amish wouldn't have a handle on law enforcement.

Hannah stood and shook hands with the deputy. "Let us know if you find out any additional information."

"I'll be in touch," Gainz said before they left the office and hurried to the car.

"There's not much to go on," Hannah admitted. Lucas opened the passenger door for her. "But it's a start."

He nodded and glanced at the sky. "Looks like a storm is rolling in. We can postpone the visit to Zook's farm until tomorrow when you feel a little stronger."

She shook her head. "I came to Willkommen to find my sisters. I don't want to give up now."

Chapter Six

Storm clouds gathered overhead and rain began to fall as Lucas pulled onto the road heading out of town. He eyed the sky, concerned about the weather and Hannah's safety. Glancing at the rearview mirror, he checked for anyone who might be following them.

The rain increased in intensity. He turned the wipers to high and activated the defroster. Inwardly, he questioned his lack of common sense for exposing Hannah to danger that might lurk along the country road.

"We should turn around and head back to the inn," he suggested, seeing the stretch of isolation that lay ahead of them. "I'm worried about your safety."

"Don't be silly, Lucas. If I'm reading the GPS on my phone correctly, we'll be at the Zook farm before long." She stared at the screen, no doubt estimating the distance they still had to drive. "It would be a shame to turn around now."

Lucas flicked another glance at the rearview mirror. The road behind them was clear. The horizon was, as well.

"Promise me," he said, "that we won't stay long.

We'll walk around the house, maybe check the barn, and then head back to the car."

"I told you, I just want to see where Miriam stayed. I won't cause a problem or dally too long."

"You're not a problem," he assured her.

She almost smiled. "Have you always been a worst-case type of guy?"

"What's that mean?"

"That you envision the worst."

"Seems you forgot that I found you hiding on the top of a deer stand."

She nodded. "Which I appreciate. I'm not sure what I would have done if you hadn't happened along."

"Knowing you, Hannah, you probably would have stuck a wad of chewing gum into the hole in the radiator, filled the reservoir from your stash of water bottles in the trunk of your car and driven to Willkommen to talk to the deputy sheriff."

"It was the middle of the night. The sheriff's office would have been closed, and I don't like to talk to law enforcement."

"But you did fine today."

"Because you were with me," she admitted.

"You've got a beef with police?" he asked.

"I'm a private person. Sharing information is difficult, especially with strangers."

"Your policeman is your friend. Didn't your mother teach you that?"

"My mother threatened me by saying she would call the cops."

The comment surprised him. "You were a difficult kid?"

"No. In fact, I was easygoing. I worked hard to help pay the bills and bring money into the family."

"But?" He stared at her.

"But my mother didn't believe everything I did was in the family's best interest. Deputy Gainz said she was suffering from Alzheimer's. That might answer some of the questions I've struggled with since leaving home. My mother hadn't been herself, only I was too stubborn to realize the deeper issues that must have played into her change of temperament. Unfortunately, I didn't see the signs. Evidently Miriam was more observant than I was, but then, that's what my mother had always said."

"That Miriam was observant?" he asked.

"That Miriam understood her," Hannah clarified. "They were cut from the same cloth, so to speak. Two peas in a pod."

"I think that's usually in reference to siblings. Perhaps you and Miriam were the two peas in a pod."

Hannah shook her head. "We were opposites. Growing up, I always wondered how we could be so different."

He glanced at her but she failed to divulge the reason behind her statement.

"The Zook farm's about ten miles from town," she offered after checking her phone again. She tried to appear upbeat, but he knew she had to be stiff and sore after the attack this morning and lack of sleep.

The rain eased and he turned off the wipers.

"It's pretty out here," Hannah admitted. "I can see why Miriam would have liked this area. She was more of a free spirit and loved animals and the outdoors."

"And you're a homebody?" Lucas asked.

"I'm content wherever, even a small apartment.

Open a window and I have fresh air. I don't need to live on a farm to feel free."

"You think Miriam loved the freedom she found at Zook's place?"

"It's hard to say. Maybe she just loved Zook."

Lucas nodded. "You're right. Love can strike at the strangest times and places."

Hannah's cheeks flushed. She turned to gaze out the side window as if unsure of what to say.

He felt equally confused. Sometimes it was better to remain silent.

Hannah had said too much. Lucas had that effect on her. He made her see beyond herself and reveal details that had been buried for too long.

She jammed her fingernail into her hand, hoping to keep her focus on anything except the man behind the wheel. His eyes were too pensive as he stared at her and his questions too insightful. If she answered any more of his queries, he would know more about her than she had known about herself for all those years.

Why did it still hurt? She should be able to move on. Maybe it was her concern for Miriam and especially for Sarah that made her feel so despondent, as if she was wearing her heart on her sleeve. She needed to tuck her heart back in her chest, under her ribs and away from Lucas's penetrating gaze.

She didn't want anything to interfere with her quest to find her sisters, especially not a handsome almost-Amish guy who dug too deep and had a knack for making her reveal more than she should.

Glancing at the road ahead, she saw the farm in the distance. "That's got to be the Zook place." A white fence circled the property. A barn and a number of outbuildings clustered in the rear.

"Looks nice," Lucas said. "Zook's got a good amount of land. His pasture slopes up the rise where those horses are grazing."

He pointed at the other side of the main roadway. "Another farm sits farther down the road. That's probably Beiler's dairy. We'll stop at Zook's place first."

The gate was open. Lucas turned onto the gravel drive and parked close to the house. The home was newly painted and well maintained. Front and rear porches gave a welcoming touch to the two-story structure.

Hannah climbed from the car and hurried to the back door. Shielding her eyes, she peered through the window and into the tidy kitchen. "There's a woodstove, a table and dry sink."

Oil lamps sat on wooden wall stands, no doubt providing light for the entire kitchen. "It looks neat and clean and inviting."

Miriam loved to bake and, for a moment, Hannah envisioned her sister flitting around the kitchen, peeling apples and pulling pies from the oven, filling the house with the rich smells that made her mouth water.

Hannah was better with numbers. She'd kept the books for her family and paid the bills. That had been the problem.

Turning from the window, she stared at the pristine landscape, inhaling the fresh air mixed with the smell of earth and nature. She could see Miriam here, finding happiness and giving her heart to a good man.

"I'll check the barn." Lucas started toward the outbuilding.

"Don't leave me behind."

He turned and smiled. "Are you okay?"

She nodded, coming up beside him. "Maybe a little on edge after everything that's happened."

He held out his hand. "We'll go together."

She slipped her hand into his, feeling a warmth. Her anxiety eased and again she searched the landscape, seeing none of the threats and only peace and serenity.

"I can imagine that Miriam loved this environment."

"Can you see her in an Amish dress and bonnet?"

She shrugged. "Maybe. I'm not sure about her joining the faith, although she always begged our mother to let us attend church wherever we were living."

"You didn't share that desire?" he asked.

"Actually, I liked the services, the prayers, the sense of being part of a faith community." She smiled. "Plus, the people usually reached out to the little girls who came alone or with a neighbor."

"They probably tried to get your mother to join you in the pew."

"No doubt, but she always objected. Evidently her parents had been strict in their faith. She left home to get away from their control. Maybe their faith, as well."

Together they neared the barn. A rustling sound floated through the open doorway. Lucas stepped protectively in front of Hannah. Her heart pounded as she peered around him and stared into the dark opening.

"Well, look who came to say hello." Lucas laughed.

Hannah glanced down at a large dog with doleful eyes who stepped gingerly toward them, his tail wagging.

"You look like you've got a lot of Labrador retriever

in you, boy. Are you all alone?" Lucas turned to Hannah. "Stay here. I'll check the barn."

Which made her concern return. "Be careful," she said as he disappeared.

She stooped to pat the dog. "You're a nice dog. What's your name, pooch?" She couldn't help but smile as he sidled closer and rubbed his head along her leg.

"Looks like we've got company," Lucas called to her as a second dog scurried out of the barn. The beagle's coat was gray with age, but he was equally as friendly and enthusiastic as the Lab.

Hannah patted her leg to encourage the smaller dog to come closer. Tail wagging, the beagle looked up with big eyes as if begging for attention.

"You're as lovable as the big guy who shares the barn with you."

The beagle barked and then scurried toward the woodshed.

Lucas stepped from the barn and pointed to the dairy on the opposite side of the road. "We might find someone at home at Beiler's place."

As they hurried to the car, Hannah looked back at the Zook house with its wide porch. "In spite of what the deputy told us, I had hoped to find Miriam."

"We can come back," Lucas assured her once he settled behind the wheel and started the engine.

What would Hannah say to her sister if they found her? Their parting had been a painful memory she'd carried for the past three years. Coming face-to-face with Miriam would bring back the hateful words they'd both spoken needlessly. If only Hannah could go back and undo what was already done.

The drive to the dairy took only a couple minutes.

Lucas turned onto the property and parked next to the house.

"I don't see signs of anyone." His voice was low and cautious.

"Two families couldn't just disappear."

He looked at the dairy cows grazing in the pasture. "Someone's milking his cows. The deputy mentioned the Amish twins who were helping Zook. The teens might be working the dairy, as well. Let's take a look around."

Hannah opened her door and stepped from the car.

Lucas headed to the house and knocked on the door. He glanced back at Hannah and offered an encouraging smile that she appreciated.

He knocked again then peered through the window for a long moment before he returned to the car.

"I'll check the barn."

A sharp wind blew from the west. Hannah shivered and glanced back at the Zook farm.

A buggy appeared in the distance. "Lucas?"

He peered from the barn. "Is something wrong?"

She pointed. "We've got company."

The buggy turned into the Zook property.

"It might be one of the Keim twins." Lucas motioned her toward the car. "Let's drive back to Zook's place."

The Lab barked as they once again parked by the house and hurried toward the barn. The young Amish man was pumping water that sloshed into the horses' trough, covering the sound of their arrival.

"Excuse me," Lucas said as they approached the youth.

The teen startled, surprise written on his narrow face.

"My name's Lucas Grant." He stuck out his hand.

The kid hesitated for a moment and then accepted the handshake. "You are not from around here."

Lucas nodded. "Not originally, but I've been working at the Amish Inn for the past eleven months. You might know Fannie Stoltz. She owns the inn."

The teen shrugged. "Perhaps my mother knows her."

"Are you one of the twins caring for Abram Zook's farm?"

"*Yah.* I am Seth Keim and my *bruder* is Simon." The slender youth gazed at the hillside. "You have seen my *bruder*?"

"We've seen no one," Hannah volunteered.

"I brought him here earlier before returning to town to help our *mamm* at the Amish Market. We have a stand. Usually my *bruder* and I both help, but the farm requires work."

"When will the Zook family return?" Lucas asked.

"This I do not know."

"I need to contact Abram," Hannah stated. "Do you have his address or perhaps a phone number?"

"The Amish do not have telephones."

"But you write letters?" she pressed. "Can you give me information about his whereabouts and whether a woman named Miriam Miller is with him?"

"I do not have an address. Isaac Beiler owns the dairy." Seth pointed to the neighboring farm. "You can see it from here. He would know how to contact Abram Zook."

"But Mr. Beiler is not at home. We stopped there briefly. Do you know where he and his family might be?"

"Simon knows. He talked to Isaac before he and his wife and son left for some type of a family gathering."

Hannah glanced at Lucas. "I guess we need to find Simon."

The big Lab trotted toward them. "What's the dog's name?" Hannah asked.

"Bear. He is Abram's dog."

"And the other pup?"

"The beagle is Gus. He belonged to Ezra Jacobs." Seth pointed to the road that passed the dairy and headed up the mountain. "Jacobs had a cabin not far from the road that leads to Pine Lodge Mountain Resort."

The deputy had mentioned Ezra.

Lucas stepped closer. "Have you been to the lodge?"

Seth shook his head. "Simon and I planned to look for work there, but it was closed for renovation. Instead we got this job. It is better to work the land than to clean hotel rooms." He glanced at Lucas. "I do not mean to insult your work at the inn."

Lucas smiled. "I handle the grounds and security, and agree with you about the benefits of working outside."

The young man glanced at the car parked near the house and the keys Lucas still held in his hand. "You are not Amish, but an *Englischer* dressed like an Amish man? This is what is done at the inn?"

"I'm learning about your faith, Seth."

"I have heard it is hard to leave your world and come to the *plain* life." The Amish lad narrowed his gaze. "Yet you look like a man who knows what he wants."

Gus raced up the hill, stopped on the rise and started to bark. Bear's ears perked up.

The Amish lad turned at the sound. "The dog has found something that causes him upset."

Lucas held up his hand. "Continue your chores. I'll see what's troubling Gus."

Hannah tagged along beside Lucas. Bear followed close behind. She inhaled the clear fresh air and glanced back at the pretty Amish home and barn, imagining Miriam walking along this same trail.

Approaching the rise, Lucas paused and patted his leg to divert the beagle's attention. "Come on, Gus. Let's go back to the barn."

"He wants you to see what he's found," Hannah said.

"Probably a dead animal. Maybe a squirrel or a rabbit."

She raised her hand to shield her eyes from the glare of the afternoon sun. Something lay on the grass. Larger than either animal Lucas had mentioned.

Her stomach roiled.

Not a rabbit or a squirrel or even a deer. Gus barked to warn them, not about *what* was lying on the dried winter grass, but *who.*

A young man. He looked almost identical to Seth.

Without doubt, they had found Simon.

Chapter Seven

Hannah gasped at the blood oozing from a gash to the teen's forehead. Lucas bent over the young man and touched his neck, checking for a pulse.

He turned to Hannah. "The kid's alive. Get your cell from the car and call the deputy. We need an ambulance and law enforcement. Now."

Heart thumping wildly, she ran to her car, passing Seth on the way.

She grabbed her cell from the console, tapped in 9-1-1 and tried to explain what had happened to the operator. "Send an ambulance and notify the sheriff's office. I'm at the Zook farm, about ten miles from Willkommen."

Hannah's head pounded and a roar filled her ears. What was happening to this idyllic Amish community? First her sisters had been captured and her mother murdered. A man had attacked Hannah, and now an Amish youth had been left for dead.

Bear had followed her down the hill and now trotted to the rear of one of the outbuildings that, from the lumber stacked outside, appeared to be a workshop.

The dog growled then started to bark as ferociously as Gus had earlier. Seemed everyone, even the animals, was tense.

"It's okay, Bear," she called.

The Lab continued to bark. Edging closer to a pile of lumber, he showed his teeth and growled.

"What is it, boy?"

She neared, hoping to calm the distraught dog. "Did you see a chipmunk?"

Hannah patted her leg. "Let's go to the edge of the road and flag down the ambulance so they know where to turn."

Again she patted her leg. "Come on, Bear."

The dog wasn't dissuaded and continued to focus his attention on the lumber.

She stepped closer. A rustle sounded from behind the pile of wood. Fearing what she might find, Hannah turned, but not in time. The man in blue flannel raced toward her.

Her heart stopped, seeing his raised hand.

She screamed. The blow sucked air from her lungs. Her knees gave way. She heard Bear bark and then darkness took her to a place of silence.

Hearing the scream, Lucas ran down the hill. "Hannah!"

A man—the same man who had grabbed her this morning—was hefting her, like a sack of flour, over his shoulder.

"No!" Lucas cried.

Bear nipped at the guy's feet.

He yelled at the dog, dropped Hannah and ran toward the woods.

Lucas raced to where she lay, fell to his knees beside her and rolled her over, fearing what he would find.

His fingers touched her neck. He let out the breath he was holding once he felt a pulse.

"Hannah, it's Lucas. Can you hear me?"

A lump formed on her forehead near the gash from last night. She was taking a beating.

Her eyes fluttered open.

"Can you hear me?" He leaned closer, needing reassurance. "Tell me you're okay."

She grimaced, raised her hand and gingerly touched her head. "The guy's persistent."

Lucas almost laughed, feeling a swell of relief.

She lifted her head.

"Easy does it," Lucas cautioned. He placed an arm around her shoulders and helped her to sit up. "I'm not sure what the guy's after, but it includes you."

"He thinks I have information about Miriam. I wish he'd realize how little I know about my sister and her whereabouts."

She glanced up the hill. "Is…is Simon…?"

"He's alive. His pulse is weak and he's lost some blood. Seth is with him."

"What happened to the guy in flannel?"

"Bear nipped at his heels. When he saw me charging down the hill, he decided to make a run for it." Lucas pointed to the wooded area. "Last I saw of him, he was headed into that densely wooded area. Probably has a car parked nearby on one of the back trails."

"Help me to my feet, Lucas."

"Sure you feel up to it?"

She nodded. "I'll wait for you in the car."

Lucas wrapped his arm around her and helped her to stand. “Easy does it.”

She leaned against him and rested her head on his shoulder. “I’m sorry to be such a problem.”

He pulled her closer. “And I’m sorry I haven’t been able to protect you.”

The faint but shrill wail of a siren sounded in the distance.

After he got her into the car, Hannah squeezed his hand. “Flag down the ambulance. I’ll wait here.”

Lucas raced to the road and waved his arms once the ambulance came into sight. Two cars from the sheriff’s office in Willkommen led the caravan and turned onto the property. Deputy Gainz and another officer of the law sprang from their vehicles.

“We’ve got two injured,” Lucas quickly informed them. “The most serious victim is in the pasture.” He pointed the ambulance toward where Seth stood waving his arms.

As the EMTs cared for Simon, Lucas told Deputy Gainz what had happened. “I’m not sure who attacked one of the twins, but the same guy we saw last night, wearing a blue flannel shirt, knocked out Hannah and was carting her off. If I hadn’t come running, no telling what would have happened.”

The deputy glanced at the car. “How’s she doing?”

“Upset and maybe suffering from a bit of shock. You need to talk to her?”

“I’ll have to get a statement.”

While the deputy questioned Hannah, Lucas hurried to where the EMTs were loading Simon into the ambulance. “We’re taking him to the hospital in Petersville,” the head EMT told Lucas.

"How's his condition?"

"He's lost quite a bit of blood. I suspect the doc will order a transfusion, maybe two or three units. The lab work will tell more than our rapid screens here on-site."

"I'll meet you at the hospital," Seth assured the lead EMT. He hurried to his buggy and followed the ambulance out of the gate.

"The other deputy and I will stay and search the grounds," Gainz said to Lucas after he had questioned Hannah. "Watch yourselves getting back to the inn."

Lucas didn't need to be told. "If anything turns up, call the Amish Inn. Fannie will pass the message on to me."

"I wish we had more information on this guy. Ms. Miller is kind of fuzzy about what she saw, but from what you said about his clothing, my guess is the same guy is coming after her. She says she's got nothing that he wants, but he's got to want something."

"I think he wants her. If he was supposed to deliver Miriam to whomever the powers may be orchestrating all this corruption, he may need another woman to take Miriam's place."

The deputy rubbed his jaw. "Sounds like you know something about what's going down."

Lucas shrugged, not wanting to go into too much detail with the deputy. "I lived in Savannah for a bit. It's a port city. There was a trafficking ring in the area, but no one could determine who was involved. Except women disappeared. Girls from the street, mainly. Some younger girls, runaways. They were never heard from again."

Gainz stared at him with a questioning scowl.

"I read it in the local papers," Lucas offered as an explanation.

"Yeah?" The deputy raised his brow.

"That's right. I doubt this small mountain operation has anything to do with the Savannah group, but you never know. They use the port to get the women out of the country, maybe to the islands. The rumor was that one of the high rollers in Savannah involved in shipping had his own island in the Caribbean. There was speculation."

"That the women were being transported there?"

Lucas nodded. "You ever hear of a guy named Eugene Vipera?"

The deputy shook his head. "He's not from around here?"

"No, but I did a little research when I lived in Savannah and uncovered a trail that led to the lodge. I'm not sure if he's in a partnership or owns it outright."

"The lodge falls under Petersville police jurisdiction, so we never go up there. From what I've heard, it's five-star and top of the line. You have to have money and be well connected to stay there."

"Anyone from town work there?"

"No one I know. You could talk to the chief of police in Petersville, but you'd need to set up an appointment first. The guy's less than helpful. There was talk that a few of his officers might be taking money under the table, but nothing's been proven."

Gainz narrowed his gaze. "All it takes is one bad apple, if you know what I mean."

Lucas did know. Greed could corrupt the best of men.

Olivia? Lucas pursed his lips. Olivia hadn't taken

the money as their chief had suspected. She'd been a dedicated officer of the law who had gotten too emotionally involved in the investigation, and she'd been set up.

Lucas glanced at Hannah sitting in the passenger seat of the car. Her face was pensive and drawn. She deserved better than what had happened to her.

He slapped the deputy's shoulder. "You let me know if you find out anything. I'll take Ms. Miller back to the inn."

"The attacker knows where to find her, Lucas."

Gainz was right. If Lucas took her back to the inn, he was handing her over to the man in flannel.

But where else could she go?

Tensions were high as Hannah and Lucas left the Zook farm. She glanced back at the house where Miriam had lived. Her heart ached for Simon and his brother, Seth. The man in flannel was searching for Miriam, just as Hannah was. The Amish lad must have seen him and questioned why he was snooping around the farm.

Or had the attacker followed Hannah there? Had she been the reason Simon was in an ambulance heading to the hospital, his life hanging in the balance?

"You're not to blame for anything," Lucas assured her as if he could read her thoughts.

"Miriam and I parted on such bad terms," Hannah admitted. "Perhaps I shouldn't have come here today."

"Yet if not for your cell phone, Simon wouldn't have gotten the emergency medical care he needed."

"Maybe." Although Hannah wasn't convinced. Lucas thought more of her than she deserved. If he knew how she and her mother had parted, he would be less understanding and probably not as willing to help her.

She glanced at him, sitting straight in the driver's seat, hands gripping the steering wheel. His eyes scanned the road ahead as well as the forested area that skirted the narrow roadway.

"You're worried." She said it as a statement rather than a question. The pensive furrow of his brow was evidence enough of his concern. "Do you think he's still hanging around?"

"The guy in flannel?" Lucas glanced at her for a long moment before he turned his gaze back to the road. "I'm not sure where he is or why he keeps coming after you. I'm wondering if it has more to do with you rather than just wanting to know your sister's whereabouts."

"Maybe if he couldn't have Miriam, he wants me."

"You mean as a trophy of sorts?"

She nodded. "For whatever reason."

"The deputy wonders if you'd be safer returning to Macon."

A heaviness settled over her shoulders as she thought back to the one-room rental where she had been holed up for six weeks. "Do you think that's what I should do?"

"No." His voice was firm. "I don't want you driving along the highway alone. The stalker's determined. I can see him following you south. You'd have to stop for gas or to stretch your legs. You'd be vulnerable. No telling what might happen."

She glanced out the window at the fading daylight. "I… I don't want to leave, Lucas."

"Then it's settled. You'll stay here."

"But he knows I'm a guest at the inn."

Lucas nodded. "That's the problem."

His shoulders tensed. Hannah felt the change more than she saw the shift. His eyes focused on the rear-view mirror.

She glanced over her shoulder. Her heart lurched and a chill swept over her. "When did that car start following us?"

"It turned onto the roadway at the last intersection. The driver's probably headed back to town."

"We didn't pass anyone on our way here."

Lucas gripped the wheel even more tightly.

"Tell me the truth, Lucas. You're hiding something from me."

He shook his head and glanced again at the rear-view mirror. "I'm not hiding anything. Let's see what happens when we speed up."

Lucas pushed down on the gas and the Nissan accelerated. Hannah's pulse thumped, seeing the vehicle behind them speed up, as well.

"There's a turn ahead." Lucas's voice was tense. "We'll take the roadway to the left that leads away from Willkommen and over the mountain to the inn. It's not a well-known route. I'm sure the car behind us will continue along the main road to town."

Fear raced down Hannah's spine. In spite of Lucas's calming voice, she recognized the very real danger that could be following them.

The sun was setting over the horizon as they made the turn. The two-lane road was narrow and not well maintained. The front right tire hit a hole, causing the car to shimmy. She gasped and reached for the dash-board to steady herself.

"Sorry. Your car's not made for bumpy back roads."

Hannah glanced over her shoulder, hoping the car behind them would bear right. Instead it had followed them to the left and accelerated.

"He's behind us, Lucas. It's got to be that same guy."

"We'll be okay."

"We'll be okay if we can escape him. His SUV is larger and faster."

"The Lord will provide."

That was what Hannah had believed when she'd attended church in Atlanta. She'd met Brian and thought they had a future together. She hadn't known he was a thief.

Which was what her mother had called her.

Tears sprang to her eyes. She couldn't escape, not from the man in flannel who kept coming after her, not from the memory of her mother's hateful words, not from the mistakes she had made when it came to her heart.

"Night's falling," Lucas said. He glanced at her. "I doubt he knows the roadway."

The Nissan's engine chugged. She grabbed his arm. "What's that noise?"

"The engine's knocking. It doesn't like going this fast over a bumpy road."

"He's gaining." Hannah watched the car draw even closer.

The driver turned on his bright lights. The reflection flashed in Lucas's eyes, blinding him momentarily. He growled and adjusted the rearview mirror.

"There's no getting away from him." Fear ate

through her gut. She clutched the console with one hand and the dashboard with the other, trying to steady herself as the car bounced even more over the pitted roadway.

A large hole appeared in the pavement ahead.

"Hold on," Lucas warned as he maneuvered the Nissan around the broken asphalt.

"We can't keep accelerating," she cried.

The last of daylight faded. Only the headlights were visible in the dark night.

"A small dirt road veers to the right around the next curve. We'll pull off there."

"He'll follow us, Lucas. We'll be sitting ducks."

The road ahead went dark as they rounded the bend.

Fear gripped her anew. "What happened?"

He didn't reply. Instead he made a sharp turn to the right. Tree branches scraped against the Nissan as it bounced along the narrow passageway.

Hannah raised her hand to her mouth to muffle her scream. The guy was right behind them, but all she could see was the darkness that swallowed them whole.

Lucas braked to a stop and grabbed her hand. "I cut the lights so he wouldn't see us. Pray, Hannah."

"Help us, God," she groaned, holding back her tears.

She closed her eyes, expecting the SUV to come up behind them. In her mind's eye, she could see the guy in flannel pulling both of them from the car. Strong as Lucas was, he wouldn't be able to save them.

Lucas chastised himself. Foolish of him to be traveling on a back road at nightfall in Hannah's old car. Why hadn't he realized the guy would follow them?

At that instant he saw the headlights of the SUV round the bend.

His heart stopped for one long moment, knowing if the guy turned onto the dirt path there would be no way they could escape.

Lucas had made a tragic mistake with Olivia. Had he made another mistake with Hannah, as well? One that would cost Hannah her life?

He squeezed her hand. Her slender fingers wrapped through his and held on tight, as if she needed him.

Olivia had needed him and she had died because of his inability to answer her call for help.

Lord, please.

The SUV passed the turnoff and continued on.

Lucas let out the breath he was holding. "It worked. He didn't see us."

Hannah gasped with relief then started to cry. "I... I was so frightened."

He pulled her into his arms. "I never wanted to frighten you, but it was the only way to get rid of him."

She nodded and sniffed. "It's okay. We made it. But what if he comes back?"

"We'll return the way we came and work our way through Willkommen to the inn. I need to use your phone to call Deputy Gainz and tell him we were followed. The cops are looking for a black Tahoe. Maybe they'll be able to apprehend him on that back road."

"And if they don't?" she asked.

"Then we'll find another way to keep you safe."

Chapter Eight

The night was black as pitch by the time Hannah and Lucas returned to the Amish Inn. Last night she had felt a sense of relief to find lodging and a place of reprieve after eluding the attacker. This morning, the hearty breakfast in the bright and welcoming dining room had wiped away the fear she had experienced the night before and made it seem almost like a dream. Then the vile man had struck again and again and again.

She glanced over her shoulder to ensure he wasn't following them now.

"He's not behind us, Hannah," Lucas assured her.

She turned back to stare at the inn, seeing the room where she had stayed. He had known she was there. He would know she was staying there again tonight.

"I… I can't, Lucas."

"What?"

"I can't stay here. He knows where to find me. Someone who works at the inn provided information about my whereabouts this morning. They could do so again."

Lucas pulled in a stiff breath. "It's late, Hannah. You won't find a motel for miles if you head south on the highway. You'd be vulnerable there, too."

"What if I just keep driving?"

"Back to Macon?"

To a one-room apartment furnished to a minimum with only a single bed, small dresser, table and two straight-back chairs. When she'd first rented the apartment, she'd been grateful for someplace to hole up, someplace cheap while she tried to elude Brian and find a way to survive. She was no longer worried about Brian but rather a new, more deadly threat.

"I'm not going back to Macon."

Lucas glanced her way. "Is there someplace safe you could stay? Maybe with a relative?"

She shook her head. "I've got no one except my sisters." Sisters who had disappeared.

He pulled into the entrance of the property but skirted the road to the front of the inn and, instead, drove along a narrow path that led away from the main lodging.

Two Amish homes, nestled on the side of a slight incline, came into view. She had hardly noticed them before due to a stand of tall pines that partially obscured the houses from view.

"Fannie lives here?" she asked.

"In the main house. She gave me lodging in the *grossdaadi* house."

"*Gross* what?"

He laughed. The sound filled the car and helped to ease the tension in her neck. "*Grossdaadi* means 'grandfather' in Pennsylvania Dutch. The Amish often build a house for their parents once they get older. The son and his wife help care for the aging folks, who are the grandparents to their children. Thus, their home is called the *grossdaadi* house."

"But Fannie doesn't have children."

"That's right. She bought the property after her husband died. The inn itself belonged to an *Englischer* and his wife. An Amish family lived on the adjoining farm with the two houses. After Fannie's husband died, she sold the property they had owned together and bought both parcels of land, the inn and the Amish farm."

"And made a success of the inn."

"The farm would have been difficult for a widow to maintain by herself, but the inn was a better fit. She had worked in the kitchen for a number of years and then moved into the other aspects of B and B management after her husband died. When the previous owners decided to sell the place, Fannie knew the opportunity was too good to pass up."

Hannah smiled at Lucas. "Evidently she also had a good eye in picking honest folks to work for her."

He braked to a stop in front of the larger of the two houses and turned off the engine. "I came here with a hard heart and a lot of anger. Fannie put me to work, knowing that physical labor would help diffuse some of my frustration. I had a bum leg and felt a bit useless."

He chuckled, as if remembering how needy he had been. "Fannie refused to coddle me. In fact, she was just the opposite. If I wanted room and board, I needed to do the tough jobs even if I was still recuperating from my leg wound."

Hannah didn't question him about his injury. Lucas was opening up and baring his soul. She wouldn't do anything to stop him from sharing a bit about his past.

"She was right," Lucas continued. "Work was what I needed." He patted his thigh. "My leg healed. My anger dissipated with time. Fannie's tough love helped me through it all."

"Which is why you've considered joining the Amish community."

He nodded. "They embrace peace. They're quick to forgive and don't harbor grudges. They rely on God—or *Gott*, as they say—and they believe in hard work. Plus, they shun worldly ways."

He reached for the door handle before adding, "I've seen a lot of corruption and hardship and filth in my time. I started to believe the whole world was dark and evil. The Amish folks made me see how good people can be. That changed my life." He glanced at her. "Maybe the Amish faith could change your life, as well."

Before she could counter his comment, he stepped from the car and slammed the door behind him.

Hannah didn't want to be saved. Especially not by a sect of people who embraced the past. She didn't need the trappings of wealth or power, but she liked a few creature comforts, namely electricity, running water and inside restrooms.

Lucas rounded the car and opened the passenger door. "Let's pay Fannie a visit. I've got an idea about how to keep you safe."

"It's late, Lucas. I doubt she wants company after a long day at the inn."

He grabbed her hand. "Trust me, please."

"I do trust you, but I still don't think this is a good idea."

She stepped from the car and begrudgingly walked

beside him up the porch steps. He could be insistent. Still, the calm peacefulness of the house was evident even on the porch.

Lucas rapped on the door then tapped again.

"She might be asleep," Hannah whispered.

Footsteps sounded from within the house. The covering at the window was pulled back and Fannie's round face appeared.

The door opened to the innkeeper's sigh of relief. "You have been gone so long that I had started to worry." Fannie looked past Lucas and reached for Hannah's hand, pulling her gently into the warmth of her home.

An oil lamp on the table bathed the room in a soft glow. A wood-burning stove sat at the side of the room, giving off heat.

"I feared some difficulty." Fannie narrowed her gaze. "What did the doctor say?"

Hannah smiled, hoping to reassure the woman. "That I need to rest."

"He kept you all these hours at the clinic?"

Lucas entered and closed the door behind him. "The doctor released her after a thorough check-over and a CAT scan. We had other stops to make."

"But it is dark now. You have been too long gone."

"We visited the Zook farm, where my sister stayed while she was in the area," Hannah quickly explained. "I had hoped to find information about her whereabouts."

"From the expression on your face, it appears you did not find that for which you were looking."

Hannah glanced at Lucas, unsure of how much to share with Fannie.

"We were followed," Lucas said, playing down what had happened. "I'm sure it was the man who attacked Hannah."

Fannie sighed deeply and patted Hannah's hand. "When will this end?"

Hannah felt the burden fall heavy on her shoulders. "I've placed you and your guests in danger, Fannie. I'm so sorry."

"Oh, child. You are not at fault. You have done nothing wrong. It is this man who comes after you."

Fannie glanced at her watch. "It is late. You have eaten?"

"We hurried to get back to the inn and failed to stop," Lucas said. "Is the dining room still open?"

"Not this late, but I will fix food to fill your stomachs."

"There's something else we need," Lucas added. "The man knows Hannah rented a room at the inn. She has no other place to go, yet she needs to remain in the area until she can find her sisters."

Lucas explained that Hannah's family had been the victims of the carjacking and the tragedy that ensued. "Which means she needs a safe place to stay where the assailant won't find her."

"Here," Fannie suggested immediately. She turned to Hannah. "You will stay with me. He will never expect to find you in an Amish home."

She looked at Hannah's jeans and jacket. "Those who work at the inn wear nothing fancy, but we can do even more to protect you. You will dress in true Amish clothing."

"You mean like Lucas?"

"That's right, except you will wear a dress, apron

and bonnet. The attacker will never look for you among the Amish. What do you think?"

Hannah glanced down at her clothes and then at what Fannie was wearing. "I think that sounds like a good plan."

The next morning Hannah awoke with a start. She glanced at the quilt that covered her and turned to stare at the pegs on the wall where a dress hung, along with a white apron.

For a moment she couldn't get her bearings. Then everything flooded back to her. She was in Fannie's house, an Amish house with simple, no-fuss furnishings.

Pulling back the bed coverings, she dropped her feet to the hardwood floor and shivered in the chill of the room.

Her own clothing lay on a small straight-back chair. She passed them by and reached instead for the cotton dress hanging from the peg. She hesitated for a moment, questioning her own wisdom about taking on a way of life about which she knew so little.

The assailant's hateful face floated through her thoughts and wiped away any indecision about dressing Amish.

Quickly she donned the blue frock and reached for the straight pins Fannie had left on a side table. Feeling all thumbs and clueless about how she could hold the fabric together, Hannah breathed a sigh of relief when she heard a knock at the door and Fannie's cheerful *"Gude mariye"* from the hallway.

"Breakfast is almost ready," the older woman said.

Hannah cracked open the door and invited her into

the bedroom. Fannie dropped the small suitcase she carried in the corner. "Lucas brought your things from the inn this morning."

"That was thoughtful of him." Hannah pointed to the waistband she held together with her other hand. "But right now, I need your help, Fannie. I'm all thumbs when it comes to pinning the fabric."

The woman's laughter filled the room with warmth as she tugged on the waistband and quickly worked the pins through the layers of fabric.

"The trick is to make certain the tips of the pins are buried within the thickness of the cloth so you do not catch your hand against the sharp tips."

"I don't know how you do it." Hannah ran her hand over the pins that now held the dress together as securely as a row of buttons.

"Practice makes perfect, as the saying goes. You will soon learn many of the Amish ways." Fannie's smile touched a lonely place within Hannah's heart. "The Amish leave the world behind and embrace hard work and love of *Gott. All things work together*, as scripture reminds us. You will remember this?"

"I'm afraid there's too much to learn," Hannah admitted. Once again she ran her hand over the row of pins. Would she ever be able to dress herself let alone learn the many tenets of the Amish life?

Fannie reached for the apron and slipped it over Hannah's head. Standing back, she nodded in approval. "*Yah*, you look like one of us."

Hannah carried too many struggles within her to be Amish. Most especially the animosity she still harbored, remembering her mother's verbal attack the night she'd left home. The night she had learned the truth about her father and the type of man he was.

Hannah had always been the outsider. Growing up, she had questioned her mother's caustic comments about her first child being born out of pain. That night Hannah had better understood her mother's all-too-frequent criticism.

"What is it, Hannah?" Fannie touched her arm and smiled with understanding. "You are remembering something that troubles you?"

She nodded. "I'm thinking of my youth. I… I grew up in a chaotic home. Love—if it was even that—had to be earned. I never seemed to do what was right."

Fannie nodded. "Perhaps *Gott* has brought you here to sort out the past. Painful memories can be like a millstone around our necks, unless we are able to cut free from that which weighs us down. Not all homes are built on love. My own home growing up was filled with turmoil. When I married Eli, I vowed our children would know love and acceptance and not harsh unforgivingness."

"But I thought all Amish homes were filled with peace and understanding."

"That is the ideal for which we strive. Sometimes people fall short of the ideal."

"Lucas said you didn't have children."

Fannie smiled. "One son. He died as an infant. I blamed *Gott* for too long. My husband was gentle and loving. He understood that we must accept what *Gott* wills for our lives."

"But God didn't want your child to die, Fannie."

"He did not. This I had to learn. Eventually, I realized I had to accept life as it was. That millstone I mentioned weighed me down until I could forgive *Gott* and myself."

"And you had no more children?"

"I have Lucas. He came into my life. He, too, was broken. I consider him the son *Gott* took from me."

"You were given a second chance."

Fannie tilted her head. "Are you longing for that, as well?"

Hannah shrugged her shoulders. "Growing up, I never fit in. My mother found fault, more with me than with my sisters. I worked to help support the family, but I also saved some of my earnings and kept the cash in my bottom drawer."

Although she hadn't expected to bare her heart, the understanding she saw in Fannie's gaze made her give voice to that which she had kept hidden for too long. "Three years ago, I decided to count my savings only to find the money gone. I… I confronted my mother."

Hannah's heart pounded, remembering the argument that had ensued. "My mother said the money belonged to the family even though I had earned it working overtime. She called me a thief. She said I had stolen from the family and threatened to turn me over to the police."

"Oh, child." Fannie opened her arms and pulled Hannah into a loving embrace. "You are not a thief. You are a beautiful young woman, yet you grieve not only for your mother but also for the love that perhaps she could not provide."

What Fannie had said was true. Hannah had grieved the loss of her family for so long. Had God brought her here to heal?

"Thank you for the clothes and for letting me stay with you, Fannie."

"You are safe with me, child. We will think of happy thoughts and not allow the past to cloud our sunshine. *Yah?*"

Hannah laughed through her tears, feeling a sense of homecoming and wholeness. *"Yah."*

Fannie handed her a handkerchief. "Wipe your eyes and then we will go downstairs and have breakfast together. I must leave soon for the inn. You can decide what you will do today."

Hannah followed Fannie into the kitchen, where the table was set for three. Fannie quickly pulled biscuits from the woodstove's oven and piled them in a basket that she placed on the table.

A cast-iron skillet on a back burner contained scrambled eggs. A plate of bacon, crisp and succulent, warmed there, as well.

"May I pour coffee?" Hannah asked.

"Many hands make light work," Fannie said with a definitive nod.

Hannah poured the pungent brew into two cups on the table and then turned, holding the pot in midair, back to Fannie. "Shall I fill a cup for Lucas?"

As if on cue, the kitchen door opened and he stepped inside, bringing with him the clean scent of fresh air. "Morning, ladies." His face warmed with a wide smile and twinkling eyes that made Hannah's heart flutter.

"I'll take a cup of that coffee," he said as he hung his waistcoat and hat on a peg by the door.

Hannah poured the coffee and handed him the sturdy cup. Their fingers touched and he gazed into her eyes. "Smells wonderful."

"You've been working?" she asked, suddenly flustered and unsure of her voice as well as her heart.

"I wanted to check the fence I fixed yesterday." He glanced at Fannie. "No one bothered it last night, but it didn't come down by accident. I fear the man who attacked Hannah wanted to create a distraction."

"Having the cattle break out of the pasture would have been a distraction for certain."

"But the broken fence forced you to be in the pasture when I needed help." Hannah voiced what she knew to be true. "You rescued me, Lucas."

"*Gott* provides when we are in need." Fannie motioned them to the table.

Lucas held a chair for Hannah and then sat across from her and bowed his head.

"We will give thanks." Fannie followed Lucas's lead.

Hannah did, as well. The innkeeper's heartfelt prayer filled Hannah with a sense of well-being in spite of everything that had happened. Glancing up after the prayer ended, she was taken aback by the overwhelming contentment that swept over her.

Her whole life she had longed for stability and love. For some strange reason, she had found it—at least for this moment in time—in an Amish home in the North Georgia mountains.

Was that what Miriam had found at the Zook farm? Was that why she had fallen in love with an Amish man who had, more than likely, disavowed the ways of the world?

Hannah glanced at Lucas. He stopped his fork, filled with eggs, midway to his mouth and gazed at her across the table. What she saw in his eyes warmed her. Understanding, acceptance, concern.

Had she stumbled onto the very place for which she had been searching?

She clenched her left hand on her lap and reached for her coffee with her right as her thoughts returned to the reality of her plight.

She had allowed a man access to her heart before but he had lied to her. She was too much like her mother, giving her heart to someone who wasn't the man she thought him to be.

Surely Fannie was an excellent judge of character, and if she loved Lucas like a son, then he had to be a good man.

But Brian had seemed like a good man, too.

Hannah had learned the truth, which had made her realize how gullible she really had been. She wouldn't make the same mistake again.

Suddenly, Hannah wasn't hungry. She was worried. Worried about the man who kept coming after her, worried about staying in an Amish home with a woman she had only just met, and worried about feelings of attraction for the man sitting across the table from her.

Hannah knew so little about her biological father but she knew her deceased mother too well. Unfortunately, she was and would always be her mother's daughter. Shame on her. Hannah needed to guard her heart and her life. Staying at the Amish Inn was probably a mistake. Hopefully one she wouldn't come to regret.

Chapter Nine

Lucas didn't want breakfast to end. Sitting across from Hannah warmed his heart and lightened the burden he had carried since Olivia's death. He hadn't thought a meal could be so enjoyable, and it wasn't due to Fannie's excellent cooking. He had sat at this very table eating the wonderful food she provided many a morning without feeling the buoyancy to his spirits that filled him today.

Hannah stared at her plate, which provided Lucas a moment to study her pretty features. He had been attracted to her oval face and crystal-blue eyes the night they'd met. Yet seeing her this morning with her hair pulled back in a bun and wearing the white *knapp*, or bonnet, made him see the deep beauty, the true beauty, she possessed.

He doubted many *Englisch* women would be comfortable without their makeup and hair products, thinking their looks would diminish without the accoutrements. Hannah, on the other hand, had grown in grace and poise and seemed to have an inner glow he hadn't noticed earlier. Even the bruises on her forehead and the scrape on her cheek seemed better today.

"Calvin fixed the wheel on one of the buggies," Lucas informed both women. "I want to make sure it won't give anyone a problem and thought I'd take it for a ride this morning."

Fannie nodded. "That sounds like a good idea. Where are you planning to go?"

"I thought about heading to the Glicks' home. It's not far if I go along the back path."

"Rosie Glick?" Hannah asked. "The Amish girl who ran off with her *Englisch* boyfriend?"

"That's right." Lucas nodded. "She disappeared three months after I came to Willkommen. At the time, I didn't think much about it."

"Such a thing has happened before," Fannie admitted. "Young girls taken in by non-Amish men who promise them all the world offers. My heart breaks for the families torn apart when their children reject the faith."

"Are the girls shunned?" Hannah asked.

"If they have been baptized and have already accepted the Amish faith, then, *yah*, they are shunned by their families and their communities if they leave the order."

"That sounds harsh."

Fannie gazed with understanding at Hannah. "Does it seem harsh? The one who leaves does not desire what we have within the Amish faith. They are the ones who turn their backs on us. We cannot open ourselves to more pain by those who do not wish to follow the *Ordnung*."

"The rule that guides each Amish community," Lucas explained.

"A mother always knows her child," Fannie continued. "Yet in these cases, the child has turned his or her back on the mother first. Repentance can be achieved. The one who left confesses the wrongdoing to the bishop and the church, and asks forgiveness."

"You mean they can gain acceptance into the community again?" Hannah asked.

"It is possible."

"So Rosie could come back?"

"If that is her desire and if she is willing to confess her actions and ask forgiveness."

"But—" Hannah looked at Lucas. "There's something you're not telling me."

"Lucas has come to feel the way I do about this girl," Fannie volunteered. "Something more is at stake here. Rosie was an impressionable young woman. She believed her heart about a young man who perhaps lied to her."

Lucas saw the pain fill Hannah's gaze as if she was all too aware of how that could happen. Was she reflecting on her own mother? Or on her own life?

"Fannie fears that harm may have come to Rosie Glick." Lucas said what he and Fannie both believed to be true.

"You're talking about foul play?"

He nodded.

"That's what the television reporter mentioned. They said law enforcement is looking anew at her disappearance."

Hannah lowered her fork. "I wish someone had information about my youngest sister. If what people have said about Abram Zook is true, Miriam may no longer be in danger. But Sarah? She's only twenty-one. I haven't seen her for three years. At that time she was so sweet and too naive. I don't know if she would have the stamina to survive."

"Yet you said your upbringing was not good," Fannie added. "She survived growing up, which may give her the stamina and determination to survive other challenges."

"I hope you're right, Fannie."

The older woman patted Hannah's hand. "We will trust *Gott*, *yah*?"

Hannah nodded and then turned to Lucas. "Take me with you when you talk to the Glick family. They might know something that could help me find Sarah."

"The man came after you, Hannah. Stay here where you'll be safe. I'll let you know what I learn."

She shook her head and grabbed his hand. "The attacker is looking for a woman in jeans and a jacket. He won't be looking into Amish buggies."

"He saw me run toward him yesterday," Lucas reminded her. "I don't want to draw his attention, especially if we're together."

Hannah smiled. "But he wouldn't be looking for an Amish couple. You'll be safer with me than if you went alone."

"I'm not worried about myself. I'm worried about you. Besides, it'll be a cold trip," he cautioned.

"Surely Fannie has a coat I could wear."

"A cape," the older woman volunteered, "and a large black bonnet with a brim that will hide your face if anyone happens by who seems unfriendly."

She patted Hannah's hand. "You are right. The man

in flannel will not be looking for an Amish couple riding in a buggy."

"But—" Lucas didn't like putting Hannah in danger, even if she was hiding undercover in Amish clothing. He didn't know much about the attacker, but he knew that the man kept coming after Hannah. Would he follow them to the Glick farm? If so, would Lucas be able to keep Hannah safe?

He had left law enforcement and didn't want to return to that way of life, but everything had changed when he'd found Hannah on the deer stand.

She needed to find her sisters, especially Sarah. If the local deputy wasn't able to carry out the investigation, Lucas couldn't sit by and do nothing. Even if returning to police work was the last thing he wanted for his life.

A young woman was missing. An Amish girl had disappeared. Lucas needed to determine if there was a connection.

Fannie was right. The attacker wouldn't recognize Hannah in the blue dress and white apron. He was looking for an attractive woman of the world instead of a pretty Amish gal with a scrubbed face and piercing blue eyes.

"All right. We'll go together. I'll hitch the mare to the buggy. Be sure to wear the bonnet and cape when you step outside. I'll bring the buggy to the kitchen door." He glanced at Fannie. "No one is to know about your visitor."

"She's a niece from Tennessee, if anyone asks." Fannie patted Hannah's hand. "I'm accepting you as kin right here and now. You are family to me." The older woman glanced across the table to Lucas. "You are family, as well, Lucas."

The words touched his heart.

She glanced back at Hannah. "And this sweet Amish woman is the niece I never knew who has only recently come into my life."

Hannah's eyes filled with tears. Evidently she was as touched as Lucas. Fannie had a big heart. She should have had a houseful of children and grandchildren, yet that was not the path God had chosen for her life.

"I'll get the buggy." Lucas rose from the table and, without saying anything else, shrugged into his waistcoat, situated his hat on his head and left the warmth of the kitchen.

A cold wind whipped around the house and tugged at his jacket. Lucas lowered his face into the wind and walked toward the barn. What would they find today at the Glick house?

He didn't know. The only thing he did know was that a man was after Hannah. And Lucas—even though he had left law enforcement—needed to keep her safe. He touched his hip where he had carried a weapon for years. Unarmed and wanting to be Amish didn't make for a good combination when evil prowled. Lucas would have to be extra cautious and use all his skills to make sure Hannah didn't end up in the wrong place at the wrong time.

"*Gott* help me," he quietly prayed. Perhaps if the Lord realized his desire to live the *plain* life, He would keep them both safe.

That was Lucas's hope. He glanced back at the kitchen and saw Hannah gazing at him through the window. What was she thinking? Was she thinking about her sister Sarah or about the wannabe Amish man who didn't understand his own heart?

Hannah slipped into the black cape and bonnet that Fannie offered, grateful for the older woman who adjusted the bonnet and tied the ribbons under Hannah's chin.

"No one will recognize you," Fannie assured her. Then, peering out the kitchen window, she motioned her toward the door. "Lucas is bringing the buggy."

Hannah stepped onto the porch, feeling the warmth of the heavy cape and enjoying the way the dress moved with her. The clothing she thought would be encumbering turned out to be freeing. She also liked the smile of appreciation Lucas flashed her way before he helped her into the buggy.

He sat next to her and flicked the reins, urging Daisy forward.

Once they passed the Amish Store and turned onto the main road, Lucas settled back in the seat. "Belinda Lapp is the young woman who works at the store. She gave Hector the note yesterday that he passed on to you. The Lapp farm isn't far. I want to stop there first."

But no one answered the door when Lucas knocked. He checked the barn and the pastures before returning to the buggy.

"Seems all the families in this area have left their farms," Hannah mused, hoping to deflect his frustration.

"They might be in town," he admitted. "Many of the folks sell produce and baked goods at the Amish Market in Willkommen. Lydia is known for her jellies and jams as well as the quilts she stitches. Too frequently, the Amish around here need to supplement their incomes. I'm sure the Lapps could use the extra cash."

"We'll come back again," Hannah suggested.

He nodded and hurried Daisy along. They rode in silence while Hannah thought of the young Amish women trying to find their way and be true to their faith in a world filled with enticements.

"I don't have a good feeling about Rosie Glick." She finally shared what had been bothering her, knowing Lucas and Fannie felt a similar unease. "Why would an Amish girl run off with an *Englischer*?"

Lucas shrugged. "The grass looks greener, as the saying goes. She might have struggled with her own parents. The Amish life isn't easy and the lure of the world can be enticing, especially for a teenager. The Glick farm isn't far. Let's stop there first and then head to the boyfriend's place after we talk to Rosie's parents."

"That sounds good."

"But we need to be careful," he added. "The guy in blue flannel is still on the loose."

Lucas seemed genuinely concerned for her safety, which made Hannah feel special. A feeling she'd never experienced around men. Initially the guy she had dated in Atlanta had been considerate of her feelings, but he'd soon changed and put his own desires first. Thankfully, she'd found out the truth about who he really was before it was too late.

"You're quiet." Lucas interrupted her thoughts. "Everything okay? You're not feeling sick, are you?"

She shook her head. "I'm just musing over what's happened. I never thought a fast trip to Willkommen to reconnect with my sisters would put me in danger."

"Nothing like this has happened before?"

She didn't like his question. "Are you suspicious?"

"Of you?"

"That I might have brought this upon myself."

He shook his head. "The thought never crossed my mind. I'm just wondering if something in Atlanta—"

"Macon. I moved there about six weeks ago."

"Then did something or someone in Macon follow you here?"

"Negative, as they say in law enforcement."

He smiled, which relieved some of the tension.

"I haven't lived in Macon long," Hannah continued. "I've got a job working retail, a small apartment, and the only folks I know, other than a few people at church, are the ladies at work. Most of whom are in their fifties and early sixties. Not a guy wearing blue flannel in the bunch."

"And in Atlanta?"

She studied the passing countryside. "I lived there for three years and had a number of friends. Perhaps I stepped on a few toes, although I couldn't say for sure."

"Anyone give you a hard time?"

"Meaning what?"

Lucas tilted his head but kept his eyes on the road. "Maybe a guy who came on to you but who you didn't like. Someone who tried to get a bit too close. Anything like that?"

She turned her head, grateful for the wide brim of the bonnet that hid her face lest he read something from her expression. Brian Walker. He would fit Lucas's profile of a person to watch.

"You've turned quiet again," Lucas said.

"Just sorting through all the guys I knew and coming up empty-handed as far as your parameters. I'm sure Mr. Flannel is a local problem. I told you he was in the filling station when I turned off the highway. I'd never seen him before that moment."

"Yet he followed you."

"Because of my sister. The news video was playing on the television. The older man commented on my resemblance to the woman in the news clip."

"Do you and Miriam look alike?"

"Some say we do. I'm taller. Bigger boned. I take after my father."

"And Miriam?

"In looks, she's her mother's daughter." So very much so.

"Yet the old guy at the gas station saw enough of a resemblance to comment about it?"

"He was speculating and probably trying to drum up a little excitement. It was the middle of the night. I doubt much happens in this part of the country that's exciting."

Then she thought of what *had* happened—her mother had been killed and her two younger sisters kidnapped.

"Look, I'm rambling." She waved her hand in the air. "And not thinking straight. Forgive me. Let me assure you I haven't seen anyone in the area who reminds me of the folks I knew or had business dealings with in Atlanta. This guy in blue is a home-grown problem who wants information about Miriam for whatever reason."

He also wanted Hannah, which she wouldn't mention. Not when she was riding in a buggy in plain sight.

Would Lucas be able to save her if the guy came after her again? That was a question Hannah didn't want to voice.

Lucas kept his eyes on the terrain around them, watching for anything that spelled danger. He flicked a quick glance into the rear of the buggy where he had stashed his rifle. Not that he wanted to use it, but some precautions were necessary, especially if he wanted to keep Hannah safe.

She hadn't spoken in longer than he would have liked, but he wouldn't interrupt her thoughts with idle chatter. A lot had happened recently that she needed to ponder. He hadn't told her about his former life as a cop and wondered if that would make a difference. At first, she had seemed hesitant to talk to Deputy Gainz when they had stopped at the sheriff's office in Willkommen yesterday. Some people struggled with law enforcement. He hoped that wasn't the case with Hannah.

Although having her mother murdered and her two sisters kidnapped was reason enough, especially when at least one of the men who had stopped Miriam's car had been law enforcement. A rotten apple could spoil the whole bushel, as folks who grew apples in this area of Georgia knew all too well.

Olivia. His hands tightened on the reins. She hadn't been dirty; she'd been set up. Lucas had tried to track down the culprits responsible. Someone had planted the marked bills in her apartment just as sure as two guys working for Vipera had killed her on that fateful night. The memory of finding her body sprawled on the dock struck him like a rock that tightened his gut and made him gasp.

Hannah turned to him. "Are you okay?"

"Sorry." He struggled to find his voice. "I must have been daydreaming."

"I'd call it more of a nightmare from the sound you made."

He fisted his right hand and tapped it against his chest. "Probably indigestion." He smiled, hoping she would buy his explanation. "Or too much coffee."

"Do you know the Glick family?"

"Fannie does. She said they're nice folks."

"What about the daughter?" Hannah asked.

"Amish children are seen and not heard, as the saying goes. Fannie knew who Rosie was, but I doubt she had any interaction with the girl."

"What about Belinda, who works at Fannie's store? Were she and Rosie friends?"

"A good question and one I can't answer. Fannie might know."

He flicked the reins and considered Hannah's question. The girl at the inn had given Hector the note that led to Hannah's confrontation with the attacker. Belinda had been seen talking to a man earlier in the day. Could both girls have been involved with men who were in some way tied in with the hijacking of Hannah's mother and sisters?

Lucas rubbed his right hand over his aching leg that often acted up in the cold. Not that he would complain. His injury had been minor compared to what Olivia had endured. Some days he wondered if he'd let her down since he'd left Savannah. His career in law enforcement had ended because he'd gotten too close to someone. Had it been Eugene Vipera?

His eyes left the road momentarily to stare at the mountain. Over the rise and on the other side was the Pine Lodge Mountain Resort, one of Vipera's many assets.

Lucas had traveled to the North Georgia mountains in the hope of uncovering dirt on the wealthy tycoon who he was convinced had played a role in Olivia's death. But the trail that had led him here had dried up and made him realize he was following a false lead. As far as he could determine, Vipera had never even visited the lodge and left the operation to a number of managers and a board of directors.

For the last eleven months, Lucas had pushed anything to do with law enforcement aside to let his body and his psyche heal. The wound to his pride had been harder to deal with than the gunshot he'd taken.

Fannie had provided a balm for both. Her motherly ways had brought him from the brink of darkness and allowed him to live again. The clear air and wholesome lifestyle had soothed his pain and made him realize there was more to life than crime and corruption.

Now he felt the pull back to his old ways and his former life. Mentally he drew a triangle between the two Amish girls and Vipera. Then he placed Hannah's sisters and her mother in the center and circled them with a bull's-eye before he glanced at Hannah.

If her family had been in the bull's-eye, she might be, as well.

"I've got a brother, but no sisters," Lucas stated. Seeing her surprise made him realize his mistake.

"Sorry," he said, hoping to clear up her confusion.

"I must have thought you could read my mind. Let me backtrack a bit. I don't know much about girls, but they like to share secrets, right?"

Hannah shrugged. "I guess they do, although I'm not a good person to ask."

"But you're a girl. You know how women think, even teenage women."

Her mouth tugged into a weak smile. "How very astute of you to realize that I'm a girl. The truth is I never had many friends growing up."

"Really?"

"We moved too often. My mother never stayed anyplace more than a few months. Children adjust, no matter the circumstances, so early in life I learned the folly of making friends only to leave those friends behind. Some would call it a protective mechanism. Maybe it was but, for whatever reason, I kept to myself."

"You and your sisters must have been close."

Hannah tugged at a strand of her hair that had escaped the bun and the bonnet.

Had she heard him? Before he repeated his question, she sighed. "Miriam and I were sisters. I wouldn't call us friends."

Lucas turned his gaze back to the road. "What about Sarah?"

Hannah's expression softened. "Sarah was different."

"Because she was the baby?"

"Maybe. I'm not sure. It probably sounds strange, but for the last few years—in fact, most of our teen years—Miriam and I seemed to be competing with each other. I never felt the need to prove myself when it came to Sarah."

"You and Miriam were closer in age?"

"Two years apart, which could have had bearing on our relationship. I don't know when the competition with Miriam started or why."

"Did your mother recognize the struggle between you two?"

"It's hard to say. She and Miriam were always close. I never felt like I fit in."

"Usually the oldest is the favorite. I'm the middle child and never felt that I measured up."

"I'm sorry, Lucas. It's not easy growing up without feeling secure."

"It may have helped me succeed."

"Meaning?"

"College, to get ahead in my job."

"You mean you haven't always worked at the inn?" Sarcasm was evident in her comment.

He'd said too much. "There was a time before the inn, but I'm happy here in the mountains."

"And the life you lived before?" she asked.

"It's over. Let's leave it at that."

Lucas was grateful she didn't press him for more information. Some things needed to remain in the past, back in Savannah, on that dock.

Chapter Ten

Lucas's comments added anxiety to Hannah's already unsettled day. She didn't like to discuss her past or her estranged relationship with Miriam. The pain of what she had learned the night she'd left her family in Knoxville remained an open wound she feared would never heal.

Her mother's caustic words still stung. Miriam and Sarah had returned home long after their mother had become enraged and hadn't realized what had transpired. Maybe that was a blessing.

Hot tears burned Hannah's eyes as she recalled her mother's accusation. "You're just like your father. He was a thief and so are you. I'm reporting you to the police."

"There's the turnoff to the Glick farm," Lucas said, interrupting her thoughts and bringing her back to the present.

She brushed her hand across her cheeks. Lucas, with his big heart and willingness to help, wouldn't understand her mother's assertion or the legacy that came with being her father's child.

Seemingly unaware of her upset, Lucas guided Daisy into the turn. The buggy jostled over the narrow dirt road. Holding on to steady herself, Hannah studied the farmland that stretched on each side of the roadway and the fallow fields waiting for spring planting. Surely Mr. Glick would be tending them soon.

The farmhouse appeared in the distance, a two-story, typical Amish structure in need of paint. Chickens plucked at the weeds in the side yard. A few head of cattle grazed on a distant pasture and a pair of horses stared at the buggy as it turned onto the gravel drive.

A barn, woodshed and outhouse sat at the rear of the main structure. A spindly tree, barren of leaves, grew near the house and would, undoubtedly, provide little shade in summer.

A child's face peered from the window. A little girl. Evidently Rosie Glick had a younger sister.

Lucas pulled up on the reins and turned to Hannah as the buggy stopped. "The Glicks have probably been inundated with police asking more questions than they would want to answer. They may have had their privacy interrupted by newsmen seeking a story, especially after your mother's death and your sisters' kidnappings were thought to be connected to their daughter's disappearance."

"You're saying we may not be welcome."

"I'm saying let's see what happens and go with the flow. I'll take the lead. You follow."

"You're sounding like a cop, and they happen to be my least favorite people."

His brow rose.

Again she'd said too much. "Nothing personal."

"Right. Sounds like you've had a problem with law enforcement in the past?"

She nodded. "Leaving rental properties when our mother couldn't pay the rent made our family cautious around anyone in uniform."

"Tough way to live as a kid," he said, climbing down from the buggy.

"Some folks have it worse."

He nodded. "You're right."

A cold wind blew from the mountain and made her shiver. She adjusted the cape and was grateful for Lucas's strong arms when he helped her down.

She glanced at the house.

Was anyone home? The child had disappeared. Or had she been a figment of Hannah's imagination?

The girl had reminded her of Sarah when she was four years old and left alone too often when Miriam and Hannah were at school and their mother had to work. Hannah should have done more to protect her sister.

Now Sarah was gone.

Hannah's heart weighed heavy as she and Lucas climbed the steps to the front porch. He moved in front of her and knocked on the door.

He rapped again and then turned to study the fields and pastures. His gaze brightened. He tapped her arm and pointed. "Someone's coming from the field."

She turned to see a man dressed in the Amish waistcoat and black felt hat.

Lucas left the porch and met him in the drive. Hannah followed then stepped back a few feet, unsure if she would be welcomed. At least Lucas looked the part, whether he was true Amish or not.

Glancing down at the blue calf-length dress and

black cape, she realized her mistake. She looked Amish, as well.

"Yah?" The farmer eyed Lucas and ignored Hannah. Perhaps women were to be seen and not heard, just like the children, as Lucas had mentioned.

He extended his hand. The farmer hesitated and then accepted the handshake.

"I'm Lucas Grant. I work for Fannie Stoltz at the Amish Inn. She sends her greetings."

"I do not know your face."

Lucas nodded as if understanding the farmer's confusion. "I have not lived long in the mountains. Fannie has given me a job and the community has accepted me, for which I am grateful."

"You are here for a reason?"

Hannah appreciated the Amish's way to cut to the chase. They didn't waste time on idle chitchat.

Lucas motioned Hannah forward. "I am here with Hannah Miller. Her mother was killed on the mountain two months ago. Her sisters were kidnapped. Perhaps you have heard of this?"

The farmer's expression never changed.

"There is speculation," Lucas continued, "that your daughter's disappearance could be tied to what happened to the Miller family."

Mr. Glick pursed his lips. "I have already talked to the police."

"Yes, sir. I'm sure you have, but the police will not share the information with us. You can understand Hannah's concern and her desire to learn more about what happened to her sisters."

Mr. Glick blinked but refused to respond.

"Could you tell us about the young man Rosie was seeing?"

The farmer's gaze darkened. "I do not need to talk about my daughter. Talking will not bring her back."

"Sir, she may have been involved with the same people who captured Hannah's sister. If so, the women may be together. The more we can learn about what happened to Rosie, the better able we'll be to find both of them."

"Rosie is gone." The father's voice was devoid of inflection.

"You probably think she left of her own volitions, of her own choice, but that might not be the case, sir. Rosie could have been kidnapped. If so, we need to find her."

The door to the house opened and a woman stepped onto the front porch. Her brown dress hung loose over her bony shoulders. Her face was drawn tight and a kerchief covered her head and tied under her chin.

"Tell them, Wayne. Rosie was a good girl. She would not leave without telling me where she was going."

The husband did not respond to his wife's plea.

"I told you of my dream," she pressed.

He stared at his wife. "We do not believe in dreams, Emma."

"And what of scripture? Has not *Gott* worked through dreams?"

"He does not work in that way today."

Hannah stepped forward, hearing the pain in the woman's voice. "Mrs. Glick, I believe in dreams."

A flicker of hope washed over the woman's face. "I saw her. I saw Rosie. She was crying for me to find her."

Hannah glanced at Mr. Glick. “Sir, if we can track the boyfriend, we might be able to find your daughter.”

Glick’s eyes narrowed. “The police have not found her.”

“The police initially thought she had run off with Will MacIntosh,” Hannah tried to explain. “I doubt they put much effort into the investigation.”

“*Yah*, it is only when the *Englischer* women are attacked that they think about the needs of my daughter.”

Mr. Glick’s comment had merit.

Lucas stepped closer. “I don’t know how the police operate here, but I do know that the sheriff has been in the hospital with a gunshot wound and the sheriff’s office is staffed by an older deputy and a few new hires. The deputies may have tried their best, but their best might not be good enough.”

“Tell them.” Mrs. Glick moved toward her husband and grabbed his arm. “Tell them about the man.”

Mr. Glick swallowed as if the words were stuck in his throat. “Rosie was a good girl. One day I found her wearing a necklace of shiny beads. She did not think I had seen them, and she tried to tuck them into her dress. The boy had given them to her.”

“Will MacIntosh?”

He nodded.

“Will lived on the county road not far from here. The police said she had run off with him. The neighbors said they had seen them together. He lived alone and worked at the lodge.”

“What happened to him?”

“I went to his trailer. His things were still there, but he was gone. I found the beads he had given Rosie broken on the ground outside. They had hurried away and had not taken time to pack. He lived over the county line in Petersville. The police there did not think anything of them leaving. I told them Rosie was a good daughter who would not do such a thing, but they told me I was naive and did not realize how a teen would want something other than the Amish way."

"What about the sheriff in Willkommen?" Lucas asked.

"He was more interested, but he said it wasn't his jurisdiction."

Hannah had thought the father unfeeling at first, but she caught a glimpse of the pain he carried.

"I do not understand," Glick continued. "A sheriff who would not search for a girl no matter who was in charge of the investigation."

Lucas nodded. "Once the sheriff is released from rehab, I'll see what he has to say. Perhaps one of his deputies will talk to you again."

Mr. Glick shook his head. "I do not wish to talk to anyone."

He took his wife's arm. "Come, Emma. We must go inside."

"But, Wayne."

He motioned her forward. She glanced at Hannah, pain written on her face. Then, like a dutiful wife, she followed her husband up the steps. He entered the house. Mrs. Glick hesitated for a moment and then glanced at them over her shoulder.

"Find Rosie," she said, her voice almost a whisper. "Find my daughter."

Mr. Glick's reaction troubled Lucas. He had, no doubt, been questioned too many times already and saw no point in revealing facts about his daughter to anyone again. The pain both parents felt had to be heart-wrenching.

Mrs. Glick's desire to obey her husband, as was the Amish way, seemed to conflict with her heart that had to be broken.

"I wonder if Mrs. Glick knows more than she was willing to share," Lucas said as Daisy pulled the buggy onto the dirt road and headed toward the paved blacktop.

"Information her husband didn't want her to share." Hannah shook her head with regret. "Why are Amish men so insensitive to their wives' feelings?"

"It might seem that way, especially today, but remember Mr. Glick is trying to protect his daughter's reputation and his family's privacy. He's been interrogated by the Petersville police. Their tactics may have been cold and callous, and even more so, considering the circumstances. Then if he repeated everything to the Willkommen sheriff without any good coming from either branch of law enforcement, he may have lost trust in the *Englisch* ways."

Hannah nodded. "When you say it like that, I can almost see his point and take his side. Yet nothing can be done if we don't know more about the young man who showed an interest in their daughter."

"Deputy Gainz provided directions to the county road, and Mr. Glick mentioned that MacIntosh lived in a trailer. When I first moved here, I took my buggy over most of this area to get to know the terrain, including the county road. I seem to recall seeing a few trailers."

He glanced at Hannah to make certain she would

agree to his plan. "We could look for a mailbox that might bear the kid's last name. MacIntosh isn't common around these parts. Most surnames are either German or Amish. A Scottish name might stand out or be remembered by one of the neighbors."

"It's worth a try."

He nodded. "The county road isn't far."

In less time than Lucas had expected, the sign for the road appeared on the left. "The turnoff's less than two miles from the Glick farm," he noted. "An easy walk, especially for an Amish girl used to hoofing it around the county."

"Did I tell you that I don't like this guy, whoever he is?"

Lucas nodded in agreement. "I don't like anyone who preys on women."

A small clapboard house sat back from the road. Lucas slowed as they passed the mailbox. "Koenig means 'king' in German," Lucas said, referring to the name stenciled on the box.

"A far cry from MacIntosh."

Continuing on, they passed a number of houses without names on the mailboxes.

Lucas was starting to feel discouraged. "We'll go a bit farther and then turn around."

"There." Hannah pointed to the right. "Behind the white house. It looks like a trailer sits back from the main structure. Let's check the mailboxes and see if we can find a name."

Pulling Daisy to a stop, Lucas peered at the two mailboxes and felt a sense of relief when he spied *MacIntosh* written on one of the boxes with what appeared to be a wide-tipped Sharpie. Someone had painted over the marker with a thin coat of white paint that failed to completely cover the ink.

"I think we've found Mr. MacIntosh's home."

Lucas pulled onto the dirt drive and slowly headed past the small house. A muscular dog with Rottweiler markings barked from the front porch.

"So much for trying to go unnoticed," Lucas grumbled.

A hand-painted sign was nailed to a tree: Trailer for Rent. Lucas turned the buggy onto the narrow path that angled toward the trailer.

Hannah glanced back at the house. "I hope the homeowner doesn't think we're trespassing."

"We'll say we're interested in renting."

Lucas pulled Daisy to a stop in front of the trailer. "Might be safer if you stay in the buggy."

She shook her head. "I'm going with you." She climbed down and hurried to join him as he neared the door.

Again she flicked her gaze back at the clapboard house. "I'm worried, Lucas."

He understood her concern. "I didn't see a No Trespassing sign. Remember we're here in hopes of renting the trailer."

A cobweb stretched across the front door. "Doesn't look like anyone's been here for some time."

He wiped the web away and knocked on the door. Hearing no one inside, he grabbed the door handle, expecting it to be locked.

The door opened.

"People in the country often forget the importance of security." He held up his hand. "Wait here, Hannah."

She grabbed his arm. "I'm not leaving your sight."

She was frightened, at least somewhat.

"Isn't it against the law to break and enter a private property?" She rubbed her hands over her arms and glanced again over her shoulder.

"That's a question for law enforcement," he answered, once again thankful she didn't know about his past.

He climbed the few stairs into the trailer and was surrounded by stale air and more cobwebs. A roach scurried underfoot. "Watch out for critters."

"Meaning—"

"Meaning anything could have taken up residence here."

He glanced at the small table and bench seats. A magazine was tossed open to one side. Lucas flipped it over, noting the name on the mailing label. William MacIntosh.

"Let's see if we can find anything the police failed to uncover." Lucas glanced around the cramped space. "If they even did a search."

While Hannah peered into the bathroom, Lucas entered the bedroom. A blanket and top sheet were strewed across the thin mattress. He walked around the bed and leaned down. Using a tissue he pulled from a box on the small side table, he lifted a white ribbon from the floor.

"One of the ties on an Amish bonnet?" she asked from the hallway.

"Maybe." He folded the tissue around the ribbon and tucked it inside his shirt.

"Anything in the bathroom?"

Hannah shook her head. "Nothing I could find."

Lucas glanced at the commode, sink and shower

before opening the kitchen drawers and cabinets. He rustled through the odds and ends, none of which provided clues to either William MacIntosh or his Amish girlfriend.

He opened the refrigerator. A half gallon of what must have been milk sat on the top shelf filled with a black rotting mass of bacteria. He checked the vegetable bin and freezer and then closed the door and turned aside to pull in a lungful of air.

Once they had searched the rest of the trailer, he motioned to Hannah. "Let's get going."

Pushing open the narrow front door, he blew out a stiff breath. His pulse raced and his gut tightened as he stared down the barrel of what appeared to be a Remington .308 rifle.

Leaving his own rifle in the buggy had been his first mistake. Placing Hannah in danger followed a close second.

"Hands in the air," the burly guy behind the rifle demanded. "Nice and slow. The rifle's loaded and, in case you didn't notice, my finger is on the trigger. Now step outside and don't try anything funny."

"I'm so sorry, sir." Hannah smiled sweetly as she followed Lucas out of the trailer, acting completely unfazed by the man or his weapon. "We are new to the area and need a place to live. I saw your sign about a trailer for rent." Her voice dripped with sincerity.

The tension in the man's neck seemed to ease. "Where're you folks from?"

"Tennessee," she answered with another warm smile. "We need lodging, but money is tight."

"I haven't cleaned up the place since the last tenant left."

Hannah batted her long lashes. The muscular guy appeared taken by her pleasant disposition and pretty face.

"If you don't mind—" Lucas pointed to the rifle. "We're not out to do any harm."

"Sorry." The landlord lowered the weapon. "I came home from work and saw the buggy."

"Our mistake," Lucas admitted. He glanced at Hannah. "As she mentioned, we are eager to find a place to live."

The guy sniffed and rubbed his jaw. "I could rent you the place starting this weekend. Soon as I get it cleaned up."

"How much would you charge per month?" Hannah asked.

The landlord quoted a figure that seemed steep, especially considering the condition of the trailer.

"The tenant must have left in a hurry," Hannah mused.

The big guy nodded. "Without paying his last month's rent."

"Any idea where he went?" She continued to press.

"No clue." The landlord looked at Lucas's wide-brimmed hat and Hannah's bonnet. "You folks Amish?"

Lucas hesitated then nodded.

"I saw an Amish girl here a few times," the guy continued. "Maybe I should have said something, but I figured it wasn't any of my business."

"How old was she?"

"Sixteen or seventeen."

Hannah glanced at Lucas. He nodded and then placed his hand on the small of her back. "If I can find work, we might be interested in renting your place."

He ushered her toward the buggy. "We'll be in touch."

"Just let me know." The landlord waved and then stepped into the trailer.

Lucas helped Hannah into the buggy and climbed in beside her. He flicked the reins, hurrying Daisy along the dirt road. They passed the white-clapboard house on the left. From the looks of the rotten soffits and peeling paint, the landlord didn't maintain his own home, either.

A dog barked.

"Look, Lucas." Hannah pointed to where the Rottweiler foraged in the underbrush. He continued to bark as if trying to get their attention.

Lucas pulled Daisy to a stop. "Stay in the buggy."

Glancing at the trailer to make sure the landlord was still inside, Lucas approached the dog, who clawed at the loosened soil and whined. Either the dog or another animal had dug a hole and had unearthed something of interest.

Moving closer, Lucas peered down at a partially uncovered shoe. A work boot that appeared to be encasing a human bone.

The hair on Lucas's neck rose.

He turned to Hannah. "Did you bring your cell phone?"

She nodded and pulled it from under her cape. "Do you need to make a call?"

"I want to take a photo of what the dog found."

She accessed the camera app and handed him the cell.

Working quickly, he snapped a series of shots and then climbed back in the buggy.

"Call Deputy Gainz." Lucas provided the number for the sheriff's office. Once they turned onto the main road, she tapped in the number and handed him the phone.

"We stopped at Will MacIntosh's trailer and found a ribbon that may be from an Amish bonnet," Lucas told the deputy once he was on the line. "A thorough search by your crime-scene folks might turn up additional evidence, but that's not the main reason I'm calling."

"Did something happen?" the deputy asked.

"The landlord has a dog. Looks like a mix of Rottweiler and some other big breed. He burrowed in the dirt and uncovered a work boot and what appears to be a human fibula."

Lucas glanced at Hannah, who was staring at him wide-eyed.

"I'll send you pictures, but you need to check it out yourself, Deputy. I'm ninety-nine-percent certain the bone isn't from a farm animal."

"What are you saying?"

"I'm saying someone killed Will MacIntosh and either dumped his body or buried it in a shallow grave directly across the path from the landlord's house."

"What about Rosie?"

"My guess is that she was kidnapped, held captive and maybe trafficked."

Lucas glanced at Hannah before he shoved the cell closer to his ear. "Or she might be dead."

Hannah could only hear one side of his conversation with the deputy, but Lucas's words chilled her. What if Rosie had been killed and buried along with her boyfriend?

An even more chilling thought played through her mind. She gasped, tears filled her eyes and she grabbed for the seat, needing something to hold on to as her world spun out of control. Only, instead of the seat, she found Lucas's hand.

"Take a deep breath." His voice was filled with concern. "Clear your mind of whatever you're thinking because I'm more than positive that they'll find the boyfriend's remains in the grave, but not Rosie's, and not your sister's, either."

She nodded and tried to do as he suggested, but she kept seeing Sarah's big eyes filled with tears the night she'd left home.

"I abandoned her." Tears streamed down Hannah's cheeks. "She thought I didn't love her and didn't care about her. Now I'm not even sure she's alive."

Hannah pulled her hand out of Lucas's grasp, wrapped her arms around her waist and bent over, unable to control her emotions.

He tugged on the reins and guided Daisy to a stop. Before she realized what had happened, his arms were around her, pulling her into his embrace. She nestled her head against his shoulder, feeling his strength and support.

The tears flowed. She cried for what had happened that night, for the terrible misunderstanding she'd had with her mother and for her unwillingness to explain the truth to Sarah. Hannah had chosen not to sully her youngest sister's relationship with their mother. In her heart, Hannah knew it had been the right thing to do, yet since then everything had turned out wrong.

"Shh," he said, his tone warm and soothing. Lucas's hand rubbed her shoulders. He rocked her like he would a child. The back-and-forth rhythm calmed her and filled her with a sense of acceptance.

"If anything happens to Sarah, I'll never forgive myself," she said, her voice raspy.

"You're not to blame for what happened."

As comforting as his words were, Lucas didn't know the truth about her past. "I left home. I left Sarah. She didn't understand."

"It was a decision you needed to make for your own well-being, Hannah. What happened on the mountain road has nothing to do with you leaving home."

"If I had remained in Tennessee, I could have insisted they stay put and not travel to Georgia."

"Are you sure? You might have agreed to the trip, as well. You could have been in the car the night it was stopped."

She shook her head. "You're wrong, Lucas."

"What could have happened isn't important, Hannah. What matters is that you stay strong. You're not at fault. Two men captured your sisters. Miriam was able to escape. Sarah is still being held, but we'll find her."

"No one has found Rosie Glick."

"Because law enforcement mistakenly thought she had run off with her boyfriend."

"She could be dead."

"She could also be alive," Lucas countered. "If this group is trafficking women, they want to keep the girls alive. That's a good thing. We just need to find them."

"There's nothing to go on."

"Not yet, but something will break now that law enforcement realizes that the two disappearances may be connected. If we find Rosie, we might find Sarah, as well."

Hannah closed her eyes for a long moment and willed her mind to clear. She couldn't think of what might be. Just as Lucas had said, she had to remain optimistic and focused on the present.

Easier said than done.

"Let's go back to the inn." He squeezed her shoulder and relaxed his hold as she pulled out of his grasp. "You'll be safer there."

For all her life, Hannah had never known anyone who was totally focused on her welfare. Not until she had met Lucas. She felt secure with him.

But she had also felt secure with Brian. Then she'd done some investigating on her own and had found out the truth about him that was both painful and humiliating. She'd been such a fool.

Maybe God was giving her a second chance, although Lucas was hesitant to talk about his past. Maybe he was hiding from something, as well. Perhaps they were alike in that way. She wouldn't give voice to her mistakes, and she was afraid to ask him to reveal the truth about his own.

She couldn't take any more disappointment. Not today after she'd found comfort in his arms. Hannah would rather live in the moment.

If only she could.

Chapter Eleven

Hannah was heavyhearted when they returned to the inn. The fresh air had been invigorating and she enjoyed the side-to-side rhythm of the buggy over the roadway and the sound of the horse's hooves clip-clopping on the pavement, but she kept thinking of the two young women gone missing.

Lucas pulled to a stop in front of the Amish Store, where the mechanic was standing.

"How'd the wheel work?" Calvin asked, glancing at the back of the buggy.

"No problems. You did a good job."

"You've got a good horse and a good driver. That makes a difference." He glanced at Hannah and tipped his head. "Afternoon, ma'am."

She smiled in return but didn't speak, wondering if the kindly gentleman recognized her. He wasn't saying and she wouldn't ask.

"We've got a new guest," the mechanic said.

"Oh?"

Hannah's pulse quickened fearing who might have moved into the B and B.

"You know Sheriff Kurtz? He was getting rehab in the Willkommen nursing home, but they released him today. Fannie said he's not strong enough to be on his own, so she insisted he come here for a week or two."

"Fannie's a good woman," Lucas said as he flicked his gaze to the inn. "I need to talk to the sheriff. What room's he in?"

"Room three," Calvin replied. "The room on the corner."

Where Hannah had stayed.

She stole another glance at Calvin, but his attention was once again focused on the wheel he had fixed. Perhaps she need not worry about anyone at the inn questioning her identity.

The horse obeyed the flick of Lucas's wrist and headed across the property and back to the barn located near the Amish homes.

Hannah kept her head down lest they pass anyone, still concerned she might be recognized. She didn't want questioning eyes on her, especially after the young woman had passed the note to Hector yesterday.

"What about Belinda?" she asked.

Lucas leaned closer. "I'll talk to her when she comes back to work tomorrow."

"Are you sure people won't recognize me?"

"I don't think you need to worry, Hannah."

Easy enough for him to say. But she was worried. Even more so after stopping by Will MacIntosh's trailer.

"Lucas, are you sure the bone you saw was human?"

He hesitated before responding. "I know it upset you, but MacIntosh probably got too cocky or maybe he no longer wanted to be involved in whatever was happening. He might have attempted to shove his weight around. Somebody wanted to teach him a lesson."

"The lesson went too far." Hannah shivered not from the cold but from the thought of a man being murdered.

The road turned and in the distance the two Amish homes were visible. Fannie's house looked warm and inviting set against the mountain range in the distance and the low foothills.

Cattle grazed in the pasture and two deer nibbled on bushes at the far end of the landscaped area that surrounded the inn. Hannah glanced at the tall windows in the dining room, seeing the twinkling lights. Was the sheriff there, enjoying a meal? If so, would he want information about her past and perhaps do his own investigation? What would Fannie and Lucas think of her if they found out about her father?

She clutched her hands together and bit down on her lip, trying to stem the worry that bubbled up within her. How foolish to think she could hide the truth from anyone.

"Coming here was a mistake," she said aloud even before she realized the words had escaped her mouth.

"You're tired and worried. Probably hungry and cold, too. You'll feel better once we get to Fannie's house."

"I'm not sure, Lucas. If it weren't for me, the guy in flannel wouldn't be hanging around. He's after me for whatever reason and he's putting everyone else in danger. That's my fault."

"No one is accusing you, Hannah."

"Thank you for that, but I know the peace and quiet of this mountain inn has changed. I'm worried about innocent people who might get hurt."

"So far the guy hasn't harmed anyone except you."

"And Simon."

Lucas nodded. "You're right. Simon was injured, but I blame it on the man who attacked him. He's the one who's stirring up trouble, not you. You're here to find your sisters."

"What were they doing on the mountain?" She dropped her head into her hand and sighed. "I can't understand why they traveled to Willkommen."

"The deputy mentioned that they wanted to find your mother's estranged sister, but maybe the sheriff will have more information."

She lifted her head, feeling a swell of encouragement. "Do you think so?"

"We can talk to him if he feels like having visitors. He was involved in the investigation of your mother's death. He's bound to know more than the deputy."

"But he probably won't divulge Miriam's whereabouts."

"He'll know if she's safe and that's the most important thing, right? If she's with Abram Zook as people have mentioned, then you probably don't have to worry. He'll take care of her."

Lucas pulled the mare to a stop at the back door of Fannie's house. He climbed to the ground and helped Hannah down, his hands holding her tight and secure.

"Thank you," she said as her feet touched the ground.

His hands remained around her waist for a long moment. He stared down at her, question in his gaze. Behind him, the rays of the sun bathed both of them in an ethereal glow that seemed surreal.

Being in Lucas's arms was so unlike anything she

had experienced before. She didn't want to move lest he drop his hands and step away from her.

She lifted her face expectantly. He lowered his lips to hers and time stood still. Everything that had happened in her life—all the darkness and pain—faded away. For one sweet instant, she was totally enveloped in goodness and hope and light.

The kitchen door opened. Hannah's heart plummeted.

"There you are." Fannie stepped onto the porch. "I was beginning to wonder if you would ever return."

A sense of loss filled Hannah as Lucas moved back and grabbed the reins. "We ran into a bit of a problem."

"Oh, no."

"Hannah can tell you about it while I unharness the mare and get her settled in the barn."

Only Hannah didn't know if she could talk about anything, except how much she wanted to return to Lucas's arms.

"Tell me, dear, all about what happened." Fannie motioned her inside. "I have water on the stove if you'd like a cup of tea."

With a nod, Hannah pulled in a fortifying breath. She needed to focus on the present instead of a handsome man who made her dream of what could be.

"Tea sounds perfect," she told Fannie. Hopefully the warm beverage would calm her racing pulse and make her forget how much she had wanted Lucas to kiss her again.

After hanging the cape and bonnet on a peg just inside the kitchen, she helped Fannie fix a pot of tea and then recounted what they had found as she sipped a cup of the inviting brew.

"Will the coroner be able to tell if the remains are from the young man?" Fannie asked after Hannah had shared what had happened.

"I believe the medical examiner or even the Georgia Bureau of Investigation will get involved," Lucas said as he entered the kitchen and overheard Fannie's comment. "The forensic folks will be better able to make an identification."

"That poor young man," Fannie said.

"He was probably involved in illegal activity, Fannie. Hopefully we'll find out more about him once the results come back from the GBI."

"The tea's hot," Fannie told him. "There's coffee, as well."

Lucas poured a cup of coffee and nodded his gratitude as he took a long swig. His gaze met Hannah's, and the memory of his kiss made her face flush.

"The temperature's dropping," he said. Then he glanced away as if not realizing what that kiss had meant to her. "I thought we could expect warmer weather, but you can't fool with Mother Nature."

"Spring will be here soon enough," Fannie assured him. "New buds are on the Bradford pear trees."

"They're always so beautiful," Hannah said wistfully, recalling the flowering trees in Knoxville that dotted the landscape. "I'm sure spring is lovely here at the inn."

A heaviness tugged at her heart. She wouldn't stay long enough to see the trees and flowers bloom. She would be in Macon or in some other small town, trying to make a life for herself.

"Did you talk to the sheriff?" Lucas asked Fannie.

"*Yah.* He does not want to be coddled, but he is not

as strong as he thinks. The man can be stubborn." Fannie smiled impishly. "He will hurt himself if he pushes too hard. I told him he could not do any work for the first week he is here. He did not like that, but it was the only way I would agree to having him stay with us."

"You and the sheriff are friends?" Hannah asked.

Fannie smiled knowingly. "Yes, for many years. He was new to Willkommen when we first met. My father did not think he was someone with whom I should spend time."

There was a longing in Fannie's voice that Hannah had not heard before. Then just that quickly, the Amish woman wiped her hands on a napkin and rose. "You have reminded me that I must check on him." She glanced at Hannah. "Lucas has chores, but you can join me. I think you want to talk to him about your sisters. You could also tell him what you found today."

"I'm..." She glanced at Lucas.

His gaze softened. "You don't have to be fearful of the sheriff."

"Of course not. I'm not afraid. It's just that—"

She didn't want either of them to learn the truth about her past and about the man who had given her life. Her gut tightened. She rubbed her hand over her abdomen, hoping to stem the rumble that ensued.

"You are tired and would perhaps want to rest?" Fannie offered.

"Yes, that's it exactly. I just need to shut my eyes for a few minutes."

Hannah pushed away from the table, carried the cup to the sink and left it on the sideboard, and then hurried upstairs to get away from both their questioning gazes. Hannah needed time to forget Lucas's kiss and gather strength and the wherewithal to face the sheriff.

She didn't like law enforcement, never had, and especially not since her mother had threatened to call the authorities. Hannah needed to run away and pretend she had never been involved with her mother or her criminal dad.

Lucas was worried about Hannah. Today had almost been her undoing. He and Fannie left her to rest, locked the doors to the house and hurried to the inn. Fannie scurried into the kitchen to help with preparations for the evening meal while Lucas knocked at the sheriff's door.

"Sheriff Kurtz, it's Lucas Grant. If you're not too tired, I'd like to talk to you."

The door opened and the sheriff, looking a bit older and more stooped than he had the last time they had met, extended his hand. "Good to see you, Lucas. Come in. Fannie said you've been involved in a new situation."

Lucas closed the door and gave the sheriff time to return to the easy chair in the corner by the bed. "Draw up that other chair," the older man said, pointing to a straight-back chair near the door. "I never knew recuperation from a gunshot wound could take so long. Guess it says a lot for my age."

"Sir, from what I heard, you took a close-range hit to the abdomen. The surgeons had a lot of work to do."

"I'm not faulting their ability, mind you. I just don't appreciate being laid up so long. I expected to be back at my job by now, but the docs insist I need more time to heal."

Gingerly he rubbed his side. "I have to tell you they're right. No way I could sit at a desk or drive around in my squad car the way I'm feeling. Fannie invited me to stay at the inn. She claims three good meals a day and fresh air will have me back on my feet in no time."

"She's a thoughtful woman, and I know she's been worried about you. We all have."

"Appreciate it, Lucas. Coming close to death as the docs said I did makes a man look at life anew, if you know what I mean."

Lucas thought of his own gunshot wound. The ache in his leg was minor compared to what the sheriff had experienced. Still, Lucas could relate. His own inability to regain his strength had been a proverbial thorn in his flesh.

"You know, Fannie took me in when I was struggling," Lucas shared. "She gave me a dose of tough love when I started feeling sorry for myself. That coupled with her chicken soup got me on the right track. You'll be feeling strong in no time."

"Just so I don't get used to the soft life."

Lucas smiled. "I don't know if I've ever heard the Amish life called 'soft.'"

The sheriff laughed heartily and then sobered. "You may have heard my story. I was raised Amish in Ethridge, Tennessee, but decided to leave the faith and moved to Georgia."

The sheriff's words took Lucas by surprise. "I'm doing just the opposite. After working here for the last eleven months and with Fannie's love for *Gott*, as she says, rubbing off on me, I'm considering seeking baptism."

"Have you talked to the bishop?"

Lucas shook his head. "Not recently. We talked a while back."

"From the sound of your voice, I take it the talk didn't go well."

Lucas shrugged. "He asked some direct questions and I answered truthfully. Seems I have a few issues to resolve before he can accept me as a member of his community."

The sheriff narrowed his eyes. "You told me you were a cop. That's not the easiest life, as we both know. Most folks thought I was crazy growing up Amish and then going into law enforcement."

"The two don't seem to coincide, do they, sir?"

"Not a bit. But there was something inside me that wanted to help. To make order out of some of the disorder I saw around me. I wanted that peaceful life for the folks I knew. No better way, in my opinion, than to be an officer of the peace."

Lucas appreciated the sheriff's take on law enforcement. Too many people thought cops went into criminal justice to carry a gun and order people around, which was the farthest thing from the truth.

"I appreciated you coming to me when you first arrived in this area, Lucas, and telling me about Savannah and the trouble you had experienced there. I told you then that I was sorry about your partner's death and knew you carried a heavy burden." The older man leaned closer. "You weren't at fault—I'm sure of that."

"She called me with information she'd received from a dubious source who I thought was taking her for a ride. We hadn't been able to find anything in two months. I doubted the new intel was legit."

"But she went in without you."

Lucas nodded. "She told me she wouldn't. Then the next thing I get a phone call telling me she's in trouble. I got there too late."

The sheriff steepled his fingers. "We all make mistakes, Lucas, although the mistake was your partner's and not yours. She should have waited for backup. But then, that's easy to say all these months later. I'm sorry for your loss."

Lucas nodded. "Thank you, sir. I thought I was over it. Then…" He hesitated. "Then I stumbled upon Hannah Miller in the woods."

Lucas told the sheriff what had happened and explained about the subsequent attacks and what they had found at Rosie Glick's boyfriend's trailer. "The two cases seem connected."

The sheriff rubbed his jaw. "You know we thought Rosie had run off. Hate to think we got that wrong and that she's been held captive all this time, especially if she's been caught in a trafficking operation."

"Did you talk to Miriam Miller? Hannah's worried about her whereabouts."

"She's safe. I've got an address to contact her somewhere in my things. As soon as I find it, I'll pass it on. Assure Hannah that her sister's with Abram Zook and he'll take care of her."

"I'll tell Hannah. What about Sarah? Supposedly she was carted off by a red-haired man."

"Which is what Miriam told us. I've had people looking for him. So far he hasn't surfaced." The sheriff shook his head with regret and then raised his gaze to Lucas. "What did you uncover in the Savannah operation?"

"A shipping tycoon by the name of Vipera. It's thought that he buys young, good-looking women and ships them out of the country on his cargo ships."

"Takes them to foreign countries?"

"Some, and some are taken to his private island where he entertains business people and government types from foreign countries."

"He needs to be stopped," the sheriff said.

"My thoughts exactly, but then someone wanted me out of the picture in Savannah. My partner was set up and they tried to get me, as well. I was politely told to turn in my badge and leave town."

"Seems the tycoon has pull, even with law enforcement."

"That's how I saw it. I had been wounded in a run-in with some of Vipera's goons and knew there was nothing I could do to change my past. I had to make a new future."

Again the sheriff stared long and hard at Lucas. "I think I know what caused the bishop to question whether you should join the Amish faith. He doesn't understand a man's need to bring the guilty to justice. Sometimes there's a fine line between justice and vindication."

Lucas didn't respond but he was relieved to know the sheriff understood. Lucas wanted to apprehend the thug who'd killed his partner even if retribution wasn't the Amish way. He also wanted to nab Vipera.

As much as he wanted to join the Amish faith, Lucas knew he'd be hard-pressed to turn the other cheek even if that was what the bishop demanded before he could gain entrance into the faith.

The sheriff narrowed his gaze. "Now tell me about this man who came after Hannah."

Lucas provided a description and recounted everything that had happened, which brought him back to today. "Rosie Glick's boyfriend worked at the lodge. Have you heard anything about that place?"

"Funny you should mention it. One of my deputies was in a vehicle accident the day Miriam escaped from her captor. He's been on a ventilator since then and hasn't been able to talk. According to his wife, he suspected something was going on at the lodge. High rollers from Atlanta and points south come in for a little hunting and fishing. My deputy suspected other things were happening, as well. The men rarely brought their wives and families, so I'll let you put the pieces together."

"Did he find proof of his suspicions?"

"Not that I know of, but his car was struck by a delivery van. The only info I have is that a small snake was on the side of the truck's paneling."

Lucas leaned forward in the chair, his pulse kicking up a notch. "Are you sure about the snake?"

"Deputy Garner spelled out a message, and I determined he was trying to say 'snake.' Could have been wrong. I'm not sure. Why?"

"It's a long shot, sir, but as I mentioned, the shipping tycoon's last name is Vipera, which is a genus of venomous snakes. A coiled snake is part of his shipping logo. In fact, the night my partner was shot, she texted me, saying she had seen the snake."

"The tycoon?"

"Actually, two of his men. Vipera has a vast wealth and lots of holdings, including the Pine Lodge Mountain Resort. That's what drew me to this area initially. I was trying to find anything that might have bearing on my partner's death, but the trail went cold soon after I got here. In my search for evidence, I left no stone unturned but could find nothing that implicated Vipera in anything illegal on this end. The lodge is run by a group of managers, and Vipera has no involvement in the day-to-day operation."

The sheriff pursed his lips. "Yet if women have been taken around here and if the same thing has happened in Savannah, then there could be a very real trafficking connection."

Lucas nodded. "Which might be the link I was looking for."

"The problem is that I'm short-staffed, Lucas, or I'd send someone in to check out the lodge."

"The resort has been closed for renovation and is scheduled to open this weekend. Fannie delivers there. Pies, fresh-baked bread, produce. They placed an order for tomorrow. I'll make a delivery and check out what's going on."

"Everything will be under wraps, Lucas. I doubt they'll show any dirty laundry. They wouldn't be foolish enough to expose themselves."

"Sometimes the laundry is on the line and in full view, especially in an Amish area." He rose and extended his hand. "Thanks for giving me this time to talk, Sheriff."

The sheriff struggled to stand. "Wait a minute." He walked to a small suitcase beside his bed, unzipped the case and dug inside. "I know you're living Amish, but if you place yourself in danger, you'll need protection."

The sheriff pulled out a Glock, along with a holster and an extra magazine. "You might need this."

Lucas shook his head. "I left all that in Savannah. The only weapon I have is a .30-30 for hunting deer in season. I took it with me today because of Hannah but—"

"I understand, and that's commendable, yet you need to be realistic." Sheriff Kurtz held out the weapon. "Take it or I won't give you permission to help with this investigation."

"I'm not involved with the investigation, Sheriff. I'm trying to find two women who have disappeared."

"Then take it for the women."

Lucas thought of the firestorm he had walked into in Savannah. He hadn't expected the shooter. He hadn't expected being injured. He hadn't expected the surgery and recuperation. Then he thought of Olivia, who hadn't had backup and who had been slaughtered on a dock in the dead of night.

He raised his gaze to the sheriff, whose open expression told Lucas that he understood the former cop's conflict. "Thanks, sir." Lucas accepted the firearm. "I'll take the Glock, but I pray I won't have to use it."

"Stay safe," the sheriff cautioned.

Lucas nodded then hurried from the room, closing the door behind him.

The gun was heavy in his hand. He hadn't handled a sidearm in eleven months. He used to live with one, but he'd changed.

Night had fallen by the time he left the inn and hurried along the path, eventually seeing Fannie's house in the distance. A light appeared in the window. Hannah was waiting for him there. She didn't know he was an ex-cop. The sheriff and Fannie were the only ones who knew.

Lucas couldn't be law enforcement and Amish. He couldn't carry a gun and be Amish. He couldn't embrace the *plain* way and be baptized into the faith and track down a killer.

But a killer was on the loose and he could have ties to the man who was coming after Hannah.

Amish or cop?

Lucas didn't know which he wanted to be.

"Hannah?" He unlocked the door and walked into the house calling her name. Only silence.

He turned and hurried back to the inn. Something didn't feel right in his gut.

Hannah? He started to run.

Chapter Twelve

"I'm glad you had a nice nap and then came to help me with the sheriff's dinner," Fannie said as she carried the meal tray and walked next to Hannah. The two women headed along the hallway to room three, the room where Hannah had stayed two nights ago.

"I wonder if the sheriff has a minute to talk to me about my sisters." Hannah kept her voice low so as to not disturb the other guests.

"We can ask him, dear. Samuel is a very considerate man, although I know he might be tired after leaving rehab."

Before entering the far wing, Fannie stopped in her tracks and sighed. "Silly me. I forgot to bring his coffee." She turned and placed the tray in Hannah's hands. "Take this to Samuel while the food is still hot. I'll get the coffee from the kitchen."

Before Hannah could offer to run the errand, Fannie was halfway down the hall, heading toward the dining area.

Hannah walked quickly to room three, stopped at

the door and knocked lightly. "Sheriff? I have your dinner tray."

She heard a muffled response. Believing he had invited her to enter, she pushed open the door, stepped into the room and gasped.

A man stood over the sheriff. One hand was around his throat and the other was fisted as if to strike a blow.

"No!" Hannah screamed.

The man shoved past her, knocking the tray out of her hands. "Get outta my way."

She fell back against the doorjamb. The tray and its contents clattered onto the floor, the china plate shattering into tiny shards of porcelain.

Hannah struggled to her feet and stumbled toward the easy chair next to the bed where the older gentleman sat slumped, his head on his chest.

She touched his shoulder, fearing the worst.

A sound at the door made her turn. Was the assailant coming back to do more harm?

"Hannah?"

"Lucas, help me. The sheriff's been hurt."

Lucas was beside her, searching for the sheriff's pulse. "He's got a heartbeat. Come on, Sheriff. We need you to come to."

"It happened so fast," Hannah told him.

"Did you see the attacker?" Lucas asked.

She nodded, trying to find her voice.

"Who was it?"

"Oh, Lucas..." She gasped. "It was the same man who came after me. The man in the blue flannel shirt."

Lucas hadn't done enough, and Hannah had been placed in danger again. Thankfully the sheriff regained consciousness and seemed to be all right in spite of a blow to his jaw.

"The guy didn't expect me to fight back—that was evident," the sheriff said as he held an ice pack to his face. "He came up behind me and called me Hannah."

He looked at Fannie, sitting close by holding ice against her elbow. The assailant pushed her to the floor as he ran down the hallway and out the door.

"He kept saying 'Where is she?'" Fannie shared.

Lucas turned to look at Hannah, her hand resting on the older woman's shoulder.

"It's my fault," Hannah moaned. "He was looking for me. This is the room I stayed in the first night at the inn. The Hispanic man had delivered the note and the young Amish girl was involved. Belinda must have told him where I was staying." She looked down at Fannie. "The keys were hanging in the entryway."

"We changed that after you were attacked. Now the staff has to come to me to get a key."

"But he got in here somehow."

Lucas went to the bathroom and saw the open window. "He climbed in through here. The screen's been removed."

"That's my fault," the sheriff admitted. "The rehab facility was so warm. I always sleep better in a cold room. I opened the window to enjoy the fresh county air."

Lucas pointed to the wall. "From now on regulate the heat with the thermostat and keep the windows shut and locked. The open window was an invitation to him. With the curtains drawn and the lights out, he probably thought he could surprise Hannah if she was in the room or wait until she returned."

Although still shaken, Fannie excused herself and hurried to the kitchen to help with the evening meal. Deputy Gainz arrived soon after the sheriff notified him of the attack, and he and Lucas walked outside to survey the exterior of the inn.

"Removing the screen wouldn't have been difficult," Lucas admitted after they found the screen discarded in the bushes. "The open window allowed an easy entry, although the sill is about eight feet off the ground."

Gainz pointed to something in the underbrush.

Lucas neared and bent low. Two wooden boxes had been shoved under the bushes.

"My guess is the guy piled the boxes one atop the other," the deputy said. "That would give him enough leverage to hoist himself into the bathroom."

"Check the boxes for prints?"

"That's a good idea. If he's ever been arrested, we'll have him on file." Gainz glanced at the driveway and main entrance to the property. "Any idea where he could have parked his car?"

"He drives an SUV," Lucas reminded the deputy. "There's a back road that runs along the rear of the property. Easy enough to cut through the woods to get to his car and then head into Willkommen."

"Did you hear a vehicle leave the area?"

"No." Lucas shook his head. "But at the time, I wasn't listening for a car. I was trying to make sure the sheriff was all right."

"We've got a BOLO out for a dark Tahoe, although the guy could have more than one vehicle. I'm just glad the sheriff is okay. We're ready to have him back at his desk. I didn't sign on to be the head of the sheriff's department. Samuel was elected. Folks trust him. They know he'll do his best to keep them safe."

"You're doing a good job, Deputy Gainz."

He shook his head and laughed. "I can warm the seat of his chair, but that's about all. Ned Quigley's the expert. He's young and smart. He's got the ability and desire to run the sheriff's office, but he's at GBI headquarters, which I believe I mentioned when you stopped by the office. I had hoped Ned would be back by now."

"Does he know what happened?"

The deputy shook his head. "He's got enough on his plate without me calling and talking about our problems here."

"You might want to contact him in case he has the choice to stay or come back to Willkommen."

"I'll do that in the morning."

Lucas wondered if the deputy was truly interested in the new, younger deputy being called in. From what Lucas had been told, Gainz had worked for the town as long as most folks could remember. Sometimes a newcomer was hard to accept.

"We'll lock down the inn tonight and rig up some type of security on the main door," the deputy shared. "Everyone will have to go through the front entrance. It might be inconvenient for the staff, but we'll know who's coming and going. I don't want anyone else injured."

Especially not Hannah.

"You're certain Miriam is safe?" Hannah asked the sheriff as Lucas and the deputy returned to the guest bedroom.

"About as certain as I can be," Samuel said with a nod. "Abram won't let anything happen to your sister."

"And he's a good man?"

The sheriff smiled. "I've known him all his life, Hannah. Abram will protect your sister."

"You've known him all his life?" She repeated his comment, her brow furrowed. "I don't understand."

"Abram's my nephew."

"You're Amish?"

The sheriff laughed and shook his head. "No, but I grew up Amish. Ethridge, Tennessee, was my home."

Hannah glanced at Lucas. He saw the question in her eyes.

"If Abram needed a safe place to hole up," she said to Samuel, "would that safe place be Ethridge?"

The expression on the sheriff's face was enough to make Lucas realize that Hannah may have uncovered Miriam's whereabouts.

"Ethridge would be a safe destination," the sheriff acknowledged with a knowing smile. "If someone needed a place to hole up. I'll rummage through my things and try to find that address just as soon as my head clears a bit more."

Lucas's heart melted at the relief he read on Hannah's face. He glanced at the deputy, who was studying the window in the bathroom and hadn't heard the discussion. Just as well. Although the deputy was trustworthy, the fewer people who knew how to find Miriam, the better.

"What about Sarah?" Hannah asked.

The sheriff shook his head. "The new deputy who took over while I was having my surgery did everything he could to find her."

"He's the guy at the GBI now?" Lucas asked.

The sheriff nodded. "That's right. Ned Quigley. He briefed me on what he had found before he left for Atlanta. I'm sorry to say nothing has materialized on Sarah." The sheriff's eyes were heavy with regret. "No one has information about a red-haired man and no one has seen your sister."

"Did Quigley have a picture of her?"

The sheriff nodded. "One of the guys involved in the carjacking had pictures of both women on his smartphone."

"He also had a picture of Miriam?" Lucas asked.

The sheriff nodded again. "It appeared their hands were bound. The women were seated on a chair, their hair was disheveled and they looked upset."

"Had the criminal sent the photos to someone else?" Lucas asked.

"All text and email messages had been deleted from the phone. Quigley took the mobile device to GBI headquarters. Their tech folks will try to uncover any contacts that might have left a cyber trail."

"Could you contact Quigley and check on the GBI's progress?"

The sheriff stared at Lucas for a long moment and then nodded, no doubt making the connection. "You're hoping they might find a trail that incriminates the shipping magnate in Savannah?"

"That would make everything fit together, don't you think?"

The sheriff nodded. "You never know what the GBI might be able to find."

"I don't understand," Hannah said.

Although Lucas didn't want to go into his past, Hannah needed to know. “I lived in Savannah. A shipping company there was thought to be involved in trafficking. I told the sheriff that it would be a huge coincidence, but the two operations might be connected.”

“Although Georgia’s not that big of a state,” Samuel mused.

“Still,” Hannah said, “it does seem unlikely.”

“Let me know if you find out anything,” Lucas said to the sheriff.

“I’ll post a guard tonight.” Gainz stepped back into the room.

Samuel groaned. “Do we have anyone to spare?”

The deputy jabbed a thumb at his chest. “You’ve got me. I may be getting close to retirement, but I can still pull surveillance and keep guard.”

“Do you need help?” Lucas asked. “I can take a shift.”

Gainz nodded. “I’ll cover the first two hours. If you want to spell me at midnight, I’ll catch a few winks then come back on at two a.m. Knowing the Amish, I’m sure some of your folks will be up by four. I’ll wake you close to that time. That will get us through the night.”

“I don’t need a babysitter,” the sheriff complained.

“No, sir, but there are other folks to think of at the inn.”

“Of course there are.” Samuel nodded. “I’m not thinking rationally.”

He wiped his hand over his eyes.

“You’re tired and need to rest.” Lucas stood. “The kitchen chores should be done and Fannie will probably be ready to return to her house. I’ll walk her home.” He glanced at Hannah. “Are you ready?”

She nodded. "What about you, Sheriff? Are you feeling okay?"

"After everything I've been through, a little scuffle and a jab to my chin isn't going to do any significant damage. You go on. We can talk tomorrow."

"How's Samuel?" Fannie asked when Hannah and Lucas entered the kitchen.

"He seems to be all right," Hannah assured her. "Although he'll probably have a sore jaw in the morning. I… I'm still so sorry."

Fannie patted Hannah's shoulder. "Stop thinking that way. You're not to blame. Is that clear?"

Fannie's stern gaze softened. "The sheriff has had worse happen to him. If he survived a gunshot to the stomach, he can survive a blow to his chin."

"Still—"

"No *stills* allowed, my little cabbage."

Hannah laughed at the older woman. "Little cabbage? Is that how you think of me?"

"It is a term of endearment." Fannie smiled. "A nickname of sorts."

"I'd rather be a brussels sprout," Hannah teased.

Fannie laughed and Lucas was relieved that both women were allowing a bit of levity to lighten their spirits.

"Ladies, your escort is ready when you are."

"Give me one more minute, Lucas. I want to ask one of the girls to take a sandwich to Samuel. I know he wouldn't feel like eating a large meal after all the excitement, but he needs something before bed."

She soon returned and Lucas helped both women with their capes.

Opening the kitchen door, he surveyed the landscape, searching for any sign of danger. Once satisfied, he motioned Hannah and Fannie forward. "Let's hurry. We'll take the rear path. Stay close, and alert me if you see anything that doesn't look right."

Overhead the moon peered between the clouds. The night air was cool and Hannah shivered. Lucas wanted to put his arm around her shoulders and draw her close, but he didn't want to embarrass her in front of Fannie. Hannah was a private woman. Plus, he needed to keep his attention on the surroundings instead of her pretty face.

Lucas had to admit that he was acting like a cop again, an undercover cop who dressed Amish. Was this why he had come to Willkommen? To protect a woman with expressive blue eyes and a sweet mouth that turned into an enticing smile?

He had to keep her safe, whether he embraced the Amish faith or not. Her life was more important than his future. Although if things worked out, his future might have bearing on her life. At least, that was his hope.

The next morning Hannah hurried down the stairs of Fannie's home and entered the kitchen just as a *rap-tap-tap* sounded at the door.

"Would you see who that is?" Fannie asked as she leaned over the stove and pulled a tray of golden muffins from the oven.

Hannah peered out the window and saw the young teen who worked at the Amish Store. His black waistcoat hung open and his felt hat sat low on his head. Shaggy blond hair curled around his neck and stuck out around his ears.

She opened the door. The cold morning air swept into the kitchen. "Come in before you let out all the heat."

The teen stepped inside, dutifully removed his hat and nodded to Fannie. "Belinda Lapp's mother said to tell you that Belinda is gone. Something happened in the night."

With a heavy sigh Fannie placed the filled muffin tin on the top of the stove. Wiping her hands on a towel, she turned to Joseph. "Do they know where she could have gone?"

The lad shrugged. "Mrs. Lapp did not tell me and I did not ask."

Yet it seemed to Hannah that the teen was holding something back. "Does Belinda have a boyfriend? Perhaps an *Englisch* boyfriend?"

The boy's shoulders slumped. "Belinda does not talk to me about boyfriends."

"Perhaps not," Hannah said. "Yet often we know more than what we've been told. Is that not right?"

Fannie nodded her agreement. "You must tell us what you know, Joseph. Belinda's well-being depends on finding her. She could be in danger."

"Danger?" The teen took a step back. "I do not think that could be."

"If this boyfriend is not a *gut* man—" Fannie stepped closer. "You remember Rosie Glick?"

He nodded. "She was my sister's age. Someone said they saw her riding in a truck last summer a few weeks after she went missing."

"A truck?" Hannah looked at Fannie. "What kind of truck?"

"The kind that makes deliveries."

"Who told you they had seen Rosie?" Fannie asked.

The teen shrugged.

Fannie leaned closer. "You are not to hold back information when asked, Joseph. This you know to be true."

He fingered his hat and glanced over his shoulder at the door as if ready to bolt. "I need to go back to the store. Mrs. Lapp tried to work, but she was worried about her daughter. Her hands could not move as fast as her mind, so she went home."

"I'll send someone to help you," Fannie assured him. "But first, tell me the name of the person who saw Rosie."

"His name is Levi Raber."

"I do not know the family. They have a home nearby?"

"On the other side of the mountain, but I do not know where. I met him at the lake last summer. He is a good fisherman. I asked him to show me the bait he used."

"And your discussion turned to Rosie Glick?"

"He asked me if I knew an Amish girl named Rosie who had left the area."

"Levi knew Rosie?" Hannah asked, trying to put the pieces together.

"He had heard about her when she first went missing. He was in town, selling his fish at the market. People were talking. He could not help but overhear."

"If he did not know Rosie, then how did he recognize her when he saw her?" Fannie asked what Hannah had been thinking.

"He had seen an Amish girl with an *Englisch* man at the lake. They were arguing. The man called her Rosie."

Fannie's brow furrowed. "What were they arguing about?"

"Levi did not tell me."

"The sheriff or one of his deputies needs to talk to Levi," Hannah said. "Does he still go to the lake?"

"I have not seen him during the winter. Perhaps he will return in summer."

"You said he saw Rosie in a truck?" Hannah prompted.

"*Yah*, but another man was with Rosie that time. He had a skinny face and pale skin and red hair."

Hannah's heart lurched. "You're sure that's what he said?"

The boy nodded. "I would not tell a lie."

"I didn't think you would." Hannah needed to find Lucas. "Did Levi say where the truck was headed?"

"It was going up the mountain toward the lodge."

"You're sure?" Hannah asked.

"That is what he said."

Hannah needed to go to the lodge. If Rosie had been seen there, Sarah might be there, as well.

Once the boy left, she turned to Fannie. "Tell me about the lodge."

"It is a resort for the wealthy. Our kitchen supplies them with fresh produce and baked goods. They often bring in guests from Atlanta and the Carolinas. Florida, too. There is hunting. They fish on the lake. There is much to interest *Englisch* men in the area."

"Meaning what, Fannie?"

"Meaning I think there may be more than hunting and fishing that attracts them now, from what Joseph has said. We must tell the sheriff."

"Lucas also needs to know."

Both women grabbed their bonnets and capes and hurried out the door, heading to the inn.

Hannah wanted to visit the lodge. Would Lucas go with her? Or would she have to go alone?

Her first priority was her sister. Hannah had to find Sarah. She had to find her now.

Chapter Thirteen

"Lucas!"

He turned. Hannah was running toward him, waving her arm to get his attention. She was breathless, her cheeks flushed. She grabbed his hand and could hardly get her words out when they met.

"Joseph knows someone who saw Rosie."

"When?"

"Last summer. On the mountain road that leads to the lodge. She was in a delivery truck." Hannah explained what the boy had shared. "The driver of the delivery van had a slender face, but here's the thing, Lucas…"

She paused, catching her breath. "The driver had red hair."

Hannah gripped his hand even more tightly. "Don't you understand? The man who took Sarah was red-haired and slender. It's the same man. The girls might be at the lodge. I'll get my car. Go there with me."

"I need to talk to Joseph before we do anything."

Together they hurried to the store. Joseph looked worried when he saw them.

"You need to tell me everything you said at Fannie's house," Lucas told the teen.

"I spoke the truth."

"I believe you, but I need more information."

Lucas took the boy into the rear of the store. Hannah joined them there. "Tell me what you learned and who told you," Lucas insisted.

The boy recounted what he had told Hannah.

"How can I find Levi?" Lucas asked when Joseph had shared everything he could remember.

"I do not know."

Frustrated by another dead end, Lucas and Hannah left the store and hurried along the path that led to the inn. When the main walkway split in a number of different directions, she stopped and pointed to the mechanic's shop. "Let's get my keys. We can take my car to the lodge."

Lucas grabbed her hand. "We can't drive there."

"What do you mean?"

"We have to go Amish."

"But—"

"We'll take the buggy, although it won't be an easy ride," he cautioned. "Fannie can get the delivery items ready while I harness Daisy."

"I'll help Fannie."

Lucas made sure both women were safely in the B and B's kitchen before he hurried to the barn. A short time later, he guided the buggy to the inn's side entrance.

Fannie helped load the buggy with the boxes filled with winter vegetables, pies, rolls and loaves of bread. "We will have cakes ready if you wait a bit."

Lucas shook his head. "We need to go now. I want to stop at Belinda's house on the way."

Fannie wrapped a loaf of bread and an apple pie in a plastic bag and handed it to Lucas. "Give this to her mother. Tell Lydia we are praying for her daughter's safety. I understand why she could not stay at work today. Tell her to come back when she can. Until then we will ask *Gott* to keep her daughter safe."

Lucas appreciated Fannie's thoughtfulness. "You have a generous heart, Fannie."

"*Yah*, and you are hoping there will be pie left when you return."

He laughed and hugged her, something he rarely did.

The older woman blushed and patted his arm. "You will have me with tears in my eyes for your thoughtfulness. Now go with *Gott* and be careful."

Fannie held out her arms for Hannah. "Be watchful, my child. And remember Amish women do not talk to strangers. Lower your gaze if you come near someone. The bonnet will protect you from being identified. Lucas will keep you safe."

The two women embraced. "Now go," Fannie said, motioning them toward the buggy.

Taking her into his arms, Lucas lifted Hannah into the seat. He couldn't help but note how light she was and how pleasing she smelled. She may be wearing Amish clothing, but she was anything but plain.

Climbing in beside her, he flipped the reins. "Let's go, Daisy."

The mare trotted along the drive and headed for the entrance. Turning onto the main road, Daisy picked up speed. Lucas's heart grew heavy as he thought of what was before them. Hopefully having Hannah accompany him to the lodge wouldn't be a mistake. She might see things he could overlook. Two sets of eyes were always better than one.

His thoughts turned to Olivia. They had been a good team and worked well together, but in the weeks before her death their relationship had changed. Another mistake he had made. He had started to see Olivia as more than a cop. He'd seen her as a woman who had woven her way into his heart.

The ride to the Lapp farm didn't take long. Turning into the drive, Lucas was overcome with a sense of sorrow. Something had happened to Belinda Lapp, he felt sure. The forlorn look on Lydia's face when she stepped onto the porch only confirmed what he was feeling. Her eyes were red. No doubt, she'd been crying.

"Fannie wanted you to have this," he said, handing her the baked goods and wishing he could do something to ease her pain.

"I could not work today because—" The woman's mouth twisted with emotion.

"Stay home as long as you need to," Lucas assured her. "Fannie understands. She sends her love and her prayers."

"She is a good woman, *yah*?"

Lydia was a good woman, too, but her daughter could have been lured into something that might prove deadly.

Lucas's gut tightened as he turned Daisy back to the main road.

Hannah's silence told him that she, too, had been touched deeply by the fear written so plainly on Lydia Lapp's tearstained face. Neither of them spoke for some time and the significance of another young woman gone missing hung heavy between them. Perhaps, Lucas silently mused, it was better if they didn't give voice—at least for a while—to the reality of what had been happening in this once peaceful mountain paradise.

The falling temperature brought both of them back to the present. Hannah wrapped a lap blanket around their legs, then tugged the bonnet down around her forehead and clutched the black cape tightly across her shoulders.

The day was cold and the sky overhead looked ominous.

"It might rain," he warned, grateful for something to talk about that didn't have anything to do with missing women.

"We will not melt if we get wet," she said with an encouraging smile.

He appreciated her straightforwardness. There was nothing weak about Hannah. She could handle any problem, seemingly. Independent maybe to a fault, but he liked women who were assertive and could take care of themselves. Not that he wanted Hannah to take care of herself. He wanted to be there with her, helping her and protecting her.

He jostled the reins and the horse took off along the road.

If only he could keep Hannah safe.

Riding along the mountain road with Lucas would have been perfect except for the reason they were traveling. Another young woman had gone missing. Hannah needed to find Sarah, but she also worried about Belinda.

As much as she wanted to believe the young Amish girl could be found, Hannah wasn't sure of anything, except Lydia Lapp's sorrow that had tugged at her heart. Some pain was almost too hard to bear. Didn't scripture say that the Lord gave only as much as some-one could carry? Surely scripture was mistaken when it came to parents and their children.

She glanced at the rugged mountain terrain and the steep slope of the road ahead. The mare was strong but would she be agile enough on the back path Lucas said they would travel? Hannah wrapped the cape more tightly around her chest.

"You're cold." His glance was laced with concern. "If we were riding in your Nissan, I could turn up the heater. Scoot closer to me, Hannah. Body heat is the only solution."

"I'm fine." But she wasn't. She was worried and frightened about what they might find in spite of her attempt to be strong. Plus, although she didn't want to admit it to Lucas, she *was* cold.

Being Amish in Fannie's warm home with the rich smells of fresh-baked biscuits and a wood fire to make piping-hot coffee was one thing. Being out in the ele-ments made her have second thoughts about the *plain* life and what she would have to give up if she joined the faith.

The thought took her by surprise. Consciously she hadn't considered embracing the bonnet. She touched the ties under her chin as if to adjust the covering, but her thoughts took in the simplicity of the Amish way, of not having to worry about what she would wear or the need to be in style or to apply makeup or to go to a salon for her hair. All of that seemed so frivolous and such a waste of time when two young women were in danger.

Lucas placed the reins in his left hand and stretched his right hand into the seat behind them. He pulled a thick lap quilt out of a heavy burlap tote and draped it over Hannah's lap.

"The quilt will add more warmth than the blanket alone," he told her. "If you're going to live like the Amish, you need to learn from them. They have warm woolen stockings and undergarments to ward off the cold. They also have outerwear and thick quilts and woolen blankets that insulate them from the frigid temperatures."

"How did you learn so much about their way of life in such a short few months?"

"It was Fannie. She made sure that I was fully immersed in Amish life. Some days I longed to catch up on the local news or find out what was going on in the world at large. She told me I had to decide whether to be of the world or not."

"And you ended up embracing the Amish way?"

"I was hurt when I came here and quite literally stumbled onto the inn. My car had a flat tire half a mile from the entrance. I had seen a small sign at the last intersection I had passed, so I hoofed it there as best I could with an injured leg."

He reached down and touched his old wound, grateful it had healed. "The first week I rented a room in the inn, but I soon got tired of having nothing to do. Calvin fixed my tire. I was ready to drive away, but I didn't know where I'd go. My life had been a jumble of confusion at that point. Fannie had a knack for seeing beneath the surface. She needed help maintaining the property and offered me a job."

"And you moved into the *grossdaadi* house."

Lucas nodded. "That's right. I sold my car to one of the kitchen staff who was going to college in the fall and needed transportation."

"Fannie had convinced you to accept the Amish way?" Hannah asked.

"To at least give it a try."

Hannah smiled. "She said you're like a son to her."

Lucas's gaze softened. "Hearing that makes me happy. She can be tough when she needs to be, but she forced me to work through some of my struggle. I said it was her chicken soup that healed me, but it was her big heart that made the difference. My extended family was scattered. My parents passed when I was young. Having a home had meant a one-bedroom rental."

Hannah nodded. "I can relate."

"She enjoys having you around," he added.

"How can you tell?"

"After eleven months, I can read her almost as well as she can read me. She's been cooking and humming and smiling more recently. I know you're the reason."

He put his arm around her shoulders and pulled her closer. "Feeling warmer?"

"Much. Thank you."

Hannah appreciated Lucas's concern for her comfort. He seemed to be adept with the horse and buggy and with the various ways the Amish would attack any problem.

"You're planning to become Amish?" she asked.

"It's been my hope."

"Do I hear a reservation?"

"Not from me, but the bishop is a different story. He doesn't think I'm ready."

"There's a stumbling block?"

Lucas nodded. "You could say that. Probably has to do with my pride. At least, that's what he led me to believe."

"Pride can be a stumbling block to a lot of things." Hannah thought of her pain when she'd learned about her father. The shock had taken her aback. Her mother's delivery had made the information even more hurtful and her pride had been wounded when she'd found out the truth.

"You don't seem like you have a problem with pride." Lucas jostled the reins and nudged the mare forward.

"Rejection, abandonment—both of those can be overscored with pride when you think you don't deserve to be treated in a certain way."

"You're talking about a guy who didn't appreciate you for who you are," he said as if reading her thoughts.

"That's not too far from the truth." Her mother hadn't made good decisions when it came to men. Hannah's father was proof of that, but she wouldn't go that far back with Lucas. "A seemingly nice guy kept showing up at the store where I worked. He invited me out for coffee. We got to know each other and hit it off, or so I thought."

She glanced at the hillside, trying to find her words. She hadn't talked about Brian to anyone. Maybe sharing some of what had happened would help her heal. "I enjoyed his attention and the nice things he did for me. Brian seemed concerned and attentive. Turns out it was a game for him. He...he lied to me about a number of things. He said a bill from his credit-card company had gotten lost in the mail. His late payment hurt his credit. He asked to use one of my credit cards to buy supplies for the law office where he worked. He assured me he'd be able to pay me back."

A muscle in Lucas's neck tensed. He kept his eyes on the road. Perhaps he thought her gullible and naive. Seemed she was both.

"Of course, he didn't plan to pay me back," she admitted. "He charged a number of big-ticket items to my card that didn't pertain to his job and seemed hurt when I questioned him. He made up another excuse and then another. Finally, I did some investigating and found an address that he hadn't told me about."

Lucas squeezed her hand, offering support.

"I went there when I thought he was home from work. We had always met in town. I thought he shared a house with two other guys, but the guy who came to the door was five years old. The child's mother appeared and then the child's father did, as well."

Lucas wrapped his arm around her shoulders. "It was Brian?"

She nodded. "I never suspected that he was married. He was using me the entire time. Here's the funny thing. He told me he worked for a well-established law firm in Atlanta. Turns out he's an ambulance chaser and not a good one. But he said if I made a fuss, he'd make certain that people would think I stole money from him." Which was a repeat of what had happened in her own home.

Hannah hung her head in shame. His hateful words echoed through her mind. *I know who your father is.*

Once the information is made public, your reputation will be ruined. No one will believe anything you say.

"I'm sorry, Hannah. You were too good for him."

"Too stupid is what I was, but I learned my lesson, that's for sure."

"Did you go to the police?"

Inwardly she flinched. How could she explain her reason for not notifying the authorities? "I… I worried that he would discredit my reputation and my credit."

"So you did nothing?"

"I moved to Macon. I turned off my cell phone and got a prepaid cell to use instead. I changed email addresses in case he tried to contact me over the internet. I didn't want him to find me."

"You weren't the one at fault."

"I wasn't sure how he would spin the story, and I couldn't risk what he might do."

"You need to let law enforcement know."

She shook her head. "It's all right, Lucas. That part of my life has ended."

"That's why you don't want to go back to Macon," he said, which wasn't far from the truth.

"Do you think I'm foolish?" she asked.

"Not at all. I think he bullied you and badgered you and told you untruths. I can help you."

"It's okay, really."

"But you have property there, your household furnishings, clothing."

"Nothing of value."

He stared at her, probably wondering why she had accumulated so little in her life.

"When you grow up with a mother who never stayed long in any one place, you learn to travel light. Anything we acquired that brought joy or comfort to our lives had to be left behind when she awakened us, often in the middle of the night, to climb into the car and leave for someplace new."

"What about your education? A kid would have to be smart to get by in that type of situation."

"Maybe, or maybe it worked because we were young. We didn't know any other way to live. We never established strong friendships because we always had to say goodbye."

"I'm sorry, Hannah. You and your sisters should have been close."

"You would have thought we would be, but Mother manipulated us with her love and played us one against the other. Especially Miriam and me. Miriam was the dutiful daughter. I dreamed of making my own way." She laughed ruefully. "And look what happened to me. You might say that I've become my mother."

"You can't believe that."

"I've been wandering through life, which is what my mother always did. She was searching for something, although I never knew what it was."

"Maybe love and acceptance," Lucas suggested.

"That was something her daughters couldn't give her."

"Of course not. You needed her to mother you and provide the love and acceptance you needed. Don't confuse the roles here, Hannah. The child is never the one who needs to take care of the mother."

"But Miriam did."

"Later in life, but not when you were growing up."

Hannah picked at the cape and lowered her head. She didn't want to talk about her childhood or her mother or her dysfunctional life. Nor did she want to consider what her life could have been like if she hadn't been so gullible when it came to Brian. She had been such a fool.

She scooted away from Lucas, needing to distance herself from his warmth and acceptance. She had made a mistake in Atlanta when she had given her heart to the wrong man. She wouldn't, she couldn't, make that same mistake again.

Chapter Fourteen

Lucas turned the buggy onto the narrow mountain path that led to the lodge. Hannah had been silent and lost in her own memories ever since she'd mentioned the man in Atlanta. From what she'd said, it sounded as if she still cared for Brian.

So many thoughts swirled through Lucas's mind that centered on pride and betrayal and abandonment. His world had ended in Savannah when Olivia died, but he'd gone after the shipping magnate and his company. The guy was well connected and his goons and minions had soon come after Lucas. He never would have backed off except for the suitcase uncovered in Olivia's personal effects and the immediate supposition that she was involved in something criminal. Olivia had never been dirty, but money didn't lie. At least, that was what his supervisor warned. The stash of marked bills had made her a suspect in a Savannah murder-for-hire case.

Lucas was thought to have been dirty by association, and he'd been encouraged, rather forcefully, to resign from the force before he was incriminated, as well.

Turning in his badge had been a necessity, but

he hadn't given up. He'd followed one last lead to Willkommen, where Vipera was said to have had holdings in the Pine Lodge Mountain Resort. An allegation Lucas could never prove.

Thankfully his search had led to the Amish Inn. God had wanted him to accept healing instead of vengeance. Although now Lucas wasn't sure he had read God correctly.

The back road around the mountain was bumpy and rough. Hannah bounced from side to side.

"Hold on," he warned. His hands held tightly to the reins when he wanted to wrap his arm protectively around Hannah. She was in another world, a world of memories, probably about the man who had stolen her heart. Lucas wouldn't interfere. She needed time to work out her past just as he had.

"We're almost to the lodge," he finally said. "We'll be watchful but appear to be minding our own business."

The buggy crested a small rise and the lodge was visible in the distance. Pretentiously grand, the stone structure rose like a sturdy fortress, and its windows gleamed golden from the reflection of the sun that broke momentarily through the clouds.

The three-story resort had a circular drive that passed under an A-frame portico at the entrance. From what Lucas had heard, many a person of prominence, whether in the sports world, business or entertainment, had visited the resort for a relaxing respite. Their privacy was protected above all else. Security guards wearing gray, down-filled jackets bearing the name of the resort patrolled the grounds to keep unwanted visitors from encroaching on the premises.

"We might be stopped as we near the lodge," he warned. "Let me do the talking."

A small security guardhouse stood to the left of the entrance road. A man wearing a gray jacket and metallic, wraparound sunglasses stepped from the protective structure. He raised his hand to stop the buggy.

Lucas pulled back on the reins and nodded to the bulky guy packing heat. "We are making a delivery from the Amish Inn," he informed the man.

"What's in your buggy?"

"Produce and baked goods."

The guard peered at the stack of boxes in the rear of the buggy and then pointed to the narrow road that curved around the side of the large stone structure. "Take that path to the right. It leads to the kitchen entrance. Someone will help you unload."

"Danke."

With a flip of the reins, Lucas guided Daisy onto the narrow side road. He glanced at the front entrance where another muscle-bound guy stood guard and wondered whether Hannah realized that both men in the security detail were heavily armed.

They rounded the side of the lodge and stopped at the entrance to the kitchen. In the distance, Lucas spotted a row of cottages nestled in a wooded area beyond the well-landscaped lawn. Although rustic in appearance, each seemed artistically decorated in accord with the resort's five-star rating. Perhaps guests who wanted a special getaway could rent the cottages to be one with nature, as the brochures for the resort probably stated.

Secluded luxury. But something else was underfoot. Lucas could sense the tension in the air. What was really happening at the lodge?

* * *

"¡Hola!"

A woman opened the door to the kitchen and hurried outside to greet them. "You are bringing us baked goods, yes?" She was short and plump, with a strong Hispanic accent.

"Pies and bread and root vegetables that just came from some of our local farms," he said with enthusiasm.

"This is good. We are opening soon after our renovation."

Hannah nodded in greeting and then followed Lucas's lead and climbed from the buggy.

"My name is Isabella," the woman said as she quickly reached for one of the boxes. "I will help you unload."

Lucas handed Hannah a smaller box containing pies and cookies, and hefted the heavier produce box into his own arms.

The inviting smell of a hearty soup, simmering on the stove, greeted them when they entered the state-of-the-art kitchen. Hannah glanced at the pair of stainless-steel refrigerators, the granite countertops and copper pots. If the kitchen was this grand, she could only imagine the ambience in the areas of the lodge open to the guests.

Another Hispanic woman, shorter than Isabella, unpacked the pies and nodded her approval as she placed them on one of the far counters.

"Hurry, Maria," Isabella encouraged. "There are more boxes to unload."

The smaller woman had no problem lifting the heavier cartons and the buggy was soon empty.

"I'll need a signature," Lucas said, holding out an invoice form.

"Yes." Isabella nodded. "You have not been here before?"

Lucas shook his head. "You'll have to direct me."

"I will take you to the food and beverage director's office. It is just down the hall."

She hurried Lucas out of the kitchen, leaving Hannah to enjoy the succulent aromas.

Maria appeared younger and more timid than Isabella, but she smiled sweetly to Hannah and pointed to the coffeepot. "You would like coffee? Maybe tea?"

As much as Hannah appreciated the offer, she declined and stared through the window at the cottages. "It's beautiful here. So many wealthy people must visit."

"*Sí*, is beautiful." The woman picked up a long-handled spoon and stirred the soup.

Hannah stepped closer. "Maria, I need information. Have you by any chance seen an Amish girl? She's sixteen and dressed like I am."

The woman's neck tensed.

"She's from the local area but has gone missing."

The woman dropped the spoon. The utensil clattered on the granite.

"She's a nice girl," Hannah continued, "but she got involved with an older man."

The woman flicked a sideways glance at Hannah and then turned to pull a gallon of milk from the refrigerator.

"Do you understand me?" Hannah asked. "The girl's name is Belinda?"

"No hablo inglés," the woman insisted as she poured milk into a large measuring cup.

Hannah doubted the woman's inability to speak English since she had offered coffee and had readily followed her supervisor's instructions to unload the buggy.

"My sister is missing, as well," Hannah continued, unwilling to be deterred. "Sarah is twenty-one and blonde. She disappeared six weeks ago. She might be with a tall, slender, red-haired man who is thought to be holding her captive. Plus, a girl disappeared eight months ago. Her name is Rosie."

The woman turned worried eyes to Hannah. Then, glancing down, she opened her mouth as if to speak.

At that moment Isabella stepped back into the kitchen.

"Your friend will be here soon," she assured Hannah. "He is waiting for the director to return to his office."

Isabella glared at the younger woman. "Maria, you are making pudding?"

"Sí." She returned the milk to the refrigerator.

Isabella smiled at Hannah. "Perhaps you would like coffee?"

"No, thank you. Maria already asked me." Hannah touched the younger woman's shoulder. "Was there something else you wanted to tell me?"

Once again Maria lowered her gaze. "No, senorita."

Realizing Maria wouldn't divulge anything within earshot of her boss, Hannah pointed to the door. "I'll wait outside near the buggy."

She shivered when she left the kitchen. Not from the cold mountain air but from the sense of foreboding that permeated the setting. Maria had something to say. If only Isabella hadn't returned so soon.

Rounding the buggy, Hannah gazed at a cluster of cottages sitting on the opposite side of the landscaped lawn. On the far right, a cobblestone path led past a wooded area and then on to one cottage secluded from the rest. Hannah glanced back at the kitchen, seeing both women huddled over the central work island with their backs to the windows.

She peered at the sun peeking through the clouds and decided a stroll to stretch her legs would be good before the ride home.

A breeze picked at her skirt and made her grab her black bonnet before it flew off her head. She again glanced back, relieved that no one seemed to notice her ambling along the path. The stone pavement led through an area shaded by tall pines. A chill settled over her and she pulled the cape tighter, knowing she should turn around, yet her gaze was drawn to the cottage that appeared to be constructed from hand-hewed logs.

Lace curtains hung at the windows and rustic rockers and pots of pansies decorated the wraparound porch. All of which looked inviting.

A flicker of movement behind the curtain on the far right window caught Hannah's attention. Someone was looking out. Perhaps one of the guests renting the accommodations or a housekeeper tidying up the room.

Before Hannah could turn and retrace her steps, the curtain pulled back ever so slightly and a face peered from the window. A teenage girl's face.

Even at this distance Hannah could see her wide eyes and sad frown. She could also see the bodice of her blue dress and the ties of a white bonnet that hung around her neck.

Hannah started toward the cabin when a hand grabbed her arm. "What do you think you're doing, lady?"

She turned, seeing the snarling face of one of the guards. His nostrils flared and the anger flashing from his eyes bored into her.

"You're trespassing on private property."

"But—"

Hannah glanced over her shoulder. The curtain had dropped into place. No one remained at the window.

"Are you interfering with our guests?" the man demanded.

Hannah hung her head and pulled in a silent prayer. She needed to appear meek, humble and authentically Amish. "Forgive me, sir. I was waiting outside and the path invited me to walk before my buggy ride home."

He jerked her forward and growled his frustration. "You folks live by your own set of rules, but we've got rules here that need to be obeyed. Now hurry along and get back to your buggy."

Hannah pulled her arm free and ran, wanting to distance herself from the hateful man.

She also needed to tell Lucas about what she had seen at the cabin.

Not what, she corrected herself, but who.

She had seen Belinda, the missing Amish girl.

Chapter Fifteen

Lucas flipped the reins, encouraging the mare to increase her pace. Hannah peered back at the lodge.

"I don't see anyone following us," she said, breathing a sigh of relief.

"What happened, Hannah? Your face is pale as death and you're still trembling."

She quickly explained about the small cottage and the face at the window.

"It was her, Lucas. It was Belinda. She was peering through a window from the cottage on the right, closest to the wooded area."

"Are you sure about what you saw? I didn't think you had even met Belinda."

She straightened her spine. "I haven't. But the girl was wearing a blue dress. White ribbons hung around her neck."

"That doesn't mean it was Belinda Lapp." As much as he appreciated Hannah's desire to rescue the girl, Lucas wasn't convinced the girl at the window—whoever she was—needed rescuing. "Did the guard realize someone had been at the window?"

"I doubt he noticed the girl. He was probably more concerned about the Amish woman—namely me—trespassing on private property."

She grabbed Lucas's arm. "We have to go back and try to save Belinda."

Lucas blew out a deep breath. "We're not the ones, Hannah. It needs to be law enforcement."

"Belinda is in the cottage. I'm sure of it."

"That may be, but she could be there of her own volition."

Hannah let out a frustrated breath. "She's sixteen."

"I know, but we need to be prudent."

"Prudent I agree with, but I think we're being foolish to leave her behind. Besides, Sarah could be there, as well."

"If we go back, the guard will stop us. I know he frightened you, Hannah. He would be even more antagonistic if he realized you had returned."

"Then what can we do?"

"First things first. You'll stay with Fannie while I talk to the sheriff."

"We'll both talk to the sheriff." She steeled her jaw and released hold of his arm, then turned to stare at the road ahead.

As much as Lucas wanted Belinda and Sarah and Rosie to be found and brought to safety, he knew going back without law enforcement would be a risky mistake. Plus, the girl at the window could be the teenage daughter of one of the guests or even a worker at the lodge.

Seth and Simon Keim had considered applying for a job at the resort. Perhaps housekeeping used Amish girls, as well. Racing headlong into a cottage because of a nebulous figure at the window, who had made no attempt to signal for help, seemed brash. Although he wouldn't use that term with Hannah. Her heart was in the right place for sure.

"When I was in the food director's office, I saw a memo on his desk," Lucas shared. "Seems a number of important people are arriving late tonight in anticipation of the big opening. Someone from the sheriff's office needs to pull surveillance and find out who those important folks are and whether they have ties to any illegal operations in other areas of the state."

"And what about the girl I saw at the window?"

"Surveillance will watch for anyone going or coming, Hannah, including young women in blue dresses."

Hannah seemed satisfied with his response, for which Lucas was grateful. Feeling a swell of relief when they arrived back at the inn, he stopped the buggy at the kitchen entrance and hurriedly unloaded the boxes.

Fannie met them there. "Did you find anything of interest?"

Lucas looked at Hannah. "Maybe. We're going to talk to the sheriff and let him decide how to proceed."

He handed Fannie the signed invoice. "Any news on Belinda?"

"Nothing new. Joseph's brother is helping at the store but both boys need to go home soon."

"Lucas?" Hannah rushed toward him and held out a scrap of paper. "I found this stuck in the corner of one of the empty produce boxes."

His gut tightened when he read the note. *I see Amish girl last night.*

"Maria wrote the note," Hannah insisted. "She

started to tell me something before Isabella came back into the kitchen."

"I'll talk to the sheriff."

Hannah hurried after him. "Not without me."

"And me," Fannie said, following behind them.

Sheriff Kurtz had been reading the newspaper in the easy chair. At least, that was what he told them when he opened the door and invited them into his room, although his eyes were puffy and he appeared to have been napping.

"I'm sorry we had to disturb you," Lucas said. "But there's information you need to know."

Hannah quickly explained what she had seen and about the guard who had stopped her on the path, as well as the note she'd found.

"There are a number of security guards on-site and they're armed," Lucas said.

The sheriff rubbed his chin. "Seems strange to have all that protection unless some well-known guest is staying there."

Lucas nodded. "A few VIPs are arriving late tonight, according to the memo I saw. If we can identify them, we might learn what's really going on at the lodge."

"It's been closed for renovation and opens this weekend," Fannie shared.

"Security is tight because of the women they're holding captive in the cottage," Hannah insisted.

"One woman," Lucas corrected.

"One that we know about," she admitted. "Although there could be more."

"If a couple of your deputies pull surveillance," Lucas told the sheriff, "we might be able to identify who those people of prominence are and whether they have ties to illegal activity. Tell your guys to watch for any young women escorted by older men who don't appear to be related."

"Sounds like a good plan." The sheriff reached for his cell. "I'll call Deputy Gainz and pass the information on to him. He'll check it out."

Which didn't seem to appease Hannah, from the way she sighed with frustration. "He'd better hurry before they transport Belinda to some other hideout."

The sheriff tried to place the call then shook his head. "I can't get service."

"You can use the phone in my office," Fannie suggested.

Even if the sheriff could reach Gainz, the deputy wasn't the most aggressive officer of the law. Could he amass enough manpower to thoroughly search the resort? Lucas couldn't stand idly by after reading the note that mentioned an Amish girl, who could be in danger.

"Sir, I'll go back to the lodge," Lucas said.

The sheriff nodded. "Make sure you don't go empty-handed. Take that Glock I gave you yesterday. You know what to do. I could swear you in as a deputy."

Lucas held up his hand. "That won't be necessary."

"I'll call Gainz and let him know you'll need backup. I'll also tell him to have at least one of our guys keeping track of arrivals and departures. Maybe we'll be able to hook some big fish." The sheriff put his hand on Fannie's shoulder and leaned on her as they left the room.

Hannah stared at him. "What's going on, Lucas?"

"You wanted me to go back for Belinda."

"But not as a deputy," she insisted. "You're not law enforcement."

"I was in Savannah."

She took a step back. "What are you saying?"

"It's the reason I came here. My partner, Olivia Parker, was killed. She was working on a trafficking investigation that could have incriminated a local shipping tycoon. His name's Vipera and he's supposed to be connected to the lodge, at least financially. Only nothing materialized until today. If women are being trafficked as that note could indicate, he might be involved."

"Then this is more about you getting even rather than trying to save Belinda."

"What?" He didn't understand her logic.

For all Hannah's earlier insistence that he needed to rescue the Amish girl, she now seemed totally against him doing just that.

"You're Amish, Lucas."

He shook his head. "I'm not."

"Isn't it what you want for your life?"

"I was wrong."

"No, you weren't, but now you think the person who killed your partner is suddenly involved and that gives you a reason to throw away your future. Is it that pride we talked about? Or is it the desire to avenge her death that you've grappled with all this time?"

He felt betrayed. "Evildoers need to be stopped."

"Stopped and brought to justice, but not stopped dead in their tracks."

"What are you insinuating, Hannah?"

"You're going back in hopes of finding the man who killed your partner or was in some way responsible for your partner's death. Her name was Olivia, right? When she died, did your dreams of a life together die, as well?"

"You don't know what you're talking about."

"Don't I? I can see it in your eyes, Lucas. It's why you were a broken man when you came here."

"I was broken because of taking a bullet to my leg," he insisted. " I told you Fannie nursed me back to health."

"And Fannie told you to forget the past and live a new life, to let go of the world and embrace the Amish way."

"That's what I've tried to do."

"But you failed, Lucas, because of the need for revenge that's hardened your heart."

"It's called justice, Hannah."

The sheriff's laptop was open on the desk. She tapped Lucas's name into the search-engine bar and quickly read the headers that appeared on the screen. "The Savannah paper seems to have a number of articles with you in the title. Let's look at this one." She clicked on the link.

"Hannah, you're being irrational."

"Am I?" The news article appeared on the screen.

"'Sergeant Lucas Grant is thought to be involved… his partner was implicated…marked bills were found in Officer Olivia Parker's apartment,'" Hannah read aloud, catching the high points of the piece. "'An unnamed source claims Parker may have been involved in a criminal activity, involving bribery and money laundering. Her partner, Sergeant Lucas Grant, denies the allegations.'"

Hannah glanced at Lucas and then back at the monitor as she continued to read. "'Another source stated that

Sergeant Lucas Grant might be involved in the corruption, as well. He turned in his badge and is on medical leave. The spokesperson claims there is speculation that his career in law enforcement is over and that he, too, will be indicted if their investigation goes to court.'"

She looked up and glared at him. "I keep making the same mistake."

"What do you mean?" He stepped closer.

"I keep getting involved with the wrong type of men."

Calvin rapped on the open door. "Sorry to interrupt you, folks, but Joseph needs help at the store. Is anyone available?"

"I'll go," Hannah volunteered.

"No, wait." Lucas grabbed her arm. "We need to talk this out."

"You've already made up your mind, Lucas." She hurried from the room.

Lucas started to follow but Fannie stopped him in the hallway. "Calvin will protect her. She'll be safe, but I don't think you will be. I know what you're planning. It's not wise. As much as I want to see Belinda saved, this is a line you should not cross."

"I can't sit by when someone is in danger. These men need to be apprehended."

"You're one person, Lucas. You cannot take them all down. I know you, and I can read your heart. You have not changed since Savannah. You're still intent on stopping the people who killed your partner."

"I'm intent on saving a young woman held captive."

Lucas left the inn and ran toward the mechanic's shed, where he grabbed the keys to Hannah's car.

He climbed behind the wheel, started the engine and pulled onto the roadway. As he neared the Amish Store, Joseph came running out. His cheek was bruised and his lip bloodied. Calvin stumbled to the doorway, holding his head.

Lucas sprang from the car. "What happened?"

"A man. He knocked Calvin out and grabbed Hannah. He said he recognized her even in her Amish clothing. He said if Miriam could not be found, he would have to make do with her."

"Where did he take her?"

"I do not know," the boy said. "But he drove away in a delivery truck."

"Get medical help for Calvin and tell the sheriff that I'm going to the lodge."

Lucas accelerated out of the yard and turned right. He'd take the narrow back road. If Daisy could pull the buggy around the mountain, Hannah's car could handle the rough terrain, as well.

He thought of Olivia dead on the pavement because he had arrived too late. He had to find Hannah. He had to find her in time.

Chapter Sixteen

Lucas drove like a madman up the hill and turned onto the shortcut that rounded the mountain and led to the lodge.

"Lord, help me," he prayed aloud. "I need to find Hannah."

His heart beat against his chest and sent a ripple of fear to weave along his spine.

He couldn't live if something happened to Hannah. "Please, Lord."

As he neared the spot where the path intersected with the main road, Lucas flipped off the headlights. He turned right onto a narrow trail that wove through a wooded area. After backing into a small clearing surrounded by trees, he cut the engine and stepped from the car.

Pausing for a moment, he listened for any sound that could alert him to Hannah's whereabouts before making his way, carefully and quietly, through the undergrowth. Drawing close to the resort, he stopped and stared for a long moment to study the stone building, the kitchen doorway and the cottages in the distance.

Hannah had mentioned a more secluded cottage nestled to the right at the edge of the woods. He moved through the underbrush until the small lodging came into view. A light shone in the front bay window as well as a window at the side of the cottage, no doubt where Hannah had seen the girl's face.

The main structure of the lodge sat dark and foreboding with only a few rooms lit on the first floor. In contrast, the landscaped walkways had recessed lighting tucked in the shrubbery and along the paths, painting the grounds in a surreal glow. How could an area so lovely harbor anything as evil as human trafficking?

Though eager to find Hannah, Lucas also knew going in blind would be a mistake.

His gut tightened. What if she wasn't there? Suppose the man in the blue hoodie had taken her someplace else? What if they were on the highway headed for Atlanta or Savannah? Lucas's hand fisted and he touched the weapon strapped to his hip.

Headlights appeared on the main mountain road. He moved closer to the edge of the tree line to get a better view of the road and felt a sense of relief when a beige delivery truck pulled into sight. The guy in flannel had taken the longer route through Willkommen, which allowed Lucas to arrive first.

The truck pulled into the drive. A guard waved the vehicle on. The truck skirted the kitchen and turned onto the side road that led to the small cottage.

The front door of the cottage opened. A man, dressed in the black slacks and gray jacket uniform of the security team, stepped onto the porch. He waited until the truck braked to a stop before he hurried to the driver's side of the vehicle.

The guy in flannel climbed from the truck, rounded to the rear and opened the door. He and the other man peered into the darkened interior.

Lucas stepped closer. A twig snapped underfoot. Both men turned to stare in his direction. Lucas held his breath and chastised himself for his stupidity. In his haste, he had made a mistake that could prove deadly.

As the men watched, an armadillo scurried out of the wooded area and raced across the path. The guy in flannel laughed before they both turned back to the van.

Lucas's heart pounded when he saw what they pulled from the rear. Hannah bound and gagged. She struggled against their hold. Her bonnet was gone and her hair had pulled free from her bun.

His pulse raced and he wanted to rush forward to save her. Before he stepped from the shadows, something caught his eye on the distant path. Two security agents walked toward the lodge, oblivious to what was happening at the cottage.

The guy in flannel untied the rope binding her legs and then shoved Hannah up the stairs of the porch. She tripped and fell. The sound of her knees hitting the steps ripped through Lucas's heart.

Her kidnapper jerked her upright and pushed her toward the door. She stumbled inside. The guard, who had been inside earlier, followed her into the cottage.

The flannel guy returned to the delivery truck, started the engine and drove around the far side of the lodge. The sound of the engine faded in the distance.

Lucas scanned the property, searching for any sign of security. Seeing no one, he approached the cottage, flattened his back against the wood siding and inched his way toward the window. Curtains covered the panes, but a slit between the panels provided a tiny view into the room.

A voice sounded, moving toward the window. Lucas ducked just as the curtain was pulled back. Huddled only inches below the window, he held his breath.

The voice became more muffled.

Lucas waited until he heard nothing and then, ever so slightly, raised his head and peered over the edge of the windowsill.

His heart stopped.

He saw Belinda Lapp on a bed. Her hair was disheveled, but from the rise and fall of her shoulders, she appeared to be breathing evenly. Hopefully she was unharmed.

The door to the bedroom opened and Hannah appeared. Her mouth was gagged and her wrists bound.

Her eyes widened ever so slightly. Had she seen him?

She struggled against the guard's hold. He raised his hand and slapped her face.

Lucas felt the blow to his heart as if he had been the one struck. If only it could have been directed at him instead of Hannah.

The guard shoved her onto a straight-back chair and retied the rope around her ankles. He raised his voice. Lucas couldn't make out the words, but from the harsh tone, the guard's displeasure was evident. A door inside the cottage slammed.

Minutes later the front door opened. Lucas peered around the corner and watched the guard jog to the lodge.

Lucas had to move quickly, but before he could move, two more security guys appeared on the path.

Were they heading to the lodge? Or coming for Hannah?

Hannah's heart beat so hard she thought it would surely beat out of her chest. Although terrified by the guards and the man in flannel who had brought her here, she was even more unsettled by the face at the window.

Had it been Lucas or a figment of her imagination?

Tears filled her eyes. She blinked them away. She couldn't cry now. She had to remain focused on what was happening around her.

The Amish girl lay on the bed. Asleep or drugged, Hannah wasn't sure.

Keeping her feet together, she raised her legs and kicked the mattress once and then struck the bed again and again. The exertion made her breathless. She struggled to pull enough air into her lungs. Frustrated, she bit into the gag, wishing she could rip it in two and be rid of the hateful restraint.

The cloth slipped ever so slightly. Using her chin and shoulder, she tugged at the fabric until her lips were free. Opening her mouth, she pulled in a deep breath, filling her lungs with sweet air.

Buoyed by her success, she kicked the bed again and wiggled her hands back and forth in the hope of releasing the rope that bound her wrists. The coarse hemp dug into her flesh, but she ignored the pain.

She scooted to the edge of the chair for better leverage and slowly raised herself to a standing position, then hopped forward and dropped onto the bed.

Using her bound hands, Hannah gripped Belinda's arm and jerked. The girl's eyes blinked open.

Relieved, Hannah leaned closer. "I'm from the inn. You've got to wake up. We have to get away."

The girl moaned.

Not to be daunted, Hannah jostled her again. "Open your eyes, Belinda. We're in danger and have to escape."

The girl blinked, appearing dazed. She stared at Hannah for a long moment then tried to sit up. "Save... save me," she whispered.

"I will, but I need your help." Hannah held out her hands. "Undo the rope."

The girl pulled herself up and grimaced as she fumbled with the restraint. "It is knotted so tightly."

"Maybe there's something in the bathroom." Hannah pointed to the adjoining bath.

Holding on to the bed frame, Belinda struggled to her feet and stumbled forward while Hannah lifted up a silent prayer.

The girl returned to the bed carrying a small plastic case. "I found a nail file and scissors."

Which wouldn't hold up against the thick rope. Hannah's spirits fell, but she held out her hands nonetheless.

Belinda didn't try to cut the sturdy hemp. Instead she snipped at each individual thread. Amazed, Hannah watched as, little by little, the rope frayed. She tugged against the remaining strands that eventually broke free.

Hannah rubbed her wrists and then undid her legs. "We have to hurry," she told Belinda.

The outside door opened and footsteps sounded in the main room of the cottage.

The girl gripped Hannah's arm. "He's come back."

Before Hannah could respond, the knob turned and the door opened.

Lucas hadn't expected the look of terror on Hannah's face when he opened the bedroom door.

"Oh, Lucas." She collapsed into his arms. "We thought you were the guard."

"Are you all right?"

She nodded. "Belinda helped me break free of the ropes binding my wrists and legs."

He looked at the girl's dilated pupils. She had been drugged, but the effects appeared to be wearing off.

"We need to leave the cabin now." He squeezed Hannah's hand before he opened the bedroom door. "Follow me."

They hurriedly crossed the living room. Lucas opened the front door ever so slightly and peered outside. Seeing no one, he motioned the women forward.

He kept his eyes on the surrounding area and then followed the women down the porch steps and into the woods.

"The car is parked through there." He pointed to the clearing.

The sound of an engine caused them to turn.

Just as before, a delivery truck braked to a stop in front of the cottage. A man stepped to the pavement. He was dressed in a windbreaker and jeans, and wore a Braves baseball cap over his short-cropped hair. He rounded the truck, opened a side door and jerked a woman onto the pavement. She gasped as he forced her up the steps to the porch. The guy stopped and turned to study the landscape before he shoved her into the cottage.

"The woman—" Hannah grabbed Lucas's arm. "I didn't see her face, but she has blond hair. What if it's Sarah?"

Chapter Seventeen

Hannah couldn't take her eyes off the cottage in the hope of catching another glimpse of the blonde woman.

Lucas gently gripped her shoulders and turned her around. "Whether it's Sarah or not, you and Belinda have to get away."

"I can't leave now."

"Think about Belinda's safety. Drive her to the inn and get help. I'll stay here and see what happens."

"What about Deputy Gainz? Wasn't he supposed to be doing surveillance?"

Lucas sighed. "He's probably still in Willkommen."

He pulled the car keys from his pocket and shoved them into her hand. "Go. Now."

She took the keys and then watched as another truck arrived, stopped at the guardhouse and drove to the cottage.

A man climbed from the truck and limped toward the porch. His phone rang. He stopped to dig it from his pocket and raised it to his ear. "Yeah?"

"It's one of the men from Savannah," Lucas said, his voice low and menacing.

"One of the men who killed your partner?"

He nodded. "I recognize him by the way he walks."

"Are you sure?"

"Of course I'm sure." He motioned Hannah toward the car. "You need to get going before someone sees you."

"What about you?"

"I'm going back, Hannah. He needs to be stopped."

"You can't. There are too many of them and only one of you. Plus, you think vengeance is sweet. You want to kill him for what he did to Olivia. Only that won't get you anywhere. You'll be outnumbered and captured yourself."

She stared at him, trying to read his thoughts. "It won't help Olivia, either."

"But it'll help me, Hannah. It'll help me get over the guilt I've carried for too long and the deep need I have to pay back the injustice done to a woman who didn't deserve to die."

"One injustice doesn't warrant another one. You're hoping to be Amish, but you're not there, and you won't be after this. If you kill that man, you'll be tied up with court hearings. You could end up in jail or, at the very least, you would be pulled back into the world of law enforcement."

"It was the life I knew."

"It tore you apart."

"Then help me heal, Hannah."

She shook her head. "I'm staying at the inn. Fannie can always use an extra pair of hands, and I need a place where I'm accepted for who I am. A place where I don't have to worry about the past or the future. Come with us now, Lucas. We'll send law enforcement to save Sarah or whoever she is."

"I'm not leaving," he insisted.

With a frustrated sigh, Hannah turned and hurried to the car where the girl waited. She had to get help. Lucas was walking into a trap. A trap that would get him killed. As much as she wanted to rescue the blonde woman, Hannah had to help Belinda first.

Sheriff Kurtz would send law enforcement, and not just Deputy Gainz, to free Sarah or whoever the woman might be.

Lord, protect her and protect Lucas.

Hannah had hoped that someday she and Lucas could have a future together and both become Amish and embrace the peace-loving lifestyle that had been healing for both of them, but Lucas was eaten up with vengeance that hardened his heart. He couldn't love her when his thoughts were still on Olivia.

Tears stung Hannah's eyes and her heart nearly broke. She could save Belinda. If only she could save Lucas, as well.

Seeing the man from Savannah brought back the pain Lucas had experienced after Olivia's death. The memories of her body lying on the pavement and her long hair matted with blood caused the anger to return.

His leg ached, reminding him of the gunshot wound and his weeks of recovery. No telling what would have happened to him if it hadn't been for Fannie. She had brought him back to life and to the faith she embraced. Now he was ready to discard everything he had learned about the Amish way and about himself over the past eleven months.

The man still held the cell phone to his ear and talked excitedly to someone on the other end. Lucas turned his head, hoping to catch some snippet of the conversation.

"Vipera." The name of the tycoon from Savannah.

Lucas glanced at the cottage, knowing he was outnumbered and could be easily overpowered by the guards. That wouldn't do the blonde woman any good, nor would it bring Olivia's killers to justice.

Vipera had top-notch lawyers that could adjudicate his release. The tycoon would never stand trial without concrete evidence to substantiate his guilt.

Lucas needed one of his goons to talk.

Slowly and surely, he crept from his hiding spot and crossed the clearing. The guy was still on the phone with his back to the van.

Lucas came up behind him.

Just as he disconnected, Lucas wrapped his arm about the guy's neck and cupped his other hand over his mouth.

"Don't move, and don't make a sound," Lucas whispered.

The guy struggled to break free.

Lucas grabbed the guy's phone and then shoved the Glock into his back. "What don't you understand about not resisting?"

The man stopped moving.

"Remember Olivia Parker, the cop you killed in Savannah?"

The guy shook his head and tried to speak. Lucas's hand pressed even more tightly against his mouth.

"Don't plead innocent," Lucas snarled. "I know you and your buddy killed her. You had orders from Vipera, but you were the one who beat her and then slit her throat."

The guy tried to shake his head. Lucas jammed the gun even deeper into his back until the struggling stopped.

"We're going to take a little walk."

Lucas half dragged, half shoved him around the side of the truck, heading for the underbrush where they'd be hidden from the guards. Before they left the protective cover of the truck, the door to the cottage opened and a guard stepped outside.

Lucas's chest tightened. Where had he come from? There had to be a back door, which made everything much more complicated and dangerous.

"I'll check and see if Xavier took the Amish girls to the lodge," the guard said over his shoulder to someone still inside. His voice traveled in the night. "Call my cell if you learn their whereabouts."

The guard descended the porch steps and hurried along the pavement.

The guy from Savannah jerked. His knee hit the van. The sound broke through the stillness.

Tightening his hold, Lucas pushed him flush against the truck.

The guard turned. He was coming back to the cottage. Lucas had to decide what to do…fast.

Chapter Eighteen

Tears stung Hannah's eyes as she drove along the path leading away from the lodge. She didn't turn on the headlights and instead followed the tree line, praying she wouldn't snag the car on a boulder or drop into a rut. Her eyes flicked to the rearview mirror to ensure they weren't being followed.

Thankfully, all she saw was the dark night that swallowed them in its grasp.

"How…how did you find me?" Belinda asked, her voice low as she started to come out of her lethargy.

"I saw your face at the window and told Lucas Grant. He came back to look for you."

"What about the other girl?"

"Sarah?" Hannah's stomach tightened. "She's my sister."

"No, another girl. I never saw her, but they talked about her. Her name was Rosie."

"Rosie Glick?"

Belinda nodded. "They said they needed to find her."

"But…but I thought they had her."

"I can only tell you what I have heard." The girl rubbed her arms. "They mentioned a basement."

"The basement of the lodge?" Hannah asked.

"I am not certain."

Hannah stopped the car and turned to face Belinda. Even in the dark she could see her wide eyes and fearful expression.

"Have you ever driven a car, Belinda?"

The girl hesitated.

"I need to go back and tell Lucas about Rosie, but I can't leave you in the middle of the woods. So answer me truthfully—do you know how to drive a car?"

The girl dipped her head. "Do not tell my father, but I have driven with the man who promised me nice clothes and pretty jewelry."

How ironic that after everything that had happened, Belinda was worried about her father finding out she had driven a car.

"I won't tell your dad," Hannah assured her. "Continue on this path. It will intersect with the main road. Turn right and you'll end up at the inn. Alert the sheriff. He's in room three."

"But what about you?"

"I need to go back," Hannah insisted.

"They will capture you."

"I have to help Lucas."

She climbed from the vehicle and held the door for Belinda, who quickly settled in behind the wheel. "Don't turn on the headlights until you get to the main road. It's about five hundred yards from here."

The girl caught hold of Hannah's hand. "*Gott* protect you."

"And protect Lucas, Sarah and Rosie, as well."

She closed the door quietly and watched as Belinda drove away. Then, turning, Hannah ran back along the path she had just traveled. She had to get to Lucas. She had to get to Lucas in time.

"Hey, Josh, the boss wants to see you." A guy cupped his hands around his mouth and called from the doorway to the kitchen.

Lucas offered an internal prayer of thanks as the guard hesitated for a long moment and then double-timed it to the lodge. Once the kitchen door closed, Lucas shoved the guy with the limp toward the rear of the truck and opened the door.

"Climb in, buddy. We'll see how you like being tied up and defenseless."

The guy dug in his heels and shook his head.

Lucas shoved him into the truck, bound and tied his hands and feet, and jammed a rag in his mouth. He tied the guy down so he couldn't roll and then quietly closed the door and hurried to the side of the cottage. Once again he peered into the bedroom window and saw the blonde woman sitting on the chair where Hannah had been earlier.

The delivery-truck driver wearing the Braves baseball hat and windbreaker came into the room, grunted and then left, leaving the door open. Lucas stretched to see into the main room, where a security guard stood, coffee cup in hand.

Two men. Could he take them?

Only if he could divide and conquer.

He rooted in the grass and found two small pebbles.

Glancing around the side of the cottage, he lobbed one of the small stones at the porch. Again, he peered into the window. The guard sipping coffee placed his cup on the mantel and headed for the door.

He stepped onto the porch, walked to the van and peered through the window. Lucas slammed the butt of his weapon against the guy's head. He collapsed without a sound.

With swift, sure moves, Lucas bound and gagged him and tucked him inside the truck along with the first guy. Only one man remained, but when Lucas stepped from the van his heart stopped.

The driver from Savannah—Mr. Baseball Cap and Windbreaker—was standing with his weapon raised. Only his weapon wasn't pointed at Lucas. It was pointed at the person held in a tight hold against his chest.

"Hannah!"

Chapter Nineteen

"I'm sorry," Hannah moaned. "I wanted to help you, Lucas, but I've done everything wrong."

The guy glared at Lucas. "Drop your weapon."

"Don't hurt her." Lucas removed the gun from the holster around his waist and placed it on the ground.

"Hands over your head."

Lucas complied.

"Who's in the truck?" the guy demanded.

"No one of interest."

"That's not smart, Amish. Open the doors so I can see inside."

"You're from Savannah. I've seen a picture of you on Olivia Parker's phone. Remember her? You killed her on the dock. First you called her and told her a woman was being trafficked. Then you ambushed Olivia when she showed up."

The guy sneered. "I didn't know there were Amish folks in Savannah."

"You didn't think anyone saw you, but your picture has been sent to law enforcement in the city. They plan to apprehend you and Vipera."

"That's Mr. Vipera to you, but you're a fool if you think he can be taken down. Mr. Vipera is above the law."

"Tell me what he does with the women."

"If I tell you, I'll have to kill you."

Lucas smiled. "You plan to kill me anyway."

"What about her?" the guy asked, jamming his gun against Hannah's chest.

"She doesn't deserve to die."

"Of course not. She'll make a nice addition to Mr. Vipera's entourage. The Amish ladies are always so agreeable."

"Where's he keep them?"

"You've heard of his island? He entertains wealthy businessmen from counties around the world. The ladies are one of the extra benefits he provides."

"Is that what happens at the lodge?"

"On a much smaller scale. The pleasure industry is lucrative and Mr. Vipera pays well."

"Is that why when a woman escaped some weeks ago everyone was upset? Someone started stalking the woman's sister. He said he wanted information, but he really wanted a substitute for the woman who escaped."

"You're talking about Tucker Davis. He had an agreement with Mr. Vipera. Once an agreement is made, the contract needs to be fulfilled. Mr. Vipera doesn't want anyone to cheat him out of something he's purchased."

"Women aren't chattel."

"Some are." The guy laughed.

Lucas stared at Hannah, his mouth dry, his heart racing. He needed to throw the gunman off with a series of false claims. Hopefully when frustrated, the guy would make a mistake.

"Two men are dead," Lucas taunted. "But they told me everything about the operation before they died."

"They didn't know anything," the guy countered.

"I called the Savannah-Chatham Metropolitan Police Department and talked to the chief. He'll make sure Vipera is arrested."

"Amish don't have phones."

"But I'm not Amish. I'm an undercover cop. What will happen to you when the chief tells Mr. Vipera that you're the snitch?"

"What?"

"I told him you blamed Olivia's death on Mr. Vipera. I said you provided evidence."

Lord, let him buy into this story I've created, Lucas prayed.

"I sent the chief photos of her dead body and said I got them from your phone," he continued. "Anything is possible these days with a good computer and a little technical expertise. I also created photos that showed Mr. Vipera at the crime scene. How long will it take his henchmen to find you once they learn you provided evidence that could send Mr. Vipera to jail?"

"Oh, Lucas," Hannah gasped.

"Shut up." The guy tightened his hold.

"No." She struggled, kicked his shin and bit into the flesh on his arm.

The guy growled and shoved her aside.

He aimed his weapon at Lucas. Hannah threw herself against the gunman and knocked him off balance.

Lucas charged. He ignored his aching leg and ran headlong into the guy, dropping him to the ground. His weapon flew into the brush.

Lucas pummeled his chest, then landed a blow to his chin.

The guy groaned and passed out.

Lucas started to get up and saw Hannah, gun in hand.

"I would have killed him to save you." Her voice was hollow and devoid of inflection. "Maybe I understand what you were feeling with Olivia."

"You thought I wanted to kill him, but I just wanted to bring him to justice."

"What about the men in the van?"

"They're both very much alive." He glanced over his shoulder. "We need to get going before the guards come back. While I tie this guy up, you go inside and free the other woman."

"Is it Sarah?"

"Hannah, I don't think—"

He wanted to warn her but she was already gone.

Hannah raced into the cottage, hurried to the bedroom and pushed on the door. "Sarah," she cried, opening her arms.

Then she stopped short.

The blonde woman was her sister's age but she wasn't Sarah.

Chapter Twenty

Sirens sounded when Hannah stepped onto the porch with the young woman. Three police cars pulled up to the rear of the lodge, lights flashing. Two cars from the Willkommen sheriff's office and two more from the Petersville police department parked at the front entrance.

One officer in a squad car stopped at the cottage. "You folks get in. I'll take you someplace safe. We're not sure how everything will go down."

"A number of security guards are inside the lodge," Lucas said as he helped the women into the car. "Three guys are in the back of the delivery van."

The cop relayed the information over his radio.

"How did you know we needed help?" Lucas asked.

"Ned Quigley's the acting sheriff in Willkommen. He just got back from GBI headquarters in Atlanta and pulled us together. The guy's good. He knows law enforcement."

It was over, almost over. Lucas put his arm around Hannah. She folded into his embrace and cried all the way back to the inn.

* * *

Hannah wouldn't let Lucas out of her sight. Too much had happened too fast. The sheriff and Fannie sat in chairs by the fireplace while Lucas stood next to where she sat on the couch. The hot coffee Fannie had made helped to steady Hannah's trembling heart.

Deputy Gainz had driven the two women home. Belinda had been reunited with her family and promised to never be so foolish as to believe an *Englisch* man who promised her pretty things. She wanted to talk to the bishop, to be baptized and to live within the Amish faith.

Hannah looked up at Lucas, seeing the fatigue on his face, but she also saw the sense of purpose in his eyes. She had been wrong. He wasn't focused on the past. He was thinking of the future. He touched her shoulder and she raised her hand to his.

The sheriff put down the cell phone. "They didn't find Rosie. In fact, everything in the lodge seemed legit. Evidently the trafficking was done in the cottage at the rear of the property. The Savannah police are on their way to Vipera's home to arrest him. The coast guard is headed to his island. Federal agents are on board."

"I hope they find the women and reunite them with their families." Fannie glanced at Hannah. "I am praying Sarah will be among those found."

That was Hannah's prayer, as well.

"Vipera will get the best lawyers," Samuel continued, "but they're confident the men Lucas hog-tied will talk. Seems that story you made up, Lucas, about being undercover and sending photos you claimed came from their phones to incriminate Vipera did the trick. Plus, the women who have been held captive will be credible witnesses. I have a feeling there will be an abundance of evidence to bring Vipera to justice."

The sheriff smiled with appreciation. "The chief of police in Savannah said to thank you, Lucas. He also said if you wanted your old job back—"

Lucas held up his hand. "No way. I'm staying in Willkommen."

"Ned Quigley's running things until I get back on my feet, but I could still use another deputy," the sheriff offered.

"And take the inn's new manager away from me?" Fannie said with a huff.

She smiled at Lucas. "I'm getting older. Having Hannah with me made me realize how much I missed spending time in my own home. I'm ready to turn over more of the inn's operation to a competent manager, if that's the type of job you're interested in having, Lucas."

He beamed with gratitude. "That sounds perfect, Fannie."

"I guess we just need to know what Hannah plans to do." Fannie smiled. "I need someone to help me in the office, if you're interested in a permanent job."

Everyone looked at her. She could feel the heat rise in her cheeks. "I… I don't want to go back to Macon, and I don't want to go back to the way I was living. If you need me here, Fannie, I'd like to stay and work at the inn."

"I need you, of course, but I think someone else does, as well." Fannie winked at Lucas and then patted the sheriff's arm. "Might be good to stretch your legs, Samuel. Your physical therapist said you need exercise."

He took the hint and the two of them left the room.

Lucas pulled Hannah to her feet and smiled down at her, causing her heart to beat wildly. Without saying a word, he drew her closer. Then he lowered his lips to hers. She molded against him, overcome with a sense of acceptance and joy.

"Everyone seems aware of the way I feel," he said when their lips finally parted.

"Everyone except me," she answered coyly.

"I've fallen in love with you, Hannah Miller."

"Oh, Lucas. I love you, too. You're a good man and I'm sorry that I thought you harbored vengeance in your heart. Evidently I couldn't see clearly enough because of my own struggle. I told you that I learned about my father the night I left my mother and sisters, but I never told you what else I learned. He was a thief and also a murderer. He gunned down three people in a church and killed two police officers as he was fleeing. All this time, I've feared law enforcement mainly because I thought they would look unfavorably on me because of the sins of my father."

Lucas started to speak but she touched her finger to his lips, needing to explain everything she had been holding back. "For the last three years, I harbored resentment toward both my mother and father. Seeing how you brought Olivia's murderers to justice made me realize that I needed to forgive my parents so I could move on with my life."

"Your father has no bearing on who you are, Hannah."

She nodded. "I know that now. I've forgiven him and forgiven my mother, thanks to you."

He rubbed his hands down her arms. "You're beautiful, Hannah, and sensitive and smart, and you make life worth living again. It's soon, I know, but I want you to hear what my heart is saying..."

Her own heart was ready to explode. She stepped even closer.

"My heart says it loves only you. Will you be my wife? Will you let me love you and cherish you for the rest of my life?"

"Oh, Lucas, I love you, and, yes, I want to be your wife. Nothing would make me happier."

"There's one condition, as you probably know."

She tilted her head, suddenly worried about what he expected, what caveat he would place on their love.

"I want to become true Amish, to be baptized into the faith and to live my life within the Amish community. It's not an easy choice, and I know you probably need more time."

Relief flooded over her. "When I thought you would return to law enforcement, I knew I wouldn't be able to follow you back to Savannah. What I've found here, in this peace-loving community with their focus on the Lord, is what I want for my life, too."

"I need to talk to the bishop. Hopefully he'll realize I no longer harbor vengeance in my heart or desire retribution. I'm free of the past and ready to embrace the future."

Again, Lucas lowered his lips to hers and pulled her more tightly into his embrace.

Eventually he eased up a bit and smiled. "We'll have children together."

She nodded. "A houseful."

"I'll work the land and manage the inn."

"I'll learn how to cook on a woodstove and how to bake bread and delicious pies."

"And we'll face tomorrow together."

"Nothing could be better." She pulled him closer and turned her mouth to his. "Now, my sweet husband-to-be, stop talking and kiss me again."

"*Yah*, kissing is a good thing. *Ich liebe dich*, Hannah Miller. I love you."

She wrapped her arms around his neck and whispered before his lips touched hers. "*Ich liebe dich*, Lucas Grant. I love you now and will love you forever. Cross my heart."

Epilogue

Hannah stood next to Lucas and peered over the clearing, seeing the green grass and the budding trees in the distance. Turning, she spied the deer stand where everything had started on that fateful night.

So many things had changed since then. Instead of her earlier apprehension toward law enforcement, she now felt only gratitude for Ned Quigley, Deputy Gainz and especially dear Samuel. She glanced at where he and Fannie stood, hand in hand, both somber and lost in thought.

With Lucas's help, the three men from the Willkommen sheriff's office had brought down a state-wide trafficking operation. Tucker Davis, the guy in flannel who had come after her, was in jail awaiting trial, along with a handful of other men who had been involved in the mountain operation. The men Lucas had subdued at the lodge had copped a plea, and because of the information they had provided, the Savannah district attorney felt confident Eugene Vipera would pay for his crimes.

Lucas slipped his arm around her shoulders. “Are you okay?”

She smiled, appreciating his concern. Glancing down at the freshly covered grave, she was overwhelmed with a sense of closure. Her mother had been laid to rest in this idyllic setting, on Lucas’s land, almost at the exact spot where he had saved Hannah for the first of many times.

“I was just thinking about everything that happened and how God protected both of us.” She hesitated, feeling the weight of concern she carried in her heart. “If only—”

He pulled her close. “They’ll find Sarah. God will hear our prayers.”

She nodded, appreciating how her soon-to-be husband always said what she needed to hear. “I’m praying for Rosie Glick, as well.”

“‘Patience is a virtue’ is what the bishop told us before we were baptized.”

She rubbed his arm and smiled. “My mother claimed I was impatient to a fault. I understand her better now. She struggled to accept God’s love and, evidently, never felt loved herself. I hate that she had to carry such a cross. Hopefully the Lord healed that brokenness before her death.”

“What about the letter? Have you opened it yet?”

She nodded. “My father hopes I’ll keep writing. He said he never knew what happened to me. My mother left him when I was six months old, but he’s kept a picture of me all these years.”

“If you decide to visit him in prison, I can—”

Hannah shook her head and held up her hand. “Not yet, Lucas. I’m not ready. Maybe someday.”

“We have time, Hannah. A whole lifetime ahead of us.”

She kissed his cheek, thankful for his strength and understanding. Taking his hand in hers, she stepped back from the graveside and together they walked to where Fannie and Samuel stood.

"Thank you for being here," Hannah told them both.

"Of course, child. You're like family." Fannie opened her arms and Hannah stepped into her warm embrace, feeling a connection and a love that she had always longed to receive from her own mother.

"You'll need a marker for the grave," Samuel said, ever the pragmatist. "Something simple with her name."

Hannah appreciated his suggestion and smiled, knowing how the kindly man seemed a perfect match for Fannie. Perhaps soon he would be ready to embrace the faith of his youth.

No doubt aware of his fatigue, Fannie patted Samuel's hand. "Let's go back to the inn. Lunch will soon be served and I know you are hungry."

As they turned to retrace their steps, Hannah stopped short, seeing the handsome Amish couple who had climbed from their buggy at the far side of the clearing.

"Looks like we've got company," Samuel announced.

Tears welled up in Hannah's eyes and her heart nearly burst with joy. "Miriam," she called as she ran with outstretched arms to her sister, her beautiful sister who had come back to Willkommen.

"Hannah." Miriam's long skirt billowed out behind her as she raced across the clearing, wisps of hair pulling free from her bonnet.

A flood of tears spilled down their cheeks as the two women embraced. "My sweet sister, I have missed you so." Miriam's words were like a balm that healed Hannah's long-ago broken heart. In that split second everything was forgiven and the wounds of the past were forgotten. Now only this present moment mattered.

An Amish man, tall with broad shoulders, shook Lucas's hand, and then the two men embraced, as well.

Fannie and Samuel joined in the welcome.

Miriam and Hannah didn't need words. They would catch up later. Now they just basked in the knowledge that yesterday had passed and they were together again.

Arm in arm, they walked to their mother's graveside, both women silent, each lost in her own thoughts.

"I'm sorry I left you," Hannah whispered at last, the words and the memories no longer painful.

"I still don't know what happened that night," Miriam admitted. "Later, Mother told me how much she loved you and missed you. She regretted her actions, but she could never muster the courage to call you. I regret not doing so. Maybe I wanted to punish her for forcing you to leave."

"She's at peace now," Hannah said.

Wiping their tear-streaked cheeks, the sisters walked to where the men they loved waited.

"I'm hungry," Samuel grumbled.

"I'd like to invite all of you to the inn for lunch," Fannie announced, taking Samuel's hand. "I hope you'll join us there."

Eager for the welcoming comfort of the inn, the two other couples climbed into their buggies. Hannah hesitated and glanced back over the clearing, overwhelmed with gratitude for the many ways the Lord had blessed her life.

Lucas kissed her cheek and then stared down at her with eyes of love. "As Fannie would say, *Gott* is good."

Overcome with emotion at the bounty of the Lord's

providence, Hannah wrapped her arms around his neck and smiled at the wonderful man who had stolen her heart. "Sarah will come home soon. I know it, Lucas, especially now with Miriam here. Today we will celebrate as a family."

"We need to tell them about our upcoming wedding."

She nodded. "We have to tell them about a lot of things, but first, I need to tell you something, Lucas Grant."

He took off his hat and pulled her closer, his eyes twinkling. "*Yah*, I am waiting to hear what you will say, my little cabbage."

She laughed then feigned a pout. "But I wanted to be your brussels sprout."

"Ah, *liebling*, you are my everything."

They laughed, and when the laughter stopped she said what she had wanted to say and would continue to say for the rest of their lives. "I love you, Lucas."

He lowered his lips to hers and all she had ever wanted was fulfilled in his kiss.

"Let's go home," he said, helping her into the buggy.

Snuggled next to him as Daisy started down the path that led back to the inn, Hannah's heart nearly burst with joy. *Gott* had given her what she had always wanted, a man to love and a place to call home.

* * * * *

SPECIAL EXCERPT FROM

Love Inspired®

Though Texan cowboy Toby Christner was raised Amish, he has no plans to settle down in the new community along Harmony Creek. But when he meets Amish nanny Sarah Kuhns, he can't help but wonder if a Plain life with her is exactly what he needs.

Read on for a sneak preview of The Amish Christmas Cowboy *by Jo Ann Brown, available in October 2018 from Love Inspired!*

Toby was sure something was bothering Sarah.

He thought through their conversation among her family's Christmas trees. She'd been distressed by how Summerhays and his wife paid too little attention to their *kinder*, but she'd been ready to speak her mind on that subject.

So what was bothering her?

You.

The voice in his head startled him. He'd heard it clearly and, for once, it wasn't warning him away from becoming too close to someone. Instead, it was telling him the reason why there might be a wall between him and Sarah.

Maybe it was for the best. Every day he lingered was another drawing him into the community. Each moment he spent with Sarah enticed him to look forward

LIEXP0918

to the next time they could be together. In spite of his determination, his life was being linked to hers and her neighbors.

That would change once his coworker's trailer pulled up to take him back to Texas.

Sarah gestured toward the *kinder*. "They're hungry for love."

"You're worried they're going to be hurt when I go back to Texas."

"Ja."

He wanted to ask how she would feel when he left, but he'd hurt his ankle, not his head, so he didn't have an excuse to ask a stupid question.

"The *kinder* will be upset when you go, but won't it be better to give them nice memories of your times together to enjoy when they think about you after you've left?"

Nice memories of times together? Maybe that would be sufficient for the *kinder*, but he doubted it would be enough for him.

LIEXP0918

SPECIAL EXCERPT FROM

Love Inspired® SUSPENSE

A serial killer is after a military nurse. She'll fight to stay one step ahead of him with the help of a heroic soldier and some brave K-9s.

Read on for a sneak preview of Battle Tested *by Laura Scott, the next book in the Military K-9 Unit miniseries, available October 2018 from Love Inspired Suspense.*

Two fatal drug overdoses in the past week.

Exhausted from her thirteen-hour shift in the critical care unit, First Lieutenant Vanessa Gomez made her way down the hallway of the Canyon Air Force Base hospital, grappling with the impact of this latest drug-related death.

The corridor lights abruptly went out, enclosing her in complete darkness. She froze, instinctively searching for the nearest exit sign, when strong hands roughly grabbed her from behind, long fingers wrapping themselves around her throat.

The Red Rose Killer?

It had been months since she'd received the red rose indicating she was a target of convicted murderer and prison escapee Boyd Sullivan.

She kicked back at the man's shins, but her soft-soled nursing shoes didn't do much damage. She used her

LISEXP0918

elbows, too, but couldn't make enough impact that way, either. The attacker's fingers moved their position around her neck, as if searching for the proper pressure points.

"Why?" she asked.

"Because you're in my way…" the attacker said, his voice low and dripping with malice.

The pressure against her carotid arteries grew, making her dizzy and weak. Black spots dotted her vision.

She was going to die, and there was nothing she could do to stop it.

Her knees sagged, then she heard a man's voice. "Hey, what's going on?"

Her attacker abruptly let go just as the lights came on. She fell to the floor. The sound of pounding footsteps echoed along the corridor.

"Are you okay?" A man wearing battle-ready camo rushed over, then dropped to his knees beside her. A soft, wet, furry nose pushed against her face and a sandpapery tongue licked her cheek.

"Yes," she managed, hoping he didn't notice how badly her hands were shaking.

"Stay, Tango," the stranger ordered. He ran toward the stairwell at the end of the hall, the one that her attacker must have used to escape.